PRAISE FOR
AWARD-WINNING AUTHOR
DORICE NELSON

Saratoga Summe: 1863

originally published as 1863 Saratoga Summer © 2000

"...A FANTASTIC READ, full of the atmosphere and unique tone of the era in 1860s New York...Five Roses!," — Kristie Leigh Maguire, *MyShelf.com*

"SARATOGA SUMMER, 1863, GRABS YOU AND WON'T LET GO! You'll go from the beautiful green hills of Ireland to New York...a city in unrest over the new [Civil War] Conscription Law..." — Margaret Marr, *Romance at its Best*.

NOMINEE FOR THE BLOODY DAGGER AWARD!!! Five Daggers. "If you never read a historical romance again in your life, you have to read *Saratoga Summer*...I cannot put into words the power Ms. Nelson puts into her characters and scenes. Power that will absolutely take your breath away." — Sue Hartigan, Member of RIO, *All About Murder Reviews*

"Ms. NELSON ALLOWS HER READERS TO EXPERIENCE the emotions of this troubled period in time through her descriptive passages." — Julie Shininger, *eBookIsle*

"...A SATISFYING STORY about love and family, don't miss *Saratoga Summer*." — Jennifer Bishop, *Romance Reviews Today*

Clan Gunn: Gerek

Originally published as The Gunns of Killearnan, *2000*

Coming Soon
Lost Son of Ireland.

Originally published as Unlawful.

May the wind be always at your back

Dorice Nelson

SARATOGA SUMMER: 1863

by Dorice Nelson

Cambridge Books
an imprint of
Write Words, Inc.
Cambridge, MD 21613

Publishers Note: This book is a work of fiction based entirely on the author's imagination. Any resemblance to actual persons is purely coincidental. Real places mentioned in the book are depicted fictionally and are not intended to portray actual times or places.

All rights reserved. No part of the book may be reproduced in any form or by any means without the prior written consent of the Author or Publisher, excepting brief quotes used in reviews.

𝕮𝖆𝖒𝖇𝖗𝖎𝖉𝖌𝖊 𝕭𝖔𝖔𝖐𝖘 is a subsidiary of:

Write Words, Inc.
2934 Old Route 50
Cambridge, MD 21613

ISBN -1-59431-192-7

Bowker Standard Address Number: 254-0304

PROLOGUE

Ireland
Summer, 1843

In the usual fashion of uncut equine males, the leggy chestnut
stallion shrieked and whinnied to attract the attention of the mares
in the next field. Head held high, he ran the perimeter of his enclosed grassy paddock and worked up a heavy sheen of sweat.

He had been at the farm for a month but still behaved in this
fashion when other horses were being led into the nearby pastures.
His shrill bellows caused eleven-year-old Connor O'Malley to glance
up and shake his head in apparent disgust. No one else seemed to
pay much attention to the stallion's nervous calls, so Connor kept
watch.

At the chestnut's continued trumpeting, Bowes Brennan, a short,
bandy-legged young man with a thatch of hair the color of ripe
straw, peered from behind the barn's double doors. He, too, shook
his head but grinned as he checked the outside area. He waved to
his wife, Annie, round with child, who sat on the top rail of the
stallion's paddock fence. He blew her a kiss and disappeared back
into the bowels of the barn.

Annie sat high on the fence, seemingly amused at the prancing
stallion's comical attempts to entice the mares. With a joyful smile
on her face, she turned and called out to the elder of her two small
daughters playing in the sand pit at the near side of the barn.
"Sinead, darlin'. Look," she shouted, her voice filled with merri-
ment. "Isn't he the most glorious looking beast?"

"Aye, Mam, he is. Pretty horsey," came the childish shout from the four-year-old. The little girl smiled broadly, displaying perfectly aligned small white teeth. "Almost pretty as you."

Annie turned back to watch again, her smile wider than before.

Now unbearably anxious, the chestnut focused on the mares in the nearby field. He snorted and called again. Suddenly, in desperation, he propelled himself into a tearing gallop. His massive muscles bunched and stretched, bunched and stretched. He ran straight at the fence, rocked back on his hocks, and propelling himself forward, leapt to jump from the paddock.

The stallion missed the top rail in his surge for freedom. He was almost over when his front hooves clipped the rail, knocking Annie—and him—off balance. She tipped backward and fell to the ground. The stallion's back legs crashed onto wood, hard and split the rail in half. The two pieces of stout logs plummeted to the ground, hitting Annie, who lay crumpled in a heap outside the paddock.

Her single scream resounded above the hushed hillsides, silenced by more than a thousand pounds of horseflesh landing atop her. The stallion thrashed and kicked in his struggle to regain his feet. He crushed Annie beneath him before he stood upright.

At the sound of the scream, Bowes, his jockey-sized body pumping his legs like pistons, exploded out the barn doors. Connor bolted from the far pasture where he had been teasing the new foals. The two girls rose and stood in the sand, dumbstruck, their faces crossed with horror and their hands tightly clasped.

Bowes reached her first. He lifted her battered body into his arms. "Annie, Annie," he sobbed, watching the blood seep from her mouth. Her eyes stared blankly at the serene sky. Her lips hung open as if that one scream would be the last sound she would ever make. "Annie, lass, don't be leaving me. Please, me darling, don't go..."

Finn O'Malley, Connor's father, stormed out of the manor house, shouting, "What in hell's name is going on out here?" Bowes was on the ground holding a body. Finn turned his head and called, "Mary, come..."

The new stallion hovered nearby, head hanging, muscles quivering, his weight on only three of his four legs, unable to move. Finn's expression was wild. He shouted to Connor, who was fast approaching from the field. "Fetch the gun from the house. Quickly now, lad."

Connor swerved at his father's command and dashed into the house, pushing past his mother, who stood frozen in the doorway, her hand covering her mouth. Finn tore across the lawn toward the accident, his face a mask of sorrow.

Bowes nestled his wife in his arms and looked up at the man standing over him. "Och, dear God! She's gone, Finn," he cried. "Me Annie-girl is gone. The babe with her. I felt the last breath leave her." He sobbed with earth-shaking, gulping howls. "Only a moment ago. Me Annie's gone and the babe she carried with her." He clutched his wife closer to his narrow, heaving chest and rocked the body. Keening, he rained kisses over her bruised and bloody face.

Face drawn, Finn hunkered down next to Bowes and put a consoling hand on his shoulder. "Here, man." He patted the shoulder then rubbed the young man's head with a gentle hand.

Tears of anguish gushed from Bowes's blue eyes and forged paths down his cheeks. He looked up at the older man with an almost vacant expression. "What'll I do without me Annie?"

"Let me take her from ye, laddie. I'll be bringing her up to the house for me Mary to care for. There's nothing ye can be doing for Annie now. See to yer girls." Finn nodded in the direction of the barn. "They're little forms are shaking yet, stiff with the fright."

Slowly, with movements meant to soothe, Finn eased Annie's limp body from Bowes's grasp and lifted her gently into his own strong arms. Connor ran from the house with a rifle grasped tightly in his hand and moved to his father's side.

The sight of the blood and gore hit young Connor him with the impact of a runaway train. He fell to his knees. He dropped the gun, crossed himself and murmured a short prayer.

Finn gazed down at his son. "Lad, yer Ma and I will be busy. We must see to Annie. Ye'll have to be taking care of that crippled creature yerself," he said quietly, pointing at the forgotten stallion. "There's none other to do it. 'Tis this very day ye'll be turning into yer manhood, son. I trust ye to do the deed right, and quick."

Fighting back tears, Connor's father turned and shuffled toward the house, carrying Annie Brennan in his arms. The quiet sound of the manor's door closing was punctuated by the sobbing of a boy becoming a man, the horrific wailing screams of two frightened children and the sound of a gunshot.

* * *

Two months later

The two little girls, eyes wide, gripped each other's hands tightly. This farm was the only home they'd ever known. Now, they were leaving it. Sitting in a narrow cart amongst their luggage, they stared straight ahead, seeming no longer to recognize the people standing on the porch of the stone manor house. Their father, unlike his former laughing, teasing self, stood morose, stiff.

"Bowes, ye don't have to be leaving. Ye know me Mary and I will take care of ye and yer lasses."

"Aye, I do that, sir." He shook his head. "But the very sight of the horses scares the girls far too much for any pleasure in them. Sinead, in her mourning for her mam, is afraid to leave our cottage. She's afraid to go anywhere near the horses."

"We can move ye to another place, perhaps, in the village. At least, ye'd know ye'd be having steady work. Ye're too much of a horseman to be leaving the beasts forever."

"Nae, Finn, 'tis better I take the lasses away from the scene of the accident."

Mary O'Malley, her soft brown eyes filled with unshed tears, asked, "Where will ye go, Bowes? Where will ye be taking those lovely girls?" She paused to look at the sad little girls, her desire for daughters apparent on her face. "I'll be missing them so. They were the daughters I've not had."

"I think we'll head toward Dublin first," Bowes said, taking off his cap and crushing it against his chest. "I have sisters there who will watch the lasses while I work." He turned away but turned back again, as if reluctant to leave. "They'll be having family around and a routine to follow. It'll be better for them."

Finn put an open hand out to Bowes. "Ye're a good man with people and a finer hand with the horses. How will ye ever stay away from the beasties? They've been yer life's work, for sure," he said, in a hopeful pleading tone.

"I think some time soon, we may travel across the pond to America. I have sisters there, too, in a city called New York. It'll be a new place, a new life for me and the girls," he said, gripping Finn's hand then letting it go and walking down the steps, saying good-bye to Mary and Finn O'Malley for a final time.

Finn followed him down to the drive. He put his arm around Bowes's thin shoulders and hugged the young man to him. They broke apart, embarrassed at the sudden show of affection. Bowes took a step closer to the overloaded cart.

Finn said in a low voice, "The money I've given ye is not near enough for the care of your girls. 'Tis not enough for me to do for ye. Bowes, ye know ye can always count on me if ever yer family runs into any kind of trouble."

"Thank ye, Finn. Ye've always been most generous to me and mine. I don't think things will ever get this bad again. At least, not in my lifetime."

A short grunt of derision burst from Finn's mouth. "There's no telling the amount of tragedy God will put into a fellow's life, just to test him." He crossed himself quickly. "But if ever ye should need me or mine, we'll be there for ye. 'Tis my solemn promise to ye, man to man."

The two men embraced again and gave each other quick pats on the back. Neither looked up to notice the grave forlorn faces of Connor and his four younger brothers. The boys stood huddled together and watched the leave-taking from an upstairs window.

Bowes trotted toward the cart alone. Inserting himself between the protruding frames, he grasped them and, with a grunt, pulled the cart down the road, away from the manor house. He didn't look back.

CHAPTER ONE

Ireland
April 1863

Connor O'Malley scanned the pasture and studied the new foals racing across the field in playful abandon. He chortled over their antics. *Lord, but I love these horses!*

Looking guiltily to each side, at the ground in front of him, and then up to the sky, he crossed himself quickly and added both his family and Ireland to his mental list of things he loved, whispering aloud, "In that order."

Connor laughed at himself for the many insignificant superstitions ruling his life. He shook his head in further amusement at his own daftness. He knew full well, whenever he got a chance, he would tell everyone or anyone who would listen or not, about the best breeding program of racing stock in all of Ireland. He smiled. And the best racing training to boot.

This morning, he was puffed up with a sense of pride in what he considered his accomplishments and downright smug in his beliefs about his future in the European world of horseracing. He was hotter-than-hell from planting oak and elm saplings in the pastures, to cover his beloved horses from the ravages of Ireland's quick downpours and shade them from the strong bursts of sunshine. It became more important each day to maintain the proper condition of their coats.

Beads of perspiration rolled from beneath the blue cloth circling his brow. He stopped digging and, with the turned-up sleeve of his grimy cotton undershirt, wiped the sweat from his forehead and looked around. Where had his four brothers gone, he wondered. *The damned fools disappear every time there's hard work to be done.*

A dull jangle of out-of-tune iron bells made Connor turn from the foals clustered around him, now shoving and poking at him, to look down the road leading to the manor. Ill-matched hoof beats of a poorly shod horse accompanied the discordant clang of the bells and drummed up thin clouds of dust on the dirt road.

Slowly, an ancient gray horse struggled into view over the last slight rise in the roadway. Connor chuckled and leaned on his shovel to watch the old gray, with an even older white-haired man perched atop him, approach the stone house.

His cousin Padrik O'Malley from the village, a pouch slung over his shoulder, sat draped atop his plug of a horse. Padrik's chin rested on his chest. His eyes were closed.

The flea-beaten horse plodded across the gravel path straight to the most vibrant green of the grassy lawn surrounding the house. Once there, he spread his front legs and stretched his neck down to graze.

The sudden movement upset the elderly man's balance. Slipping and sliding in the leather saddle, almost falling, Paddy grabbed a handful of mane and pushed hard to right himself. He looked around him with a silly and guilty expression on his face, obviously startled by the rude awakening.

"Good day to ye, Cousin Padrik," Connor called while moving steadily toward the old man.

"Aye?" Paddy called in return. He looked around with a vacant stare. "Aye? Och, there ye are, Connor, me lad," he shouted. Cupping his ear as if he could barely hear, he beckoned Connor closer with his free hand. "A good day to ye, laddie. Come closer," he bellowed, his voice growing louder the closer Connor came. "Yer horses are looking right fine, a rompin' in that new field at hill's bottom. Sleek-looking, a gleamin' in the sun they are."

"Why, thank you, cousin," Connor said. He grinned, suspecting Padrik had been sound asleep when he passed the lower field. "'Tis a beautiful day for taking leave from your duties and traveling a bit. A visit to me da, is it now?"

"Nae. 'Tis me duty I'm doing. As post fer the village, I'm deliverin' a packet to yer da."

Connor strolled to Paddy's side and lifted the horse's head to wipe the half-chewed grass from his mouthpiece. He handed the reins to his cousin. "Padrik, I think the packet's for me. 'Tis expecting one from an English breeder I am."

With the mail pouch clutched to his chest in a tight grip, Paddy shook his head. "Nae, Con. The packet's addressed to your da, it is." He leaned down and whispered in a gravelly voice, "Lots of papers shoved inside, it has. Givin' it some bulk. Came from across the pond, it did. Important, I'm thinkin'."

"America?" Connor frowned. "Well then, it's surely not for me." Connor edged around the horse in the direction of the pasture. "Have yourself a short nip while you're visiting with me da," he said as an afterthought.

He wheeled around and strode back toward the pasture, mumbling to himself, "As if you hadn't thought of that nip all by your wee self."

Connor briefly wondered how a packet, from America no less, would concern his da, but he shrugged off his thoughts and marched back to the field. Why should he worry about something from America? He had everything he needed to keep his life content. His horses, his family and Ireland itself were the very things on this earth to fill him with supreme happiness.

I am blessed!

* * *

Four days later

Only minutes earlier, a heartbroken Finn O'Malley rang the huge iron bell on the manor's porch to summon his five 'boyos' from the

11

fields. He let the bell peal on by itself while he retired to the library.

Finn's eyes filled. He let the wetness slither down his face as he stood at the tall windows waiting for his sons to appear in the distance. Vivid sunlight danced over his face in flickering movements. He shaded his eyes from the glow, for its very brightness made a sad mockery of the dark deed he would commit this day.

He wondered what the mother of his sons, his sweet Mary, gone these past ten years, would think of him. What would she think of his promise and of his newfound scheme to honor it? Would she sling curses from heaven upon his head for severing the family life she so cherished?

Over the years, Finn presumed the vague promise, barely remembered, would never come to pass. How could he explain to his grown sons the promise made so long ago, before they were adults? In twenty years, no mention of it crossed the O'Malley threshold. Now, Bowes Brennan had called it in, a Bowes Brennan from the new country, a Brennan who desperately needed an O'Malley.

Finn's heart filled with sadness. He knew he would lie to his lads. One of his sons must…

They appeared in the distance. Finn shook his head to chase his dour mood away. With pride, not unlike Connor's, he watched the young men leap the pasture fences with an agility born to them. Each stopped long enough to pat every grazing horse they passed before they met in the center of the biggest field. There, they jostled and shoved each other around in their usual roughhouse ways.

Finn carefully studied them, committing to memory each and every precious feature. They were of the same sturdy stature — tall, with corded muscles thick and deep from daily dealings with the land and the animals. Their coloring, different for each one, was not unlike their rainbow temperaments — from fiery redheaded, green-eyed Egan, the youngest, to enigmatic, dark brown-haired, dark-eyed Connor, the eldest at thirty-one.

He watched them enter the house and knew they would clean up before entering the library. When he heard the shuffle of their feet in the hallway, he turned to face the library door.

* * *

Connor stood in the doorway of the library, his hand resting on the doorknob, his brothers elbowing him to see past his shoulders into the room. He peered in and located his da, half-hidden by a heavy curtain, in the glare of a tall, sunny window. Connor saw his father's serious, gray face, streaked with tears. No doubt the man had important things on his mind, important things to say to them all.

With a smile, Finn stepped forward and gestured. "Come in lads, come in. Sit ye down. I'm having a sore need to talk with ye. In a most straightforward fashion as is my wont."

Connor took note of his father's tone of voice and hesitantly stepped into the room. The four others filed in behind him, concerned with their usual poking, shoving and trying to get past their older, larger brother, who turned sharply and frowned at them.

Finn stood in the middle of the room, waving them in as if anxious to talk to them. "Hurry in, boyos. Don't be playing about with yer usual antics."

The twins and Egan, the three youngest, looked at each other then swiveled around to look at Connor, who shrugged. They each must have perceived something unusual in their da's demeanor, for they came in quickly and settled themselves, according to age, in chairs lined against the wall, just as they did when they were children.

Each looked expectantly at their father, who continued to wave at them. "Nae, boyos. Bring yer chairs closer. Be drawing them into a warm, comfortin' circle. 'Tis a family thing, this is."

The scrape of chairs filled the small room, the sound somewhat muted in the thick covers of leather-bound books crowding the bookcases. Finn waited until they were settled and grouped together facing him. "We're going to have a lottery, boyos."

"A lottery?" Connor's eyes widened, surprised, not understanding the message. He stared at his younger brothers, who always trusted him to come up with answers. Again, he shrugged. He was baffled, with no concrete answers to this rare situation.

"A lottery. That's what Da said. Don't be dense, Con," said Egan, the youngest brother, whose face now matched the brilliant carrot-red shade of his hair. He spoke with a touch more animosity than Connor would have accepted under ordinary circumstances. Perhaps he, too, noticed their da's serious demeanor.

Finn coughed loudly, capturing their attention. "Aye, a lottery it's to be. Ye see, boyos, there's a friend, a Brennan, who once gave your great-great-great— Dammit, I don't know how many greats. But 'tis one of yer forefathers, afore there were real O'Malleys, I'm thinking."

Finn's hesitant manner and downcast eyes belied what his smile conveyed. Da is not being truthful, Connor thought. "Is this to be a history lesson about our forefathers, Da? If so, I'll pass. I've work to do with the horses and the trees," Connor grumbled, half rising from his seat, while glaring at his brothers.

"Sit down lad," Finn growled. "I must tell this to you all, and all together. I'm wanting no blame put here on anything but circumstance."

Finn stared down at them with what Conner considered his sternest mien, so Connor smiled, hoping to lighten the terse words he'd spoken. "Well, hurry, Da. The bay mare is in season. I'd like to be putting the stallion to her before this day is out."

"Ye best hear the whole story as I know it. 'Tis an important piece of O'Malley history that must be fulfilled if we are to persevere." His father looked down at the floor then raised his head with deliberate slowness before beginning. "In the fifteen hundreds or so, the chief of a Brennan clan saved one of us O'Malleys from the gallows." He sighed softly. "'Twas a Grace O'Malley, daughter of a chief, and a foolish woman I'm thinking. Fighting the English, or something, she was. A deal was made then and there for an O'Malley to come to the aid of a Brennan should a severe and odd emergency exist."

"I take it from your expression, Da, that such an emergency exists," said the more serious of Connor's blond twin brothers, Arlen, who sat shoulder to shoulder with his brother, Darren like a mirror image. They both had their hands clasped together in front of them, elbows on their knees. "How does it affect us, Da? Is that why you called us together?"

"Right to the penny, son. It seems a Brennan has fallen upon hard times." Finn shook his head up and down in agreement. "Powerful hard times."

"Harder than the famine itself?" asked the muscular, brown-haired Bartley, who was a year younger than Connor.

"Aye. A widow woman is to lose a child entrusted to her by her deceased husband. That is, if her husband's in-laws have their way. I believe they've threatened to drag her through some sort of legal do, but I guess 'tis a long story. I don't know the whole of it. Besides, 'tis for the widow to relate if she chooses."

"Well, what are we supposed to do? We've no lawyers among us," Connor asked, suspicious of the story told by his father, thinking it strange indeed. All the brothers nodded in response.

"Are there no O'Malleys nearby to help the poor woman out?" Egan asked. "Doesn't she have folks of her own?"

When his da shook his head in answer to both questions, Connor asked, "What would you have us do to help?"

"Marry the widow, I presume," Bartley said. He patted Connor's back and shook his head as if mimicking their da.

Finally realizing the full import of the situation—the widow woman, the lottery— Connor leaped to his feet. "What are you talking about?" He stared at his father. "Da? Ye're not telling us a wee tale, are ye? How could any of us take care of a woman with a child when we can barely take care of our horses, our villagers and ourselves? 'Tis a foolish scheme ye have, old man."

"I'll not be telling ye again. Sit, Connor! Ye may be within yer thirty years, but 'tis respect ye'll be showing for yer da. And 'tis no foolish scheme, I'll have ye know."

Finn stood with his arms crossed over his chest and waited. Connor sat down. He scowled at his father then at his brothers.

Darren, the younger of the blond twins quipped, "Now, lads, show some consideration for a poor unfortunate who might be losing a child of her very heart. No doubt a wee one she has come to love with all her being."

"I apologize for my quick temper. But the shock was into me," Connor said, trying to smile. "But we know you too well, Da. You've a plan in mind."

With his mouth opened wide enough to stuff a full-grown bird in the round 'o' it made, the older twin turned to the rest of the brothers, stared at them for a second then turned to their da. "'Tis one of us you're fixing to marry off."

Connor spoke quickly. "Well, it won't be me, for sure. Not right now at any rate. If we're to match the English in Ireland's racing scene, I need to keep breeding and training the horses. Once I beat them to a 'fare thee well' then maybe — just maybe — I'll marry that sweet thing from the village, the very one I've had me eye on for the last few years. She'd be a real help with the animals, and I kinda' fancy her."

His father paced to the windows, anger apparent in the redness of his face. He gulped once then turned and sauntered back, seemingly relaxed. He stood directly in front of the twins. "Ye're right, boyos. Marriage in the offing. That's why we'll be having a lottery. Ye'll each start out equal in this."

Finn paused and moved off in another direction but he kept talking as if he couldn't stop. "'Tis a deed that must be done. Was promised way back when. The Brennans did for us, now we'll do for them, just as our forefathers would have done. As I would do, were I a younger fella'."

Finn pointed to a small oak table at one side of the room's stone hearth. "There are five pieces of straw placed on the table. Drawn from one of our own bales they were. Different lengths, each and every one."

Aware of the drama of the scene but still wary of what he considered a false tale, Connor watched his da slowly pick up the straws.

Finn laid several in his hand. Glancing briefly at his sons, he made a fist and pushed all the straws down into it. What could be seen were mere pieces, all the same length, one indistinguishable from another.

Connor's attention was riveted on Finn's hand. All the straws were level at the top, each one facing in a different direction. *This is not right.*

"Well, now, boyos, ye're going to do this. 'Tis an obligation secured for a lengthy time, and it's fallen to us O'Malleys to equal the original favor."

No one moved. Still as cats ready to pounce or run, all the brothers sat, staring at their feet. A premonition took hold of Connor. A chill passed over him. He looked up and drew a large breath. He knew his father would not have any of them shirking of their duty. One brother had to 'pay the piper' and repay a deed done in kindness. *Never let it be said an O'Malley didn't live up to his honor-bound duty.*

"Well there, Connor. Ye were in such a hurry to stand earlier. Have ye no feet, except to look at?" his father asked. "Stand up lad. Ye're the biggest and the eldest. It's up to ye to decide whether the shortest or the longest straw gains a wife and a child. Choose long or short."

"Long."

"Long, it is. Whichever of ye boyos gets the longest straw will marry the lass and sail to America on the quickest ship to go there."

Egan leaped to his feet to stand next to Connor. "Sail to America? What do you mean by that?"

"Whoever gets the long straw will marry here in Ireland with a priest in attendance so that the marriage vows are approved and sealed by the church. But the widow-woman lives in America. It'll be a proxy wedding, so ye'll have to go to America in order to consummate the marriage, proper-like. She can't travel over here. The folks causing her problems want to keep the tyke and won't let her take him out of their sight, much less to Ireland."

"To America?" Egan's face grew redder than his hair. His light green eyes doubled in size. He whispered, "I heard 'tis a terrifyin' trip. To America." Then he raised his voice louder. "Besides, I'm too young to marry some stranger."

"Nae, don't ye get any ideas, my lad. Ye'll choose like your brothers do." Finn shook his fist at Egan.

"We'll all choose," Bartley said, slightly backing away from the rest.

"Aye, we will, Da, but Connor first." Arlen turned to Connor. "Hurry up, Con. Choose a straw. Go ahead. You're the oldest."

Connor spun around. "You're in such an all-fired hurry, you draw. You're not the only one who wants to stay here, at home, in Ireland. America be damned."

"I'll be having no battles over this, lads. It'll be done right and proper. Connor, ye're the oldest of me sons. Ye have the right to choose whether ye want to go first and pick or go last and have the final straw yer brothers might be leaving in their wake."

Connor moved next to his da. He stood head and shoulders above him and glowered down.

Finn was not in the least intimidated. "Stop yer dark faces at me, Connor, laddie, and choose yer fate."

Connor studied the straws in his da's hand then picked the straw farthest from him. He shoved it behind his back so quickly his da couldn't see it. Nor did Connor want to look at it. The tips of his fingers grew warm. The straw seemed to burn a trail of fire into his hand.

"Now, Connor, don't be breaking the straw so it's shorter. I'm watching ye careful-like," Bartley quipped, stepping forward to pick next.

The others stepped forward and drew according to their ages. When it was Egan's turn, he bounced forward and took the last one. He didn't put it behind him. He opened his fingers and stared down at the brittle yellow piece. "Mine is short." He gave a chuckle then his face paled. "Da, why are we doing this? None of us is wanting to go. Not me brothers, nor me. I, for one, would hate to be marrying so young. To a stranger. 'Tis a hard thing you're asking."

The younger of the blond twins whispered in Eagan's ear. "'Tis the long straw that goes to America." He opened his fist and displayed another short straw.

Egan ignored him and continued, "But since I have no lass in mind, any will do. I'll sacrifice myself for one of me brothers and go to America."

"That'll be the day. When you sacrifice yourself for one of us," Connor retorted with a grin. "It would be a first. So hush now and let Da speak."

Finn ignored them both. "All of ye, put yer straws on the table in the order ye drew them. Connor, you go."

Each straw placed on the table was shorter than the first. They all turned to look at Connor. He backed away from the table when he realized his was the longest straw. "Aye, Da. You've made your point. I'd be doing the deed but how am I to leave the horses?"

Egan shouted, "Aye. Who's going to train the horses?"

Connor shouted back. "I will. I'll take them all with me. I could not go without them." All the air left his body and his voice softened. "I've worked so hard to keep them well-bred and sturdy. They're me life, Da."

Finn started to disagree but raised his hand instead.

"At least, would I be able to take the stallion and our best mare?" Connor asked, his voice loud and forceful, as if he couldn't stop talking. "Our villagers are doing well, better than most of Ireland. We did our best to save everyone during the famine. 'Tis not that I'm swell-headed." Connor sat, leaned his elbows on his knees and lowered his head to his hands. In a pathetic whisper of lost hope, he moaned, "But I cannot leave the horses. I just can't. Some must go with me — or I'll not go, I'm telling you."

Egan faced his older brother, his hands on his hips, his legs splayed. "You can take a stallion. Not the mares. There must be mares in America. Besides, you don't know how to handle a mare, anymore than you know how to handle the lasses. Females are different. They're sensitive. You can't boss them around like you do all of us."

"You don't know what you're talking about, Egan. You seldom do," Connor snapped, his lip curled in distaste.

Egan's expression changed, his face grew white.

Connor was sure Egan would say something he'd regret. He gave him a dark look, hoping to stay his words for the time being.

Egan kept on. "I can imagine how you'll handle the widow you're to marry. You don't know anything about females."

"And I suppose you do, Egan. How come you don't have any of the village lasses chasing after you when we go to market?" Connor shot Egan a malicious, one-sided grin.

"You just don't see them, ye bloody fool. You're too busy looking at the horse flesh," Egan spat back.

Connor jumped up. He suspected their argument would escalate into a battle were it not stopped, but he couldn't give in to this feisty, smaller brother. Not now. He noticed Bartley had moved closer to the two antagonists, the twins farther away.

"Both of ye. Enough!" Finn interrupted with a loud snarling grunt. "Yer darling mother died too young. She never had the chance to socialize ye properly once ye were grown, much less teach any of ye the wonder and glory of a good and caring woman. She'll live on in our memories, from this day, in shame if ye continue yer silly battles."

At the mention of their mother, they stopped moving and bowed their heads. They each made the sign of the cross. Their mother's memory was dear and sacred to them all.

Without raising his head, Connor knew his da had their attention now. Somehow, he understood his time of happiness had come and gone in the space of a moment. The little people—those Irish leprechauns — had made a mockery of his overbearing sense of pride. It was time for him to pay the piper.

Bartley moved to stand by Connor and said, "Con, ye'd be pressed trying to take the stallion and any mare of yer choosing and handling a new wife, a child and a new country. Besides, all of us would lose out as well if ye took them with ye. The horses fit our lives, too."

Finn uttered a sharp gasp and snapped his fingers as if he had a wonderful idea. The lines in his forehead smoothed out but he hesitated. He turned to look at each of them. "Listen to yer da, son. It's a long voyage to America. Ye don't know what conditions ye'll be facing, Connor, me boyo. Trying to handle a stallion and a mare that might come into season during the voyage will tear ye down and them as well."

One side of Finn's mouth creased upward and he broke into a smile. "Instead, take Egan with ye. He's been bustin' to go to America since he was but a wee mite. He was ready when the first group left the village in '48 and him only a wee lad."

"Take Egan? Toss him into the sea on the way, no doubt. I'd probably kill him before we landed." Connor glanced at his youngest brother. He studied him. *Egan would make good company and a willing hand if horses were involved in America. And horses had to be in his future...* He made a half-turn away.

"Con, take me. I'll behave, I promise. Take me with you." Egan grinned up at his brother, who seemed to ignore him. He moved in closer to face him. "What's the matter, Con? Afraid I'll take the sweet widow-woman away from you?"

"Who cares?" Suddenly, Connor let a big, booming laugh erupt into the room. The sound of it reverberated against the stone of the fireplace but stopped abruptly as he made up his mind to include his brother. He spoke directly to Egan. "Why not? Aye, I'll take you with me, Egan. I've heard America's big — a scary place — but with lots of room. I hate to be going alone someplace I know little about. The two of us together...?" Connor flung his arm over Egan's shoulders then gave him a hug fit to break the younger man's ribs. "But, little brother, you'll be listening to every word I tell you."

"Och, for sure, Con," Egan said with a smirk, shaking his head in agreement.

CHAPTER TWO

Ireland
Late May

Knowing he falsified his story, Finn O'Malley felt ill about sending two of his five sons to a place called New York, a place where crass strangers ruled. Only the good Lord above knew what went on in such a barbaric place. What he had feared most was one of his boyos going off alone and being left to the monsters he envisioned lived in America.

Even worse, he was sickened and ashamed by the lie he was compelled to relate, but, for some inexplicable reason, he was hesitant to tell them the truth or to remind them of the tragedy that happened twenty years before. At the time, he prayed their young minds would forget the sorrow of the days following the tragedy of Annie Brennan's death. Now, on a continual basis, he prayed his Mary would forgive his lying.

He wasted several weeks, hoping something might occur to change his decision to send them. One week passed, then another, before Finn finally gathered Connor and Egan close for a manly talk. Not only was he faced with losing one son; he was to lose two, both going far from home.

Perhaps it was better this way, he thought, pacing to a window and back. Finn knew there was little for his sons in Ireland, with memories of the famine and the cruelty of the English still setting neighbor against neighbor at the strangest times. All his sons should go, not stay in a struggling Ireland where the Irish had so little respect from those who seemed to rule them.

Connor and Egan would keep each other company, so he spoke to them quietly. "Connor, make sure yer marriage is properly consummated and yer bride has the child safely in her custody, with no one wanting to take it away from her." Finn made note of Connor's grim face and his heart grew heavy. "Lads, ye don't have to stay in that foreign place forever, ye know."

Connor nodded at his father's words, but Finn could see the lad still felt uneasy about the reasons for doing this. Finn understood something in Connor's demeanor gave credence to the idea he'd heard the lie. Finn knew his boys recognized the fact.

Nevertheless, Finn went on. "Once everything's settle proper-like, ye'll be free to bring yer new family back here. Yer horses will still be where ye raised them, and ye'll be back in the home ye love. Think on it, boyo."

Connor nodded and Egan patted him on the back.

"Boyos, I want ye to keep this old country and its proper behavior uppermost in yer minds. Keep yer religion close to ye. There'll be folks who'll want ye to stray but the faith will bolster yer senses and keep ye well."

"Aye, Da," Connor mumbled, his dark eyes saddened with burdensome grief.

"Aye, Da," Egan said, his green eyes dancing with glee.

Finn studied both Connor and Egan. They were good sons. Each and every one of his sons were fine, fine men. He was as proud of them as any man could be. He breathed a sad sigh at losing any of them to another world beyond the confines of their small breeding farm.

With regret uppermost in his thoughts, he raised himself to his full height, standing straighter and taller than he had since getting the packet. "Well, boyos, 'tis off to the priest we go."

He turned back for a moment. "Connor, take the papers from that table by the fireplace. They're in the top drawer. We need to take them with us for the priest. We'll have a ceremony all fine and legal. Signed and sealed by Father William."

Egan rushed to the table before Connor. He dragged open the drawer and was about to take the papers out when his brother's large hand encircled his wrist.

"I'll get them. Don't be getting ahead of yourself, little brother. I'll be wanting to do this myself."

"Aye," came the soft answer.

Finn smiled and started for the door. "Och, I think the widow's name is somewhere on one of those papers."

Connor opened the drawer and took the papers out. He studied the top one then shuffled through them all until he found what he was looking for. A name. "Sinead Cavanaugh, soon to be Sinead O'Malley."

Finn's smile widened. This would work.

* * *

New York City
July 11, 1863

The day dawned hot and sulky without a breath of wind to cool the troubled times Bowes Brennan knew were heading for the city of New York. He could feel the horrors of everyone's reactions to the Conscription laws permeateing the air. Things were too quiet around his boarding house and the area where he lived, too subdued and peaceful not to matter.

He sighed, wiped the sweat from his brow with the back of his hand and settled his two matching grays into their places at the front of the open carriage. Once finished with the last belting of the harness straps, he climbed up onto the driver's seat, took the reins in his hands and clucked to the horses to move forward down the street.

Rounding the corner into a main thoroughfare, the hasty movements of pedestrians and carriages caught his eye. An endless river of people, each pursuing his or her own destiny, marched steadily for the business districts of the city.

Bowes figured the lottery drawing for the draft had already begun at the Conscription offices on Third Avenue and Forty-sixth Street. Rumors were that the authorities intended to start in areas of vacant lots and isolated buildings—so as not to upset the more vocal populace in heavily crowded areas. But he knew the draft would be a clash of race, classes, religions and nationalities, a jam of unrest and tumultuous desires. That was New York, a dissonant chorus, a city of hurried and sparkling waters, a city of spires and masts.

He pushed such incongruous thoughts from his mind. It was time to pick up his daughter, Sinead, and go with her to meet her new husband. Ablaze with plans and possibilities for her, he had coerced her into participating in one of his schemes. He had wanted a good man for her and was surprised he was able to talk her into marrying one, just by her taking her da's word for everything. His heart would break with grief if she and little Robbie couldn't make a fresh start in life. It would be his fault.

Bowes vaguely remembered young Connor as being a stalwart youngster, but twenty years passed since he's seen him. Now, he needed to make sure the man was worthy of his daughter, that Connor had grown into the kind of man she could admire and respect.

* * *

Sinead Brennan Cavanaugh stood staring at her empty room. She was mentally exhausted, physically nauseated and frightened. Disgusted with herself beyond belief, she had done the unimaginable. Stupidly done it. And not for the first time in her life.

Whenever she followed one of her da's schemes, the pit of her stomach housed the same sick feeling. The man had a million ideas for the future since arriving in America. None of them were remotely successful.

This time, her da's scheme seemed right to her, even honorable, until the sorry excitement of this morning dawned. But, as usual, her da's plot, along with the enervating heat she hated, made a mess of her thoughts, her nerves. Now, she wished she had more time to enjoy the last hours of her freedom.

The entire city of New York lay under the siege of an unexpected and oppressive early summer heat wave. Coupled with the people's escalating opposition to the Conscription Act, tension reigned throughout the city's boundaries and beyond. The very thought of what might come in the next few days succeeded in making Sinead short of breath and ill.

The wet, stifling hot air refused to move and its torment didn't help her frame of mind. The overbearing humidity settled on her head, her shoulders and clung to her narrow frame. With a deep sigh, she longed for cooler places, less-confining garments and no tension.

Moisture gathered on her brow and slithered down the side of her face. She brushed at it with one hand then pushed unruly hair back up into the tightly coiled back loop where it belonged. The quick swipe of her forehead didn't stop a rivulet of moisture traveling down her neck. A drop of wetness trickled into the valley between her breasts. She grabbed a soft, lacy cloth from inside her sleeve, dabbed her face and shoved the cloth between her breasts and her far too-tight corset, hoping her dress wouldn't show a stain. It was important to keep up appearances.

The heat and her inability to accept a second marriage conspired to make her more nervous, with an edginess that wouldn't go away. Her new husband, a man she'd never met, was to arrive from Ireland today. Worse yet, she was to meet him then bring him here to the Dewitts' household. How could she bring a man she didn't know, here, to this grand but empty wasteland?

She scanned her surroundings. Not a particle of dust marred the wood floors. No warm, colorful carpets covered the wide-boards. No soft drapes hung from the windows. No bright, lively pictures graced the walls. There was little charm or warmth to enhance the dull gray of the suite. The lofty rooms sparkled with such bare cleanliness they gave off a sterile purity. A deep sigh, sounding more like a groan to her ears, escaped Sinead's mouth.

Often shy, sometimes bewildered, Sinead knew she was only a simple girl with simple tastes and few airs above her lowly, Irish station. Dewitt House was too grand, too elaborate for her and too devoid of any type of character, except for the stultifying atmosphere perpetrated by Dewitts in their often futile attempts to enter the city's ranks of high society. Sinead slammed her fisted hand down on the tall dresser and pulled out a drawer to destroy the symmetry of the room.

Startled by another elongated sigh, her unhappiness grew, as it had with every moment since the proxy wedding. "I'm not ready to greet a husband," she said aloud. "And I won't bring him here to live."

Despite the intense heat, Sinead stalked to the windows and looked out on the street. Staying with Robbie was the one thing she didn't regret since her deathbed promise to Robert Cavanaugh. She mumbled to herself. "Where else can I bring him? I have nothing of my own."

The tap of heels on the wooden steps of the main staircase caught her attention. Adelaide Dewitt, Robert Cavanaugh's mother-in-law, called out from the landing, her tone unpleasant. "Jane, you'd best hurry. The ship will arrive long before you get to the wharf."

Adelaide's voice was high-pitched, reedy, cold, with a sharp edge to it. The very tone indicated her usual inability to wait for whatever she wanted.

In response, Sinead's temper rose. She reverted to the feisty Irish lass she was before she was moved, under duress, into this house. Mimicking Adelaide's voice, she answered in a sweet but false way. "Remember, the ship might be delayed and not even arrive this day. The wharves might be filled, the berths closed, unable to handle another ship."

The moment she made the statement, she hoped the ship would

never arrive at all but added with a touch of spite, "Why, Adelaide, I'd not be missing the first sight of young Robbie's new father for anything in the world." She let the words hang in the air and peeked out the door of her suite of rooms to see the reaction.

Mrs. Adelaide Dewitt stood midway on the stairs, waiting, her foot tapping a slow rhythm. She made impatient, fussy gestures at herself in the huge, ornate mirror secured to the wall of the landing, and fiddled with her even more ornate hat, trying to pin its cloth bird in a secure spot.

The heat of midday, plus Sinead's generalized apprehension, threatened to bowl her over. Her corset was too tight. It scraped her ribs. She could barely catch her breath. Her knees threatened to give out on her. She grabbed a doily from the dresser, wiped her brow then fanned herself with the cloth.

Her heart beat too fast, with an irregular beat. She took a deep breath and forced herself to stand tall before stepping from the small comfort of her suite.

She walked down the long corridor of the second floor, stopping by another ornate mirror to take a quick look. Her curly, blush-blond hair curled in the heat and fell out of its bun, leaving tendrils to frame the sides of her face. She spit into her hand, pushed the long, wiry strands up and slapped her shallow lace-trimmed bonnet onto her head. With a free hand, she secured it to her piled up locks with a long pin, blew the remaining hairs off her face and tried to tuck them behind her ears.

She angled her body slightly to watch in the mirror. Mrs. Dewitt and her maid, Tibia, a tiny, sprightly Dutch girl, stood on the landing. Each had a foot poised on the next step and were swaying like two cats ready to pounce. Sinead wheeled around to face in their direction. She hid her bothersome thoughts with a pained smile. "There. See, I'm ready after all."

"And you look your usual charming self, Jane," Mrs. Dewitt said, with emphasis on the 'usual.' She turned and smiled at her maid, whom she called Tibby when not fussed at her. "Come Tibby.

Lead the way."

Sinead stopped and looked from one to the other. "I don't under..."

Mrs. Dewitt straightened and moved onto the next step of the landing. "My dear, certainly, you are not planning on going to the docks by yourself. No one else in the house seemed prepared to accompany you, so I just..." She paused and clucked her tongue. "It would be distasteful for you to go alone."

"I've been to the docks before — before I lived here," Sinead stammered.

She stared at the floor, knowing the lecture coming next. There would be no point in arguing, yet she tried. "As a girl I went — "

"How often must I tell you? You are no longer that girl. As young Robert's nursemaid, you now have a position to maintain, dear."

Sinead looked up, ready to argue that she was Robbie's mother but could barely contain the giggle rising in her throat. The fashionable bonnet Adelaide wore, perched on the side of her head with the bird nestled on top, began to droop. When she spoke, the bird tilted to one side, its beak near her ear.

Adelaide seemed not to notice. She stiffened and gave a curt reminder to Sinead. "You are living in a grand home and must abide by its customs. You will not be seen on the streets of New York without a proper chaperone. As you can tell from my clothing, I shall accompany you myself. Remember, dear Jane, you haven't seen this gentleman before, if what your father has told my husband was correct."

Her pronunciation of 'father' showed her bias toward Sinead's da, Bowes, and made Sinead bristle in defense. She drew in a deep breath, grimaced and stood taller than before.

Adelaide did not recognize Sinead's preparation for battle and continued on. "You might not even recognize your husband, dear, from the puny description he sent you in the short note he wrote."

Both Adelaide and Tibia smiled, with almost identical facial expressions. Sinead's heart skipped a beat. What Mrs. Dewitt said was true. She had no idea what her new husband looked like, only that he was tall and had brown hair.

The two clipped, but respectful letters from Laird O'Malley, basically indicated her future husband's deep and fervent interest in horses, an animal she hated since watching her mum struck down by one. Fear predominated and made Sinead less anxious to confront the man she was to live with forever. Horsemen are a hard lot, she thought.

Totally unsure of whom she would find waiting for her at the docks, she was sure the man was no more anxious to marry a stranger than she. Nor was he interested in coming to America, if the subtle indications in the notes he included in his da's letters were true. Would O'Malley harbor resentment over being forced to marry? No doubt, she would have to live the rest of her life through another loveless marriage built on gratitude and her own usefulness to a man.

Adelaide tapped her foot again, this time with a stronger beat. She cleared her throat several times and mumbled something to herself or to Tibia.

Sinead, lost in thought, looked up. She couldn't think of the right words to get Adelaide to stay home. "Och, I do not wish to trouble...discommode ye." The words tripped from her mouth in a series of slurred consonants and vowels. "I'll take someone with me. Perhaps, Robbie's governess."

"Robbie? Robert. And who would care for the child while you were both gone? He's far too active. You know that boy is difficult for me to handle by myself and there's..."

"I'll take Robbie with me. He'll..."

"His name is Robert, my dear Jane. Surely you don't want to confuse him with pet names. Right Tibby..." Mrs. Dewitt turned back to reexamine herself in the mirror. She readjusted the hat, which slid again when she turned back to Sinead. "Besides, Robert doesn't need to mingle with the riffraff who call the docks their home. And your going there without a member of the family is totally unsuitable."

"I wouldn't let Robert out of my sight. I'd hold his hand every second."

Tibby stepped back and turned her head, smiling, a hand to her pursed mouth. She coughed delicately.

Mrs. Dewitt drew herself up, as if preparing to create a grand scene. "As I said before, dear, it's unsuitable without a member of your family."

"Then I'll ask my da to accompany me."

"He is totally unsuitable all together," Adelaide shrieked. "I will go with you and Tibby will accompany us. I hired a coach for the occasion. I'm sure the driver will keep us from harm — that is, if he wants to be paid for his services."

She gave Sinead a hard look. "Jane, do not frown so. It makes you so homely. You cannot go alone. You know how the Irish on the docks are. Now more than ever."

Mrs. Dewitt's comment about the Irish verbally slapped Sinead. Not that such a remark was the first to come out of Adelaide's mouth. This time, Sinead's face grew warm, her breathing hard, as she tried to control her annoyance. Tibby tittered into her hand in an attempt to control the widening smile growing on her mouth. Sinead wanted to slap the foolish girl.

Any defense of her Irish heritage would fall on deaf ears, so she capitulated. "I'd be delighted to have ye come with me," she lied. "Then, perhaps, I can take Robbi — Robert — with us?"

"Darling Jane, how I hate to repeat myself. Unsuitable! Robert shouldn't have to gaze upon such indecencies as is perpetrated on those wharves. My Josef doesn't even like to go near there. The docks are dangerous. Besides, it's not as if that man is the child's father. He is simply your husband, one acquired with surprising alacrity after my son-in-law's death."

Sinead had no answer. The statements about her husband were true. Bowes, her da, had arranged the circumstances of her marriage to the O'Malley stranger. Fond of little Robbie, he shouted his disapproval far and wide about the priggish, Protestant Dewitts raising an Irish, Catholic lad to manhood. He thought to thwart the Dewitts by giving Robbie a da who came from the old sod and maintained his Catholic roots.

Sinead tipped her head in Mrs. Dewitt's direction. "It shall be as you wish," she quietly said, knowing it wouldn't be any other way if she was to retain her relationship with Robbie. "Well, Mrs. Dewitt, we'll be going then. You lead. I will follow." *As usual*, she thought.

Adelaide turned on the landing. She poked Tibby to precede her. With chin protruding, inches ahead of the rest of her, Adelaide swung the back of her dress to one side, swished around on the landing and glided down the massive staircase.

Tibby reached up to offer her hand before Adelaide got to the bottom of the stairs. Sinead followed them, holding her temper in check, biting her lip until she drew blood and tasted it on her tongue.

The butler held the foyer door open. Adelaide sailed out and down the porch steps, like a steamboat under full power. The butler followed and helped her into the waiting public carriage. Tibby climbed in and sat next to her mistress. Adelaide shoved her over. With a wave of her hand and a pat on the middle seat, she summoned Sinead to sit between them.

Since the butler retired to the house after handing Adelaide into the carriage, Sinead climbed up the narrow step and over the maid. She desperately wanted to step on the girl's feet before she plopped down on the tiny space left to her. Squashed between the two ample women, the heat became overbearing. Perspiration coursed down Sinead's face and trickled onto her dress.

The cart's driver, who didn't have the decency to help them enter the carriage, gave a loud cluck. The two horses moved off at a fast pace, careening around the very next corner. Adelaide clutched her throat and hung onto the door handle. Tibby shrieked and Sinead's heart beat in an over-fast rhythm, frightened beyond measure by the quick movement of the horses.

"Driver, slow down," Adelaide shouted. "This instant, I say."

The carriage continued to bounce down the cobbled street, its pace uninhibited by any tug on the reins. Adelaide hoisted herself forward, bending her considerable chest over her round knees. She screeched at the driver, "Slow down. Immediately, I say!"

Sinead could barely breathe. Her corset pulled on her. The heat winnowed every ounce of strength she had in her and made little dancing spots in front of her face. Her innate fear of horses terrified her, and her breathing became more labored.

Without turning, the man in the front box called out in a rich Irish brogue. "'Tis a wee bit too fast for ye, is it? Yer servant told me ye were a mite late for the docking of a mighty ship from the land of the green." The man chuckled. "Of course, missus, with a pleasant 'please' from yer mouth, I'll slow these fellows down."

Sinead frowned, and groped in her small reticule for a handkerchief, but she was hemmed in on all sides it seemed. She tilted her head to one side and listened carefully.

Adelaide held the falling bird on her hat in a tight grip with one hand and the door of the carriage with the other. Her knuckles were white. "Please. Yes. Oh, please. Slower," she called out, tears streaming down her face, her hair somewhat askew.

"Och, that was much better," the driver hollered. He slowed the horses to a brisk walk. "See, they feel much more confident in their steps when ye speak with a softness to yer voice." The man loudly laughed. "'Tis a lovely day for the docks!"

This time, Sinead heard the voice clearly. It was her own da's voice, Bowes Brennan's voice, a voice with all the teasing ways of the old sod and it came from the front of the carriage. She wanted to howl with gladness but her heart beat too fast. She was dizzy, sick to her stomach, and closed her eyes.

* * *

The longer it took Bowes and the ladies to get to the docks, the more the sun beat down on their heads. Traffic stopped their carriage in all directions on several occasions. People gathered in groups, with no obvious purpose in mind, forced others onto the busy thoroughfares. The continual starting and stopping motions of the carriage, plus the heat and humidity, made Sinead physically ill.

No matter where they turned, what street they tried to go down, people seemed to be milling about, shouting, not hurrying from one place or another but clogging the streets. Carriages jockeyed for space to drive and, once they arrived at their destinations, took their time trying to park as near to newly opened shops as possible.

Invariably, wagons, carts and carriages lined the broad thoroughfares making up the business area. Dust spurted into the air from broken cobblestones. The entire scene filled Sinead with tension, the noises loud and frightening, and it was getting later and later.

After several hours of delay and rerouting, they arrived at the overcrowded piers of South Street and Wall Street, The East River bulkhead. Men were already lighting the gaslights lining the shipping areas.

Odors of decaying fish, spices, and garbage thrown about and left to rot, made Sinead even more nauseous. Unbearable heat, nervousness over her future and the tensions in the streets of the city regarding the new conscription laws further added to her discomfort. Hard pressed to hold it all together, Sinead leaned against the hard back of the carriage seat and closed her eyes, covering her mouth with her hand to control the bile building in her throat.

Bowes brought the horses to a partial stop and maneuvered them into a waiting area, across from the docks and screened from direct access to the ships. He stopped completely and leaped from the high seat in a single bound then stood on a wheel to reach under the driver's seat.

Sinead gulped, letting out an elongated sigh, until she saw her da pull out a large printed sign with something written on it. With a wave back at the ladies, he ran onto the pier and hastened over to a large steamship.

Sinead watched him raise the sign and circle in every direction within the milling crowd surrounding him. For a moment, she lost sight of him in shouting groups of vendors scattered around each ship and the passengers trying to embark. Every voice called to passengers or tradesmen, and she assumed her da was doing the same with his hand cupped to his mouth and his lips moving.

Every moment of sitting in the waning sun distressed her more. Faint from her fear of horses, the humidity and the pressure of the two women on each side of her, her heart fluttered like a moth beating against a glass lampshade. Her anxiety built a furnace inside her.

She breathed a sigh of relief upon spotting her da going up the gangplank of the steamship. She could barely see him talking to someone at the end of the gangplank and lost sight of him when he turned to go to another part of the ship. She could no longer see him and the pulse in her neck beat hard enough to make her gasp for breath. She didn't dare look at Adelaide or Tibby.

* * *

Carrying the placard with the name of O'Malley boldly emblazoned on its front and back, Bowes Brennan rushed onto the wharf and held the sign aloft. He turned in every direction and shoved the sign into faces of passengers embarking from the steamer.

"Do ye know these lads I'm looking for?"

Most were frightened-looking newcomers to the country, clutching their slight sacks of worldly goods to their chests. They looked at him with suspicion and pulled away, their heads shaking a negative response. Bowes waved the sign in all directions, until his arms tired of holding it so high.

He showed the sign to several of the stevedores who were already unloading cargo and to some of the sailors carrying passenger-goods onto the dock. "The O'Malleys. Do ye know the lads?"

One of the men pointed a finger to the steamer. "They haven't disembarked yet. They're still on board, waiting on someone to fetch 'em."

Bowes walked in the direction of the gangplank. He looked about him in hopes of spotting one of the lads, as if he could recognize them. He pushed and shoved to get through the noisy crowd of those arriving, those leaving and those bargaining to carry goods away.

His thoughts were a bit distracted. Most of the letters that had passed from one country to the other were between Finn O'Malley, his old friend, and himself. Bowes didn't tell Sinead about those private letters, so she thought the two short ones he delivered to her were all there was to know.

He couldn't remind her of the previous relationship between the O'Malleys and the Brennans. She wouldn't remember. She was too young when they left the farm in Ireland, although she did remember the accident. Would either of the lads Finn said were coming recognize him? Would Connor, the eldest of the lads, remember him? Bowes moved toward the ship. When Connor last saw Bowes and the two little girls, he was only eleven, though already taller than Bowes.

Bowes snorted to himself. No sense in worrying whether they would recognize each other or not. The deed was done. The priest had joined them in holy matrimony. Now, Sinead would keep young Robbie. He reached the gangplank and looked up at the ship. She'd be happy with that set of circumstances. The two youngsters would have to make the best of everything.

Hundreds had done so before, for less constructive reasons.

CHAPTER THREE

The steamer docked early on the morning of July eleventh. Connor made Egan rise from a sound sleep and dragged him up onto the deck. The temperatures below deck had taken a sorry toll on several passengers during the course of the voyage. Egan was one of them.

The steamer had sailed across the sea, like a silver fish, until the last week. Egan got seasick during the last ocean storm and collapsed shortly thereafter in the unbearable heat of the hold, while trying to help others sicker than he.

Connor knew Egan hadn't recovered fully. A fever and weight loss diminished his strong body and left him with a slight cough. Now, as they stood on the deck of a transatlantic steamship, Connor listened to the deep breaths Egan took, without coughing, and was somewhat relieved.

The lad was getting better by the moment, he thought.

The air was thick and scratchy, dense with odors of the many ships docked at the wharf. Egan waved back and forth, pointing to everything in a matter of seconds, his mouth keeping up a commentary of "Och. Con, look there. And there, too. Did ye see that?"

Transfixed, Connor stared with astonishment, his gaze moving from one area to another. For the first time in his life, he felt dwarfed by things far bigger than he. He was not in the least comfortable with the feeling, nor with this world into which he was being thrown.

The two brothers noted the activity with interest. A conglomeration of piers, docks and slips were lined up at what the sailors called the East River bulkhead. Mighty bowsprits and carved fig-

38

ureheads reached over the immediate wharf area into the street beyond.

The port was noisy, with pilots and crews jockeying for berths and merchant traders calling out their wares. Schools of sloops and lighters darted in and out amongst canal boats, schooners, barges, ferries and two thousand ton steamers. The offshore chaos gave rise to onshore mayhem as goods were transferred to hacks, carts and wagons, each competing to tote bales and barrels.

Still holding on to Egan, Connor, muttered, "How the devil do they expect a person to think with all that going on at the dock?"

"This is New York City. They don't expect you to think."

Connor laughed, shaking his head at his brother. They moved companionably toward a part of the railing nearest the wharf. Connor had never in his life seen so many things happening at once, all in one place, all at one time. He glanced at Egan's face to gauge his reaction to this tumult and was pleased to see it animated with interest in his surroundings. His normal ruddy color was returning.

"Och, 'tis a busy place this New York City. I'm hoping we don't have to stay here too long. I don't like the confusion," Connor said woefully.

"Con. Look around," Egan said, again pointing to the people on the dock. "'Tis exciting. People all moving about with a purpose. 'Tis better than our quiet farm. I'm in favor of spending lots of days here, I am." His smile grew broader. "I'll be mixing with the riffraff and the elite of the world, I will."

"Och, Da must have sent you with me for a purpose. Now, I'll be having to look after you, it seems," Connor said, looking down, his fists stationed on his hips. "Keep ye out of trouble will be my job, no doubt."

"I couldn't hear ye, Con," Egan snapped back at him, his eyes growing darker with the beginnings of anger.

The din was terrific. Several hundred iron horseshoes struck the cobblestone pavements. Boxes being lifted and carried rattled in

39

their crates. Drivers cursed at each other in different languages and dialects.

The throng and rush of crowds along the waterfront thoroughfares was enormous. A fight broke out in the street, just beyond where Connor could see clearly. No one seemed to pay any attention to the fisticuffs, no matter how near it got.

"Con, look at the buildings. Look at the size of them. Reaching for the sky they are."

"Some look to be five or six stories high. Warehouses the lot of them, I bet. The designs are peculiar, different than our wooden ones at home," Connor said with great distaste. "Some have… Is that white marble on the front of them? I can't quite tell from here."

"Neither can I," Egan replied, his eyes wide with delight.

"I would like to get off this ship," Connor said, scanning the dock for someone who might have arrived to fetch them, lost in a world he didn't know or understand. Although he had the address, he assumed his new wife would send someone as her letter stated.

Noticeable in his easy grin, Egan's joking ways returned. "Why don't we see if we can find your widow-woman?"

Connor grinned back but shook his head. "Not a good idea. Look at us. Beards down to our buttons, it seems. We look a fright, the two of us. We don't want to scare the woman, do we now?"

"Aye, you're right Connor, me lad. What say we get a room for this night, clean ourselves up a bit then call on the lady, all proper-like? You have the address. I'm sure some kindly soul will direct us."

"But she did say in her letter someone would be coming for us." Connor scanned the wharf. "How do people live in this place? There are buildings sitting on buildings. Look! They go on for miles," he commented, gesturing toward the sky. "As far as you can see. 'Tis glad I am now, we didn't bring the horses. The journey would have been hard on them and where would we put them in this wasteland of huge buildings and noisy people? Too much activity..."

"Aye. There's little room to move about. 'Tis what I expected though," Egan said, his chest puffing up in pride. "I thought New York City would be a large place, with excitement running rampant in the streets and life brimming with new worlds to conquer."

"Did you now?" Connor paused. "Something's been hanging on to the far reaches of my mind. I've been wanting to know for some time, so today I'll be asking you, Egan, for the first and last time. Why did you come with me, little brother?"

Egan looked up at him and seemed to consider his answer in a thoughtful manner. He smiled briefly. "I don't know. Rather, I'm not positive, for sure," he said. He turned away for a moment before continuing. "Adventure, excitement, a fresh life, different from the old."

"Were you not happy with the horses?"

"They were always more da's life, Bartley's and yours. The twins and I had other things to interest us. There were few opportunities in our area but for the horses or some kind of farming. Of course, I could have worked in one of the pubs, but I didn't think Da would approve. But never mind. We managed to be happy, the twins and me."

Connor was puzzled. "Are you thinking the twins wanted to come with us to America?"

"Aye. I know they did, but they wouldn't leave Da in a fix. They'll be here sooner or later." A slow smile crept across Egan's face. "Besides, none of us thought you should be going off alone. You don't know how to take care of yourself proper-like."

Connor leaned back and let loose one of his booming laughs. "Nae, I agree with you. I sure haven't taken care of meself. I've been taking care of you, wee brother, and a thankless job it's been."

"That you have and kindly, too. Surprised me, it did. But don't let it give you any ideas. I won't be beholden to you."

Connor let his gaze wander the docks. "Och, 'tis a busy place this New York City. I know. I keep saying that. I'm hoping we don't have to stay here too long. I don't like the place at all," Connor said woefully.

"Con. Look around. See what's out there. Give it a chance. You might even like it."

Connor shook his head. "I doubt it."

"So let's go. I want to see more and more. We could take a carriage to the address on the letter you got."

Connor had the address in his pocket. Across the thoroughfare, carriages lined the street. "I wish my newly acquired wife sent someone to meet us as she said. Her letter didn't sound like she was eager for a new husband, or a new life, and her comment, about disliking horses, doesn't bode well for our future together."

"Let's wait a bit longer, then. At least, until late evening. That's when we have to be off the ship."

"Con." Egan pulled on Connor's sleeve like a child. "Connor, look over there," Egan shouted, pointing in the direction of a milling crowd.

"What is it ye see, laddie?"

"See." He tugged Connor's sleeve again. "Nae, over there. A wee man. He's carrying a sign that has our names on it. And he's weaving in and out of the crowd fast, coming toward this steamer."

Connor sighed in relief at the sight of the placard the man carried. He'd never been to a city this size before, a city with so much activity, so much pushing and shoving, and he didn't like it at all. He had his plans ready. He would consummate this marriage quickly and hurry back to Ireland and the family he loved. His father was right. The beloved horses would still be there.

* * *

Bowes stopped at the ship's gangplank and called up to the first officer, who stood at its head. "Hey there, officer, can I come aboard? I have some passengers to find. I know they were coming on this steamer."

"Aye, you can. But be careful. Don't be pushing those who want to get off, or I'll toss you into the drink," the man replied in a stiff, superior tone.

"I wouldn't be thinking of doing a thing. I have me own calling. As long as I find the men I'm looking for. Do you know the O'Malleys?"

"O'Malleys? Oh, the big one, dark is he? And the other, a mite smaller, fresher mouth and red-haired?"

"If they still look somewhat the same, that would be them, I suppose. And where would I be finding them?" Bowes asked with a bit of deference.

The officer pointed his finger at two men who stood at the rail, away from those departing the ship. "Those be them. At the other end of the railing."

Bowes glanced over. A fiery-haired lad, looking a bit peaked, stood talking to the huge dark-haired fellow standing next to him. Bowes experienced a short flash of memory of them as children but couldn't remember which one was which, so mixed up they were in his mind.

After twenty years, what should he expect? Which one had married his daughter? The redhead might tickle her fancy. The big one, handsome under that straggly hair, might scare his poor daughter half to death. He chuckled to himself. But not for long, if he had any guesses left to him about men and women.

"Ho, O'Malleys. If that be you two. 'Tis Bowes Brennan at your service, lads," he called in a loud, raucous voice. "Are either of ye ready to meet the bride? I'm her da."

"Och, Lord," Connor commented, poking Egan again. "Me new wife's father. We certainly weren't expecting him. There's something about him that looks familiar. I wonder what he wants here."

"Probably to check you out, Connor. I'm sure he feels his daughter is worth more than you do. And that's a fact, for sure." Egan grinned. "And 'tis fitting." Egan stared at the man. "He does look familiar. He looks only a mite bigger than a leprechaun. Ye've seen a million Irishmen who look just like him."

"Aye, you're right." Connor slapped Egan on the shoulder for good measure. "Mr. Brennan? 'Tis us, sir, the O'Malley brothers, Connor and Egan," Connor said, drawing himself up to his full height.

Bowes Brennan marched toward them but stopped about three feet away, hoping they wouldn't recognize him. He carefully studied them then tossed the placard over the side and into the water, where it splashed and bobbed away on the current. "Well, ye don't look like much now but I suppose ye'll do better with a bit o' cleaning up. Which one of you is Connor, me son-in-law and husband to the only daughter I have left to me?"

"And good day to you, Mr. Brennan," Connor said in a voice filled with annoyance at the man's suspicious stare. "We've just come over the pond from Ireland. It was a long and tedious journey. We spent most of our time caring for those who sickened on the journey. 'Tis lucky you are I didn't bring my horses with me…"

Bowes stepped closer to the two younger men. "Horses? Me favorite animal. I would love to see an O'Malley-raised horse. I've been driving a common carriage here to the docks and back again for so long, I've almost forgotten what good horse flesh looks like." Bowes smiled, loving the effect he had on the two youngsters, who stood rooted to the deck, glancing at each other and looking utterly bewildered.

"Well, enough o' that. Follow me, Connor. Leave yer brother here to guard yer things or ye won't be having them when ye leave the ship."

Connor started after the man but turned back. He stared at Egan, opening his eyes wide then staring up at the sky. He made the sign of the cross and smiled when Egan laughed, nodding and gesturing him to go forward.

Bowes Brennan, thinking Connor was behind him, continued talking. "…bringing yer bride and the Mrs. she's staying with to the docks here. We got caught up in some unusual traffic, more than on most days. Got the feeling there's something afoot. Maybe 'tis cause of the heat."

He stopped, turned and looked Connor over once again. His voice carried over the water. "Well, I guess ye'll have to do. To be honest, there was no one else I could call upon but yer da. With such a short notification and all."

Egan, who had followed them, chuckled into his scruffy beard. "Well, I guess you're in for it now, Con. Seems as the widow has a randy-like da."

Connor swung around to face his brother and said behind his hand, "I'm thinking this is not a funny situation. If my wife looks anything like her da, then I'm in far more serious trouble than you think. Our mares are finer looking."

He turned back to Mr. Brennan. "Listen, man, if you want, I can get cleaned up. But, I'll be wanting one evening to myself to do it in. Can you get us a room at an inn?"

"There's no time, laddie. Ye're a married man now. Ye need to meet with the woman ye married — even if ye do look like the hordes of hell."

"Well, you're no raving beauty either. If the woman looks like you, I'll be hard put to make it right."

Connor stepped toward the man. Egan followed them a bit more. "Let's get the deed done. If I scare the poor woman to her grave then I'll be a free man, ready to turn right around and go back to Ireland. Now, let's march and have done with this bloody mess."

Bowes spun around and stomped toward the gangplank. "Hurry up, laddie. The sooner this part is over with, the happier I'll be. Try not to scare the lass."

"'Tis not the lass I'm worrying over." Connor turned back to Egan and shouted at him. "You stay here. Guard our things. I'll go find out what I can."

"Aye," came Egan's reply, muffled from the laughter he was holding in. "Go ahead now, Con."

Connor frowned at his brother for taking this entire affair so lightly. "I don't even know what the woman looks like."

"Didn't she write you about her appearance?" Egan asked, in an abortive attempt at seriousness.

"You know what lasses say when it comes to how they fancy themselves. Besides she told me more about the boy than herself. All she said having to do with herself is that she would meet the ship." Connor groaned. "Have your fun now, Egan. There might be the devil to pay later."

"Och, Connor, I'm thinking you see only the bad in things. For myself, I think we'd be better to wait until she sets her eyes on you. Sure an' ye'd scare the devil himself, looking all wild with that dark beard, long hair and those dark eyes. Go on with ye now." Egan turned away and went back to the rail, murmuring softly to himself in Gaelic.

Connor wondered what he was doing here in America, a place he never desired to see. He spent countless hours from the day he drew the long straw until the day he left on the ship, haranguing his brothers, pleading for one of them to take his place. Even during their good-byes he tried to weasel one into going in his stead.

His da wouldn't allow him to go back on his word. The man was well aware Connor didn't want to participate in this fiasco. But the marriage certificate bore his name. He had to go.

His dread of the woman with whom he must share the rest of his days, regardless of what difficulties they might find, made him shuffle his feet in a slow, then even slower, march. *And she hated horses?* That was the most stunning blow of all.

Once on the gangplank, he looked about, hoping beyond hope the widow wouldn't be displeasing to the eye enough to put him off. Plus, he would have preferred their first meeting be in a somewhat secluded area, so they might be able to conceal their initial distaste for one another.

Having become accustomed to the motion of the ship, the lack of it made him shaky as he stepped off the plank and followed the short man in front of him. The mass of people gathered between the sailing vessel and a grand steamer in the next berth did nothing to ease his frame of mind.

He felt out of place here, in a city. His former life was one of farms and animals. He knew he looked like a stable lad, not the heir to a fine Irish home. He looked down at his clothing and tried to brush it into some semblance of cleanliness.

The outfit was faded from washings in the ocean waters and grimy in spots. He took a cloth from a pocket and tried to wipe some of the grime away. When that didn't work, he shoved the cloth back into the pocket. He really didn't care. His one dark suit would stay wrapped in its package until he was more comfortable in his new surroundings.

If he were to have something worthwhile to do in this country before traveling back to Ireland, only horses would do it for him. He had to find some horses. He mumbled an oath to himself. "Raising horses is what I know and what I understand. I'll work with some horsemen here then take their knowledge back to Ireland with me."

Ten or more carriages lined up on the nearest street to the docks. Several of them contained women, but none contained only a single woman. It never occurred to him that women did not travel alone in the city like they did in the villages back home. He glanced at the crowded wharf, at the people who jostled and elbowed each other.

All at once, a great cry arose from the crowd. It seemed to be directed at someone emerging from the steamship. Connor turned in a circle as people surged toward the steamer, crying and shouting a name he couldn't understand. Either they were excited to welcome a family member or it was some kind of celebrity.

Bewildered, Connor rushed across the wooden beams beneath his feet toward the carriages parked along the roadway. He kept Bowes Brennan in view. In one carriage where the man seemed to be heading, three women, their faces turned in his direction, stared across the thoroughfare.

He stopped in his tracks. One of the women was a bit older than the other two. Her sophistication, seemingly regal bearing and tight lips made Connor nervous. Afraid she was his bride, his heart plunged. He stepped back and sharply looked around. Egan, standing on the deck, waved to him. He started toward the ship but stopped himself before he had taken two steps. He made himself smile and whirled around to face the carriage.

The two younger women in the carriage looked like servants. Neither was dressed any better than the other. The one furthest away stared at him boldly. The lass in the middle acted shy and partially hid herself behind the older woman. To his practiced eye, she seemed virginal, unsure of herself, like an untouched village lass.

Bowes Brennan stopped at that very carriage. Connor straightened and moved forward. He dragged his feet, reluctant to hurry up this meeting. With every step he took, the bones in his body ached. He longed to be back on the steamer, sailing to Ireland and his horses.

The closer he got, the more outrageous the entire situation seemed to him. His mouth turned down, and he half-closed his eyes. But as an O'Malley, he promised he would make the best of it, no matter what.

* * *

All of a sudden, Sinead spied her father shoving his way through a crowd of people toward the carriage where she waited. He had a broad smile on his face. His chest was puffed out like a peacock's. He turned back and motioned to someone.

The women in the carriage gasped. *Oh, no,* Sinead thought. *This can't be my new husband.*

A dirty-looking man, all dark beard and dark eyes, followed closely behind her da. His hair stood up like a rumpled haystack. He was a giant Irishman with icy dark brown eyes, like those of a gunman.

He must be her new husband's groom from the looks of him and the state of his clothing. Of course, that was it. A laird's son wouldn't be traveling alone across the ocean without a manservant of some sort. Laird O'Malley did mention his sons were horsemen. Naturally, a horseman would have someone crudely vulgar as a hireling. Sinead sighed in relief.

The man was muscular, fit as a groom should be, and totally Celtic looking — a black Irish thug, for sure. He looked as if he hadn't shaved in weeks. A straggly beard hung down below his chin and obscured much of his face. His hair touched his shoulders, but a lot of it was pulled back with a cord. His clothes, worn-looking with the colors faded, were wrinkled as if he'd been sleeping in them.

Her emotions raw, Sinead had no stomach for the first meeting with either this groom or his master. She wished the entire business of the marriage hadn't happened in the first place. Wanting to hide her distaste, she slid farther behind Adelaide and pursed her lips into a sneer. The approaching rogue's master should have seen fit to come to her himself, to introduce himself properly.

What could she expect of the ignorant son of an Irish laird, who was probably spoiled by far too much undue attention? Well, there was nothing she could do about it now, being already in the soup with the deed done.

She stole a peek at Adelaide, whose eyebrows were raised, almost to her hairline. The bird on her hat was sitting at her ear. Her eyes bulged out as she leaned forward over the carriage door. Sinead wondered what the woman thought of this spectacle of a groom coming to meet them instead of the man himself.

Her da, so short and wiry, moved swiftly across the crowded wharf, wending his way between people and carts. The giant, towering over most people on the wharf and dodging wagons, vendors and sailors, continued to step closely after her da. Several times, the big man wheeled around and darted one way or the other. He scowled at every person who bumped into him.

The closer the two incongruous men came to the carriage, the harder Sinead's ribs moved in an out in an erratic rhythm, the warmer she became. Her ribs slammed against the boning in her corset. She drew closer to Adelaide, as if for protection, and grew

49

faint.

Sinead's head throbbed. She had an odd, dizzy feeling. Little spots like insects danced before her eyes. No doubt it was due to the heat. Bile rose to her throat and lodged there. Then, an old Irish statement flew into her mind, 'the devil ye know…' She almost swooned.

When her da stopped at the carriage, the tall man did, too. The black-haired giant pulled in a bit of air through clenched teeth, frowned, then he straightened himself. He seemed to grow even larger, more intimidating, trying to look pleasant by leering at them.

His dark eyes looked directly at Adelaide. He tilted his head and nodded, saying, "Sinead O'Malley, I presume?" He extended his hand as if expecting someone to take it.

With the heat wave, the atmosphere choked her. Dizziness assailed Sinead, thick as the damp mists of Ireland. She couldn't speak. The devil had filed down the edges of her tongue. She pressed her hands against her chest in prayer or supplications then couldn't move.

Adelaide gasped and fell back against the carriage seat, her mouth opened wide. She gulped and asked, "Are you the Laird O'Malley?" Her mouth opened wider. She made a choking sound.

"Well, madam, not until me da's gone to his rewards…"

* * *

Connor studied the three women in the carriage. One hid behind the older, uglier woman — the one he assumed was his wife. From what little he could see of her, she was far more attractive than his wife. Both seemed to be struck dumb.

The buxom lass with straight hair the color of wheat looked him over carefully. She seemed to like what she saw, for she fluttered her eyelashes at him in a decidedly coy manner. Rather a brazen hussy at that, but one he was sure Egan would find amusing.

Connor waggled his eyebrows back at her, figuring the two younger ones were probably daughters or servants. He glanced at the older woman wondering why she looked at him with such wild, stricken eyes.

He knew he needed a bath, a shave and a change of clothing. He groaned into his beard and looked at the ground for a moment to gather himself. He scuffed his feet in the dust of the roadway. His wife seemed much more mature than the others, but none the less, extremely well-dressed and rather attractive. Connor tried to smile.

A fight broke out, not far from the carriage. His wife shrieked. The buxom lass laughed at the antics of the men battling. The one in the middle sat with her eyes and mouth open. She stared vacantly at the fisticuffs.

Totally bewildered by the amount of noise and activity emanating from the surrounding environs, Connor turned to scan the area as if he could quell the chaos with a look. Then he realized that no one had spoken in minutes. The women in the carriage and the driver, his wife's da, merely stared at him.

His wife asked, "Are you the Laird O'Malley?"

He tried to smile at her but could only sputter. "'Tis a strange question you've asked me. Am I the Laird O'Malley? Well, I'll tell you as I told you in me letter. Not until my da meets his Maker. Is it a problem?"

His wife spoke up yet again. "We were led to believe…" She turned to the younger woman next to her and yanked her forward. She put both her hands behind the girl's back as if to hold her upright. "I'm Adelaide Dewitt. This is your Jane O'Malley. This girl here. She's your wife."

Connor heaved a loud sigh of relief and stared at the lovely creature, now bent over, half crouching as if ready to attack. Although she listed to one side, at a funny angle, her blue eyes stared up at him. Tendrils of hair, the soft color of unripened strawberries, fell down the sides of her flushed face. They curled and tangled over her ears. She was breathtaking, despite her look of horror.

Now, he smiled broadly. Tipping his head in her direction, he said, "'Tis a lovely afternoon, wife. Allow me to introduce myself.

Connor O'Malley, your husband and servant."

"You certainly look like someone's servant," the older woman exclaimed.

His wife's mouth fell open. The racing of her heart pulsed visibly in the vibrant stretch of her neck. She tried to speak but words wouldn't come out of her mouth. She gasped for air.

Fascinated, Connor watched her eyes roll up into her head and her body pitch across the older woman's lap in a graceless heap. Connor was shocked. The one who was truly his wife had fainted away at the very sight of him.

He turned to Bowes, his dark eyes further shaded by the twisting of his eyebrows, the furrowing of his forehead and the length and unruliness of his hair. The women's obvious fear made him push away from the carriage, eager to leave, His need for acceptance was a thumping bass counterpoint to the high pitch of their anxiety.

"With your permission, I'll return to the ship, retrieve my brother Egan and our belongings. I seemed to have caused your lass some difficulty. For that, 'tis most sorry I am."

"Aye." Bowes Brennan howled with laughter. His body doubled over and tears of good humor ran down his face. He straightened, tried to put on a serious demeanor, but slapped his knee instead. "Ye're an Irish laddie, after me own sweet heart. Call me Bowes, son."

Connor grinned. He shook his head and turned back toward the ship. Still shaking his head, he mumbled aloud, "'Twas not the welcome I expected but…well, there's nothing to be done for it now."

CHAPTER FOUR

Adelaide Dewitt was angry, more furious than she had ever been in her life. For whatever reason this Irish marriage thing happened to help Jane in her attempts to wrest young Robert from his blood family, it was more than Adelaide could bear. Her face flamed and her fists balled into angry hammers.

No doubt, her husband would be ashamed of what she knew would be poor behavior. With escalating rage, she refused to worry about his feelings.

I have rights!

Her eyes felt like fire, burning with unshed tears welling up in them. She glared at Jane, who had fallen across her lap. No help would come from that direction. The girl was as limp as a dead varmint…totally incapacitated.

Adelaide shoved the foolish girl from her lap and onto Tibby's. "Here. You hold her sorry Irish self."

With a look of disgust on her face, Tibby pushed Jane up against the back seat and held her upright shoulder to shoulder. Jane's head lolled back onto the small headrest of the carriage. Her mouth hung open.

Glowering at Jane with utter distaste, Adelaide lost absolute control of herself. The cool, calm outer demeanor, along with any former dignity she might have garnered over the years, fled with her fury. She reverted to the little barefoot Dutch girl she was while growing up in the wilds of Albany, before her husband visited that city and saw the financial advantages of marrying her.

Any sophistication she had gained in her life was gone. She stood up. The carriage swayed. Her balance was off and she tottered back, half onto the seat, half onto Jane. She quickly rose again. This time, she spread her feet on the carriage floor and held onto the side of the carriage for a moment to balance better.

Connor watched her without moving. He seemed intent on the ensuing scene. No doubt, he had never seen a woman act like this. He looked as if he wanted to help Jane but was afraid to step into the fray.

Adelaide knew her mouth was moving as rapidly as her thoughts, but no words came out that she could hear, only gurgling sounds. She gasped for breath, trying to speak. Distressed that her words of condemnation wouldn't surface, she decided to take action.

With the long cloth handle of her reticule grasped tightly in her hands, Adelaide swung around it around her head several times until its momentum nearly carried her out of the carriage. She stood, teetering and swaying, her balance askew, the reticule ready to fly out of her hands.

"I should have known this whole rotten thing was your fault," she screeched with venom. She swung the reticule at Bowes Brennan's head. "This is another mess you conjured up with your foolish little people and your silly ghosts of days past."

When the handbag connected with Bowes's head, Adelaide swung it around in the other direction and missed Connor's head by the narrowest margin.

Bowes ducked and swayed from one side to another. He rolled on the balls of his feet and took several steps back until he bumped into Connor.

"All you Irish are the same, from that Cavanaugh who married my daughter, then yours, to the one you brought here. And just how do you think this marriage will go?"

She swung the reticule yet another time and missed Bowes's head again. "You insect, you. This was all your fault. Your fault...your fault..." Adelaide's words were garbled. "You've made

my husband's life a misery with your schemes. You have no understanding of people or their needs…all for the sake of a small boy
who barely knows you."

Bowes took a step closer. He reached out to Adelaide. "Now,
missus, don't be getting yerself all riled. Yer mister would be quite
upset if he saw ye now or if ye were to arrive home all flustered. And
for no godly reason."

"No reason. It's you. You're a schemer, an unreasonable seeker
of your own way."

"My way?" he asked in a soft voice. "Just because it doesn't
agree with yers? Is that the whole of it, now?"

"It was your fault Jane married that hulking brute Cavanaugh in
the first place. Your stupid suggestions sent her in his direction to
wheedle and nag at him. He was too sick to refuse…" she screeched
while still trying to whack him.

"It wasn't me choice. I didn't want her to marry an old, crippled
man who would never be able to give me grandbabies to dance on
me knees. She did it for the boy. 'Twas her promise to save the boy
from Protestantism and the misplaced Republicanism of his grandparents that got her married."

Adelaide's eyes narrowed. She scowled at Bowes with undeniable hatred. "You lie. As always. You thought it would make your
daughter rich."

Bowes turned away with a look of disgust on his face. He
shrugged and turned to Connor, a manly scowl on his face. "Ye just
can't talk to women. 'Tis something ye should learn, boyo. Aye,
learn it now while ye're young enough. Women have their own
female ways of dealing and doing things. They'll hear nothing from
any man of sense. Isn't that the way of it, now?"

* * *

Connor stood dumbfounded as he heard parts of his wife's story
for the first time. He didn't understand it all but paid close attention to the Dewitt woman. Her accent being somewhat foreign to

him, he missed some of her tale of woe. He was not pleased with the little he could understand. Did Sinead fool him, filling him with lies? His muscled arms crossed over his chest and a scowl deepened the angry look on his face.

And, why did the Dewitt woman continually call Sinead, Jane? Connor wondered while watching the young woman start to move.

Sinead groaned as she tried desperately to rise and sit upright. Her face was bright red. She wobbled, as if she would faint away again.

Connor's long arm snaked up to grab the reticule from Adelaide, who still swung it with abandon. "Madam, 'tis not the way to handle difficulties. Peace is to be desired above all. If ye have it, any difficulty can be solved. Always."

He moved closer to the carriage and gently settled Adelaide back in her seat. He bent over her then took his wife's elbow. With little effort, he helped Sinead to sit up straight. "There, lass, that should help ye in your struggles to rise."

He saw Sinead's face was pale with bewilderment. She looked around as if she didn't know where she was. She shook her head and looked directly at Adelaide. Perhaps, she hadn't heard what the Dewitt woman said. "Are you feeling better, lass?" Connor asked.

"That I am. Thank you. 'Tis the heat, and me worries over this day." She reached between her bosoms and pulled out a lace hankie. With careful strokes, she blotted the moisture from her cheeks and chin.

"Aye. I agree. 'Tis over-hot, and the situation does seem to be a bit awry."

"It is at that. We'll talk later." The sadness in her blue eyes drew him in closer. She spoke directly to him. "Maybe later, we'll see if we can make some sense out all this. 'Tis a bit of a turmoil, for sure."

Shouts erupted from another wharf and from the street just ahead. Everyone in the entire area turned to see what caused the ruckus. Many people climbed back onto their carriages, vendors closed up their carts and moved on. Sailors scurried back to their ships. Connor wondered what could be going on terrible enough to make everyone leave the area.

Bowes moved to the front of their carriage. "Laddie, I have to get these ladies safely home. There are things afoot in this city that are not going well for those involved. See a bit of the way down this very street? There are a few Irish pubs for the local seamen. Fetch yer brother, yer trunks and wait for me in one of them. They all know old Bowes. I'll escort the ladies home and come back for ye young fellows."

Connor saw the distress written on the man's face and answered, "Aye. I'll do that." He turned away from the carriage toward the steamer but quickly turned back to say, "I'll be seeing you a bit later, wife." He stared at her lovely face, hoping for a reaction of some sort, but none was forthcoming.

Sinead nodded and looked down at her lap. "Da, let's go."

"Aye, we'd best go home quickly. We'll sort all this out later, daughter."

Bowes settled the ladies securely in the carriage and climbed up on to the driver's seat. He cracked his whip and gave a jerk of the reins. The horses took off weaving their way around several of the carts that remained in the waiting area near the piers. Within moments, he managed to get onto the street and down it. He drove away from the harbor without a single glance backwards.

Connor watched them go, shrugged and turned back toward the ship. He'd get Egan, their goods and go to one of the taverns Bowes suggested. He wasn't quite sure which one. Well, it was of no consequence. He was hungry and could use a pint. He knew Egan would enjoy that too. He smiled as he thought over the events of the day and chuckled when he thought of the beautiful woman he'd have at his side. Suddenly, consummation of the marriage seemed much more appealing.

* * *

Egan stood by the steamer's railing, exactly where Connor left him. Their trunks were safely tucked behind him. Connor could tell by Egan's frown and foul expression that he had kept his gaze on the actions at the carriage.

His first words proved it. "What was going on over there? From the little I could see with the ships swaying into my way, one of those ladies took exception to your presence."

"Not mine, particularly, although I'm thinking one of them did," Connor said, puzzled. "I don't quite know what to make of the whole situation." He frowned and pushed his hair from his forehead.

"Well, through the haze from the heat and the light rising from the waters of the bay to make things fuzzy, seemed like they didn't have much respect for your wife's da either." Egan began to laugh then snickered, while patting Connor on the back. "I thought the swinging handbag would take his head from his shoulders."

"I think the older woman, Adelaide Dewitt she's called, has a problem with my marriage, and with Bowes Brennan, who must have been the one to perpetrate the occasion. I don't quite understand the reason for it all, but I'll find out before long, for sure." Thoughtful, Connor stared out at the ships in the harbor. "And why do those names, Bowes and Brennan, sound so familiar to me?"

"'Cause Da mentioned them for days on end before we left. It almost seemed like he was testing us with the name to see if we liked it. Didn't want us to forget it, I'm thinking."

"Why, I wonder. Well now, it sure does ring a bell, regardless of the reason." Connor smiled at his brother, bent and swept his trunk onto his shoulder. "I think it's time to be moving our feet to shore. Do ye think ye can carry your trunk? If not…"

"Aye. I'm not really ill any more. I think ye enjoy fussing over the likes of me, me being younger, of course," Egan said, struggling to lift his trunk. It wobbled, tipped to one side but Egan caught it and managed to settle it on his shoulder.

Connor watched him to make sure he could heft the trunk with ease. Egan seemed to be under no strain, other than the slight buckle of his knees with the initial swing. Connor nodded, and the two headed out, wending their way through crates and barrels left on the lower deck of the steamer.

When they reached the gangplank, a deckhand saluted the two of them. "It's a good thing you're leaving now. We're about to pull the gangplank back onto the ship. Can't take any chances at night here in this area."

"We'll be off in a second," Connor said with a smile. "And thanks for the lovely voyage. I enjoyed most of it until everyone got sick."

The hand smiled and nodded. "It usually happens once with every crossing." He chuckled over his own joke. "I hope you get to your destination safely. This is a dangerous place at night, especially on a Saturday when folks don't need to work the next day. Watch out for gangs of men or boys lolling about in the shadows away from the gaslights."

Connor and Egan marched down onto the dock. They turned and gave the deckhand a hearty wave. For some reason, the entire nest of piers looked strangely desolated.

Connor wondered why the frantic activity had stopped and where the people had gone. Although there were some wagons and carts on the wharf, a quiet, muted atmosphere hung over the area, except for the slapping water against ships in their berths.

Having little to say at the moment, the two crossed the street and stood under a lighted gas lamp. Egan shifted his trunk to his other shoulder.

"Is it too heavy for you?" Connor asked, frowning with concern.

Egan grimaced but laughed. "No. 'Tis light as a feather, for sure. Only needing a few rocks to weigh it down more."

Connor decided to tease him to see if he could recapture some of Egan's usual humorous bent. "I'll take it if you want, wee brother."

Egan shook his head, quirked up a corner of his lip and tried to shrug. Connor relaxed. He glanced down the thoroughfare at the number of pubs, taverns and saloons located there.

"I'll be…I don't remember which pub Bowes told me to visit while we wait for him. I wish we could go someplace to get cleaned up." Connor crossed the street and said, "I get the feeling Bowes Brennan might not be too reliable."

"I wondered about it meself when I first laid eyes on him." Egan replied while following Connor over the cobblestone street. He adjusted the trunk a bit and pointed to a small pub, tucked between two larger ones, which were much seedier and dirtier-looking. The small pub looked quiet and clean. "That pub over there looks a likely place. At least, it has an Irish name on the front. Let's go there. Get some food. I'm starving."

"That's a good sign. Makes me heart flutter with happiness," Connor responded. "You weren't hungry the last few weeks of the voyage." He looked up at the sign hanging across the front of the building above the doorway. "Clancy's Saloon. That's a new one— saloon." He headed for the doorway. "Well, come on Egan, Clancy's, it is then."

The brothers stood near the building and watched as sailors, day laborers and journeymen, all Irishmen, darted in and out of the saloon. None of them stayed for any length of time. A few left with pails of lager. Each time the door opened, a fog of tobacco smoke and the sour smell of porter floated out the doorway. Connor looked at Egan, who shrugged, smiled and nodded at the door.

Connor could hear a noisy argument emanating from the inside. He pushed the swinging door in with his foot and held it open so Egan could precede him. The inside, with dark wooden slats halfway up the walls, was dim. As the two entered, all conversation in the bar stopped.

Once inside, the brothers stood still for a moment, letting their eyes adjust to the interior. They glanced around the long room to get their bearings. The entire bar gave off a somber air, as if something was going on there, which couldn't be seen by the naked eye.

Connor scanned the deepest parts of the establishment. His shoulders prickled with unease. He turned to look at the door and vowed not to go too far from it. Nevertheless they placed their trunks down, near the only bank of windows decorating the front of the place.

A single wooden bar, shining and glistening even in the gloom, ran the length of one side of the room. Only soft gas lamps, connected to the back wall, lighted it. Off to the right, there was an alcove, with a stage covered by a long, dark velvet curtain. With only short candles, on tables, for illumination, the furthest reaches of the barroom were nearly black as night.

A few stools faced the bar, two taken by men, crouched over and sitting half in the dark. Most of the men stood around the bar, singly or in small groups of two or three. Toward the back of the long room, another group of men sat at the three small, round tables.

Not wanting to disturb the strange, ominous silence, Connor moved to the bar and softly spoke to the barkeep. "Sir, would it be possible for me brother and me to get a bite of food?"

"All I got is Mulligan stew. Just about to the bottom of the pot," the man retorted.

"That'll be fine. It'll stick to our bellies, I'm thinking." This city definitely wasn't a place to inspire one with the notion of wild and free, Connor thought to himself.

The barkeep walked the length of the bar and announced loudly, "Two new ones, just off the boat. Give them a break for what's probably their first meal on shore, and mind yer manners." He disappeared behind a small door set at the end of the bar.

All eyes focused on the two newcomers.

Connor turned to Egan and mumbled, "I don't like the feel of this place."

"Neither do I, but I'm starved. Let's just eat our stew and be gone from here," Egan said, sitting down on a vacant stool. Connor sat down next to him.

Men continued to rush into the bar and dash out again. Some of the men in the back were playing cards. One man kept offering toasts, but most just drank, cursed and quarreled. Connor could hear snippets of their conversations.

A sailor rolled in on bowed sea legs and plopped down at one of the tables. He was the first to be heard when he shouted, "Low-browed, they said."

Another man added, "Bestial savages they called me."

One man who was there from the start vulgarly quipped, "Hell, to describe us Catholics, the bastards compare us to wild apes. I've heard it all and I'm sick of it."

An Irishman, well into his cups and leaning on scrawny elbows piped up, "Ye have only to show them different, I keep telling ye."

The barkeep returned, his hands filled with two wooden bowls. He toted two large crusts of bread, one shoved under each arm and held close to his body. "Here's sustenance for ye both," he said, placing first one bowl and a crust on the bar in front of Egan, then the second bowl and bread in front of Connor. He plunked a fork and a cloth napkin down before each. "Eat hearty, lads."

The barkeep continued to stand there. "Would ye like a pint of lager with yer meal? To wash it down?"

"Aye, that we would," answered Egan, bringing his hand to his heart. "A lager would hit the spot after the long journey we've endured."

"Have ye just arrived from the old country?"

The question seemed innocent, but Connor felt it was weighted with some unheard meaning he didn't understand. The saloon was too quiet. "Aye."

The man continued. "By the way, I'm Clancy. The owner of this establishment." Clancy held out his hand for Egan to shake.

Out of the corner of his eye, Connor noticed several of the men from the back had crept soundlessly forward into the light of the bar, where they stood quietly. They appeared to be listening to the conversation between his brother and Clancy. Their coming close to them in a group, practically surrounding them, was not to Connor's liking.

He turned slowly, stood up and faced them. He straightened to his full height, towering over all of them. "Gentlemen, is there something I can help ye with? Is there something about me brother and me that stirs your curiosity?"

Clancy called out. "Men, go back to yer tables. Let the lads eat a decent Irish meal, fer God's sake. They've just arrived from the Green. I believe, they'll be willing to answer all yer questions when they've finished."

With a great deal off grumbling, the men shuffled back to their original places. They pulled the chairs from beneath the tables, turned them toward the bar and plopped down in them. The sat with their legs extended, waiting.

Connor took a long swig of the lager and let it roll around his mouth before swallowing. After the heat of the day, the lager was just what he needed and wanted. He dipped his crust of bread into the stew and savored the first taste of Irish cooking he'd savored since he and Egan left their home.

"'Tis good stew. Thank you, Mister Clancy. It hit the right place in my stomach and I'm hoping it sets there for a while."

"Just Clancy, son. 'Mister' in this city refers to no Irishman I know. At least not of late."

It was obvious the condition distressed the barkeep, but Connor decided not to say anything. He kept shoveling the stew to fill his belly and assuage his hunger.

"Why is that?" Egan asked with a mouthful of food slurring his words.

"The bastards who run this city have no respect for the Irish. They spit on us when we're no' even looking in their direction. Use derogatory names as well."

Connor continued to eat and listen to every word spoken. It was better to know what the situation was in a city this big, especially when you were trying to find your way around.

"What do the people who govern you act like?" Egan questioned. "It certainly doesn't seem the decent way to behave." Connor elbowed him, but Egan continued. "Who runs this city then?"

"The Republicans and the Protestant do," an older, gray-haired man groused in a nasty tone, from the end of the bar.

"And we are none of those," a young man, with a pimply face and a long, lean body, shouted from one of the back tables. He leaped from his chair, adjusted his red shirt and came forward to join the man at the bar, the man who spoke first.

He leaned an arm on the older man's shoulder before he spoke with obvious pride. "Me name is Ryan, Jimmy Ryan at that. I'm a fireman. From the Black Joke Engine Company, number thirty-three. Tops in the city we are — and, an all Irish fire company to boot."

Friendly as ever, Egan volunteered, "Sounds like something I might like to do if we stay here for very long."

"What's yer name, laddie? So we'll be expecting ye."

"O'Malley, like me brother said. Egan's me first. Call me that."

Ryan chuckled. "'Tis is right fine Irish moniker, to be sure."

All the men in the bar laughed, but Connor felt there was an edge to their good cheer. Connor put one booted foot on the floor, ready to stand up quickly if necessary. He leaned an elbow on the bar and cocked his head, listening to all the grumbling behind him.

Something was afoot in this bar. It did not bode well for him or his brother. Yet, politeness was in order until he learned he might have to behave differently. He slowly stood, unfolding his large body.

"I'm Connor, the oldest of his brothers," he said, gesturing with his thumb at Egan. "We've three more just like us, still at home, with our da."

Another man from the back tables sidled up in back of the brothers. He laid a seemingly innocent hand on Connor's shoulder, digging his fingers into the muscle as if trying to force Connor to sit. "I'm McCarthy, Jack to the two of you. I'm curious. How come ye left yer family and came to this bloody country? Going to start a new life are ye?"

"Ye'll not be doing that in this city, lads," said the gray-haired man at the end of the bar. "I'm another Jack but call me Quinn.

Everyone does. Why did you come here? Now, when there's a war on?"

"I married an Irish woman from here and came over to join her, before I bring her home to Ireland." Connor replied, thinking it was none of the man's business. Annoyed, he sat back down on one of the bar stools.

"Aren't there any women left in Ireland?" Quinn asked. He laughed louder than he did earlier, as if his joke were the finest one ever made. Seeing him laugh, both McCarthy and Ryan laughed with him. McCarthy removed his fingers from Connor's shoulder and moved over a space or two.

There was a distinct edge to Quinn's laughter. Connor was embarrassed by the rude question and crude hilarity. He shrugged and caught a glimpse of Egan out of the corner of his eye. *Och,* he thought, *me young brother is getting perturbed.* His Irish temper was on the rise and beginning to show in the blushing red color of his face.

Connor thought to deflect the situation he believed was approaching too fast. "Egan, maybe 'tis better we leave," he said in a low voice, hoping no one overheard him.

He swiveled on his barstool to face McCarthy, who still stood nearby. "Let me ask all of you gentlemen a question." At the expectant expressions on their faces, he smiled. "Where would two rather grimy and long haired fellows go to freshen up a bit?" he asked. "I don't want to scare the wife out of future years."

"Why can't ye go to yer own home to 'freshen' up a bit?"

Clancy the barkeep interrupted, "You boys can clean up here in one of the back rooms, if you like." He glared at the men who now crowded around Conner and Egan. "What are you men doing? These boyos are merely a couple of greenhorns. Let 'em be. Go on now. Move yourselves back some."

Quinn answered quickly. "Aw, now, Clancy, don't be having a fit behind that there bar. These two are no boyos. They're full grown men, capable of learning what's right and what's wrong. And they might as well learn right here."

Quinn seemed to be the leader of the group now encircling the two newcomers. Connor let the rest of his stew sit in its bowl and stood with his back to the bar. Egan stood as well and took a similar position. They both leaned back in a relaxed manner.

"Och, two tall ones," said McCarthy, the fireman.

"Aye. That we are."

He moved closer and shouted into their faces. "Do ye greenies have any idea of what's going on in this country, in this city? Do ye know of the damned draft? The damned Conscription Act?"

"No, we know none of it. We arrived in the harbor, this very day. It'll take us some time to understand the way of life over here in this huge city. From the looks of it, 'tis much different than in our village."

Quinn shrieked from his barstool, "Cities are all the same, religion and politics, politics and religion. The rich and the poor. Are there no big cities in Ireland, boy?"

Clancy began to move whiskey bottles from the high shelf above the bar to a lower one. He shouted out for all to hear. "Don't ye men be starting trouble here in me tavern. I'll be sending for the police if ye don't mind yer manners and shut yer mouths."

A single glass, filled with lager, slid across the top of the waxed bar and hit Egan's elbow. He looked around. Men hemmed in both Connor and him. The glass came from the vicinity of Quinn's stool at the end of the bar.

Within moments, the other men in the bar followed suit. Each man put his glass on the bar and slid it toward Connor and Egan.

Clancy shouted again. "Och, be quitting the shenanigans, men."

As Clancy spoke, McCarthy took a swing at Egan. Egan ducked and plowed his fist into the man's stomach. At the same time, Connor swung and caught the man on the side of his face. McCarthy fell to the floor in a heap.

The fight was on.

Clancy grabbed the remaining bottles standing at the back of the bar and put them on the floor. He covered the glasses with a large cloth and swept the ones left on the bar in a cloth sack.

In the time it took Clancy to clear the bar of breakables, another man, who didn't bother to introduce himself, took a swing at Egan. Egan hopped on his feet, from one side to another, and managed to receive only a glancing blow to the side of his jaw.

The comments, snickers and actions angered Connor. His body temperature rose. Again, he stood, this time with his back to the bar, his fists clenched at his sides.

He'd be damned if anyone would start a fight with his wee brother when he was around. "If it's a fight ye're wanting, bring it on. This may be a new city but a fight's the same regardless of country..."

Connor swung a massive clenched fist at the man who tried to hurt Egan. "Ye'll not be picking on any brother of mine."

The man went down like a puddle of lager. Then every man in the bar leaped into the fray. Quinn stood in the background, shouting orders to the rest of the men. Clancy cleared the bar and tried to break up the deadly battle for survival, to save his saloon from destruction. Someone hit him with a chair. He fell to the floor, holding his head in agony and groaning.

Connor was furious and beginning to breathe hard. He was bound to protect Egan, who had done nothing. He raised his fists high in front of him, ready to strike the next man who approached. Men were coming at him from all angles. He wheeled around in each direction, daring men to come after him.

Clancy struggled to his knees and crawled to the front door. Connor heard him screaming outside in the street but couldn't hear what he was shouting. McCarthy ran outside and dragged Clancy back inside. He lifted the barkeep and threw him over the counter onto the floor in back of the bar. A crash of broken glass accompanied Clancy's louder groan of agony.

This was fast becoming an unfair fight. Connor and Egan were outnumbered. Someone smashed Connor in the eye. He knew it would shortly blacken and make a lovely picture for his new wife.

Another caught him on the chin.

He felt his knees give way, but Egan shouted to him. "Don't give in now Con. We'll win this thing yet. O'Malleys never give up."

With a whoop, Egan leaned against the bar and brought his knees and feet up in the air. Their very height gave Connor the time to recuperate. Ryan and another man raced toward his brother. Egan's two feet sprung straight out and hit them square in the chest, knocking them both to the floor. He grabbed the bar stool from in back of him and swung it left and right, keeping others away from him.

Ryan dragged himself from the floor, brought out a knife and came toward Connor, who rose to fight anew. Ryan threw a punch and connected with Connor's lip, which began to bleed profusely.

As Connor bent forward, Ryan tried to stab him. Connor grabbed his wrist, lifting it upward. He squeezed it until Ryan dropped the knife. Connor shoved him aside toward another of the gang who was directly in front of him. McCarthy came at Connor from the side and clipped his cheekbone, tearing the skin. Quinn shouted orders to all of them but refused join in the fight itself.

A short man moved along the floor and tried to bite Connor's leg. Connor kicked out, and the man went sprawling across the floor into the opposite wall at the bottom of the stage. Connor bent and lifted Ryan from the floor. He tossed him into McCarthy. They both went down.

"Egan, laddie," Connor shouted. "Are ye doing all right? Don't let them separate us. Stay with yer back to the bar."

"Aye. I surely will." He gave a laugh of excitement. "What a kind welcome this is to the city of New York, in America, no less! Da and the boyos will never believe this story."

McCarthy stood up. He reached down to raise Ryan and seemed to whisper something in his ear.

Connor lost sight of them and assumed they were fleeing the fight. He continued to punch those who came at him from the front or sides. Still, men were able to land blows, beating both lads for every blow that landed. There were too many for the brothers to take them all down in one fell swoop.

An arm snaked around Connor's neck and squeezed. "Did ye think to have me down for the count, boyo?" It was McCarthy. His grip was firm, and he twisted his arm upward, trying to cut off Connor's wind.

"Egan' be careful... They're climbing on the bar — to get in back of us. Remember the old trick...we did once before."

"In the village...pub?" A breathless Egan asked, pummeling a man near him.

"Aye." Connor gurgled as McCarthy tightened his grip on Connor's throat. "Okay...now...Egan...go..."

The two O'Malley brothers reached over their heads and grabbed the men in back of them, raising them high. They continued to hold them aloft. Both men squealed to be let down.

"Put me down, ye bastard," cried McCarthy.

"Don't drop me, ye fool. Ye'll break every bone in me body." Ryan screeched at the top of his lungs.

Just then, there was a commotion at the door to the saloon. Some man in a uniform banged on the wall. "Okay, now, lads. 'Tis enough of this battling," he hollered above the noise of the fighting.

"Break it up, now. Break it up," yelled another voice.

"Quit yer battling, ye stupid fools," came from a voice laden with authority.

Men dressed in the uniforms of constables moved over the floor strewn with limp bodies. One man stood directly in front of Connor and Egan. "All right, lads, let's just ease those bodies down. Nice and slow-like. Ye wouldn't want to be hurting any more of these men, now, would ye?"

Connor set McCarthy on his feet.

Egan did the same for Ryan, giving the man an extra shove and then looking at Connor. "Jesus, Connor, what have they done to ye. Ye're covered in blood. Are ye all right?"

The first policeman, who had ordered the fight to stop, said,

"Och, the man looks to be just foine. Just the usual cuts and bruises that ye always get in a fight."

Ryan moved to the man. "Mick, these boyos from the old country started a battle royal over nothing." Ryan turned around to those who could still answer. "You fellows know me brother, Captain Michael Ryan, don't ye now? Mick, let me tell ye what happened. Me and me friends were just sitting around here, having a lager or two, when these two fellows came charging in and started insulting everyone." Again he turned to his bar mates. "Isn't that right, boyos?"

"Ayes," came in a chorus.

The captain strolled up to Connor. "'Tis sorry I am, but I'll have to be taking you men into the jail."

"Officer, we didn't start anything. We stopped in here to get a bite of food in our bellies and were attacked," Connor said. "We didn't do anything or say anything. We just got off the boat and wouldn't even know the proper insults to give. Ask Clancy, the owner."

"Where is he?"

"Someone threw him behind the bar. He might be hurt."

Mick gestured to one of his men to check.

"Oh, God, Mick," Ryan said. "Clancy's out like a light. He's all bloody, too. We'll have to get him some help. And get me out of here before there's more trouble."

"Ryan, go get a doctor to look at Clancy, while I take these two bozos down to the precinct," Mick said, nodding toward the door. "Sorry to do this to Irish laddies, but I'll need to keep ye close until I sort out this whole thing."

CHAPTER FIVE

Late in the evening, Bowes scoured the entire waterfront searching for the O'Malley brothers. No matter what saloon he stopped in, he heard no word of their whereabouts. He was afraid they left New York City.

He was about to go to the police to inquire, when one of the local barkeeps, Mulligan the Madman as he was called, gestured him over. The man acted like he had some secretive gossip to dispense, so Bowes approached slowly, not wanting to be bothered with gossip.

"Bowes, it was like the old days, when we first arrived here," old Mulligan exclaimed in an excited voice. He wiped his hands on his apron and described the fight at Clancy's Saloon, earlier in the evening.

Bowes laughed at the man's obvious glee over the incident, but wondered if the brothers were embroiled in one of the local bar fights. It was unlikely anyone would want to attack either of those two large men. Nevertheless, he asked. "Was there a huge man, with brown hair?"

"Aye. There was. He was a mite bloody so I couldn't see his features. And, there was another almost as big. But he was red-haired." Mulligan drew in a breath and leaned closer to Bowes.

"Anyway, all them men fighting that damned federal draft hang out in Clancy's most nights and don't seem to be very considerate either. It seems Clancy has his hands full with the likes of them, not

71

to mention trying to quell the happenings of this very evening," Mulligan added, his voice low and tense. "You know how us Irishers get riled over what might turn out to be nothing."

Bowes nodded his head in agreement. "Och, I know it for a fact." Worry creased his forehead. "I should have warned the boyos not to go into that place. They're new here."

"Aye, that ye should. Why didn't ye send them here? I would have taken good care of yer friends, for sure."

"That you would. I should have come with them meself, but me daughter fainted upon meeting the man she married. She'd never seen him all grown up. I had to drive her, and the nasty woman she lives with, home to that East side mansion those Dewitts call a home."

While continuing to worry over the fate of his daughter's husband, Bowes gestured to Mulligan to go on with the story.

The older man chuckled. "Well, anyway, the boyos in Clancy's got to feeling their oats, I'm thinking, and created a riot, such as we've not seen in a long time. Clancy had to drag himself out to the street to call for the police."

"It must have been a sight, for sure." Bowes knew he couldn't hurry Mulligan into telling the story any quicker, so he smiled and listened carefully.

"Och, that it was."

"Did the police take any of the fellows away?" Bowes asked, becoming more irritated by the minute. He tapped his foot several times in aggravation.

"Aye, they threw four of them into one of their conveyances. I heard one of the officers say they'd sort it all out in the morning, if and when everyone was sober." Mulligan gave a hearty laugh and slapped Bowes on the back.

"Mulligan, I'm thanking ye for the information. I think one of those boyos was me daughter's new husband."

"Och, then Bowes, ye better be getting her and bringing her to the precinct, otherwise they'll be sending those fellows home again to

Ireland," Mulligan said, his head shaking in commiseration.

"I'll go prepare my daughter for the possibility. Right now. This very night. We'll be going down to the precinct in the morning to spring those boyos from their cells."

Bowes left Mulligan, but not before he thanked the old man. Bowes hurried back to his carriage, mentally cursing himself and trying to figure out where he could get the money to buy their release. Regardless of the consequences, he needed to see Sinead tonight, to discuss this with her and to beg her forgiveness.

"Och, hell and be damned. I'd better pick up the boyos' gear. I bet they left their trunks in Clancy's."

* * *

Night descended by the time Bowes arrived at the Dewitts' mansion on Fifth Avenue. He tied the horses to a post left near the street for that purpose. The streetlights lit his way to the closed iron fence of the mansion. He reached up and pulled the chain to the bell at the entrance. Its tinkle broke the stillness of the night.

He knew it was late to call on people like the Dewitts, but his parental obligation to explain to Sinead why her husband didn't join her as planned had grown to unreasoned importance in his mind. He needed to relate what had transpired, to describe what she must do now and how she must behave in the morning, no matter what the police or anyone might say to her.

A bit of heat dampened his brow and trickled down his face. He wrung his hands together before clenching his fists them behind his back as he waited for someone to answer his ring. The very idea of the upcoming interview with his feisty daughter made him more uneasy than anything he'd experienced of late.

Nevertheless, he marched up onto the small circular porch of the mansion's entrance, to the huge wooden and glassed-in red door. With nervous fingers, he brushed off his jacket, straightened the rest of his clothing and rapped loudly on the door. In an unconscious gesture, he rubbed the knuckles of his hand, more from nerves than necessity.

He understood from Adelaide Dewitt, only this morning, he was not welcome in this house. "No fault of me own," he grumbled, moving from one foot to another. "Them Dewitts and me never did agree on the upbringing of young Irish folk. Like me daughter. Gave her fancy ideas, they did."

No footsteps were heard near the entranceway. No one came to answer the door. Bowes beat on it again, a bit harder this time. He was determined to rouse someone.

Still no one came, so he kicked the door with his heavy boot in defiance and guilt at the unpleasant turn of events since the O'Malley lads' arrival. He beat his fist against the door again.

Annoyed at being kept waiting for so long, Bowes gave the door one last kick with the side of his foot and turned to go down the steps. When he reached the stone of the sidewalk, he heard the door creak and turned back to the now opened door.

A decidedly stuffy white-haired man, in servant's livery, with a smug look on his face, stood in the entryway. He spoke with extreme politeness in the high and mighty accent of all the English Bowes knew. "You have the wrong entrance, sir."

"Is this not the home of Ludwig Dewitt?"

"Yes, it is, but you, sir, need to go to the entrance at the back in order to deliver any goods." The man smiled and went on to give directions. "If you go down the narrow street to your right, you'll see a small lane to your left. Come to the back door of this house. It's designated."

Bowes face grew hot with embarrassment. "Are ye finished with yer speechifying? If so, let me tell you, I'll be doing nothing of the sort. I've come to see me daughter, I have, and I won't be going to another door, no matter where it may be."

"Your daughter?" The man's nose wrinkled. His eyebrows were raised in disbelief. "I doubt your daughter would be here, sir, much less live here." The man gave Bowes a look of superiority. "Even if she were, I'm sure you would need to go to the service entrance. It's clearly marked, so there should be no problem in you finding your way."

Bowes grew more annoyed by every minute he spent talking to this guardian of the door. Things needed settling before those lads were shipped back to their da, and he needed to discuss the situation with Sinead. He had the distinct feeling only Sinead could fix the problem.

The man turned to go and attempted to shut the door. Bowes slipped his foot between the doorjamb and the door itself. "Find me daughter! I know she lives here. I intend to stand on this very porch and wait until she's called."

"I beg your pardon?" The man turned back to Bowes, his face a stiff mask.

"Ye don't need to be begging me pardon or any such thing. Is this the home of Sinead O'Malley and her son? I seek entrance if it is."

"There is no one by that name living in this house. I keep telling you that, but you don't seem to listen well."

A maid arrived in back of the man standing at the door. She whispered something into his ear. It was the lass who earlier traveled to the piers in the carriage with Sinead. With a giggle and brief wave to Bowes, she scurried away to another part of the large house.

"Oh, my," the man said. "I'm so sorry. I didn't understand and was given no directions. Are you Mister O'Malley?"

"Nae. I'm not. I'm Bowes Brennan. Da, I mean father, to Sinead."

"I'm so sorry. I mistook you for a tradesman. In fact, didn't I see you driving the coach my mistress rode off in this very morning?"

Bowes glared at the man. "Aye. I was driving that carriage, just to see that me daughter made it safely to the proper wharf to meet her husband. I know exactly what ye took me for, and I don't appreciate your fancy, hell-bent-to-those-in-trade attitude."

"I am sorry. Allow me to introduce myself. I am Nigel, the majordomo of the house." He nodded in deference.

"Majordomo is it? What in God's good name is a majordomo?"

Nigel ignored the question. With his hand and a brief nod of his head, he ushered Bowes into the foyer. "Might I offer you some advice, sir?"

Bowes, irritated by the condescending treatment, answered. "What advice might you be offering me that I would listen to?"

"First of all, Mister Brennan, a gentleman would remove his cap."

"He would, would he now? Well, thank ye kindly for yer advice," Bowes said, grabbing the hat from his head and shoving it in a pocket of his trousers.

"Secondly, there is no Sinead in this house. We do have a young woman, who lives here, called Jane. She is nursemaid to Robert, the Dewitts' grandson."

"Jane? Can't ye even call her by her rightful name, a name given to her by her blessed mam who passed on to her reward?"

Nigel stuck his nose in the air and looked down at Bowes. "In this house, the young lady is called Jane, as my employers wish. If you want to see her, call her by that name."

By this time, an angry flush came to Bowes's face. He knotted his hands into fists. He hated to be treated like a lesser being, an animal. "I don't care what ye or yer employers care to call her, I want to see my daughter."

A distinguished-looking man dressed in a tailored suit, his dark hair showing a bit of white at the sides and at the temple, appeared in the doorway. "Nigel, why are you standing in the foyer with the door open? You're letting in the heat from the street. What seems to be the trouble? Close the door, please."

The man moved to return from wherever he'd come when he noticed Bowes. "Excuse me. Sir, did you wish to speak to me? Nigel, please close the door before more insects invade the house."

Nigel pointed. "This gentleman wishes to speak to Jane, sir." Nigel stood directly in Bowes's path.

"Jane? Well, she's not feeling well. Heat-struck, I believe. And for the very same reason, I do not wish to speak to anyone myself." He turned away from the entrance to move back into the bowels of the house. "Nigel, tell the man to come back in the morning. Miss Jane is not receiving at the moment."

Bowes pushed his way past the majordomo, trying to face the heavy-set man who was about to leave. "'Tis me daughter ye're keeping from me, and I'll not be having it," he shouted. "And who are ye anyway that ye know the personal state of me daughter's health?" He raised a fist.

"Er, um…" Nigel took a fearful step backward.

"Not you, man. Him." Bowes said, pointing to the man in back of Nigel. "Will ye not be answering me? Who are ye?"

"Why I'm Ludwig Dewitt, master of this house. And you, sir, I presume are Jane's father?" he asked in a condescending manner.

"Aye that I am." Bowes puffed out his chest and looked Ludwig Dewitt squarely in the eye.

"Let me say this once again. I'm Ludwig Dewitt. Your host." Ludwig nodded. "Do come in. Come ahead," he said politely, gesturing Bowes inside the home. "The family is gathered in the drawing room. You're welcome to join us there."

"Nae, I don't think it would be a comfortable thing. I'll just be seeing me daughter, Sinead, if ye'd have her fetched for me."

Ludwig nodded to Nigel. "Please ask Tibia to fetch Jane to my office."

"Yes, sir. Immediately," Nigel agreed and left the hallway, going somewhere to the back of the house.

"Why didn't ye just have someone bring me to her room? I could speak to her there easy enough."

"I'm sure my wife would not feel it appropriate."

"There's not much that lady feels is appropriate, save fer crashing me skull with her handbag."

"I beg your pardon." Ludwig cocked his head to one side, puzzlement written on his face.

Bowes thought Ludwig Dewitt might ignore the snide remark. He smiled at his own bravado.

"I'm not quite sure what you're talking about. I was not aware you knew of my wife, Adelaide."

"I can't say I actually know the woman," Bowes said, grinning. "Let's just say, I've had some dealings with her in the past."

"I certainly will discuss it with her shortly but, in the meantime, let me escort you to my study, where you can speak to Jane in relative peace. If you'll follow me."

Ludwig turned. He tipped his head in a specific direction and made his way across the foyer. He continued down a long hallway before opening the door to a small room. Half the room was filled with books, neatly arrayed on wooden shelves. A large mahogany desk faced the door and one leather chair nestled beneath it and two others, one to each side.

Ludwig walked to the desk and lit the gas lamp sitting atop it. The light from the lamp created a warm glow but left the room dimly lit. "I do hope this light will be enough for your meeting with your daughter."

"It will have to do, for sure," Bowes said, ignoring the man and glancing around the room, somewhat awed by its grandeur.

"Make yourself at home then. If you need anything, just pull on that rope," he said, pointing to the bell rope that hung in the corner. He smiled, but it wasn't a pleasant smile to Bowes's way of thinking. "I'm sure Jane will be here momentarily."

When Ludwig opened the door, Sinead stood at the threshold. "I'll leave you two to your discussions." He sidled past the girl, gently shoved her inside the room and closed the door.

Bowes's body trembled as he gazed at his daughter. *Lord but she looked like her mother, except for the slight rose color of her hair.* Just looking at Sinead made his heart ache for the woman who had been his only true love, in a lifetime filled with loving women.

* * *

Sinead didn't move away from the door to come nearer or greet him like a daughter should. Instead, she glared at him through narrowed suspicious eyes. "You've come calling? At this hour?

Well, Da, what have you done now?" Her eyebrow moved up an inch. Her distrust was apparent in her expression.

Bowes couldn't move under her scrutiny. "Och, Sinead, don't be talking to me in that old lady's tone of voice ye use on the Dewitts or their servants. Remember, ye're me daughter, not me ma, nor me boss."

"I feel like your ma. You've made me old beyond my years."

Bowes gasped. "That's a terrible thing to say to yer very own da."

"Something has happened. I know it. You wouldn't be here at this hour, or at all, for that matter, if everything was fine. Do you want to tell me about it, or do you intend to sing and dance your way around the situation, with your wee bit o' Irish rainbow sitting on your shoulders to tease me?"

"My God, child, ye sound so harsh to me. I know ye're annoyed, but am I that much in yer disfavor, lass?"

Sinead heaved a great sigh. She moved to sit in one of the chairs at the side of the desk and gathered her skirt around her, pausing in what she was about to say, as if reconsidering it. "Da, 'tis your schemes that are in my disfavor, not yourself. I love you madly, and I treasure all the things you've tried to do for me over the years. I just wish you'd stop the doing of them."

Bowes sat in the chair at the other side of the desk. He gazed across its expanse and tried to smile, a smile that did nothing more than show some creases on his mouth. He felt like getting down on one knee to beg her forgiveness. But he couldn't imagine the thing he should be forgiven for, so he tried to explain.

"Sinead, please understand. Ye're all I have left in this whole world, the only thing I truly value now that yer mam and sister have gone on to their rewards. Besides, being older, I know how truly ferocious the world can be. I'm not wanting to see ye suffer, like I have."

"Da, you only suffer because of your plans and schemes for me. You try so hard to make everything right in the world. That can't happen, not even for me, no matter how badly you might be wanting it so." She stretched her hand, palm up, across the wide desk to his.

He grasped it in his and squeezed tightly. His smile broadened further when she patted his hand and laid her other one over both of theirs.

"Sinead, we may have a wee small problem," Bowes said, clasping her hand even tighter.

Sinead shook her head and twitched a corner of her mouth. "I thought that might be the case when neither you nor my new husband showed up at the mansion. Do I need to ask you about it, or are you going to tell me of your own volition?"

"Volition? Och, ye mean by meself." Bowes grinned. "Ye gotten so learned and refined. I hardly recognize me own daughter."

Again, she shook her head. "Da, don't be going on with unnecessary compliments I don't deserve. I'm still me, a little green lass from Ireland. Now, if you please, tell me what's happened to the man from Ireland, the man I married a few months ago and have barely laid eyes on."

Sinead felt it was her time to smile and when she saw his answering one, she felt relieved. The hardness of the meeting was over. "Now, start telling me what brought you to this house, this late. What disaster do we face now?"

Still reluctant to speak, Bowes hemmed and hawed. "Ye see. It's about yer husband and his brother..." Bowes bowed his head, looking at the rug, looking everywhere but in her eyes.

"I gathered that. You best tell me what it is before I allow my imagination to soar onto the most unimaginable things."

Bowes took a deep breath then blurted out, "The boyos are in jail."

Sinead gasped, stood, then sat back down. "In jail?"

"Aye. That's what I said, lass. In jail. At a precinct down near the docks," he said with emphasis.

"How could they be in jail?" Sinead's eyes narrowed. "They just got here to America. They don't know anything or anybody. What have you done, Da?" a horrified Sinead asked, her words bubbling together in what seemed like one sentence.

"Well, I didn't do much at all." Bowes hung his head. "The fact is I didn't do enough. I did get all of their material goods though."

"Da, why don't you just tell me what happened. Stop the play-acting. At the beginning, please," she said, crossing her arms across her chest.

Bowes's words slurred together in his attempt to justify what he did. "Well, daughter, ye weren't feeling well and I had to be getting you and that Adelaide woman home in one piece. What with her carrying on something fierce and distracting me mind from me tasks, I told the lads to meet me at any one of the several dockside saloons I frequent. I was thinking I'd be back with them in a short time, for sure."

Sinead glared at him. "Obviously, you weren't, or you would be in jail with them. And that's probably where you belong tonight."

"Sinead lass, don't be so harsh on me. The day was so warm and the humidity high…" Bowes frowned, the creases on his forehead digging deep into his hairline, emphasizing hair that was slowly graying.

Sinead grabbed at his sleeve and gave it a yank. "And?"

"And I stopped off for a wee pint of the lager on my way back to the docks. Just to freshen me…"

"And you met some friends…" Her mouth pursed in displeasure.

"Nae, not really friends, ye might say."

"What then, Da?"

"I met a woman I hadn't seen in many years. At one time, long, long ago, shortly after I came to America with ye and yer sister, may God bless her child's soul in Heaven," he said crossing himself with a quick motion. "I had a soft feeling for this woman, but she married another. I only stopped for a wee chat…"

"But it turned into more is what you're trying to tell me."

"Aye that it did, lass. We had a lot of catching up to do. She's single again, widowed, ye know — moving up north to Saratoga. Asked me to visit." Bowes puffed up his chest, his pride in himself evident.

Sinead began clasping and unclasping her hands. She rubbed them on her skirt as if they were damp. She murmured in an accusatory tone. "Did you totally forget about the lads, Da? Did you leave them to their own devices? In a place neither of them knew enough about?"

Bowes shook his head in response. "Nae. I didn't forget them. Aye, I did think about them. I thought about them the whole time I was talking to the lady. I just didn't do anything about it."

Sinead stood and walked to the window behind the desk. She looked out into the blackness of the night, staring at nothing. "How long were you with the lady, whose name you're not giving to me?"

Bowes stood and joined her at the window. He placed a hand on her shoulder. "Och Sinead, were only an hour or two, darlin'. I knew those boyos would be needing to get their gear off the steamer, but not until midnight." He paced to one side of her "I didn't figure they'd come off there so soon. I assumed on such a hot day, they'd be wanting a touch of the lager to clear the taste of the sea waters from their palates, then go back to the steamer to wait fer me."

"And you basically left them on their own, on the docks? Knowing what you know about the area? What did you think would happen to them in a place like that?" Sinead turned to stare at her father. "I can't believe you just left them."

She walked away from the window, her distress apparent in the way she held her shoulders and the rigidity of her neck. She leaned against the desk and absently rubbed the shiny surface with her fingers.

"Being greenhorns, I never thought they'd be starting any trouble. But I guess they did." Bowes gulped and moved, trying to face Sinead again. "Must be they're a bit more feisty than I knew them to be." He put his hands up to take her in his arms.

Sinead returned to the chair next to the desk and didn't look at her da.

Bowes came around the desk and went to the seat he sat in earlier. He looked at her as if asking for her forgiveness. "Lassie?"

"You knew they wouldn't have to start the trouble. In that area, the trouble finds you when you're not even aware it's looking for you. How could you leave those two greenies, straight from the old sod, to the likes of those who frequent the dockside saloons?" She turned away from his gaze.

"I told the lads to be mentioning me name wherever they went. Everyone knows me down there." Bowes's arms raised, palms outward, as if the palms were searching for the right words to say.

A look of disbelief crossed Sinead's face. "And were you thinking the name Bowes Brennan would be enough? Just your name? How often do you frequent those establishments? How well are you known by the newer places that have sprung up along the thoroughfare across from that pier?" She looked straight at her da.

"Not very often since the announcement of the Conscription. Too many hot heads there now." Bowes shook his head and pounded a fist on the desk.

Sinead gasped, leaned her elbow on the desk and lowered her temple into her hand. She rubbed each side of her forehead. In some terrible dream state, she formed words but none came from her mouth. A brief image of her husband's handsome face interfered and she gasped anew, surprised that his features were so clear to her. "But how did you expect those lads from Ireland to know about the draft, or the hotbeds of those saloons or…"

Bowes jumped quickly to his explanation. "I pointed out Mulligan's to the big one. It seems they went elsewhere."

Sinead closed her eyes, hoping to drown out the hazy picture her da's words conjured up, a picture of a lad she knew long ago. She shook her head in dismay then opened her eyes wide, concentrating on the matter at hand. "Not to Clancy's? Da, tell me they didn't go to Clancy's."

Bowes lowered his eyes and stared at his knees. When he lifted his head again to look about, a single tear of frustration slid down Sinead's face, making him feel guilty of forcing this marriage on her.

"They did, lass. They must have wandered into Clancy's and got embroiled somehow in one of the strong arguments, the very kind usually going on in that place."

"What was the argument about?" she whispered, resigned to her father's messes.

Bowes shook his head. He hadn't even asked Mulligan about that. "Lass, I don't know. By the time I got back to the docks, the police had already taken four men away. Connor and Egan were two of the four."

"Did you go to the police station to see them?" Sinead stood in a flash and looked down at her da.

Bowes stood and she shoved him back in his chair. His hands raised in protest. "I only found out about it an hour ago. I went into Mulligan's to find out if they put in a show there, or if he knew anything about them. They didn't go in there at all." Bowes gestured and said, in all seriousness, "I know Mulligan would tell me the truth. Connor would be hard to miss with him being so big, and young Egan, with that red hair, and almost as big, would be a remembrance in a barkeep's mind, for sure."

Sinead sat down, looked up toward the window, before looking at her da. There was hope in her eyes. "Did you talk to Mulligan?"

"It was Mulligan himself who informed me of the gossip on the street there. He must have watched it all. When I described the lads, he told me they were definitely two of the men taken."

Sinead leaped to her feet, distraught. "Why didn't you go right to the police station and have them freed? Och, my God, what will the Dewitts think? Now, they'll never let me keep Robbie, without a court fight."

Bowes stood. He tried to take Sinead in his arms to comfort her. "Daughter, 'tis sorry I am for..."

Her anger surfaced and her breath was hot on his face. Her voice rose to a louder pitch. "How's your being sorry going to help? We have to do something." Her body shook with disgust. "We can't be leaving them there to rot. You best be thinking up one of your fine schemes, Da. And it better be a right good one."

Bowes patted her back. "Easy, lass. Nothing can happen until morning. Just pretend we had a social conversation if anyone in this house asks ye. Tell them I came to find out about yer health after yer faint this afternoon."

"What good will that do, I'm asking? No one will believe me."

"Sinead, think, lass, think. Ye have all the marriage papers in that envelope I gave ye for safekeeping?" Bowes took one of her hands in his. "I couldn't do anything earlier anyway. The police will only release them boyos to someone who can give proof of their right to be here."

"And how am I supposed to get out of here tomorrow morning without giving the Dewitts a reason?" She wrung her sweat dampened hands together then wiped them on her skirt.

"Ye, have a reason, girl. Ye have to go to church with yer da. Ye're a Catholic and must pay yer respects to yer priest and to yer God." Bowes watched her reaction out of the corner of his eye. He began to pace, thinking up a scheme as he moved along.

Sinead paced alongside of him, resistant, pulling on his arm. "You know I can't leave Robbie all alone, with no one to care for him. His governess is gone from here every Saturday night and most of Sunday." She moved away from her da. "Adelaide would never allow it. Mister Dewitt would vote in her favor, and…" She swung around to face him, her brow furrowed with lines.

With a snap of his fingers, indicating a new idea, Bowes blurted, "We'll take Robbie with us. The lad is Catholic, too, ye know. His own mother, the Dewitts' daughter, signed the conversion papers and agreed to have the lad brought up in the Catholic Church. That has to stand for something." Bowes stood straighter and gave his daughter a huge smile, positive he solved the problem and pleased

85

with himself.

"They only let me take him to church last Christmas and haven't since. They keep saying it isn't good for him to get confused, specially since they intend to bring him up in their church, now that Cavanaugh's dead and can't do anything about it. They claim they never signed any paper."

"Ye've got the paper. We'll read it over another time. Tell them ye have to visit the church with yer new husband."

Another thought crept into Sinead's mind. "What if they ask where my new husband's been this whole day?"

Bowes paced the confines of the room until an idea occurred to him. "Tell them he and his brother took a room in an inn in order to clean up, and they were so tired they decided to stay the night. Aye, that's a good one. Tell them yer da came to tell ye that…"

"Och, to me, this sounds like another of your schemes. That always makes me fearful." Sinead began to pace alongside her da.

"Don't worry this time, lass." Bowes stopped in his tracks. He took Sinead's hand and patted it. He looked deep into her eyes and nodded to her.

"Ye can pull it off, lass. I'll be arriving during the morning in me carriage to take ye and the youngster to church, where ye're supposed to be each and every Sunday. We'll say it's to meet with yer husband. Tell the Dewitts, he wants to meet with ye on neutral ground to discuss things pertinent to the marriage and for the first how-do-you-do."

Sinead trembled in fear. She was afraid to take a chance on another of her da's schemes. "Och, Da, this will never work. The Dewitts are suspicious of me as it is. I overheard them talking about it."

Bowes grabbed her by the arms. He shook her a bit. "Listen to me, Sinead, this is not the time to get weepy or scared. Ye've got to be a brave Irish lass and fight for what ye think is right. Ye have the papers that say Cavanaugh married ye, fair and square, and appointed ye as mother of his only son. Use that. Threaten if ye have to, but ye've got to get out of this house in the morning."

Sinead drew in a deep breath and let it out. She took control of herself. "All right, Da, I'll do it. I'll insist upon taking Robbie to church to meet his new da." Sinead chuckled low in the back of her throat and grinned at her da. She shook her head in glee, becoming a coconspirator.

"Good girl. I'm proud of ye. Proud to be yer da..." He grinned back and then stared at her for another moment. He coughed a bit, not sure of what he needed to say. "And Sinead, bring some old clothes with ye."

She frowned then smiled. "Whatever for? I don't dress that way to go to church."

"Ye'll need old clothes at the jail. Trust me. I know the best way for ye to get them boyos released without anything terrible happening."

"Och, you have another scheme. I can feel it." She closed her eyes and sighed.

"That I do, but I won't divulge it until morning. I have to think on it some more. So, bring yer oldest garments and all yer papers with ye." He paused. "And ye'll have to do some pretending once we visit the police."

"Yet again, without my full consent, I'm involved in one of your plans. Will it never stop?" Even as she spoke, she rolled her twinkling eyes.

Bowes grinned broadly. "Probably not. Probably not ever."

"May the saints help and forgive us..."

CHAPTER SIX

July 12, 1863
New York City

A cloudless sky promised another sun-kissed day with far too much heat and no wind. Every shop and office was closed until Monday morning. Bowes worried about the smothering atmosphere in the city. People started drifting out of the stifling tenements and into the taverns. They'd seen the list of unlucky draftees published in the Sunday papers.

He noticed the working-class families in his boarding house pore over the names and exclaim each time they recognized someone they knew. All around the city, men discussed the situation over glasses of whiskey. Their wives and mothers would shriek wild denunciations against the Conscription Law. A variety of protests, a goodly number promoted by Irishmen he knew, would be launched.

Yet on this seemingly quiet Sunday, church bells rang throughout the city of New York. They filled the soft, warm air with a steady rhythm and called the religious of many denominations to services.

Bowes, Sinead and Robbie joined the Sunday parade of churchgoers, traveling through the streets at a subdued pace, unlike yesterday's mad dash to the piers. People around them traversed the streets with unusual dignity and decorum. The world seemed in slow motion.

Sinead's black thoughts of doubt over her original decision to marry the man from Ireland made the trip to the jail quiet for her.

Her mind traveled over every mistake she ever made in her life.

Robbie's continual questioning over the sights and sounds of the city interrupted Sinead's train of thought. Each one of his questions grew more excited than the previous one and demanded some answer. He laughed and chattered. Without knowing it, he single-handedly kept the ride lighthearted and filled with tender humor.

Time seemed to stop. Sinead's frustrations began to seep away. She was unable to berate her da this morning, something she would not do in front of her son. But now, she thought some of her da's ideas should be discussed if she wanted to get her husband out of jail.

Her mouth held in a straight, grim line, she mumbled, "I have my oldest clothes with me. I stuffed them into my handbag. They're probably wrinkled beyond repair."

"All the better. Aye," he said, shaking his head up and down. "I'm thinking 'tis much better if ye seem to be a work-worn and frazzled lass."

The subtle rise and fall of her breathing altered. "Whatever for?"

"Ye're supposed to be getting a drunken Irish husband and his foolish brother out of jail, after them drinking up all the money to feed the little ones," Bowes answered, twisting his head slightly around toward the back of the carriage, a frown on his face as if he thought his daughter stupid. "Ye have to make those men in blue think ye're a poor, suffering Irish woman, trying to bring up yer large family of lads and lasses to be decent folk, and mixed up with a sot, ye are."

Sinead looked at her da, who was smirking, then at Robbie. She wondered how much of her da's words Robbie understood. He didn't seem to be paying any attention to them, his curiosity over the different sights on the streets overwhelming him. At four, he seemed quite alert and intelligent but still only a little boy.

Her thoughts veered off in another direction, her reluctance to send the child off to school. She clasped the boy close to her for a swift hug. He wriggled out of her grasp, with a giggle. He wasn't ready for a military school to which the Dewitts wanted to send him. Sinead had no intention of letting him go.

She shook her head, and her notions drifted back to the subject at hand, her husband and her da. At times, her da's smug, self-confidence infuriated her, but she needed his advice now. "Tell me, Da, what you have me do with the clothing I brought with me. It's just an old shirt and skirt I had years ago, when I worked for the Cavanaugh's as the upstairs maid."

"Good. Perfect, in fact." Bowes rubbed his hands together with glee. "Sinead, do ye think ye can struggle into those clothes here in the carriage? While we're moving, that is?"

She looked at her da as if he were crazy. "Probably. For heaven's sake, why, though?"

Keeping one hand on the reins, Bowes opened one arm wide and nodded to Robbie. "Young fellow, come up here. Sit with Grandda Bee."

"Nae," Sinead shouted, reaching out to grab her son, who was trying to climb over the front carriage seat. "He'll not be sitting up there, near those horses. Absolutely not."

Bowes pointed his finger at her and shook it. "Daughter, ye're doing the wrong thing to the boy, a great disservice. He has to experiment, learn about new things in life." He shrugged his shoulders in distress and annoyance. "Och! Until man invents some other way of getting around this big old world, horses will be the very animals young Robbie needs to know about."

Sinead's own innate fear of anything having to do with horses gripped her. Her face grew warm with anger over her da's disagreeing with her upbringing of the boy. She needed to gain control of the situation, of herself. And she figured she'd better be nice to her da if he was going to help her in today's endeavor. "Perhaps, another time. I'm too flustered this morning to think of anything but getting those lads out of jail before the family I'm living with finds out where they've been."

"Ye think and care too much about the Dewitts and what they

might be thinking. But, I guess in this case, ye have reason to."

Sinead hadn't realized she was so tense. She smiled, sensing her da's unspoken acknowledgment of the truth, and leaned back in the carriage.

The thoroughfares were less clogged today, although groups of men were standing around on the street corners as if discussing something important. Many of them spoke in loud, angry voices. Their gestures were animated. Some even shouted. One raised his fist like a cry for justice.

Sinead wondered what was going on but wasted little time worrying about it. She had her own job to do. She chuckled to herself. Lots of angry men hung about the city streets of late — men without jobs, men against some political force or another, men in disagreement with something or someone — and now she was going to the Tombs to gain the release of just such a one.

Time was getting short. The carriage was nearing the Tombs, lower Manhattan's main jail on Centre Street. She knew she should compose herself and start thinking of the actions she needed to take, when her da's voice broke into her thoughts.

"Sinead. Listen to me. Put the damned old clothes on. I want ye to appear to be a hardworking Irish washerwoman. I'm sure ye can still speak in the Gaelic if ye have to and punch up yer native brogue."

Sinead stared at her da's back. "Of course I can. The Dewitts don't like it if I do it in front of Robbie."

Hearing his name, Robbie looked at Sinead. He pointed at ships berthed at one of the piers they were passing. "Mama Jane, look. See the ships, the big ones. Over there. How are they tied up? Can we go see them?" he asked in one stream of hurried words. But he was quickly distracted. "Oooohhhh, look at that man up on the top of the big one. Is that a clipper? What kind?"

Robbie wriggled around in the seat in order to see well. His knees pushed on the leather seat of the carriage then he climbed up onto his feet, leaning on Sinead, pointing and gesturing in every direction. She hung on to him in fear he'd fall and get stepped on by the horses. He put his arms around her neck and squeezed.

Although she couldn't really see what he was pointing at, she thought to mollify him. "Aye, darling. That's a sailor. He's working on the ship, probably repairing the sails or tying something up high."

Bowes nodded and said, "The clothes, Sinead. We're almost there. Put them on, lass."

"Robbie, get off that seat and sit. Turn around in the seat, so Mama doesn't have to worry about you falling out and bumping your head." She pulled him down and gave him a quick kiss on the cheek.

Being the good child he was, Robbie swung around in the seat, leaped into the air for one breathless second of disobedience and sat back down, grinning. He couldn't pull his gaze from the ships. He twisted around everyway possible to get a better view and kept up a running dialogue about them.

Sinead sighed, content for a brief moment. While Robbie was busy with the sights around him, she held onto him, with one hand on his legs to steady him. With her other hand, she slipped the frayed, gray skirt over her head and over the clothes she'd been wearing.

"Da, stop the carriage so I can stand. I need to fix the skirt."

Bowes did as asked. When the carriage slowed, Sinead teetered but stood to smooth the overskirt skirt down over the Sunday one she already had on. She smiled grimly. All this clothing made her look fat.

Bowes took off again. The carriage bumped over broken cobble-stones. Sinead was forcefully thrown down onto the seat again. The jarring impact ripped a seam in the skirt, making the waistline, still open, too big. Sinead took a large pin from her reticule, gath-ered the skirt in a bunch and pinned the waistline closed.

She noticed another big rip across the bottom of the hem. Think-ing it wouldn't matter if she looked poor, she eased herself back in the seat and pulled a limp and tattered shirt out of her handbag.

"Look at the birds, Mama." Robbie pointed, then suddenly noticing her activity, asked, "Whatcha' doing?"

Over the screeching calls of gulls near the waterfront, Sinead tried to explain. "Mama Jane has to stop someplace before we go to church. It's a dusty, dirty place, so Mama is putting on old clothes. I don't want to go into the church looking dirty and ill kempt."

"What's ill kempt?" Robbie asked, his face intense with concentration.

"I guess 'tis just another way to say dirty. Maybe 'messy' would be a better explanation for you." Loving his interest, his curiosity, she smiled down at the young lad who so filled her heart.

"Can I go with you?"

"Nae, darling. This is something Mama has to do by herself. You'll stay with Grandda Bee."

Robbie stood in the carriage. Sinead clutched him as if he were going to fall. "Don't, Mama. I want to talk to Grandda Bee." He poked Bowes in the back with a forefinger. "Hey, Grandda. Are you going to take care of me while Mama Jane goes into the dirty place? Can we get out and walk? Can I pet your horses? Can I…"

"Aye, laddie. We'll think of things to do, until yer new da comes out. Then ye'll be wanting to pay all yer attention to him," Bowes answered before Sinead could say anything more about horses.

"I'm going to see my new da, now?" Robbie turned to Sinead with eyes wide. He shook his head up and down in pleasure. His smile was as broad as could be. "Really? A new da?"

"Aye. I'm going to get your new da," Sinead said, slipping the shirt over her head and letting it fall where it may. "See, now I'll stay clean."

She didn't bother to tuck the shirt into the skirt. It completely covered her own clothes and made her look much heavier. But if her thoughts were correct, it was the way her da wanted her to look.

"Why is my new da in a dirty place?" Robbie frowned.

At a loss how to answer, Sinead looked at her da.

"He's been helping men repair some things wrong with the place. It takes a big man to do lifting."

Sinead's nerves got the best of her. Her heart beat faster than usual. Her tongue felt like it was sticking to the roof of her mouth. "Da, what am I going to say when I get in there?"

"Be yerself, lass, with just a bit more of Ireland in yer speech." Bowes's lips curved into a grin. "Be a bit more like yer old da." His laughter filled the carriage. Robbie laughed with him, just for the joy of laughing. "That's me wee lad!"

"This is not the time for foolishness, Da. I have to know what to do."

"Show them yer papers. Crush them up a bit now, will ye? Ye want to make it look like ye've been married for a while and they've been stuffed in a drawer somewhere." Bowes snapped his fingers. "I've got it. Pretend yer husband is a wee bit of a drunk, sometimes going a smidgen overboard. Specially when he gets with his brother."

"Do ye think the police will be believing me?" The sound of the lilt in her ear surprised her. "Aye, Da, this might be fun after all." A corner of her mouth turned up in a grin. She straightened her shoulders and set her expression into a grimace.

"And daughter, don't be forgetting to give that drunken husband of yers, and his weak-kneed brother, a sound lashing with the back of yer fierce tongue." Bowes chuckled and wiggled his finger at her. "Be sure to do it in front of the police. They'll think it's hilarious and send you and the two men on your way with a lot less trouble."

A grin crossed Sinead's face again but disappeared quickly. "I have never been a shrew. Ye're teasing me, for sure, old man."

"Ye only need a wee bit o' practice." Bowes held up his hand to stay her words. "But I want ye to act the shrew until the men are set free, in our carriage, and we're off. Then ye can apologize if ye're wanting." He paused. "Ye may not be wanting to just yet, 'til ye see the lie of the land." He nodded toward the building. "Now, go."

The possible seriousness of the situation struck Sinead. Her body recoiled in distaste. What if the Dewitts found out about this little excursion to the city's jail? She shouldn't have brought Robbie with her. "Da, I can't be doing this. I just can't. I don't have it in me."

"You sound funny." Robbie giggled. "What can't you do, Mama Jane?"

Bowes laughter floated to the back of the carriage as he turned a corner onto Centre Street. "Och, Robbie, Mama Jane can do most everything she sets her mind to. She's the smartest woman I've ever known."

"I know. Me, too," Robbie said, shaking his head up and down. He looked at Sinead with love shining from his eyes.

Sinead chuckled despite the tremors she was experiencing. In her own way, she enjoyed the way the two males she loved best teased with her. As much as she complained about her da's schemes, most often she found herself caught up in them. Even now, when her heart beat with a fast rhythm.

And, playing a part might be fun at that, she thought. "All right, you two fellows. Mama Jane can do everything. Right now, she's going to get yer new da for ye, laddie."

"You still talk funny." Again, Robbie giggled but grew interested in another sight. He pointed to a brick building. "What's that place?"

"A hotel," Bowes answered before Sinead tried to explain. "'Tis a lovely, very expensive hotel." He turned back to Sinead. "Which reminds me, daughter. Did ye bring some money with ye? In case palms need to be greased."

"Aye. This old washerwoman brought enough to bribe an army." Smiling, she held up a battered old reticule.

"Are you going to the army, Mama Jane?"

"Nae, darling. 'Tis just an expression I use sometimes."

The puzzled look on Robbie's face made Sinead chuckle. She understood she was working herself up to put on an act, one to make her da proud.

She put on the broadest Irish accent she could. "Besides, Da, that handsome lad of an Irishman, him who now called himself me husband needs to be brought down a peg or two."

She tucked her shirt into the skirt and stared straight ahead. She brought her chin up and stuck her nose in the air. "Aye, the fool needs to be learning he's not going to be controlling me life. If anything, 'tis more the other way around."

The carriage stopped across the street from the Tombs. Several men in uniforms lolled on the steps leading to the big double doors at the top. They seemed to be deep in conversation.

Robbie poked her with a finger and whispered, "Are those men the army?"

Her heart beating far too fast, Sinead stumbled over her answer, not sure how to respond. "Um, nae, I mean, aye. They're members of the army." At least, if she agreed with his assumption, the Dewitts wouldn't find out about the jail.

Bowes turned around. "That's me lassie. Ye're getting into it now. I can feel it, and 'tis a lovely thing to see. Do yer job proper-like, and ye'll be having those lads out here in seconds."

In disgust, Sinead shook her head, nodded toward Robbie and narrowed her eyes. Her irrepressible da grinned at her. "Right. Well, I'm as ready as I'll ever be. Wish me luck…"

"Luck to ye lassie," Bowes said with a solemn tone.

"And take off yer fancy hat. Mess up yer hair some," he continued, folding the reins in his lap. "Better yet, let some of it hang loose in strings. Put some dirt on yer face as ye go through the doors."

Now that the carriage was completely stopped, Sinead stood. The sides of her neck ached from the rigidity with which she held herself. She tossed her hat down on the carriage floor and looked around her. Thinking she would start playing the part now, she kicked at the carriage door. "Aren't ye going to opening this door for me, ye sod of a carriage driver?"

Bowes shouted back, "Ye think I'll get down from me perch and open the door for the likes of you?" He sat up straight in his seat and crossed his arms over his chest, beginning to play along with her. "Not for heaven's sake or all the tea from England would I be doing that. I'm probably lucky if I get paid a cent for this wee trip," he groused in a loud voice.

"Grandda Bee, don't holler at my mama," Robbie shouted, tears welling in his eyes.

"Och, hush, Rob. Yer grandda's not hollering," she bent and whispered in his ear. "He's just playing…you know, for fun."

She lifted her son into her arms for a second, then squeezed and tickled him until he giggled again. "Stay with Grandda, son. He'll keep ye safe from worry…"

"Och, Robbie lad, I'm not really hollering. Yer mama and I are just playing a game." Bowes whispered, too. "If ye want to play with us, when she gets across the road, scream at her to get yer da, quick-like, and stamp yer feet in the carriage. She'll think that's funny. Just don't scare the horses."

Sinead smiled at them both, stepped from the carriage and crossed the street under the watchful eyes of the policemen standing in front of the building. She stared straight ahead, ignoring their looks.

"Mama, you better bring my da or I'm going to be mad at you," Robbie screamed across the street, his little hands cupped around his mouth.

Sinead turned, grinned and shook her fist at her da but answered Robbie with a sweet tone. "Aye, I'll be doing that for ye, laddie, mine. Don't ye be worrying yer wee head."

* * *

Gingerly, Sinead moved onto the sidewalk and stared at the unpleasant-looking building in front of her before putting a foot on the steps. Tingles vibrated up her spine. She drew in a deep breath and, grasping the wobbly iron railing connected to the stairs, she started up.

Several members of the local precinct, dressed in their navy blue uniforms, their shiny badges worn high on the front pockets of their shirts, stood by the sides of the doors, smoking. The men stared at her. One dour and mule-faced man made a comment to another behind his hand, as she reached the last step before the double doors. The three guffawed then snickered.

Sinead spun around. "Something ye gentlemen find so funny, ye have to be laughing at me?" she asked.

"Something ye gentlemen find funny," a young man, his mouth curved in sardonic amusement, mimicked. "Aye. Coming here to be getting yer man out of jail, are ye?"

She went back down a couple of steps to face him. She conjured up a picture of an absolute, angry gesture of the most hateful Irish women she'd known and imitated their facial expressions. With her chin jutted out, she sputtered, "Now, why were ye whispering things about me? 'Tis not necessary to be making such fun of me speech or me dress," Sinead snapped, practicing the rhythm of the brogue, letting it sit comfortably on her tongue.

Her tone was quiet but her temper edged toward high. Her face was flushed. She hated being the object of ridicule, much less from the very men who were supposed to help in her current endeavor.

"Sorry missus, but we were wondering what a fair, young lady like yerself was doing down here at this precinct. 'Tis the Tombs, ye know," said an older, more respectful man who was taller and more imposing.

"Aye, here ye are, to a place for hardened criminals, missus," said the first, the heaviest of the three, who spoke while keeping a cigar stuck between his teeth.

"A neighbor said me very own husband was brought here. To this ugly place. I cannot figure out why, unless it was the demon rum what caused him to lose his senses," she said, letting her speech slur and her body tremble, as if she felt upset, lost and bewildered.

"Lately, since the Conscription draft came to the City, the only men brought to this jail have been the 'down and outers' from the saloons down by the piers. Lots of workers from the piers. Or from the slums. Most of them men who waste their time and stir up the folks around the ships," said the man who whispered in the first place.

The man with the cigar laughed. "We bring 'em in every Saturday night, steady as clockwork, and drunker than fools."

"Yeah. And women like you, lady, do not come to pick them up too often. Ye seem a finer sort than the ones who usually have their men sitting here, waiting for release," the older man added.

Sinead took his remarks to heart. *Aye*, she thought. Women who were refined, socially educated to some sort of upper society, did not visit jails, much less the one in this district. She knew she would have to change her tactics once she got inside, be more downtrodden, dissolute.

She dropped her reticule on the step in front of her, bent and retrieved it along with a great deal of dirt. With a small gesture of pushing back the hair that had fallen into her face, she rubbed some of the dirt along her cheek and down her neck. "I'll be going in now," she politely replied.

"Lass, go to the man at the desk inside. He'll get yer husband for ye," the heavy policemen said before turning back to his cigar smoking.

The older man added a bit of advice. "Speak nicely to the fellow. He's a mite quick to take offense. It's been bad today and only looks to get worse. Oh, and if ye have any papers to prove a man inside be yers, take them out as ye go through the doors."

"Thank ye. The information will help me," Sinead responded, clutching her handbag and squeezing it to crush the papers inside. "'Tis the first time I've been here," she added as an afterthought.

The man continued, "And I hope, for yer sake, it's the last. 'Tis not a nice place to visit. The row of holding cells in there are dreadful." He moved to the doors. "Here, now, Missus, let me hang on to these doors for ye."

Sinead patted the man's arm. "Thank ye so much. Ye've been a help, ye have." When he nodded, she went inside.

The interior was dingy and saved from utter darkness by thin strips of gaslight. The narrow hallway resembled the nighttime streets at the corner of Five Points, one of the city's worst slums, a place her da no longer frequented or allowed her to go to. Dominated by the Irish, Five Points was filled with rotten wooden houses and tall tenements crammed with poor families. Violent brawls and pitched battles broke out with frightening regularity between rival gangs who lived there.

The smell, wafting from another room farther in the building, almost overpowered her. Unwashed flesh and human wastes, combined with unmoving air, made Sinead feel much like she had the day before, dizzy and faint.

Turning to leave though, was not an option she could exercise. There was too much at stake. She wondered how the many policemen who milled about could stand to work in such an environment. Perhaps, it was the same for the men employed by those in charge, too much at stake to leave.

A rotund policeman, jaw slack and eyes dull, came from one of the offices to the right and passed her in the hall then turned back. "Lady, can I help you with something?"

"Aye, I'm wanting to see someone in charge. That is, if it's all right to do so."

"What do you want here? I need to know so I can take you to someone who can really help you." He stared at her with glazed eyes.

Sinead repeated what she told the men outside. "A neighbor told me my husband was here. Picked up for fighting he was, or so I was told."

"Come with me. I'll introduce you to my commander." He stared at her with contemptuous appraisal and lifted an eyebrow. "What's your name, lovely lassie?" He grinned at his own cleverness.

Humiliation heated Sinead's face. She was embarrassed by the man's blatant looks and outraged by the disrespectful tone of voice.

When she didn't answer, the officer asked again. "I need to know your name, darlin', otherwise I can't introduce you or fetch your husband when I'm told to do so."

"Sinead O'Malley, sir. Me husband's Connor. He was brought here along with his brother..." Sinead's eyes filled with tears. She was about to lie about Connor and his brother, whom she hadn't even met. "Please, be taking me to yer commander or someone who can be helping me get me stupid husband and his drunken brother home to the children and their mother, who's in mourning and would like to die just for the sight of her two darling boyos."

"Come this way," he snickered, leading her toward the office he'd just exited. He held the door open and let her precede him into the room.

The grimy office was filled with too much furniture, chairs propped up against one wall, desk lined up in the center. Although there was a window opened, the room was stifling. Little air circulated through the dim light infusing the room.

Sitting behind a large, gouged oak desk, a light-haired man with a huge, thick mustache held the focused attention of four men who stood at attention before him. The man's eyes were narrowed, and the look of anger on his face was enough to quell Sinead and stop her in her tracks.

The man shouted at the men facing him. "And the next time ye do something stupid like that again or I get another complaint from the wrong people, ye'll be gone from yer jobs. Now, get the hell out of here — and behave yerselves on the street. I have no more time for the likes of ye four." He coughed into his hand. "But keep yer eyes open from here on in. There's too much going on with the new law for us to relax our vigilance."

The four saluted him and turned on their heels to leave the room. They marched as if in a drill.

"Wait, ye fools, ye can't leave without yer badges to pin on." Exasperation and resignation dotted the man's face.

The four turned as one and moved in cadence back to the man's desk. Their hands reached out at the same time as if a single string attached them, and they took their badges.

"Jaysus, ye're like a bunch of puppets," the officer shrieked. When the men retreated, he shouted at them, "Och, get out of here." He waved his arm to the door.

This time, he looked up and noticed Sinead waiting quietly and timidly in the doorway. The expression on his face changed, grew softer, as if he were embarrassed to have sworn before a young woman. "Now what would a sweet thing like you be doing here in me office?"

All the snappy answers she had ready caught in her throat. Her ideas fizzled to nothing. With a keen sense of disappointment, she merely stood and stared, unable to mouth any words, while the man's dark blue eyes, hooded like a hawk's, stared at her.

"Well, now, lass, ye' can speak to me without fretting. I'm here to help ye with yer troubles, I am. I'm William Ryan, Commissioner of this motley group of madcap officers."

Sinead's lower lip quivered. She drew a trembling breath and tried to smile at him.

He gently smiled at her. "Let me guess. Ye're here to get yer drunken, brawling man out of jail. Right?"

Sinead felt a sense of freedom, having him take the burden of worry off her shoulders. Murmuring a prayer, she sighed and said, "Aye. And his brother, too."

"Och, the big ones, the O'Malley brothers, I'm betting." The policeman laughed. "I put them in a holding cell together. I knew they weren't part of the rowdy bunch we brought in from Clancy's Saloon. They seemed a bit dazed, not quite sure of where they should be going or what they should be doing."

"They're not usually rowdy. Only when they're together," Sinead blurted then realizing what she'd said, clenched her fists against her worn skirt and bowed her head. Her lungs felt thick, and the humidity of the day was making her perspire.

The commander stood and strolled from behind his desk. He approached her.

Sinead stepped back, his square body and swagger inspiring fear. What did she know about policemen, other than they supposedly were vicious and corrupt?

He extended his hand. "Do ye have papers, lass, saying the man is yers and that he belongs here in this city?"

"Aye, that I do." She pretended to dig through her reticule until she'd mashed and wrinkled her paper more than they already were then dragged them out. "Here. Connor and I are legally married. By the priest and everything. And he brought his brother here with him."

The commander looked the papers over. With a face full of distant pity, he asked, "Why would such a newly-married man bring his brother with him to celebrate?'

The stiff hollow question made Sinead wince. She opened her mouth to answer but the man spoke before she could fasten her mind around a single thought.

"Never mind. 'Tis none of me business. Just wait here. Ye might not like what ye're going to see." With that, he stepped past her to the door, pulled it open slightly and hollered out, "Charlie, bring those two O'Malley boys here. Quickly, man."

The name O'Malley acted like a douse of cold water on her fried mind. Her tongue slid along a dry bottom lip from corner to corner, wetting it.

The commander turned and remarked, "Yer man is being brought here. 'Tis best I leave the two of ye to settle things together. He's a sight. Don't be fainting on me either, lassie."

She nodded, heard the footsteps coming closer to the room and paused. She saw the commander leave and gesture someone in.

Connor O'Malley, his face bruised and battered but expressionless, stood in the doorway and pinned her with an angry stare. The very sight of him cut off her oxygen.

CHAPTER SEVEN

Connor O'Malley's huge body filled the doorframe of the Police Commander's office. He stood, tall and stiff, arms braced on each side of the frame, glaring at her with an angry heat coming from the depth of the one eye that wasn't swollen shut. The look pierced her. One raised fist seemed ready to do the same.

With flattened lips and a sneer, Connor snapped, "Well, 'tis most kind of you to arrive. I'm assuming you intend to get Egan and me released from this hellhole your da led us to when he didn't return to the steamer's pier. And, for your added information, my brother was sick on the journey over here and this set him back. I do not thank you for it."

Sinead, who had watched his expected entrance from under downcast eyes, looked up and stepped back until the oak desk hit her backside. Burning up, and freezing at the same time, a defensive bile rose into the closed throat. A breath caught in her mouth and made a dry, gulping sound.

The skin around Connor's eyes was purple, red, blue and yellow, colors of the most beautiful rainbows seen in Ireland. A beige substance oozed from the closed eye. Dirt outlined the seams of his face and neck. His lips were cut in more than one place and bled slightly. His entire face was bruised, battered beyond recognition, in the foulest of cruelties, and his clothing was torn and tattered.

Fetid air returned to her lungs in a slow wheeze. A loud gasp flew from the mouth, hanging open to receive air, making the loss of emotional control palpable as Connor's swollen face came into clearer focus. She stared at him. Warmth, like a pillow, jammed against her face. Hands, buried within the pendulous pockets of the billowy, creased skirt, fisted. Her lips sagged with shame, yet any attempt to close them went undone. Tears welled up and spilled out of sad eyes.

Connor stepped farther into the room and let the door swing shut in back of him. The reek of raw sewerage gathered around him. He arched an eyebrow, which must have caused pain, for he grimaced.

Feeling as if she needed to do something, Sinead ran to the wall, grabbed a chair and dragged it across the floor to him. "Och, Lord, I'm thinking ye better sit before ye fall."

"I'll not be sitting another minute in this place. I've had enough of its hospitality in the hours I've already spent here. Can't we just leave?" he asked in disapproval.

The stiff, hollow question made her wince with rejection. She covered a strong urge to pout, swallowed the protest over his behavior and wondered why the terse words bothered so much.

Remembering what her da said about proper behavior inside, she shrieked, "It wasn't my fault, you and that poor fellow were lying about in the roads, roaring up to the skies. It wasn't my fault you and your brother got into a drunken brawl."

"Drunken brawl is it! Neither of us had a chance to take more than a bite of food or a good swallow of the lager before some of your friends started an argument with us, an argument they were looking for."

Sinead huffed and puffed and pulled herself up straight. "There are no friends of mine in that saloon, or any other, for that matter."

"Then they were friends of your da's. Maybe that's why they were so crazy to pound us into the floor of the establishment."

Her eyebrows lifted at his tone of voice, a tone that scraped across the very edge of thinning patience. "Neither my da nor I had anything to do with your fighting."

"So you keep saying. Forget it, for now," he said, glowering in a threatening way, bunching his fists and unconsciously aiming one at her. "I just want to leave here and take my brother to a place where he can regain his strength." He glared with controlled dislike— hard, cold and immense.

Sinead strove to remain cheerful. "I don't know where to take you. I can't take you to the house where I live. Not with all those bruises and your eyes blackened. The Dewitts will know you've been fighting in saloons." She turned away from him and shook her head, her eyes downcast. "I don't know what they'll think of me for marrying a man such as you."

"Now, isn't that just too bad what you think you know. Or what they think. Those attitudes sounds perverse, like they…"

She wheeled back to face him. "Aye, it would do immeasurable harm to Robbie's future. I would not have them know anything bad about you," she whispered. Her body hunched and began to tremble with fear, then anger erupted. "I don't suppose you've even given a single thought to the happy and excited child, who's waiting in the carriage to see his new da."

Hands fisted, Sinead stomped back and forth in front of the desk, fully understanding the foolishness, which had caught her in its net. A refusal to go along with her da's scheme would have been the thing to do.

"Take Egan and me to your da's home, or if you're that embarrassed, take us to a hotel," he hollered. "You don't seem to have a choice." He pointed to the door in a wide, expansive gesture. "We must go somewhere, preferably as far away from you and this situation as we can get." He pounded his closed fist into an open hand for emphasis.

Sinead swayed then squirmed. A trickle of sweat made its way from her armpits across her chest. Her underclothes clung in sticky folds. She put a hand over her mouth as her breakfast slid upwards in her throat. She struggled to regain control.

She stopped pacing, coughed once. With hands folded in solemn piety and utmost patience, she looked up and tried to explain the situation to this ill mannered oaf who was her husband. "You don't understand. I have no house. I live at the Dewitts'. That's where I take care of Robbie. And my da lives in a small room at a boarding house."

"Then take Egan and me to your da's, where we can get a room, or a hotel," Connor said with finality, as he stepped closer.

"There are no vacant rooms. They're all taken and they're not in the best part of town."

"I don't care about that. Take me to a hotel if you have no other place. I have to tend to Egan's and my wounds."

"Och, for heaven's sake." Sinead stamped one foot. "That would not be right and proper. You'll need care." She tilted her head and asked in a voice huskier than usual, "Does your brother look as bad as you do?"

She ogled him, trying to look calm and expressionless but hanging on every word in an attempt to come up with a solution to their dilemma. How did this fiasco get to be *their* problem? The very idea made her furious, but another thought hammered away in her brain.

Robbie would see him. Connor might scare a small boy under ordinary times, just with the size of him, but he was doubly scary now. What tale might the child carry home? What might the child say to his Dewitt grandparents?

Her hand was gripped, none too gently, in a hot, immovable grasp. She needed to keep her wits about her and keep her feet on the ground.

"Well, are you going to answer me?" Connor demanded. "If not, just get Egan and me released. We'll find our own way around town."

Suddenly, she remembered her da's advice about screaming to amuse the police. Perhaps, it might distract Connor. Sinead raised her voice in a way she never had. "Find yer own way about town, is it? Aye, like ye and yer foolish brother did last night?" Fascinated, Sinead watched his anger surfacing in slow waves.

His voice was low, threatening. "All you had to do lass, was send your da back for us. 'Twas wrong of you to keep him at your side."

The lower his voice went, the higher hers rose. "I didn't, ye know. Me da dropped me off and let others help me into the house." She brought one boot to the floor in an angry stamp. "I was heat struck, too weak to do anything except escaping to me bed. Me da left immediately." She scowled up at Connor. "How was I to know anything? I thought he went right back to get ye. I only learned later he was delayed."

"Delayed, is it? A likely story," he shouted.

Fury swept through her with the swiftness of a summer storm, hot, steady fury that sustained and protected her from further wounds. "And a true one," she screamed, surprised at her vehemence. "If ye don't believe me then take it up with me da," she added in a loud, shrill voice, wanting to lacerate him further with the scythe of her tongue.

"I will at that." Connor's face turned ashen. A jaw muscle twitched, and his mouth set in a firm line. He reached for her elbow then swung her around toward the door. "Now, dear, sweet wife, let's get out of here."

His grasp pinched. Someone pounded on the door and pushed at it. Discordant notes from their fight hung in the air.

"Come in," both Connor and Sinead called out as one.

A haggard Egan poked his head in. "Connor, if the two of ye are through with yer fussing, could yer lovely wife come out here to sign some papers?" He took a deep breath. "I have to get out of here. I'm getting sicker by the minute, just from the fumes of the place."

"Aye, Egan. We're coming, lad."

Without letting go of Sinead's arm, Connor went to the door. He made an elaborate gesture of holding it open for Sinead. He yanked her close. "And that, dear wife, was the brother you maligned. Did you see how poorly he's feeling?" he asked, shaking her arm, none too lightly.

Sinead tore her arm from his grasp and stalked past him. She marched out of the room into the narrow hallway and almost fell over from the cloying smells, which had gotten worse. Connor and Egan followed her.

Connor caught up to her. This time, he took the elbow with less force. "You don't want to be walking about in this place without some protection, lass."

"Missus, you'll be having to sign papers at the tiny desk. There, at the far end," Egan said, pointing down the hall and smiling politely. He nodded. "And hello. I'm Egan, the misfit's youngest brother. Glad to be finally meeting up with ye."

Seems that *one* of these brothers was softer and more humorous, she thought, raising her eyebrows a bit. At least, Egan showed humor and a bit of manners. Most men made advances like bulls, awkward and rough.

Sinead wiggled her arm away from Connor and stormed the length of the hall. The closer she got to the desk where she needed to sign the release papers, the closer she came to the bars of the holding cells and the more she wanted to gag. Men reached out between the bars. They made coarse remarks.

The smells of urine, stale whiskey and vomit were overbearing. They floated toward her like the rapids of a rushing stream. She almost turned away but looking up at scowling Connor who walked beside her, she noticed the men grew quieter as he passed their cells.

The policeman behind the small desk called out. "Those men can't leave here until you sign these papers, lady. I have them ready for you. All you have to do is put your signature to them. If you can." He chuckled to himself then shouted, "If you don't know how to do that, ma'am, make an 'x' where you see the mark."

Holding her breath against the odors surrounding them, Sinead moved to the desk, bent and signed her name with a flourish on two sheets. One had Egan's name at the top, the other Connor's. Once they were signed, she turned swiftly and bumped into Connor.

He caught her before she fell to the floor. Grimacing from pain and cursing softly under his breath, he propelled her around in the right direction to leave the building and grabbed Egan's arm, too. "Come. The odor in this place will kill you. Let's go outside. Then, I'll get us a carriage.

She stopped. "I told you. My da is out there, waiting for us. He has the carriage he drove to the piers yesterday. It's his and he'll take you any place you want to go," she mumbled, trying to pull her arm away from his grasp.

"I just want to get away from the smells of degradation and wastes permeating this place." Connor turned to Egan. "Are you able to maneuver, laddie?"

"Aye," came the reply. "I'll stay right behind you and the missus," Egan said, although his steps were slowing. "Och, Connor, I'm not feeling too steady right…"

Connor whirled around and caught Egan before he fell. He lifted him in his arms and cradled him like a baby. "Don't be conking out on me now, laddie. I need your smiling face and foolish ways." Egan was limp, his arms hanging over his brother's, his head back and his eyes closed. "Egan, are you there? Can you not answer me, lad?"

"I'm all right. Just need a bit of rest, I'm thinking," Egan responded, bringing his head erect and struggling to stand by himself.

"Och, God. Let's hurry, Connor. I'll hold the door for you," Sinead cried out, her voice packed with nervousness. "Come now," she continued while holding the door open. On she went as if she couldn't stop her tongue from flapping as she turned to Egan. "We can't be letting this young fellow give in to sickness on his second day ashore, now, can we?" She jostled his arm. "Speak to us, Egan."

"Later, lass, later," Egan croaked and seemed to faint away.

Connor hurried down the stairs of the Tombs with Egan in his arms and passed the policemen, who were laughing and smoking.

One tipped his cap to the two of them. "Yer brother still drunk? Glad she got ye both out of there."

The man with the cigar, who merely mouthed it now, shouted, "Good luck to ye. I hope yer wife won't be too hard on ye." He laughed uproariously.

The carriage was no longer across the street. Bowes had turned it around until it was directly in front of the jail. He gestured to them. "Hurry lads. Hop on in here." He jumped down from the driver's seat and helped Connor get Egan onto the backward seat. "Here ye go. Put this rug over yer legs, so…"

"Nae. Don't be doing that. It's too hot, Da."

Bowes nodded in agreement and hopped back up onto the driver's seat. "Robbie, son, come sit up here with Grandda Bee."

Robbie shook his head and looked to his mama.

Sinead smiled at him. "Nae, son. You stay right here next to Mama." She patted the seat.

She turned back, laid her hand on Egan's brow and quickly removed it. "Och, Lord, he's feverish."

Connor grabbed her about the waist and hoisted her up into the carriage. He leaped into the back and sat beside Egan, shoving him over a bit in order to rest Egan's head in his lap.

He spoke in Gaelic. "Egan, don't be going away from me. I'll take care of you, I promise. Da, would never forgive me if anything happened to one of his boyos. I'd be losing my head, everything."

A soft voice whispered, "'Tis all right, Con. I'm just a mite off me feed. I'll be right as rain by morning. Let me sleep some. Too noisy last…"

Connor rubbed his hand over Egan's face, pushing the red hair from his brother's forehead.

Sinead was amazed at the tenderness she saw in Connor, and, for one brief moment, wondered how those very same hands might feel on her brow, on her body. Heat rushed to her temples. She pursed her lips to release a contained breath. She looked away and hugged Robbie, who sat close.

Bowes flapped his whip in the air. The horses took off at a smart trot, and the carriage bounced over the cobblestone road. Egan groaned slightly.

Throughout all the activity, Robbie barely took his eyes off Connor and Egan. He tilted his head to one side and up, staring at Connor, before asking, "Are you my new da?"

Sinead gasped. "Robbie, this is not the…"

Connor tried to smile. He could hardly move his damaged lips. "Aye, I am that, son. I'm to be your new da. Is that all right?"

Robbie sighed. "You're ugly for a da!"

Egan must have heard for he began to chuckle. Bowes let out a huge bellow of laughter. Connor joined in, seconds later. Sinead thought them all crazy but was glad for the release of tension.

* * *

The carriage hustled over dirt and cobblestone streets to get Egan to a place where he could rest. By the time they got to Bowes's boardinghouse, Egan was asleep with his head on Connor's lap, a snore or two rising from his mouth.

"Jaysus, the lad's exhausted. Had to be, I guess, to fall asleep like that, what with the bumpy roads and all," Bowes commented while drawing the horses to a stop. "Well, we'll get him settled in my rooms. Then he can sleep the night and the day away if he chooses."

Robbie sat in the carriage watching everyone but his gaze returned to his mother. "How are they going to get that man up the stairs to Grandda Bee's? He's too big."

Connor looked down at the boy and ruffled his hair. He spoke through swollen lips. "But I'm bigger. I'm going to carry him, as I've done before when he's been in his cups."

Robbie tugged on Connor's trousers. "What's 'in his cups'?" He mimicked the funny way Connor said the words.

Connor again tried to smile at the lad. It took too much painful effort. He looked at Sinead instead. "You handle that wee one, will you now, lassie? I don't know how you want it explained to the child."

Sinead did no more than stare at him. Connor shrugged, slid

from under Eagan's body and stepped from the carriage. He pulled Egan over to the door then hoisted the limp man onto his shoulder.

Robbie's giggle followed them to the boarding house's painted red door. There, Bowes, carrying Egan's trunk, preceded Connor inside. Connor followed the man up the stairs to a second floor bedroom.

He deposited his brother on the bed Bowes indicated. "Don't worry, Bowes, I won't be breaking or stealing any of your valuables. I'll just be fixing my brother. I'll clean away some of the grime, if you'd be giving me a basin and some cloths. I'm sure he'll be walking around and sassing everyone within a day or so."

"I surely hope so. Other than the bruises he's carrying, the lad seems quite fit."

"Aye that he is." Connor looked out the single window and around the sparse room. "This neighborhood doesn't look too comforting," he mumbled and turned to Bowes. "Should I go back downstairs to wait in the carriage with Sinead and the boy. I wouldn't be wanting anything to happen to them. Once they're settled at their home, I'll come back and tend to Egan."

"Yer right, laddie. This is a great place for terrible things to happen, but don't ye be worrying. I'll get me body down there to watch and bring the two of them into the parlor. Don't be too long, now. Make yer brother comfortable, and I'll be coming back here to feed him shortly. And don't ye be worrying about things, like I said." With a slight wave of his hand, Bowes smiled and went out the door.

Sinead, her da and Robbie waited in the downstairs parlor while Connor stripped the barely-awake Egan down, bathed him and put a sheet over his clean body.

Slightly revived, Egan rolled to one side. "Con, I thank ye mightily and well ye know it."

"Aye, I know, laddie. But you'd do the same for me, I'm sure. Listen carefully. I won't be staying here. Not enough room." He stood and gestured around the small room. "Bowes will bring you

113

food later, after you've had a good sleep, and he'll care for you during the night."

"Con, what do ye intend to do about yer new missus and the boy...about the whole relationship?" Despite the bruises, Egan's face was clear, except for the scowl.

"'Tis not sure, I am. I'm not favorably impressed with a lass who can scream like a shrew."

Connor stood by the window. He glanced out as if the whole world had crumbled. So dejected was he, his lips turned down. He leaned against the window frame. He rubbed his forehead with his thumbs.

Egan coughed to get his attention. "Con, ye have to be making up yer mind to make this thing work." He yawned then murmured, "Maybe, change *yer* attitude toward the lass."

Connor whirled around to face his brother. "Perhaps she should be changing attitudes. I didn't ask to marry." He stared out the window. "Now, at this point, all I want is to consummate the marriage and return to Ireland, the family and my horses. I swear they're the only things that kept me sane over the years."

"I think ye're being a bit impatient." Egan yawned and lay back against the pillow with a sigh. "Ye've only been in this country less than two full days." Another yawn overtook him.

"And I haven't liked a single thing I've seen in this country, not this city, not..." Connor flashed a look at his brother, who had curled up on his side, holding the pillow close to his face.

Egan was asleep. Connor shrugged and descended the stairs. Standing at the bottom of the stairs, in the archway to the parlor, he heard soft voices and peered in.

Sinead and Bowes were sitting on a sofa, lit only by the three windows in back of it. They fell silent when he appeared. Even Robbie, playing on the floor with a top, barely moved when Connor walked farther into the parlor.

"Well?" Connor frowned. He stood in the center of the small rug, his hands across his chest. He looked about him, at them, at the room. The dark color of the furniture and the dim light from the windows made the room dingy, somber and depressing.

A thick layer of apprehension lay upon his tongue, muffling the voice to a low murmuring. "I've made a decision, lass. After the boy is taken care of, we'll stay the night in a hotel." He paused and refused to look at her. "We'll settle our differences there, later."

The huskiness of his voice irritated Sinead. She wanted to shout at him that he wasn't her boss, but couldn't. Not in front of Robbie. Her eyes narrowed but she stayed seated.

"Are you dictating or asking, Connor O'Malley? Did you not hear my words?" Sinead asked softly but with malice. She plastered a smile on her face and stood slowly, her head cocked to the side. She was livid, flushed with red-cheeked, suppressed anger. Her eyes flashed green fire at this bully of a man.

Rage made her stutter. "Do you expect me… just to obey… your every word…? If so, I'll be wanting…to know…why.

She jammed her emotions into a wee box, slammed the lid down tight and locked it. Glumly resigned for a brief moment to a fate, to which she had agreed, she glared at Connor before snapping, "If you expect me to obey, because you're legally my husband…you are so wrong. Nothing makes you my lord and master." Her mouth settled into a thin line, even as she tried a smile more like a grimace. She took a deep breath. "But you are right about one thing…We *will* discuss this later."

She whirled around and stamped out of the room. The males reluctantly followed her out of the house to the carriage.

* * *

Darkness descended before they traveled the full route to the Dewitts' home. Connor unwillingly left Egan to sleep off the ravages of Saturday evening in Bowes's further care, after he dropped Sinead at the Dewitts' house and Connor at a hotel.

A bewildered Connor spoke to Sinead with great respect. "Lass, we'll drop you and Robbie at the Dewitts' for a bit. Shall we wait for you?" Connor asked, not wanting to irritate her further than he already had.

"Nae. You go ahead to the hotel and wait. My da will come back for me. I'll need some time to put Robbie to bed."

"I'm not sleepy. I don't want to go to bed," Robbie piped from the corner of the carriage, where he huddled, half-asleep.

"No matter, love." She pushed the hair from his forehead. "'Tis past your bedtime, so I'll just settle you in."

"I want to go with my new da."

"Not tonight. 'Tis important for you to listen for tonight." She kissed his cheek and turned to Connor. "After my son is settled, I need to inform the Dewitts I'm leaving for the evening, what my plans are and when I intend to return."

"Aye, however you wish it, lass. But allow me to ask, do you always treat them with such respect and obedience?"

Inside, she boiled with outrage and shame at the fact that she did. "They're older than I. They're Robbie's grandparents, and, as such, they deserve respect."

Yet, the embarrassment of discussing such circumstances with the Dewitts made her legs rubbery. Humiliation turned her innards to water, but she got out of the carriage without a word to anyone. She lifted Robbie, set him on the ground and took his hand in hers.

Robbie yanked on her arm. "I want to say good night to my da."

Sinead sighed and lifted him up to the door of the carriage. Connor bent and gave him a quick kiss on the nose. He ruffled Robbie's hair. "Good night, laddie. Sleep tight in your bed."

"Night, Da. Night Grandda." Robbie slid his arms around Sinead's neck and hugged her. "Can we watch them go away?" he asked sweetly.

"Aye." Sinead set him on his feet on the stone sidewalk and took his hand. The two of them stood gazing after the carriage until it turned the corner.

"Come on, sweetheart," she said, pulling on his hand. "Mama Jane will put you to bed and tell you a story."

On the porch, Sinead picked Robbie up so he could ring the small bell. Its clear tinkling made him giggle

Nigel answered the door. "Ah, Jane," he chortled with his usual superior air. "The Dewitts wish to see you upon your return. They were a bit worried, thinking you kept Robbie out a bit later than usual."

"I know I did." She pushed past Nigel. "And I'm rushing to get him down in his bed for the night. Please, tell them that I will report in as soon as he's asleep," she said, crossing the foyer and going up the center stairs. "I don't want to drag his evening out any more than it already has been."

She hurried up the stairs, wanting to get Robbie to bed without allowing him to tell his grandparents about the day's activities. Sinead took him to his room, bathed him and told him a story until he fell asleep.

She dashed to her room in the suite she shared with Robbie and scoured her dresser for clean clothes fit to take with her. Her hands fluttered as she discarded one outfit after another.

As she packed the few decent garments she owned, fat tears tracked down her cheeks. They settled in the corner of her mouth then dribbled over her chin. She sighed and took a deep breath. In order to regain some control over her emotional well being, she mopped the tears with a towel she used to cleanse her face.

She grabbed her beads from the dresser. Rosary clasped in her hand as if to fight off the devil himself, she waited, her lips moving in a fervent prayer, hoping to rid herself of a hard core of germinating resentment.

Condemned! Headed for the gallows! She bowed her head and slid to her knees at the side of the bed. "Does every woman feel like this? God help me, if that's true…"

CHAPTER EIGHT

Bowes stopped the carriage a block before the entrance to the Fifth Avenue Hotel, the grandest of all the hotels in the City of New York. Its layered levels and its clean, shining facade were impressive as they reached for the night sky, their gas lit lamps twinkling as bright as stars.

"Lord, that building is huge," Connor said, craning his neck upwards and sideways. "Bigger than some of the castles in England and Ireland."

"It's the biggest and most beautiful hotel in the City. Everything in there is done on a grand scale. They have rooms for everything imaginable, including a place where ye can clean up, son." Pride in the city brought a glow to Bowes's face.

Connor grinned at him. "'Tis large, for sure, and I can readily believe it's the most beautiful in the world. 'Tis most magnificent, with its pure shimmering pink and golden touches from the fading sunlight."

"Och, the lyricism of the Irish. Lord, how I miss it," Bowes chortled. Suddenly he became serious. "Listen to me, laddie, the folks in there are not going to be too pleased to serve ye."

"Probably not with the look of me right now, but I imagine money speaks as well in America as it does in Ireland. And I have enough of it with me." He patted his pocket. I have a pouch strung around my waist by a cord."

"The police didn't take it from ye while ye were in their care?"

Bowes asked, a surprised and puzzled look on his face. "They usually do, ye know." He nodded. "Maybe ye and yer brother were just too big for them to risk it."

"Maybe they thought I was just another downtrodden Irishman with no funds. Both Egan and I looked that way coming off the steamer. Besides, that's something we heard stories about, all the way over in Ireland. My brother and I discussed it on the voyage to America and decided to keep most of it in our trunks. Not show it around much." Connor chuckled. "'Tis all we have with us."

Smiling, Bowes shook his head in approval and climbed down from the driver's seat. "Och, 'twas a good plan, also a good thing I was able to get yer trunks from Clancy's before anyone noticed them. Clancy's an honest saloon owner, but he gets caught up in things with people he really doesn't understand. Being hardworking like he is, he'd be thinking everyone else is too." He tossed his whip into the back of the carriage.

"Well, I'd best be going in and seeing to a room," Connor replied, untying his trunk from the back of the carriage and hoisting it up. He winced as it settled on his shoulder.

"Still hurting, lad?" Bowes asked with compassion.

"Aye, a bit," he said, slightly readjusting the trunk and looking down the block at the hotel. "Does this hotel have a place where I can get rid of this scratchy beard, get a haircut and bathe my sore body?" He chuckled. "All your poor daughter's seen is me frightful parts and I've never looked so bad."

"Connor, lad, the hotel has some private bathrooms. Be sure to ask for a room with one of those. They're purely luxurious. 'Tis the Hotel's way of being better than those sprouting up around it like weeds. Bowes leaned into the passenger part of the carriage and dusted off the seats. "Plus, they have a mighty group of workers, about four hundred I've heard, many of them Irish, ye know."

"'Twill make it a homecoming to have some decent Irish around." Connor eased the trunk to the ground with a grand sigh and rubbed his shoulder. From the corner of his eye, he watched the uniformed man, standing at attention in front of the hotel. The man stood that way until he needed to greet people. Whenever they approached him, he ushered them in, opening the hotel's front door with a grand gesture and closing it after them.

Bowes gave out with a hoot of laughter. "Once ye make it in the door, ye won't have to be carrying that trunk much longer, boyo. They'll be grabbing it right away from ye," Bowes commented. "Looking for a bit o' yer change, I'm thinking."

"After muscling thousand pound horses on our farm in Ireland, this trunk seems light weight, once it's up there on my shoulder. I'm just a mite stiff and sore but I've been that before."

"What do ye intend doing here in America, son?" Bowes bent forward. His face glowed with a strange eagerness for the answer. "As your new da, I think I have a right to ask. After all, it's me daughter ye've married."

"I don't intend to be doing much at all." Connor strolled over to the carriage horses, looked them over carefully and stood, unconsciously rubbing the neck of the nearest one. "Nice animals, Bowes."

"Aye. They've served me well." Bowes dusted a part of the carriage door with the elbow of his shirt. A young couple came over to the carriage. He shooed them away. "I'm off for the evening after me next call."

Connor moved back toward him and said in a low voice. "Bowes, I'm wanting you to know, I have enough money for a year or two of living careful, and there's more where that came from in Ireland. After a time, I'm hoping I'll convince your daughter to return to Ireland with Egan and me to our manor." A spate of homesickness assailed Connor "I'll inherit it all someday, you know." Connor puffed up his chest with a bit of pride in what he considered his.

"Ye'd never be able to hang around for a year, doing nothing, laddie," Bowes commented as he continued to dust the shiny parts of his vehicle. "Not with caring for the horses most of yer life. 'Tis not in yer blood, I'm thinking. And Sinead, she'll not be leaving Robbie, for sure." Bowes voice was definite and restrained.

"'Tis not a problem. The boy's as welcome at the manor as she is. In fact, I'm thinking my da might look forward to having a youngster on the farm." Connor looked around him, puzzled at the way folks were walking. Strolling couples seemed to give Bowes and him a wide berth, wandering past them with exaggerated steps.

Connor straightened his clothing, brushed some of the grime off it and turned back to Bowes. "My brothers are grown, Egan being the young one of the five of us — and none of us married. Except for me, that is."

"Son, I don't think ye see the whole picture yet," Bowes said in all seriousness. "The Dewitts are a troublesome family. They're a stiff-necked, proud, moneyed family, but I think there's more behind their desire to have their grandson near at hand than just loving the youngster. They seemed to be more interested in being in high society, with wealth galore, than in being fair or truthful."

"Aye, my da indicated people were like that over here." Connor leaned against the carriage and stared up at the hotel. "I haven't even met the Dewitts yet, but I don't like them, sight unseen."

Bowes patted his arm. "I don't like to speak ill of others, but I think ye'll find there's going to be great trouble getting the lad out of their clutches. 'Tis common in the city for the wealthy to worry over their image in society and what their money will bring them. And that youngster is a good part of the Dewitts' image..."

Connor interrupted, stood straight and turned to Bowes. "But once Sinead and I come to our agreements, we'll see to the laddie in due course."

"Laddie..." Bowes's voice softened.

Connor frowned at the sound of it. "Aye?"

"Be gentle with me Sinead." Bowes looked away, the subject touchy. "She's not had a good life. Her mam died young. Sinead's been working, in one form or another, since she was a wee lass of twelve." He looked everywhere but at Connor. "Ever since her younger sister died and there was no one to care for at home, she's not been comfortable with herself. Always thinking of betterment she is."

Connor rested his heavy frame on the side of the carriage again. He thought for a moment before answering. "This marriage will be good for your daughter. She'll have all sorts of things she couldn't imagine and a fine family to boot."

"I'll enjoy seeing her in that situation." Bowes chortled once and slapped Connor on the back. "Might even bring me back to the old Sod meself."

"The marriage needs to be considered legal in the eyes of the Church. That part I will leave up to your daughter." A red-faced Connor looked down at his booted feet. Not sure of what he should say, he blurted, "I'll not be forcing any lass to partake of my favors."

Bowes nodded, his face frozen in a half-smile of discomfort. "Just take yer time, lad. Be taking yer good old sweet time. That is, if ye're wise." He coughed into his hand. "Lovely things don't happen overnight."

"They'll have to happen soon if she wants to return with me to Ireland. I have to get back to my horses." Connor bent over, about to pick up the trunk again.

Bowes's grasp restrained him. "There are horses in America, some fine ones, I might add. Do ye intend to be raising some here in America?" Bowes asked with a more avid interest than he showed before in the conversation. He paused, then, shook his head and climbed up onto the driver's seat. He tweaked his lips together and made a clucking sound in his mouth. "There might be a wee problem for ye. Sinead hates horses, she does. She has her reasons."

"She'll just have to get over her hate. 'Tis my very life, she'd be against." Connor blinked as more lights came on in the hotel, and the night grew brighter. "I don't think we should be discussing Sinead any more. I barely know her other than her fainting at the sight of me."

Bowes erupted into laughter. The horses, who had been dozing off in their traces, awoke and pulled on the reins. Bowes grabbed them in his left hand and pulled.

Connor continued to mumble. "And screaming, shrieking like a shrew when she came to the jail."

Bowes laughed harder and slapped his knee. "Och, she's a good lass. Listened to her da, she did."

Connor shook his head, not understanding the reasons for Bowes's laughter. He decided to change the subject, so he answered Bowes's original question. "I surely won't be raising horses in this brick city of yours. I might look around for a good stallion or a couple of mares, but I'll be shipping them back to Ireland if I find any worth keeping."

"Well, be off with ye, now," Bowes called out, shaking his head as if in disbelief at their conversation. Laughing, he cracked his whip, clucked, and the horses moved away from the curb. "I'll be bringing Sinead back here before ye know it. Settle yerself in the hotel. I'll take care of the rest," he shouted going down the street at a slow pace. He turned and waved.

* * *

Connor hefted the trunk onto his shoulder and watched Bowes turn a corner. The last he saw of his father-in-law that evening, the man was still shaking his head as if talking to himself. Connor chuckled, angled his trunk a little bit more comfortably and turned toward the entrance to the Fifth Avenue Hotel.

He stood for a moment and watched uniformed men outside the hotel helping others to and from carriages, carrying luggage and scurrying about. None stepped forward to help him, but it didn't bother him. He knew he resembled all the devils in hell right now and hated entering such a grand place in his present condition, but the choice was made.

He had to find a room for the night, clean up in order to feel human again and make an attempt to solve his current dilemma. Passengers flew down steps of carriages and rushed past him into the hotel. Astounded as he was by all the activity around him, it didn't stop him from admiring the fine horses lined up in front of the hotel.

One carriage pulled up and a young couple descended. The man turned back. A small lad with flaming red hair jumped into his arms, reminding Connor of Egan, Ireland and the horses waiting there for him. The sight nearly brought Connor to his knees, with an ache in his stomach.

The hotel lobby teemed with activity. It smelled of expensive perfumes, gleamed with polished ornaments and glowed in the light of huge, glass, gas chandeliers. Richly decorated chairs, edged in gilt, lined the marble lobby.

People moved in a steady river, ebbing into, through, and out of the great entry hall. Some sat, talking on huge, lavishly upholstered lounge chairs set close to small tables. Their voices, although muted, carried throughout.

Giant plants, which seemed to be growing in gigantic pots, dotted the corners of the room and reached for the frescoed ceiling. The chandeliers lit the room, tinting it, gilding it, as if from wands of Ireland's little people, elaborate and golden. The walls glittered and frisked brightly in the gas flames of the chandeliers.

Connor was so much in awe, he turned and turned, eventually backing up to the long reservation desk that stretched the length of one full alcove in the lobby.

"Can I help you, sir?" a high-pitched but masculine voice asked from somewhere behind Connor.

Without turning around Connor murmured, "Aye. I need a room for the evening for my wife and myself. And I'll be wanting one with a bathroom attached. I've heard you have such."

"I'm so sorry, but we're all booked up," the disembodied voice said with rigid politeness. "Perhaps, you'd prefer to check into one of the hotels a few streets over, nearer to the shipyard?"

Connor turned.

The man gasped. His eyes grew large and their color deepened. He stared at Connor.

"Nae, I would be preferring this establishment right here,"

Connor said in a low, tense tone that brooked no refusal.

"My word, sir, have you been in a fight?" the man asked, moving a step back from the desk.

"Ye might say that. It was sort of one way. My brother and I were defending ourselves from a group who thought two Irishmen new to this city should learn about America."

With a slight nod of his head, the man tried to smooth the situation over. "Sir, I'm so sorry your entrance into America was so violent, and I'm even more upset to tell you this. We don't take sailors at this hotel."

"What are you meaning by that statement?" Connor asked, heated anger beginning to rise.

The man put his hands together in an effort to still them. "Well, sir...sailors usually prefer to stay in one of the hotels closer to the piers."

"Well, first of all," Connor said, splaying his large hand on the counter. "I'm not a sailor but a visitor to your fine country." He drew himself up to his full height and settled his face into a stern expression. "And, as I said before, I'm wanting to stay in this particular hotel."

In an attempt to gain control of the situation, the deskman smiled and then superciliously said, "The Fifth Avenue is very expensive, sir, particularly if you request a private bath connected to the room." The deskman coughed into his hand.

Connor smiled the very best he could. "Would you mind if I put this trunk down on the floor? It's gotten a tad cumbersome to be holding it on my sore shoulder. And if it's money you're wanting, just tell me how much. I'll gladly reward you, however you need to be rewarded, but I want a room. And quickly."

"Let me call my manager. I'm sure he'll be glad to help you," the clerk said, backing another two paces away from Connor.

Connor glanced at the nameplate on the counter. "Mister Collins, is it?" he asked politely, pointing to the sign. "Are you Mister Collins?"

Mister Collins nodded. "Yes, I am," he said through gritted teeth. He raised his hand and signaled another employee, a gray-haired, bearded gentleman, who was dressed in an elegant suit and standing in another part of the lobby, in deep conversation with two other men.

The man looked up when he noticed the waving arms, finished his conversation and strolled over to the desk, where Connor stood waiting. "Can I help you?" the man asked, a small, tight smile crossing his mouth, bringing his lips into a straight line as if he were angry at being disturbed.

"Your name, sir?" Connor asked in a low voice.

"James Thorne, at your service. Manager of this establishment," he said, gesturing to the entire lobby in an expansive motion and avoiding looking into Connor's bruised, somewhat swollen face.

Connor confronted the man. "Mister Thorne, I would like a room in this hotel and a place to bathe. I would like to have things well settled before my wife arrives."

Glaring down at the man, Connor softly continued, "And don't be giving me any more nonsense about moving to a hotel closer to the piers." He glared at Thorne. "I am not a sailor. I have plenty of money and I wish to stay here." Connor yanked a pouch from his pocket and slammed it onto the counter, letting the coins and bills spill out. "If this isn't enough, I've more."

The sight of money so freely thrown onto the counter changed Thorne's expression to one of supreme accommodation. "Why, no sir, that's more than enough. How long do you wish to stay?" he asked with great politeness.

"Only for the evening."

Thorne's eyes narrowed. A sly look dotted his face, but he said nothing.

"My wife and I might wish dinner sent to our room." Connor pulled himself up to his full height before adding, "And we'll be wanting a bathroom."

Thorne smiled in man-to-man fashion, lowering his eyelids. "The only room we have left, sir, with such an attraction is one with a large single bed in it, or might you like two connecting but separate rooms?"

"Whatever for? I'll take the first room, Mister Thorne." Connor glanced around the lobby and turned back. "Allow me to introduce myself. My name is Connor O'Malley, newly from Ireland," he offered, pointing to the quill, inkstand and guestbook that he was ready to sign in.

Having listened carefully to Bowes explanation of the workers who would look for money to carry a trunk, Connor tossed some change onto the counter. "Ask someone take the trunk to the room and give me a key."

Thorne signaled a tall, stout lad, dressed in what Connor assumed was the hotel uniform, and motioned him over. "Joseph, take Mister O'Malley's trunk to Room 403 and return to the lobby."

Connor swiveled around and found the sign he'd seen before. He pointed to it. "I noticed the emporium as I came into the lobby. For shaves, haircuts. I would like to go there before I go to my room."

"Oh, I think that's an excellent idea, Mister O'Malley," Collins squealed from behind the counter. "Our barbershop has no comparison in this entire city. It's that fine."

Mister Thorne looked at Collins and nodded, a gleeful look on his face. They smirked at each other with raised eyebrows while Connor scoured the lobby.

He watched the activities with his mouth agape. The stout lad placed the trunk on a rolling cart and headed for an ornate contraption, which looked like a gilded iron cage. He wheeled the cart into it, stepped in himself and closed the cage door. The lad, the cart and the trunk rose above the floor with a whirring noise and kept on going up. Connor staggered from the counter to view its ascent to other floors.

When he turned, both Thorne and Collins were smiling.

"Fascinating, isn't it?" Collins asked.

His face suffused with awe, Connor nodded, his gaze still following the cage.

"That's our newest acquisition," Thorne commented. "We call it our little Parlor Car." He turned to face Connor. "Everything shall be as you wish, sir." He nodded to Collins. "Give Mister O'Malley the key to room number 403," Thorne commanded before his voice changed to a subservient one, and he graciously smiled. "It's a fair walk up, sir, unless you would like to take our little parlor to raise you to the floor...?"

Connor swung around and looked at another ornate cage into which guests stepped with care. A young man seemed to be driving it. The entire cage moved slowly up between the floors with a series of pulleys and ropes. Connor gaped again, his mouth opened wider when he saw the first cage come down from between the floors.

He nodded, with our taking his gaze from the car. "I'll do that when I return. Have my wife brought up that way, too, if I have not returned from the barber." Still gaping like a child at his first carnival, he continued, "Her da will see to her comfort until I reach the room."

"As you wish, sir." Thorne's smile was more genuine this time.

Connor returned the smile then adopted a high society air, an air he'd seen used by Englishmen throughout Ireland. He raised his head grandly, gave Collins a brief nod and said to Thorne, with a superior tone. "Lead me to your emporium and your shops, please. Perhaps, I'll be buying an outfit to surprise my wife."

"Certainly," the manager said. "Please, follow me."

* * *

Hearing the noise of the carriage pulling up outside the Dewitt mansion then her da's loud command to the horses to stop, Sinead swallowed the nausea that rose in her throat. Embarrassed, she grabbed the little bag that held her clothes, clutched it to her body and hurried to the front door. Without saying good-bye to anyone in the house, she sped out to the street.

Her da stood at the door to the carriage, holding it open. She took his hand, climbed up the step and into the carriage. She took a last look at the house before her da urged the horses up the street. A curtain moved in the upstairs window. Someone saw her leaving.

* * *

Ludwig Dewitt watched Sinead run down the outside stairs and leap into her father's carriage. He let the drape fall from his fingers and turned to his wife. "Adelaide, I don't believe this new marriage thing is going to work to our advantage."

Adelaide looked up from her painstaking needlework and exclaimed, "Don't say that Luddie." She smiled grimly. "Trust me, the girl will not stay with that man, who calls himself her husband, and leave the child."

"She's a grown woman. She will want a life of her own." Ludwig stretched and patted the vest, which barely covered his ample stomach.

"Look how she let us sell Cavanaugh House and all its goods. She didn't want a bit of the money for herself," Adelaide retorted, plying her needle through an intricate part of the hunting scene she was stitching.

"She allowed us to put it all away for the boy because she had no real knowledge of it." Ludwig lumbered over to his humidor and pipe, sitting on the small table at the entrance to the room.

"And look what that money has done for your business," Adelaide offered with a languid and sly smile. "In the long run, she'll choose the boy to the man, just as she has from the very first."

"What if she falls in love with the man? What then?" Ludwig tapped tobacco into the bowl of the pipe then used it to scratch his beard while he paced.

"That oaf? You should have seen him at the pier. He was dirty, with tattered clothes and a shaggy, unkempt beard." Her voice rose with pretended horror as she described Connor. "Grimy dark hair fell onto his face. His dark eyes glared at me, while all the time he tried to belie his appearance with pretty speechifying." Adelaide laughed as she remembered the scene at the pier. "Definitely an Irishman to the core. And you know she no longer associates with them, especially since you do not allow Robert to do so." Adelaide snapped. "The only one she seems to favor is that stupid, coarse father of hers."

"I know. I know. It seems she still goes to church and all with her father. Just now, I just saw her get into his carriage. They were obviously going somewhere."

"She told me she intended to spend the evening with her new husband in an attempt to get to know him a bit better," Adelaide said in a mocking voice, nervously crossing and uncrossing her legs in discomfort.

Ludwig strolled over to a mahogany sideboard, which stood against one wall of their bedroom suite. He put down the pipe, took a cigar from the humidor lying on top of the sideboard, clipped one end and stuck the other in his mouth. "The whole thing infuriates me," he said, chewing on the end of the cigar before scratching a match to light it.

"Luddie, you just lit your pipe. Please, smoke one or the other," Adelaide admonished. She pricked her finger with the needle. "Damn it!" She reached into the pocket of her gown, drew out a handkerchief and wrapped it around her forefinger.

"I don't have the time or patience to spend traipsing through court after court to get the custody settled," Ludwig groused, pointing the end of his cigar and moving toward her. He waggled it back and forth beneath her face, until she sneezed.

Smiling, he lit the match, puffed until the rosy glow at the cigar's tip brought the smoke to his mouth. He drew deeply then exhaled, sending a stream of smoke toward Adelaide. She picked up a fan from the table next to her and waved it about. The smoke drifted toward the ceiling.

Adelaide coughed politely into her hand until Ludwig moved back toward the window. "We have to spend the time, Ludwig. We have to. Think what it would do to your business if you lost the child's money." She watched her husband and saw the greedy look he wore. "Besides, what would our dear departed Lucinda think if we left her child to the care of another, one who was not of his blood?" she sweetly asked, knowing it would rile him.

"Adelaide, do not fool yourself into believing things that were not so." Ludwig whirled on his wife and glared.

Adelaide stood and responded angrily, "I beg your pardon. What exactly do you mean?"

Ludwig puffed away on his cigar and paused. In an unconscious movement, he flicked ashes onto the floor. Adelaide frowned but held her tongue. She waited to hear what else he had to say about their daughter, a child he hadn't cared for from the very beginning.

"Lucinda didn't want a child. She only had one for that Cavanaugh, so he wouldn't leave her!"

Adelaide gasped. She quickly laid the fan down, sat and grabbed at her needlework. She needed to be doing something other than listen to this fat husband of hers go on about her daughter, a daughter made in her mother's image.

"I will never understand that," she said, shaking her head and working hard to recover her composure. Her hand shook as well. "Lucinda was such a beautiful, kind and sweet girl. How could any man want to leave her?"

"Lucinda was never kind and sweet, my dear, not from the day she was born. She made Cavanaugh's life a living hell with her flirting and spending habits. But I will grant you one thing. She was beautiful." He looked over at his wife, whose expression mirrored her distaste of his last remark. "Not as beautiful as you, of course, my dear."

Adelaide smiled up at her husband. He always knew the right thing to say to her when she was upset. "Lucinda did other things for that man."

"Ach, yes, she converted to Catholicism against my advice, putting us in a precarious situation. Then she died in childbirth..."

Adelaide huffed at him. "Well, she didn't die on purpose. It was through no fault of her own that she died giving birth." Vitriolic words spurted from her mouth. "That stupid doctor Cavanaugh hired to care for her was at fault."

"You don't know that, Adelaide. Although I wonder…" Ludwig stopped in the middle of his thought as another surfaced. "Might the doctor have been in cahoots with Cavanaugh regarding the birth?"

"My God, what are you suggesting, Ludwig?"

"No, it's a terrible thing to think about, much less say."

Adelaide stood and swayed over to her husband, with grace. She drew the draperies tighter than before and laid her hand on his arm. She looked up at him in the fetching way she knew he admired. "What do you mean, you darling man?"

"It's just a thought, just a thought," he said, staring off into space. "Could it have been that Cavanaugh was already interested in our little Jane?

Adelaide laughed. "I doubt it. She's so plain looking. That Cavanaugh was interested in more attractive things. Why, he even flirted with me once."

"You never told me that."

"You probably wouldn't have believed me anyway," she said with a smile crossing her face. She made her eyes twinkle, and she patted his arm before going back to her pillowed chair. "And what could I possibly say about my daughter's husband that would have made anyone believe me?"

Quiet, seemingly morose, Ludwig let his dirty cigar drop more ash onto her lovely, bright oriental carpet. When he spoke, he spoke slowly as if testing the idea out in his mind.

"Perhaps Cavanaugh felt that way about Jane before Lucinda got with child. Jane had worked for them for several years before the birth." He tipped his head to one side. "I know Lucinda said otherwise, but might another love be the real reason he hired that doctor instead of the midwife we suggested?"

"How could any man love another when Lucinda was present? It was just not possible, although I do rem —" Adelaide leaned back in her chair, stuck herself with the needle she was using and let her needlepoint fall to the floor. With her hand raised to her mouth, she sucked the tiny spot of blood from her finger.

"If that is so, I'm glad he was injured in the accident. He tried to tell me that, on the night of the child's birth, as soon as he got word of its coming, he hurried back from club," she said with a cold vehemence, coming up from her toes. "It crippled him forever." She chuckled. "Once our daughter died, he could do nothing about his abnormal sexual drives."

"How do you know about sexual drives, my dear? I had no idea you were so worldly." Ludwig wriggled his eyebrows at her, a gesture he often used to change the subject.

She giggled, letting him think he was distracting her. "Ach, Luddie, you know I'm not worldly-wise. I'm searching for answers to our daughter's death, something that shouldn't have happened to such a young and lovely girl. I couldn't think of anything else that might have precipitated the events."

"Don't think on it my dear. Your thoughts will change nothing. How is your new chair seat coming?" he asked, crossing the floor to pick her needlework up.

"Why, Ludwig, you heard what the doctor told Cavanaugh. Lucinda was too tiny to bear such a large child. She should never have married Cavanaugh or tried to have his child."

"But dear, she kept telling us she was desperately in love. That's why we gave our permission when she was so young, why we hired Jane to be her maid and why we've let Jane take care of the boy for all these years. Lucinda wanted everything her own way."

"For no good reason. And with a blackguard who married Jane within three years, despite all his crippling injuries, insisting his child be brought up Catholic, as if that makes any difference. Sinead, that stupid name was what he called our Jane. She was the only mother the boy had ever known he kept saying. We felt sorry for him, for the constant pain he was in, and we went along with all his machinations."

Tears of self-pity rolled down Adelaide's cheeks. "Oh, stupid us." She took a soft silk handkerchief out of her sleeve and dabbed her eyes with it. "Does that give her the right to take the child away from us?"

"It shouldn't, but how are we to take care of a young boy? Our son, up in Albany, and his wife don't want the responsibility of another child, and we're too old to have a child disrupt our lives."

"The ultimate decision is up to you, Ludwig. It is your blood, as well as mine, you give up in the long run," she said, still daubing the streaming tears.

"My darling, don't cry. We'll think of something."

"What do you think of nursemaids until he old enough to go to the school your parents sent you to? Please Ludwig, for me."

Ludwig began to puff on his cigar again, taking deep inhaling breaths of pure smoke. "Decent and hardworking folks are hard to find. That's why our Jane is so wonderful for the boy. Perhaps we can find another who will suit and…"

Adelaide interrupted. "Definitely not an Irish one. I'll never have another Irish servant in my household," she said with a great deal of bias.

"Adelaide, do you feel as if you could take care of the boy by yourself, with the help of another?" Ludwig asked calmly as though he already knew the answer.

"I wouldn't have to. I thought you promised he would go off to a dormitory school when he turned five?"

Ludwig patted her shoulder then went back to the curtains. "Definitely. He'll go to the schools that I did. At five."

"He just turned four," she said, letting a single tear slide from her eye. "How on earth will I manage until he's five? We'll just have to keep our hands on Jane until he's old enough to go away to that school."

Ludwig paced in front of the window, his face getting redder and redder as plans came into his mind. "I'll send the boy to all the schools I went to. Once he graduates from my college, I'll take him into the company."

"That nice, dear," she said, smiling to herself.

"You know, you're right Adelaide. I'll not give up my daughter's child, nor do I intend to bring him up Catholic, particularly once Jane leaves us."

"His father insisted though. It was part of the marriage agreement with Lucinda and again with Jane. That's why he married a low class Irish maid, so the boy would be brought up in that religion."

"The whole idea disgusts me, my dear. Such a savage religion!" Ludwig's pacing grew more intense.

"Well, then we'll just have to take the whole thing to court, don't you think so Luddie. Especially, now that there is another involved. Lord knows what that husband of Sinead's has up his sleeve, but I'll bet it's something. You know how those Irish are."

"Never fear, wife, we will surmount this obstacle as we have every other. I didn't get to this position in my life, and in this City, by not solving problems. This, too, will pass. Let Jane go wherever she wants. She's just not going to take our grandchild with her. And that's my final word on the subject."

"Ach, husband, you do thrill me," Adelaide said, grinning broadly. "And now that you've made up your mind, let's retire to our summer home upstate. The heat of the city is getting to be too much for me."

CHAPTER NINE

Sinead said little during the carriage ride to Fifth Avenue and the Hotel. When she was this wrapped up in her thoughts, she didn't feel in a conversational mood. Her tension regarding the next meeting with her husband, for only the third time, was overwhelming. She barely noticed the busy streets, unusual for Sunday, when most stayed at home with families.

Bowes reined the horses in from their smart trot and slowly walked them the rest of the way to their destination, something he seldom did. He sat up straight in the driver's seat, showing pride in his rig and the well-mannered behavior of his horses. His attempt at dignity made Sinead briefly smile.

A liveried servant rushed to the carriage. Another hurried to hold one of the horse's heads, patting the creature's neck and murmuring to him in a voice too low to hear. The first fellow opened the door to the carriage and helped her down the short step.

"Thank you," she said, watching him reach for her clothing bag. She turned to her da, moved to the driver's seat and asked, "You'll come back here no later than noon tomorrow? Please, Da, do this without argument."

"Shouldn't ye be spending a full day with yer husband? Showing him the sight of this big city, although I'm not too sure if that's what he'll be interested in seeing," Bowes said, raising his eyebrows at her.

A blush crept up her face and, with it, all the thoughts she was trying to avoid. How could she possibly be cozy with a man she didn't know, a man who looked, for all the world, like the darkest of devils? "Da, I can't. As you well know, I'm responsible for Robbie's care." She spun away but turned back to say softly, "I will never get any peace from Adelaide if I'm derelict in my duties."

Bowes waved his arms in a useless gesture. "Och, you'll never get any peace from that old…"

"Da! Please, pick us up here." She almost stamped her foot but stopped when it seemed others were listening to the exchange. "We'll get Robbie and take him with us to the park or somewhere. After the treatment Connor and his brother received here, I'm not sure he'll want to go anywhere, except to check on his brother."

"All right, darlin'," he said, shaking his head. "I won't be fussing at ye this evening. I suspect ye have enough on yer mind as it is. Count on yer old da. I'll be here around eleven."

Bowes gathered the reins and nodded to the servant holding the horse. He turned back to her. "You best be remembering, lass, just go up to the desk in that lobby. Tell them what's working there who ye're looking for."

"Da, I know what to do." She giggled from nervousness.

'Well, don't let them tell ye he's not around. I know for a fact he's here already. Dropped him off myself an hour or so ago."

Despite her frowning, Sinead smiled up at him. "Don't worry, Da. I'll find my way," she said, turning to the servant, who held her small cloth bag in his hand, waiting for her.

"Follow me, missus," he said, leading her toward the gilded lobby. She heard her da's cluck to the horses. She sighed, looked down at her feet and followed.

The gas chandelier lit the inside of the lobby with moving flashes of fire, making it seem like daytime. Sinead glanced around then stared at the people milling about, talking and gesturing with ease. All were elegantly dressed. She peeked at her outfit, which was several years older than the newest fashions, and felt more the servant than ever before.

The hotel was fancy, filled with glitz and glitter, from the long expanse of shiny counter to the upholstered lounge chairs. She didn't belong here anymore than she belonged with the Dewitts.

Did Connor want to embarrass and show her up? They were out of place here. Why did he come to this particular hotel, she wondered, looking at the gilded décor woven into the marble flooring. She touched it with her toe and looked up, embarrassed.

All the while Sinead followed the young man, wending his way past people who stared. She kept turning around to feast her eyes on sights she's never seen before. Huge chandeliers lit every corner of the room. A golden railing at each side of wide carpeted stairs led the way to another floor, labeled The Mezzanine.

Looking elsewhere, she bumped into the young blond man who carried her bag. "So sorry. I didn't mean to bump into you." His red uniform, with its gold trim, blinded her for a moment.

Doing a slight side step, the young man stopped and held out a hand to steady her. "People often do that, ma'am. Especially, if it is the first time they've been to this hotel." He smiled and gave an expansive bow. "Don't upset yourself. Come."

He brought her to a long desk running the length of a curved alcove. She handed him a coin and watched him nod his thanks then move away to another part of the lobby.

Behind her, a man coughed politely. "Can I help you, missus?"

Startled, Sinead turned. She eyed the clerk and spoke with as much dignity as she could muster. "Why yes, I'm looking for my husband, a Mister Connor O'Malley, please."

The clerk pointed to a specific corner of the lobby. "Why yes, madam, he's across the lobby, reading the Tribune. He's been most anxious for your arrival."

Sinead looked in the general direction the clerk pointed and noticed several tall, very handsome men reading the newspapers under the chandelier and another gaslight affixed to the wall. Two of them glanced over at her, one waggling his eyebrows.

She gave them both a huffy look, sticking her nose into the air. She continued to look around for someone who was inappropriately dressed for a stay in this hotel. No one remotely resembled anyone of that nature. *Where was Connor?*

She turned back to the clerk. "I'm sorry. I do not see him."

"There, madam, straight ahead," he said before returning to his work.

Sinead gazed up again. The tallest of the men, who peered at her, a man she didn't know, approached her. He sported a big smile. She peeked around to see if another person stood behind her. Only the clerk, writing something on a paper, stood there, his head bent to his work.

She looked up again. No, surely this couldn't be Connor crossing the lobby. In large strides. With a swagger in his walk. She retreated until her back was against the counter. And studied the man carefully from beneath her lashes. The traces of discoloration under the piercing brown eyes were recognizable. The beard and longish hair were gone, along with much of the swelling.

She drew in a deep breath. Conflicting emotions crawled up her throat and burned her face. She couldn't bring herself to believe it was Connor who now stood directly in front of her.

"Sinead, I was afraid you weren't coming," Connor said softly, a hint of worry in his voice. He gently took her elbow and drew her away from the counter.

"What have I to be afraid of?" She refused to let herself be intimidated, either by his size or their marriage circumstances. "You are now my husband. I will obey your commands, if possible…" She broke off midpoint, caught up in a grip of confusing emotions.

Puzzled at her expression, Connor pulled her to one side of the alcove, away from people who might overhear them and the two older women, who with their heads nearly touching, seemed to be watching the reunion. "I hope this is not the way our marriage is to be, with you merely obeying my rules. 'Tis not what I'm wanting." He smiled down at her. "I'm thinking you might have some commands of your own."

"A woman has little to say once she marries. And if she does, it's generally to no avail in a world ruled by the stronger sex."

Connor drew back and stared at her, his head tilted to one side. "Lord, but you have a harsh attitude for such a young woman." Although he hadn't planned on touching her in any way yet, he laid a large hand on her arm. "But hear me well, I'll bear with harshness for a brief time until you get your bearings in this marriage, but not forever, Sinead."

Sinead felt the color drain from her cheeks. "Fine," she snapped, then tore her arm away and straightened her body along with her dignity. "Anytime you've a mind to not deal with me, just let me know. I will burden you no further at that point." Sinead, her head held high, moved away from him and walked into the middle of the lobby.

Connor strolled after her, whispering in her ear. "Are you throwing the gauntlet at me, lass? If so, I'm not liking it very much."

"So very sorry. I thought I wasn't supposed to just accept." She wheeled around. "Perhaps, you spoke too quickly, or I did." A myriad of emotions swept across her face, until only heat and anger remained.

He leaned closer, his height closing out some of the lobby light. "Aye you did at that. I have no definite thoughts on your acceptance of what fate has handed us, but I don't need your nastiness," he snapped back. "The truth is the best way to handle problems." As he berated her, he heard his voice, ugly with quick temper. He drew in a deep breath, slowly let it out and grinned. "Now, would you be liking some supper before we go to the room to discuss our situation?"

Softly, with shadowed eyes, she answered him, ever so politely, through gritted teeth. "No thank you, Connor. I ate a bit of supper with Robbie when I brought him home."

Connor stepped back and studied her as if he were trying to hold onto his temper. Still, there was a devious twinkle in his eye, and his arms folded across his chest as he said, "Well then, will you be joining me in that little parlor over there? 'Tis really a cage that carries a person up onto other floors of the hotel."

All eyes and trembling lower lip, Sinead nodded and whispered, "I've heard about such things but I've never been on one." Staring at the contraption with great suspicion, watching it lurch up and down, while people streamed out through the bright brass grill doors, made her feel nauseated. "Is it frightening to ride on that thing?"

"Nae, 'tis reasonably smooth until you come to your floor. It stops hard there, sometimes several good bumps before the operator gets the floor exactly right." He touched her elbow. "Come, try it."

She opened her mouth to respond but nothing surfaced. The door slid open. The grating sound caused her to tremble. The idea of going up in the air with nothing underneath the flooring was perturbing, yet she followed the man who was her husband, hesitating before he stretched out his hand to help her into the steel cage.

"Don't be frightened."

His amused voice almost silenced the protest. "I'm not…" Sinead pressed lips together to hold back a denial. Once inside, the door slammed shut. She moved to the furthest corner and clutched the bars of the cage until the skin of her knuckles flashed bone white. As the device lifted them above the lobby floor, she drew in a deep breath and held it.

Connor laughed, enjoying the reactions reflected in his wife's face. "You don't have to hold your breath or…"

"How do you know what I have to do or not do?" Embarrassed at the too quick response in front of the young man handling the device, she bowed her head and mumbled, "Sorry, I didn't mean to growl at you."

Connor didn't say anything, but his deep brown eyes flickered with amusement.

They reached the fourth floor in a matter of minutes. Again, the person running the cage opened the door, which gave out a clattering squeal.

Connor slid out the door and put his hand back in to help Sinead up a slight step.

She trembled from the touch of his fingers curling around hers. A shivery thrill of apprehension created a wonder in her. What might she be afraid of, the parlor car or him?

Connor dropped her hand, preceded down the long narrow corridor to their room and slipped the key in the lock. With little effort, the key turned in the lock. The door opened quietly, and he ushered her inside by nodding his head toward the room.

When he turned on the gaslight, the opulence of the room was a surprise. Sinead concealed the expression before Connor could notice. Throughout their life, the Brennan family moved from one relative's house to another's, in Dublin and New York City.

When they came to America, Da proclaimed he would find great wealth, in the horse business, but still she slept in other people's beds, sharing the quarters of relatives. She never possessed a bed she alone chose, much less slept in by herself.

And even in this opulent room, there was only one bed. Her gaze flicked from one side of the large room to another, searching for another bed. Would she have to share this one with the man she barely knew?

All of a sudden, her stubborn streak, most often controlled, grew into complete resentment. Anger brought a flush to her face as if she was possessed by a demon leaping from cracks in the earth. She wanted to scream in rage, wail in pain. Instead, she squeezed her eyes shut, trying to overpower the urge.

"Well, lassie, we're here. Why don't you take off your shawl and sit?"

"I will after a bit. I've developed a slight chill," she lied, sweltering in the heat of the damp night but clutching the shawl closer.

Her lungs felt thick with the closeness and humidity pressing into the room. She sensed Connor close behind, smelled the very essence of him and stepped away. She was uneasy, too uneasy to talk about anything of importance.

Some sort of idle conversation might fill the void. She walked to the window and looked out into the street. "Traffic is heavy tonight. That's not usual for a Sunday."

Night had fallen, shrouding the sky in pink and purple shadows above the trees. The moon glowed like a fiery red ball, promising another day of overbearing heat.

Sinead wished the hellish days of this heat wave would end. Perhaps then, Robbie and she, along with the rest of the Fifth Avenue mansion staff, could leave for the Dewitts' summer home in Albany.

Connor's voice was hoarse and seemed to come from a great distance. "Lass, pay attention, please. I'm not here to beat you into to some sort of wifely submission to a husband's lust."

Breath stuck in her throat. He delivered the statement with smooth skill, but the force of his attention was unnerving. Her stomach clenched in distress. The knot turned to nausea. Was she wrong to assume the worst might happen? Sharp nails dug into the palms of each hand.

"I thought if we could be alone for a few hours, we could talk. Perhaps, get to know something more about each other, since we've been coupled together with little regard for knowing."

Connor stood still, waiting for a reaction. When she didn't answer, he continued. "A little knowledge never hurts between a husband and wife. And 'tis a fact. I am your husband. You are my wife."

He stepped closer. "The Church blessed our marriage. We must live with that conclusion. Let's proceed with what we know about each other."

He seems so sure of himself, she thought. She didn't know how a husband and wife should act with one another, especially when they only knew each other a few hours. She brushed her hair away from damp temples. All she knew about marriage was learned from those within her family, days with the Cavanaughs and days of watching the Dewitts. How should she act?

Her husband merely stared. *What was he expecting?* The carnal act that supposedly transpired between husband and wife? She already made a vow not to participate in such coupling until she was ready. This marriage was in name only, not unlike the marriage with Cavanaugh, who was so crippled he could not walk.

In the space of a heartbeat, Connor moved closer to the window. A delicate shudder rippled up her back. Quivers of fear tore through her.

Mustering the strength to face him, she wheeled around. "What are you doing?"

"Lass, I've done nothing more than step to the window to enjoy the sights below with you." He nonchalantly leaned against the window frame. "Perhaps, you'll tell me about his city called New York. 'Tis quite different from any city I've been in. Far too big, far too busy."

Conflicting emotions regarding their presence in this room annoyed and angered. She shrugged narrow, tense shoulders and turned her body to move him away. "What can I tell you? It moves. This city is in constant motion. 'Tis easy to get lost within it."

"I've seen that. I don't believe I've ever seen so many carriages, carts and wagons clogging the streets." A muscle in his jaw twitched. "'Tis too much activity for a simple farmer to understand."

Taking a breath, she raised her gaze to him. "I don't understand this city myself. The politics are corrupt if the things I hear are true. There's terrible unrest threatening to explode over the new draft laws."

"Why do you stay here then?"

She tensed, hand tightening into a fist, but she managed to murmur, "For Robbie and my promise to bring him up in the Catholic faith."

Noticing the distress when she mentioned Robbie and seeking to change the subject, Connor said, in a conversational tone, "Tell me more about this city. If I am to stay here for a few weeks, I would know of those things I might have to face."

The tenseness she harbored since entering the room left when he changed the subject. She sighed, relaxed and softened her voice. "Sides are chosen by the people. Alliances are made in the conducting of business, which affect the entire world. People work to secure money, more to buy the new items that appear every day than to feed their children. The city moves far too fast for me. I feel like I'm running but I can never catch up with what's happening on those streets."

Connor grinned. "Then perhaps, you'd not be averse to returning to Ireland with Egan and me?"

He cradled her chin in the crook of his finger, tipped her head back until she was forced to look into brown eyes that assessed. He put a hand on her shoulder.

She inched away from him, feeling the imprint of his hand burning through her clothing. Glancing up and noticing three upholstered chairs grouped around a small round table, she darted to them and sat in the one furthest from the window. She refused to look up.

Connor shrugged and turned to watch his new wife. Every small gesture he made, she rejected. Puzzled by the woman's reactions to him, he pondered what to do next then sat on the edge of a window seat set in a curved part of the window. All he could do is stare at her extraordinary beauty.

Connor understood his intent gaze made her nervous, obvious to him in her every move away. What would relax her enough to talk to him? He stepped toward the chair. Something softened in him when he noticed a scowl of resignation on her face.

"Come, let me show you the rest of the room. It will be a surprise."

She stood. He went into the bathroom first. A large, claw-footed tub stood near the wall. He moved forward to turn on the taps. Warm water gushed from the faucet.

Sinead jumped back. "Oh, my." She looked at him with great

wonder. Excitement lit her eyes. "Would you mind terribly if I took a bath?" Heat burned in her cheeks. "I don't get much of a chance for a full bath at the Dewitts'. Robbie gets too frantic when I'm not around him."

A tiny bell went off in his mind. He directed the full force of his gaze on her. "Robbie is their grandson. Am I not correct?"

She nodded.

"Then why can't his mother find the time to bathe properly, in a house like the Dewitts', a house which probably has many servants? I'm afraid I don't understand the whole situation."

Her gaze drifted away, back to the tub. "It's — complicated."

"I'll tell you what. You take a long, hot soak, while I finish reading my paper then we'll talk some more, if that is all right with you."

Again, she nodded but didn't speak. Connor left the room and heard the key turn in the bathroom lock. He strolled back to the window and peered into the darkness. A second later, he spun around toward the bathroom, charged across the room and lifted his hand to knock on the door. Not a clever notion, he thought and wondered how he could possibly make the rest of this night tolerable.

* * *

Sinead came out of the bath, fully dressed and looking refreshed. She smiled. "That was so lovely. I thank you for it."

Connor was struck by the joy radiating from such a dainty person. "Lass, you don't have to thank me. I like the fact that you can relax in my presence. Would you like something to eat or would you prefer to retire now?"

Sinead gasped, jerked her head up and stepped backward. A hand came up to hide her mouth. "I'll not be sleeping in that bed with the likes of you," she said, a flash of concern registering on a surprised face.

Her skin took on a deeper, rosier glow. Exasperation filled him at her stubborn defense of herself. "I'm sorry. There's only one bed in this room."

"Then take it yourself. I don't even know you. If you think I will sleep with a man I do not even know, you're more foolish than I thought you to be."

Concern mixed with bewilderment. It wavered between a desire to comfort and a temptation to confront.. "And where will you sleep?"

In a tone edged with quiet panic, she answered. "On a chair. I've done that before when my son has been ill."

Connor moved forward, turned away then faced her again. He ran his hand through his hair. "That's something you'll have to explain to me so I can understand your situation better. Something doesn't seems to settle itself properly in my mind. The Dewitts are young Robbie's grandparents. Right?"

A deathly hue leeched all the color from her cheeks. "I don't feel like discussing this now," she mumbled.

Sinead marched past, nearly elbowing him to one side. She thrust herself into the chair she had used earlier, angling it so her back was against the wall.

The defiant look she shot in his direction brought heat to Connor's face. He followed and folded his long body into the chair facing the one on which she sat. Only a small table stayed between them. He stretched his legs, until they protruded under the table. She drew hers back.

Connor studied his wife. Pink suffused her cheeks. She was beautiful but seemed to possess an otherworldly quality, like many Irish women. Ethereal yet physical and earthy at the same time, she looked as if at any moment the air might part to reveal a different world beyond.

This woman had come into his life and upset the balance he'd worked so hard to achieve, upset his entire life. And now? She didn't feel like discussing the problems? Holding back his strong emotions, he glared at her.. His mouth tightened into a grim line.

147

His mind brooded. He was unaccustomed to asking a question more than once and grimaced at his own awkwardness. Connor was uncertain how he wanted to proceed, but proceed he would.

Slowly, relentlessly, he flexed his large hands before saying, "I'll ask you again. This time I'll be expecting an answer. The Dewitts are young Robbie's true grandparents. Right?"

Comprehension entered her eyes. "Aye," she answered, eyes downcast.

He intended to further invade the protected private space and pushed his way into the cave of her mind. "And Cavanaugh was Robbie's father?"

A terrible choice reverberated through heart and soul, to lie or not. Owl-eyed and harried, she answered. "Aye."

"And yet, you are not, in any way, related to the Dewitts. Is that not so?"

Sinead twisted in her chair and scowled fiercely. She fixed him with a stormy gaze. "What is it you want to know so badly but will not ask me outright?" Noisy, breathy, like rushing wind, the high-pitched question slapped off the walls and reverberated throughout the room.

Connor heaved himself up out of the chair and crossed the room to the window. The outside was dark and deserted, quiet like a graveyard filled with stones of the dead. He turned back to Sinead and held out his hands in a placating manner. His lips twisted in an ugly smile, sensing an unspoken acknowledgment of what he assumed was the real truth, but he needed to ask, to hear her say it.

Glowering with determination, he asked, "Are you Robbie's mother?"

She groaned like a body dying, then with fury and purpose, she screamed at him. "The only mother he's ever known, from the moment of birth to now."

"But you did not give birth to him."

"Nae, Lucinda, the Dewitts' daughter did, but she died before she was ever able to hold him close." The anger she experienced dissipated in a rush of breath and the rest of what she told him she said quietly. "Lucinda hated her parents because of their treatment of the husband she adored."

Eyes downcast, she continued, "She bled to death within hours after giving birth but before she met her Maker, she begged me to care for Robert's son. I promised, gave my solemn word, to remain his caretaker."

"And this Cavanaugh she married? You bear his name. What of him?"

Sinead put fisted hands on the table, bent and rested her head on the fists. She continued, as if the events carried too much pain. "Robert Cavanaugh was in a dreadful carriage accident while rushing home to be with his wife at the difficult time. The doctor Robert hired to care for Lucinda told him she might be too tiny to bear a large child. She sacrificed for Robert, who wanted to share her ordeal."

Connor raced around the table, scooped her up in his arms and sat on the sofa against the far wall. "'Tis all right, lass."

He brought her close before more pain registered. He held her in a tight grip and murmured comforting words. "You have a need to tell the whole story, so we'll know where to begin our joint venture. What happened to Cavanaugh?"

Sinead rested her head on his shoulder, feeling strangely secure. "The police took him to the hospital."

She sat up straight. Words sputtered out. "I didn't even know where he was until the same men came to my door. I couldn't leave the baby in order to see him myself."

Tears welled up in Sinead's eyes. "I sent a message that the baby boy lived but Lucinda didn't. It was months before I saw him. He arrived home on crutches, but his condition deteriorated over the years."

"When did you marry him?"

"He begged me to marry him, so Robbie would have the only mother he knew…"

Tears overflowed and ran down to streak her cheeks and chin. They dribbled onto Connor's waistcoat. Sinead pulled a handkerchief from a skirt pocket and dabbed at his chest, trying to smile. He patted his wife's hand and eased her back against him, while he rocked back and forth.

She sobbed out the rest of the story in spurts. "I finally agreed in January of this year to marry him. He died…at the beginning…of March. The Dewitts took all the money…to save for the baby…I didn't want it. They sold Cavanaugh House…and took me to live with them so I could care for Robbie…I've been there ever since."

Connor found neither joy nor hate in the tale. The comforts he could give were few, but he covered her cold hands with his. When the anger and pain dulled in moist eyes and the tears dried, he kissed his wife's forehead and hugged her close, hoping he could control his own anguish and resentment over this marriage. Bitterness gripped his innards.

CHAPTER TEN

July 13
Monday

Shortly before sunrise, Bowes stood in the gray-weathered wood barn located at back of his boarding house. The framed building housed the stalls for the carriage, the two grays and all the necessary equipment. There were nine stalls in all, several rented out to friends of the landlady. It was Bowes's job to keep it clean and tidy, a job he actually enjoyed, and it paid for his use of three stalls.

All the horses were fed and watered, as they were every morning by this time. Their stalls were cleaned and fresh straw bedding laid down. The two geldings were groomed and waiting to be tacked up. Bowes needed to get out on the streets early in order to make his money.

First, he'd find out if Egan was well enough to see the sights of the city. The lad had slept the night through, and his color was good this morning. Bowes didn't realize how lonesome he was over the years since Sinead worked for others. He grinned. Daughters were lovely, but it was nice to have young lads around to keep a man company.

A clamor in the street, along with considerable shouting, filtered into the stables. Bowes rushed from the back of the boarding house to the front. Waves of men, the majority Irish immigrants, spilled out of some of the nearby tenements and houses. Ragged-looking and coatless, they roamed up the street in gangs of four or five, waving and screaming to one another.

The men carried strange weapons. Iron bars, brickbats and huge chunks of wood rested on their shoulders. Women ran with them, carrying copper pots they smashed together at every opportunity, all the while screaming louder than the men. With every house passed, the crowd increased.

The people moved west. Bowes could feel trouble in his bones. He figured the slowly building army of people was headed toward the draft office on Third Avenue. The list of names printed in the black and white of Sunday's papers spelled out the reason for the difficulty. He turned to rouse Egan. Together they would pick up Sinead and Connor.

One of the neighbor men Bowes recognized hollered to him. Although they weren't exactly friends, they had sipped a pint or two together on occasion. "Hey, Bowes, are ye joining us in this?"

"After I get me chores done," Bowes answered, with a smile on his face. He wasn't taking any chances of incurring the anger of this mob.

A man carrying a NO DRAFT placard shouted to him. "Brennan, get yer arse down here with the rest of us Micks."

"Come on there, fella'," called another, also carrying a NO DRAFT placard. "'Tis time to be showing those politicos what's the right and the wrong of the draft."

"Aye, I'll be hanging with ye in a trice. Got to see to me guest first," Bowes shouted back, waving in good fellowship.

The three men stopped. "We'll be waiting right here for ye. Aye, that we will," the first man said. The three sat on the raised curbing of the street. One of the three scowled at him.

Bowes realized he had to get away from them before his plans were rearranged. "Nae, ye go ahead. I'll be with ye in seconds, I will. Ye're going to see the provost marshal at the draft office, aren't ye?"

"That's where we'll be going. Make sure ye join us there…" The words rang out as a threat.

When the three nodded and moved forward to catch up with the

rest of the crowd, Bowes breathed a sigh of relief. No sense in starting troubles near his boarding house and neighborhood. He
wouldn't be joining them but let them think he would. There were
responsibilities in his life, and he was not about to disregard those
commitments to run off and play at what could turn out to be a
nasty affair. He must get to his daughter.

Once the crowd moved farther down the street, about to turn a
corner, Bowes wheeled around and trudged back to the house. He
tore up the stairs to his room and charged through the partially
open door. His delight at seeing Egan already up and dressed eased
his heavy disgust over what looked to be the start of a terrible day.

"'Tis good ye're up, son. We need to be leaving here immediately."

"I thought something was amiss. The shouting woke me up. It
was off to the window, I was. When I saw the goings-on and heard
the men shouting to you, I knew something out of the ordinary was
happening," Egan said, stuffing clothing into his trunk.

"Aye, it is that, laddie. I'll tell ye quick as I can." Bowes grabbed
his carriage purse, with all his documents in it, from the pine dresser
and shoved the strap over his shoulder. "Ye see. 'Tis this way. The
government's passed a law saying all men will be drafted into the
army to fight in the most uncivil Civil War."

"I take it these men and women marching in the streets don't
think much of that law." Egan lifted the trunk to the bed.

Bowes heard more noise and rushed to the window. A large
group of unruly men, who sounded drunk, heaved tumultuously
down the street. Bowes clucked his tongue, shook his head and
turned to Egan. "Ye want me to carry that, lad?"

"Nae, I just wanted to get it up a wee bit higher, so it wouldn't be
so far to reach," Egan said, swinging the trunk up and settling it on
his shoulder.

"That's a lad. Do ye have everything ye'll be needing?" Bowes
asked as he started out the door.

"That I do." Egan followed him out and shut the door with his foot. "I'm right behind ye, I am."

"And we'll be sneaking out the back to me horses. Then we'll find me daughter and yer brother. I sure hope they're up and ready to leave the hotel. I have a feeling this is going to be a nasty day for everyone."

* * *

After two overtaxing days, one day on the steamer waiting to land and one in jail for foolish reasons, Connor's exhaustion from lack of a good night's sleep plagued him. Throughout the night, he had twisted and turned on the narrow sofa, unable to get into a comfortable position.

This morning, he felt frayed, worn-out, his energy burned up. His legs hung over one end of the sofa arm and his head rested high on the other, making his neck stiff and his feet numb. Even though the draperies were drawn, dawn light filtered through, bringing with it the beginnings of another bright, sunny day, already hot to the point of mugginess.

Conner yawned and stretched to ease his many aches and pains. There was little sense in trying to sleep further. He stood, grabbed his shirt and jacket, slipped on his shoes and moved to the bathroom, barely glancing at Sinead, who was curled into a ball and seemed to be sleeping soundly on the bed.

He splashed water over his face. The sensation of cold helped him to waken further but also created a strange prickling feeling at the back of his skull. He bathed himself as thoroughly as possible in the low sink and dressed, trying to smooth the wrinkles from the clothes he had slept in. His mind raced with a thousand thoughts, few of them pleasant.

He came out of the bathroom and gazed at his wife. The sight enticed him beyond anything reasonable. Something in the silky curve of her chin brought a flash of indistinct memory. He shrugged it away and, taking his key, quietly left the room.

Deciding to walk down instead of suffering the clanking noise of the little parlor, so early in the morning, he headed in the direction of the stairs. Noises drifting up the stairwell from the lobby puzzled him. The garbled shouting was frantic in its intensity. Sounds of hurried activity needled and poked at him. Wondering what the buzz was, he sailed down the stairs two at a time, passing others going up and down the same set of stairs. He nodded politely to everyone but continued his steady march down.

The mezzanine rang with strident voices, none of which he recognized, carrying up from the lobby. "Board up the windows."

"Push the lounge chairs together near the entrance."

"Keep those front doors locked."

Many folks rushed about, from one end of the wide, curved steps leading to the lobby to the stairs leading to the rest of the hotel. Connor went to the railing near the lobby steps to look down, unable to dispel the uneasiness caused by the strange commotion and hurried movements.

The lobby seemed nearly empty of the many servants who usually scurried about trying to help the hotel's guests. The clerk, who usually stood behind the registration desk, frantically gestured and called to uniformed men who stood, trying to secure large slabs of wood to the front windows. "Be careful. Don't let the board tilt toward the windows."

Other employees were turning upholstered lounges and chairs upside down and pushing them to toward the big glass doors leading into the lobby. "Whatever you do, don't damage the goods," the clerk shrieked.

"We're being as careful as we can." The reply rose over the sounds of grunting.

Chills ran up Connor's spine. He heard noises from the street, noises sounding like pans being beaten together. It was not unlike the pot lids his mam banged when she wanted to attract her sons' attention from the horses. Besides, the O'Malleys heard such sounds often enough during the worst of the famine years in Ireland. Those agonizing memories haunted Connor still.

His shoulders tightened, his head ached. He ran his hands through his dark hair. He strolled to the desk clerk, not wanting to add any more nervous energy to the already excited people in the lobby. "What's going on?" he inquired.

"It seems the whole Lower East Side of the city is up in arms. The Irish and the rest of the immigrants are marching uptown."

"What for?" Connor asked, trying to ascertain the crux of the problem so he could dismiss his own worries. "Egan and Bowes are down in that area," he muttered.

"What, sir?"

"Nothing to concern you. Go on with your story."

The clerk picked up a newspaper and shook it aloft. "It's the draft, of course. The damned Conscription laws," he said, frowning and pointing to an article.

Another clerk surfaced from a back room, his white hair shining under a gas lamp. "They're taking men away from their families, leaving the wives and children to suffer more poverty and want. Just to fight a war against their very own brethren to save some black men who'll move north and take their jobs." He raised a fist in anger. "The men around here tell me that's what the damned government's thinking."

The first clerk chimed in. "The Irish will have no more of it, I've heard. And the foolish newspapers printed the names of those the government's looking for."

Although fearful of the news, Connor craved more information before he took action of any sort. "I came over from Ireland but two days ago. I don't know what might be happening to your country. We weren't getting much news of the world, coming over on the steamer."

The white-haired man shook his head. "The people of this city are marching in protest against the powers-that-be. He lightly slapped the counter. "Over something they don't have a chance of fixing. I have a feeling these sad affairs will get bloody before this day is through." He turned and went back into the inner office.

"I don't mean to be rude, sir, but I have to get this hotel secured from the mob that's roaming in the streets. At any moment, they might take it into their heads to come up Fifth Avenue. My advice to you is, gather your family together and leave this city as quickly as you can."

"Aye, I'll be doing that immediately, but I have no idea where I could be going with them all." Connor responded, wheeling about and crossing the lobby at a run.

The clerk shouted after him. "Go north toward Albany or thereabouts.

Connor rushed up the stairs to the mezzanine, three at a time. His heart beat hard against his sore ribs with the effort. Sinead would know where to go for safety. "The lad. She'll be wanting to get the laddie."

By the time he reached the fourth floor, ragged breaths puffed out from his mouth. He inserted his key in the lock of their room and swung the door open.

Sinead shrieked. She stood half-clothed in the shadows, one hand at her bosom. He stopped short, one hand tightly gripping the door, and stared at the lush sensuality of her.

"Er…" Flushed, Connor backed out, slightly closed the door and banged on the outside of it with his fist. Struggling not to smile at the innocent posture he'd glimpsed, he called out, "Sinead, something's wrong in the city. We have to leave the hotel, quickly, I'm afraid."

She came to the door in an instant and flung it open, pulling it from his grasp. Embarrassed, her eyes were red and teary, mouth drawn and pinched but a white blouse was somewhat in place. "What more can go wrong with my days?" Arms limp at her sides, she scooted backwards to grant him entrance.

Taking a step farther into the chamber, his gaze drifted against his will to her open bodice. She met his gaze. It took all of his strength to look away. "You've no time to be weeping, lass. There's something going on, outside, in the streets. The hotel workers are barricading the hotel for some sort of invasion. Get dressed. We're leaving…"

Shadows masked her face under a sooty fringe of lashes. Her eyes were downcast. "I'll not have you rushing me, Connor O'Malley," she said, moving away in a stiff, stubborn motion.

"Aye, I will." He covered the distance between them in a single step and grasped her arm. "Did you not hear me, lassie? I'm trying to tell you…there's something wrong…outside…in the streets of this city."

Her look of concern sent daggers of guilt into him for being so rough, but his senses told him they had to leave quickly. He breathed a sigh of relief when he watched her refasten the rest of her clothing, tuck it in properly and pack her things into the bag she brought with her the night before. Now, her motions were quick and sure.

She turned to him. "Now, let me tell you, Connor O'Malley," she warned, repeating her newly assumed name, "we'll not be leaving here until my da arrives. He said he'd come by to pick us up."

"If what the clerk of the hotel said is true, people are marching up and down the streets. I'm thinking, your da might not be able to get through."

"My da will get through anything. He has a gift of gab in his every word. He said he'd be here and be here he will," she retorted. She sat in one of the chairs at the table, put the bag on her lap and clenched her fists over it.

Connor glared at her. Exasperation filled him, along with a sense of defeat greater than any he'd ever known. With or without his liking, this marriage was a fact, and it was his responsibility to see her to safety. He suppressed a shudder rolling through him and struggled to adjust his expression before he spoke.

"Lass, we'll go to the lobby and wait there for your da. At least then we'll have some idea of what's going on," he murmured, taking her bag from her lap. "Now, Sinead, now," he added in a tone that would tolerate no further argument.

* * *

By sunup, disturbing reports of crowds roaming the streets filtered into police headquarters on Mulberry Street. By eight-thirty, an urgent dispatch went out from headquarters — *Troubles brewing. Telegraph lines cut. Rush large force.*

People poured out of tenements and boarding houses. They began to barricade specific areas within the city, cutting down telegraph poles that connected local police precincts to the Central office. Rioters pulled down fences surrounding vacant lots to make huge clubs and battering rams.

Some rushed toward the trains high above ground. They stopped Second and Third Avenue railroad cars. New Haven commuter trains were stoned. Irish women, working together for a change, pulled up the tracks of the Fourth Avenue line, with crowbars.

A scowl etched on his face, Bowes swiveled around in his seat, trying to look everywhere at once. He roamed streets and paths he seldom used, trying to get through the rash of people converging on the area.

"Come up here on the driver's bench with me, laddie." He gestured to Egan while dodging irate knots of rioters. "This doesn't look good to my way of thinking. I believe we're going to have a sorry ride," he groused, in a voice shaking with annoyance and dread.

Egan swung himself up and over the carriage seat, sitting a foot taller, next to Bowes. "Don't be forgetting, Bowes Brennan. I'm a horseman like yourself. We'll manage." His face cracked in a brief smile. "Where are all these folks going, anyway?"

"To the draft office, I'm thinking. But this crowd ye see, mostly Irish to boot and marching around with little on their minds but creating trouble, are the dregs of the city's foreign folks. Come from the filthiest cellars and dens of the city, they have, and this morning they're running about, seeking others just like themselves. They're going to make a fuss, for sure."

"And they're increasing, everywhere I look. Coming out of every building we pass," Egan said, craning his neck to see the road behind, which was slowly filling with more and more people.

Bowes shook his head in bewilderment. Hundreds of workers, many of whom he recognized from driving them to railroads, machine shops, shipyards and iron foundries, began streaming up the West side. The carriage was caught in the middle, pushed along by those following.

Fear built in him for the troubles he felt were coming far too fast. He tried to keep the carriage on the edge of what was becoming a far-ranging gang of folks, but they hemmed the carriage in with sheer numbers. Along the way, they closed shops, factories and construction sites then, together with building and street laborers working for uptown contractors, moved on to a brief, loud meeting in Central Park.

No matter which way Bowes turned the horses to get to the hotel, the streets were packed with marauding gangs of angry men and women. At the moment, he dared not cross their lines without incurring a fight. He let them drag the carriage toward Central Park, figuring it would be better if he knew exactly what was going on.

As if with some preplanned signal, one or two groups of workmen employed on the Central Park Project left their employment and marched back downtown from their workstations. What with people moving uptown and downtown at the same time, the carriage slowed almost to a stop. The horses began to prance in place. Rollie, the gray gelding on the left lifted a front foot from the ground and pawed the air.

"Dammit, man. Keep those animals under control," shrieked one man who was being shoved to one side.

Rondo, the gray on the right, swung his huge head into the crowd. A man screamed, clutched his ear and hopped around on one foot. "Ye damned fool horse. Can't ye be watching yer parts?" He shook his fist at the horse.

"Don't ye be laying a hand on that animal," Bowes hollered

back.

Egan stood, as if ready to jump out to pummel the man.

"No, laddie. Sit." Shaking like a leaf, Bowes took the opportunity of a break in the crowd to shuffle the horses off to one side of two different groups. There, from their high vantage point. Egan and he watched gangs march to places where large bodies of men worked, cajoling, inducing or forcing them to leave and follow the fast-growing mob.

"Come along," a red-haired man shouted. "Don't be letting them take ye away from yer families and friends."

"Think of yer bairns," a rotund man wheedled another, whose arm he linked with his own.

"Don't be dictated to," cried another. "Let's give them officials hell!"

The crowd's numbers increased to thousands and pushed the carriage along with them.

"Och laddie," Bowes yelled to Egan. "I've never been so fearful in all me born days. I'm moving these horses. I hope we can get out of here with all our pieces." He clutched the reins with a tight fist, instead of the easy hands he ordinarily used, and noticed Egan hanging onto the sides of the carriage with white-knuckled hands. Bowes had to hand it to the lad. He didn't cry out in terror, not even once.

By nine o'clock in the morning, the unruly, disorganized mob had grown to five thousand. By the time they reached the draft office at 677 Third Avenue, it had swelled to fifteen thousand. At ten-thirty, with a huge crowd in attendance and guarded by sixty hurriedly gathered policemen, the draft lottery selection process started up.

A group of Irishmen chanted, "We'll not fight yer rotten war. We'll not fight yer bluidy war!" They pushed to the doors of the draft office. Not even the contingent of police could contain them.

A tall, thin man, who stood on a large rock nearby, bellowed above the crowd. "We've already lost too many of our fellows fightin' fer this country." He raised a fist in the air, "Go get 'em, laddies!" he cried, jumped off the rock and charged through the front door of the building.

"This country vomits on us," a stout female with a barking voice shrieked, followed quickly by the clashing clang of pots being clapped together by several of the women staggering behind her.

A chorus of "ayes" reverberated from the people, who picked up another chant. "No draft...No draft...No draft..." They hooted and called. People stamped their feet.

The noise was deafening. Egan couldn't believe his eyes or his ears. Not even during the famine had folks acted with such abandon. In the distance, the light of several torches flashed.

Bowes wriggled his nose. The smell of fire made him want to sneeze. The violence Bowes knew was coming began in earnest.

Enraged people beat through the scanty police guard and smashed the doors of the office building. They pushed and shoved each other to get inside. The men carrying the torches ran from the back of the crowd into the building and set fire to the draft office.

Flames streaked out the window. Smoke rose to fan the sky. The Black Joke Fire Engine Company, Number thirty-three, arrived in full regalia, ostensibly to fight the fire.

Bowes identified several, having shared many a pint with them at Clancy's Saloon. He pointed them out to Egan. "See, that fireman over there?" He pointed to a particularly tall man with an enormous engorged belly covered by a red shirt. "'Tis me friend McCarthy. Have a pint and a hand of cards with him every now and again."

He glanced at Egan. The boy's stare was fixed on the fire truck. His mouth hung open. "Old McCarthy told me the men of the thirty-three were in a good old fury at having lost their exemption from the war. They'll not be taking this kindly, today, I'm afraid."

The firemen formed a line. They wound a long hose from their fire wagon, tied it off to a tree and held off the police who were trying to stop the gangs. When other firemen came to quench the flames coming from the building, they forced them back until they couldn't get close enough to splay out their hoses.

Egan gasped in almost a howl, "My God, Bowes. What are they doing?" He screeched the question over the sound of the crowd cheering.

It was obvious to Bowes what they were doing. The firemen of the Black Joke must have decided over the weekend to halt the draft proceedings and to destroy any evidence that fellows in their unit had been drafted.

"Och, Jaysus," he screamed with an inward breath. "Och, they're going to be doing things would shame their mothers from this earth."

The two men watched with fear and horror, as the firemen stoned the building and drove off the police reinforcements who rushed to the scene. Bowes and Egan watched the men from the Black Joke smash the draft wheel. With great glee, they poured turpentine everywhere, fired the structure and drove away every fire company that came to assist in putting out the fire.

The smell of smoke inundated the area and hung over the crowd. People screamed in both delight and terror as the flames seemed to touch the sky. Bowes horses reared in their traces. The heat, coupled with the humidity of the already hot day, took the energy out of everyone. The crowd slowly grew silent. Muffled conversations surfaced with each puff of smoke. The people stood and watched.

With a chest feeling like it would break apart, Bowes knew it was time to flee before the mob turned even more violent. "Egan, hang on, laddie. We have to be getting out of here. Our lives will be worth nothing with this group of lunatics." He tried to turn the horses around but folks were standing in his way. Inch by inch, the animals were able to sidle over a bit.

Breath short, Bowes dropped a rein when the mob's fury fell on a detachment of thirty-two militiamen who were racing into the fray. His hand flew to his mouth in horror.

Burly men beat and kicked one soldier to death before turning on another, whom they grabbed. They tossed him back and forth over the top of the crowd. The soldier shrieked and cried. He kicked out at those who held him, trying to get loose.

A gang of strong men finally got their hands on him. Holding the poor soldier above them, tossing and turning him in the air, they took him to the top of rocks near the office. Urine stained the soldier's pants. Onlookers were caught up in the actions, their eyes glowing, faces flushed with maniacal ecstasy.

Men stripped the uniform off him, pointed to his private parts and hollered. After beating the mortified man almost to jelly, they threw him over a precipice some twenty feet high, onto hard rocks beneath. His blood spattered over the crowd. Women in the mob, holding the hands of small children, screeched their approval, laughing and cheering. He died without much of a struggle.

His body shaking in disbelief and tears rolling from his eyes, Egan grabbed for the one rein Bowes let hang loosely from his grip. He pulled it taut, grabbed the other and shoved Bowes with his hip. "Move over man. I'll get the animals turned around if it kills me."

He leaped over Bowes to switch seats and reached for the whip. He cracked it over the horses' heads.

The animals screamed their protest. Feet high in the air, they swerved into the crowd of people, who shoved each other aside to make way for the great beasts. In a mad frenzy, people struck out at the horses, trying to beat them to a standstill. Many swore and threw whatever object they clutched in their hands.

A squad of men sent by the police to form a line across Third Avenue marched north toward the burning draft office. They were met by the mob throwing paving stones. The squad broke and ran.

The incident gave Egan a chance to get the horses further out onto the edges of the crowd where he found more room to maneuver. The devastating action of the people brought more tears to his eyes. Not even in the worst of the famine years had he seen such atrocities done by one group of people to another.

"Tell me which way to go, Bowes. We've got to get out of here the best way we can. We have got to get to that hotel."

It was already eleven-thirty in the morning. Rumor raced through the crowd that the federal draft was officially suspended in all of New York. Members of the mob cheered then moved on to other areas.

A man on the fringe of the crowds shouted. "There are skirmishes spreading throughout the city.

Someone screamed with laughter. Another bellowed. "Detachments of police are being sent into other areas instead of this one. I guess we're all over the city."

"A bunch of Irishers stomped them and smashed their faces," a German immigrant squealed with glee. "They stripped their bodies."

Three men scrabbled onto a tall rock. One reached the top and raised his arms high above his head and brayed, "A gang just came from other parts. They told me, anyone even suspected of giving refuge to the police are being burned. Finally, the Metropolitan Police are getting theirs."

With those words ringing in their ears and the smoke sitting on their shoulders, Egan and Bowes fled across town to the Fifth Avenue Hotel. No matter what street they traveled on, they saw the resentment of the city's immigrant poor. Their rage exploded at every street corner with act after act of destruction and all either Bowes or Egan could do was flee.

CHAPTER ELEVEN

Egan watched the crowds of rampaging men and women, causing havoc wherever they went. They marauded up and down the avenues. It shocked and frightened Egan that people could act in such base, uncivilized ways. The scenes on Third Avenue, the appalling destruction he saw, made him want to gag. The ever-present nausea he felt while at sea came back tenfold.

Screams resounded to the side of him. Egan turned slightly. His gaze rested upon huge columns of smoke rising from burning buildings. He drew in a deep breath, laid a restive hand around the reins of the now-skittish horses and spurred them forward. He instinctively knew he could not allow them to be stopped for any reason.

With a strong pull on one rein, he brought the carriage out to the fringes of the crowd. By following Bowes's directions, they made a roundabout cut to the far side of Third Avenue and went west. They traveled over side streets, journeyed into strange alleyways and narrow paths before backtracking over lesser-known thoroughfares to get to the hotel.

* * *

It was well after one o'clock. The day grew hotter and more humid. Heavy clouds of smoke cast dark shadows over the city. Although the density of smoke obscured the hot July sun, it cut off all circulation of air. The streets fumed with the usual rotting debris and excrement, the smell worsened by the stifling heat and humidity.

The lobby of the hotel grew warmer and more tense as the hours of waiting for news laid a burden upon the folks trapped within the hotel. Tempers flared amongst the guests and staff who carried the news inside. The manager and his clerks tried to stave off verbal battles between certain members of the staff and those registered as paying guests.

To Connor and Sinead standing impatiently inside the Fifth Avenue Hotel, looking for Bowes's carriage, time seemed to drag on minute by minute. Sinead's main objective was to get home to her son. After overhearing several of the stories filtering in from the outside, she needed to make sure nothing terrible happened to him.

Although she knew he would come for her, sooner or later, she worried about her da. The fact that he was so late frightened her. Connor paced up and down near the outside doors. She tried to keep up with him but his steps were too long.

"Connor," she called after him. "Wait. Please…"

Connor's steps took him from the door to check on further rumors and back across the lobby to report what he'd heard.

Constant rumors navigated into the lobby from the street, brought by strangers, who ducked into the hotel for a brief respite from the agonies outside. Connor bent an ear to listen.

Sinead refused to believe their stories, especially when they made horrific comments against the Irish. "You can't be believing all people say."

"Well, I can smell the smoke, now, can't I?" was his retort. "So some of it must be true."

Sinead's temple creased with worry. Would her da be able to get to them if the rumors of the riots and fires were true? An aching desperation to reach Robbie rippled through her. "Robbie…"

"See the man over there?" Connor asked, pointing to an older man in a top hat. "He told me a huge mob gathered at the draft offices, on Third Avenue, just when they were ready to start the lottery. Dissenters burned it to the ground."

Connor pointed to another man sitting on a chair near the door, his face blackened with soot. Blotches of blood dampened the front of his shirt and sleeve. "With the help of some of the city's firemen, I think the man said."

"Why, such a thing sounds crazy. Why would people do it?" Sinead's heart rumbled in her chest. Something terrible was going on outside, and she was stuck in this hotel, unable to do anything about it and or to find the ones she loved.

"There's worse." Connor put a hand on her shoulder. He looked down into her eyes. "I don't know if you want to hear more, lass?"

Her body trembled under his hand. He reached over and grabbed a chair, setting it right side up. He took Sinead's elbow and led her to a chair. "Sit, lass. You won't be liking what you hear."

She sighed. "Aye, but 'tis best you tell me. I'm fit to burst with worrying over what I don't know."

"I can feel it in you, but bursting will do no good until we find the truth of the matter. We can't be leaving here until your da and Egan come."

"I know. Then tell me what you've heard." Sinead stared up into his saddened dark eyes and wondered about the confidence she felt when she was near him. It was almost as if they known each other before.

Connor knelt on one foot in front of her, loomed over her and studied her for a moment. "Sinead, lass, the mob. They're trying to take over the city, burn it to the ground, through riot and mayhem. They've done some killing and maiming, they have. And other things too horrible to mention to a lady."

She stood and nearly knocked Connor to his feet. "Don't be saying such things." She turned to face him. "Don't be saying such things..." Tears rolled from the corner of her eyes and cascaded down her cheeks.

Connor gathered her into his arms. "You don't know me yet, lass, but I'll protect you with my dying breath. Nothing will happen to you, if I'm here."

Sinead pushed him away. "'Tis not myself I'm afraid for. 'Tis your brother and my da, who are out in the riots. I know they're trying to get to us. Nothing will stop my da." She raised her arms in a gesture of hopelessness. "And what might happen to Robbie? I've got to get to him." She crossed the lobby in quick, determined steps, preparing to climb over the barricades and go out the front door.

Connor followed and laid his hand on her arm. "You're not going anywhere, until your da gets here. What does your leaving here solve? What if Egan and he manage to get through the mob and are on their way? They'll get us to Robbie faster and safer."

He turned her around. "Please, lass, running off without knowing what or where you're going, will not be helping us in any way. Stay calm."

Sinead's body seemed to fold in on itself. She leaned into his chest and sobbed out her anguish. Her body shook with the wretchedness of her fears.

Connor didn't know how to behave with her. He couldn't remember the last time he'd seen a woman cry. All he could do is put his arms around her, pat her back and let her get it out of her system. "Easy. Easy," he crooned and kissed her forehead. He reached into his pocket and found a cloth, which he shoved at her. "Here, take this. Wipe those tears from your face, lass. We must continue to think everything is going to be all right."

Sinead nodded and took the cloth from his hand. Without a sound, she dabbed at her eyes, trying to dry the flood of tears.

The clerk, his arms spread wide in supplication, approached them. "I'm sorry sir, but we have to clear the lobby. Please return to your room."

Connor stared down at the man. "And I'm equally sorry. What you're suggesting is impossible. We intend to wait right here for my wife's father."

He continued as if he didn't hear Connor. "Truly, sir, the employees of the hotel are very sorry. We've gotten word the city is in a state of siege. There are mobs outside committing arson, murder and rape. It's going on right now in different parts of the city."

Sinead's eyes opened wide. They were still glossy and blurred from the tears. She tugged at Connor's shirt and begged him with her expression. "Where?" she asked in a whisper.

"Where?" Connor asked but didn't wait for an answer. "Never mind. We'll be waiting right here for a while longer."

Sinead turned to the clerk. Her eyes were red but drier. "My father is to come here to pick us up in his carriage. Once we're settled in it, we're going home to get my son."

A loud call came floating across the lobby from the doorway. "Connor O'Malley. Call for Connor O'Malley."

Sinead and Connor turned in unison toward the door. Egan must have spotted them for he leaped the lounges and chairs placed at front door and raced to them. "Och, Connor. 'Tis glad I am to be seeing you again. I possessed some doubts, I did."

Connor clasped his brother to him. "And 'tis glad I am to be looking at your sorry, freckled face, too." He poked him on the arm then swung him around in a mighty hug. "No matter how ugly."

"Where's my da, Egan. You haven't come alone, I suspect." Sinead laid a hand on his arm. "I'm glad to see you, too. I am that. To see you in one piece and walking about. Now, where's my da?"

Egan grabbed Connor by an elbow and Sinead by one of hers He propelled them forward toward the main doors of the hotel. "Your da's in the carriage outside, holding onto the horses for dear life. They're mighty spooked. Beyond their knowing or understanding."

"You'll be after telling me, won't you, laddie?" Connor helped Sinead over a lounge chair and held the door open.

The carriage stood outside in the street. The horses twisted every way they could in a desperate attempt to get out of their traces.

Sinead barreled through the main door first. She saw her da, ran across the sidewalk and threw herself up onto the driver's seat. Her arms went about her da's shoulders to hug him. "I've been so worried about you. We kept hearing rumors about what was going on outside, but we weren't allowed to leave the hotel."

Bowes struggled with the horses. "Easy, darlin'. Easy. We'll be moving on soon enough." He turned to Sinead. "Calm down, lass, and listen to me. 'Tis not over yet. Folks have gone crazy with rioting and pillaging anything they can get their dirty hands on. They're all over the city. We've got to get out of here. And quickly."

"Da, where can we go? I have to get Robbie. I have to make sure he's all right." Sinead rested her head against her father's brow.

Connor approached the carriage. He reached up to the driver's seat and clasped Bowes's hand. "'Tis good to see you, sir. And my brother. What would you be having us do?"

"First of all, climb into the carriage. We have to find me grandson, I guess. Make sure everything is all right at the Dewitts'." Bowes stared at Connor. "Can ye drive, laddie? I know your brother can. Can you?"

"Aye, I'm a good hand with the carriages back home. You want me to be driving this rig?"

"I'm thinking ye look more fearsome than I do. People would be more inclined to let ye pass by than they would me. I'll sit next to ye, in case ye need some added instruction. Sinead and Egan, sit in the back to balance the carriage over the cobblestones."

Connor put his hands around Sinead's waist, lifted her from the driver's seat and gently placed her in the carriage. Egan leaped up beside her.

Connor shut the door and turned. "Damn it. The trunk. I left it inside."

Bowes spoke up. "Leave it there son. The people in the hotel will hold it for you, I'm thinking. At least, it will be safer there than out on the back of this vehicle, going like we might have to go."

Connor nodded. "I won't be needed much now and will come back for the trunk later tonight. I've most of my important papers and my money in the inside pocket of my jacket." He swung himself up onto the driver's seat and took a firm hold on the reins. He slapped them twice and clucked loudly. With great reluctance, the horses moved forward at a fast trot.

The heat, humidity and stench of pestilence took its toll on the occupants of the carriage. Wavy lines and dots swam before Sinead's eyes. She felt as faint as she did on Saturday and urged Connor to hurry. The more she saw, the more worried she became about Robbie.

Connor and Egan were exhausted. Egan leaned against the stiffly cushioned back of the carriage. His eyes scanned the streets in constant motion, back to front, side to side. Although Connor kept a tight hand on the reins, his eyes were almost as alert as Egan's to those around the area. Disbelief and something far more dangerous shone on Connor's face and turned his eyes dark.

Disbelieving what he saw, Bowes gave Connor directions to the West side of the city, hoping to avoid the vicious activity displayed in the streets on the East side. It was impossible to go straight to the Dewitts' home or to get through the massive crowds, who were shouting and rumbling up and down the thoroughfares.

In an effort to reach the Dewitt mansion without incident, they circumvented most of the avenues where the wild and dangerous activities occurred. The going was difficult, but they made slow progress to the West side by going crosstown.

Sinead blew out an elongated sigh of relief.

A man lumbered out of the crowd, his eyes hideously cold and empty. With a ghastly grin plastered across his face and rolling his eyes, he leaped onto the side of the carriage, hung grimly on the door and grabbed her arm with a bloody hand. "My," he cackled, "aren't you the lovely one."

Sinead writhed in her seat, pulling back with all her might. She twisted out of his grasp and struggled to throw off the wave of darkness washing over her.

With a cry of anger, Egan rose from his seat and smashed the man's hand with the heel of his own. He grabbed the man's shirt. With a heave, he shoved him from the carriage door and into the street where he disappeared from view, lost in the crowd.

"Good lad," Connor called from the front. He reached beneath the driver's seat, grasped one of the crops Bowes had and tossed it into the back. "Here. Use this next time anyone touches the carriage or anyone in it." Connor's teeth locked tightly together.

The carriage swayed from the motion of the crowd rubbing up against it. Sinead clutched the edge of the door, her Irish anger beginning to churn. "Do you have another?" she asked Connor, her voice ranging higher than usual.

"Aye." Again, he reached under the seat then tossed back a crop. "Don't be afraid to use it lass. Wield it around your head if it be necessary," he called, just as another man reached for her.

Sun bounced off the cobblestones as Sinead brought the crop down on the man's head and shoulders. The force of the movement made her wince. The man squealed with pain but backed off.

Voices pierced the distance and drew closer. A roar rose, deep and primitive, like the caws of crows swooping in black flocks to scavenge on carcasses. A sudden change of mood struck the mob to the left of the carriage. An ugly second front began. Bands of Irish longshoremen, quarrymen, street pavers, teamsters and cartmen began chasing people of color in every direction. Others were attacking the homes of blacks, only yards away from the carriage.

"Kill all niggers!" one shrieked.

"Get him—him, too," cried a man who moved through the crowd, pointing to every black man he saw.

"Don't let any of 'em escape," many women screamed.

Frightened, Sinead looked around, aware of every movement in the street. A shiver progressed down her back. Blacks were being dragged from their homes, off streetcars and from anywhere they were found. She bleated a name. "Connor..."

With mouths agape, everyone in the carriage remained speechless, unblinking and unmoving but, with the tumult around them, came images. Against the sun's glare, flashes of color, of faces, sent a fit of nausea to Sinead's throat and brought her hand to her mouth.

Egan grew pale. Connor tensed, his hands tightening on the

reins. Bowes slumped in his seat, horrified. He pointed ahead.

A boarding house owner he knew was being robbed and stripped, his place of business on fire. At one restaurant they passed, the crowd tried to attack the black waiters but was repulsed by men with knives and huge pieces of lumber.

Bowes bowed his head in shame and turned his face away from the violence, only to be met with more on the other side. Another house was trashed as paving stones smashed the windows, then people ran in and ransacked, looking for anything they could sell.

Those in the carriage could do nothing. They were hemmed in by the mass of people, by the reckless, bitter cast of the crowd, by unbridled fury and hate. The horses were leaping in their traces, striking out with their hooves.

Connor's voice rose over the mob, cold, clear and sharp as a razor. "This is more than I can stand, this waste of fragile human life. Let's get out of here."

The sound of his ragged voice chilled Sinead more than the danger they faced. She realized her new husband was a man who would walk fearlessly into violent situations, if necessary, but he would keep his fear hidden until he dealt with the danger.

Caught up in the fury of the mob scene, Connor cracked his whip with a purpose, high above the horses. They curved forward, their muscles stretching with newfound strength, and moved sideways, shoving the crowd from their path. He continued to flick the twanging, crackling whip in the air, in repeated thrusts.

Willful, spiteful, and determined to win this clash of wills, the mob began to plunder and burn, lending a wild aspect to the scene. Light smoke began to float out of windows.

Pulsing in time with the gallop of a thousand heartbeats, it seemed the beastly ruffians were masters of the situation in the city, and the group in the carriage hadn't even gotten to the Dewitts yet.

Sinead lowered her face into her hands. "What more might await us on the way there?"

* * *

Throughout the day, the carriage wound through almost impassible streets. Those in it watched with revulsion and awe. With sheer untarnished power, savage gangs stormed up and down the city. They ripped down telegraph poles and wires, destroyed streetcars and train tracks. They looted and burned everything and anything that seemed to offend their frantic sensibilities.

Undermanned Metropolitan Police were seen on every street and avenue over which the carriage moved. They fought bravely wherever they could. In one instance, Bowes pointed out members of the harbor militia. Even with those reinforcements, the police were horribly outnumbered by members of the rioting mobs.

By two o'clock in the afternoon, unbearable heat and humidity flooded the city. Smoke infiltrated the air and pushed it downward on those in the carriage. The horses walked more slowly, their weariness apparent in each footfall and in the drooping angle of their heads. On less congested streets, past less-intimidating gangs of the city, they maneuvered the carriage up the West side of the city, a far distance north of the Dewitts' East side mansion.

Worsened by the day's heat, heavy silence enveloped the occupants. Connor and Bowes managed to steer the carriage across the upper regions of the West side to Fifth Avenue. There they stopped to give the horses a rest and a drink. Their problem then became to find a way down the East side without incident.

"How are you faring, lass?" Connor turned in his seat to stare at her. He leaned on the seat with one knee flexed.

Sinead heard the tired, husky note in his voice. It rumbled in her ear. "I'm fine. Just anxious."

Bowes turned to her and said, "Sinead, ye been brave, lass. We'll get to the lad as soon as we can. We can't be riding on top of all the people in our way, can we, lassie?" A smile made his mouth quirk in a funny position.

His words smashed into her snug world, the world she'd lived in before Saturday. "Da," Sinead said in a soft voice, "let's be moving on. I have a bad fear in my heart and the fear for Robbie is pounding its way through my mind."

Connor took the reins in his hands and slapped them once against the horses. "I'm thinking these horses cannot go much faster than a walk. Their bones and temperaments are weary from all the excitement and tension."

"Fine," she grumbled. "What good are they then? Maybe we'd be better off afoot."

""I'm thinking it wouldn't be wise. To be on foot," Egan complained. "I'm thinking these beasties might come in handy later on."

"I'm in agreement," Connor added.

"Me, too." Bowes turned to Sinead and raised a finger to his lips.

She sighed. "Then I am overruled. So be it."

Not another word was spoken as they traveled down Fifth Avenue, which seemed deserted. It was only two-thirty in the afternoon. Before long they came to Fifth Avenue and Forty-third Street.

There, an infuriated gang surrounded three sides of a rambling, wooden building. The sign in front read "Orphanage for Children of Color." It was home to more than 200 children under the age of twelve.

Carrying torches, brickbats and paving stones, the gang started screaming, "Burn the nigger's nest." The one cry fostered others, wild sounds like the barks of jackals, an unconscious animal response.

"Kill them wee bastards," a man shouted, a ghastly grin on his face.

"Why are we fighting for them?" The question sounded coarse, mean, threatening. "Burn the nigger children..."

Warning bells jangled deep inside Sinead. Struck with shock, her heart thudded. Connor's ruddy color leached from his face. Blood rushed to his heart, drawn there by the violence of driving, crashing waves of people destroying themselves and others. It was the reality of the moment.

"My God," he cried. "There are children in the building. They have to be gotten out."

Paving stones were tossed sporadically at windows. Men and small boys began smashing the sashes and climbing inside. They tore the blinds down and began to throw out light articles, books and crockery.

Connor stopped the horses and turned in his seat. "I cannot stand by and watch this devastation any more." He tossed the reins to Bowes. "Take the carriage around to the back."

"Where are you going?" Sinead cried out."

"To help those wee children. 'Tis none of this their fault. Come on, Egan. They'll be needing us." Grim purpose etched every line of his face.

Connor jumped from the driver's seat. He ran to the other side of the carriage and threw open the door. Egan eased himself out. "Lass, get up in the front next to your da. You'll be safer there, with him."

"What about Robbie? I have to get to Robbie."

Connor, who already started toward the asylum, wheeled around. He ran back to the carriage and glared at Sinead. "I'd be hoping the Dewitts contained enough sense to keep their grandchild from harm. If not, you've been living in the wrong place, lassie." He turned and ran to catch up with Egan.

Bowes grabbed the reins and whipped the horses around. They went down the street at a fast clip. Bowes turned them at the corner, and they went around the block to the back of the building. He stopped them a short way away from the building.

"Do what yer husband says, Sinead. Climb in front with Da."

The idea sent a fit of nausea to Sinead's stomach. "I'm afraid to get near the horses."

Bowes turned to her, his eyes narrowed, anger written on his face. He scowled fiercely.

"Ye've too many fears for such a young lassie. Ye're too obstinate and set in yer ways, too reluctant to do new things, to live yer life. I guess ye'll have to be deciding what ye're most afraid of, daughter."

"Well, really, Da!" Her cheek burned with awareness of his appraisal.

"Is it yer new husband whom ye barely know anything about, the horses who have done ye no harm or the mobs of crazy folk busting up this once fair city? I wash me hands of yer fears. Ye should have gotten over them through the years. I have wee patience with ye anymore."

Bowes turned away from her and hunched over, ending any conversation.

CHAPTER TWELVE

Connor and Egan watched the carriage turn the corner, then, pretending to be part of the crowd, they moved closer to the building. More and more people, like an elemental force of nature, converged on the orphanage. They screamed and shouted to one another as if they were enjoying a grand picnic in a park.

Suddenly, the mob began to move in great waves to the interior of the home, pushing and shoving each other out of the way. Connor and Egan followed the crowd inside. They stood off to one side, watching, aghast at what they saw happening.

With sharp and gleeful faces, filled with macabre amusement, men ran about the ground floor, shrieking racial epitaphs. They smashed pianos and much of the furniture in what looked like a main parlor. Some ripped off wallpaper and kicked holes in the walls with heavy work boots. Others carried off carpets, lamps, iron bedsteads, or anything that looked like it was worth anything. Women, a mammoth chorus of harping magpies, rushed in to grab linens, kitchen ware and other small goods.

Stunned by the sea of people, of the violence they displayed, and to avoid being taken down by the mob, Connor and Egan rushed from the stairwell where they were crammed and took the stairs three at a time, just ahead of the crowd. They tore up to the third floor, where they found some of the children, crying in terror, huddled behind curtains and furniture, in alcoves and closets. Their eyes, filled with fear, were wide and white in their brown faces.

One little boy stretched out his hand. "Please, Mister. We didn't do nuthin'."

With the soft speech of their Irish forefathers, the brothers gathered as many children together as they could. "Come now, children. Ye've no time to fear me brother or me. Ye've got to be getting out of here as quickly as yer wee legs can carry ye," Connor said, leading several of the children by the hand and carrying another in his arms.

He brought them to a set of rickety back steps that must have been for the servants, at one time or another. "Use these steps to get down to the outside," he said, giving them gentle shoves toward the downstairs. "Hurry, now."

Egan grabbed two toddlers and handed them off to some of the bigger girls and boys. "You'd best be carrying the wee ones."

"Take each others hands and start down these back stairs. Don't stop till you get to the rear of the property. Then run and hide."

Connor stopped two of the bigger boys. He lifted smaller children onto their backs and tucked small hands around the bigger throats. "Here," he said to the older ones. "Hold them like this. You have to be taking care of the wee ones. They cannot do this by themselves."

He moved on down the long hallway, opening every door, shouting, "Come, come, everyone. Ye have to be getting out of this house before more bad things happen."

Two little boys and three girls came through doors, most sobbing, their frightened faces streaked with dust and tears. Connor patted them. He put their little hands together, made them grasp tightly and led them to the back stairs. Egan charged right behind him with four more children. They got most of the children to the top of the back stairs, before people pounded loudly up the main stairs, coming toward them.

Connor sent Egan down with three small babies in his arms. "Take care of Sinead if anything happens to me. Marry her yourself, if necessary, to save young Robbie. She's fearful of losing him."

Egan turned back and came back up one step. "Maybe I'd better stay with you. I don't want to be married. Frankly, now, I'd just as soon have been back in Ireland."

Connor smiled down at his youngest brother, who continued, "Ye better not let anything happen to ye, Connor. I'll be damned to hell trying to explain it to our da or our brothers." Egan shook his head. "The twins would not be taking me death well, I'm thinking."

"Och, Egan. Go on with you. Better yet, I'll go partway and check the second floor." He grumbled to himself. "This is a most terrible welcome to America. This day is the devil's own work..."

From the second floor landing, Connor watched Egan go the rest of the way down and saw men uproot trees, sheds and fences at the sides of the Asylum. Connor saw them tear up the ground in a terrible frenzy of madness, digging, stamping, ripping pieces of turf and tossing them into the air.

The noise of many footsteps tramping loudly overhead brought Connor to an awareness that many men had reached the floor above him. He kept his back to the wall of the stairs and inched several steps toward the window on the landing. What was happening now?

Something sailed past the window. Connor drew back against the wall. The men above were dropping chairs and mirrors into the back yard. He saw them heave a huge dresser from a window. He watched it travel to the ground, amid the remains of a riotous garden, until it struck a young, dark-skinned girl of about ten, in the head. With a loud scream, she fell to the dirt beneath the bulky piece of furniture.

From horrified eyes he saw Sinead, dodging falling debris still coming from above, streak across the yard to the little girl. She tried desperately to lift the dresser. Bowes jumped from the carriage and ran to help her, his short legs pumping away. When they managed to get the girl out from under the dresser, Connor saw Bowes shake his head. Her face bathed in sorrow, Sinead lifted the girl in her arms and turned away from the scene.

Whether for the child or for the woman who held her so gently, tears blurred Connor's vision. He turned away and rested his head against the wall to get his emotions under control. He wondered what he had gotten himself into by marrying this woman.

A frantic roar from above gave warning of something extraordinary happening. Thunderous footfalls streamed across the upper floor and charged down the front staircase. The noise of those stamping feet quickly brought him to his senses.

An outrageous, primitive scream of rampant rage, and then one of victory, came from the crowd outside the building. Connor felt his blood rush and roar in his head, felt the chug of his heart beating to a rhythm faster than usual. Smoke pumped and poured up the stairwell from the floors below. Realization stamped a burning brand across the far reaches of his thoughts.

The bloody bastards had set the building ablaze!

A sensation of ice cold water trickled down his spine. It was difficult to breathe, difficult to think and even more difficult to push the events of this day from his mind. His anger burned hotter than ever before in his life.

For a moment, he was completely disassociated from reality. He had crossed some threshold between rational thought and being trapped like an animal, like a horse. Smoke made him turn left, then right, going nowhere, just like a horse would do. The thought of a horse's reactions to fire became a chilling reminder to worry more about the danger he faced this moment rather than a past that could never be reborn.

He heard a whoosh of fire coming alive, the sound of windows rattling in their frames and their workings bursting from their mounting. Glass encased within the frames shattered almost soundlessly. Dark smoke climbed the back stairs, searing and choking. Then he snapped out of his trance.

Intense heat from the fire racing up the front of the building caressed his face like fingers of desire. His body thirsted for air and water. A stream of smoke poured down on him. He ducked beneath it with a primitive, instinctual quickness. With supernatural reserve of strength and endurance and a sudden need to survive, he dipped down to one side to avoid encroaching flames moving toward the back of the house and tore down the stairs.

The back hallway was narrow and poorly lit except for the reflected light of the infiltrating flames on the glass of the door. Smoke clung to him. He coughed, slightly upsetting his balance. His toe caught on a piece of debris, which dropped onto a step. His arms wind-milled above him. He slipped and toppled over, rolling down the stairs to the bottom, where he lay in a crumpled heap, his breath gone, the flames moving ever closer.

Connor heard a soft, disembodied voice call his name. "Connor..." It sounded like his sweet mother. He wondered if he were dead.

Egan looked to the upper stories, slowly being engulfed. He shouted, "Connor, where are ye laddie? Dammit, the fire's engulfing the whole front of the Asylum, and it's coming nearer to the back. That's where I left him. On this side of the house."

Sinead cried out over the roar of the fire. "We've got to find him, Egan. He'll burn to a crisp in those flames. I'll not be having his death on my conscience, even if I have to go in there myself."

"Give me a piece of your skirt to put over my face. I'm going inside to find him."

With a total lack of modesty, Sinead reached under her garment and ripped a huge piece of cloth from her white underskirt. "I'm going with you."

"Nae, lass. Your skirts are too wide. They'd catch fire, sure."

"Then I'll take them off."

Connor heard them speaking from a distance. He struggled to catch his breath but didn't dare draw in a big one, so he took little, short gasps of air. "Egan..." flushed from his mouth in a tiny murmur.

"Connor, Connor, lad. 'Tis me. Egan. I'm coming in. Where are ye, laddie? Answer me." He waited and listened. "Don't be getting the both of us killed, now, will ye?" Egan opened the door to the back stairs. Flames shot above his head, making him duck.

"Here, Egan. Here. On the floor. Not far from you're feet."

"Oh, Jaysus," Egan cried. "I see you. Don't move. I'll be dragging ye out as soon as I get on me belly." Egan fell to the floor. Using his elbow, he inched forward on his stomach. "How'd ye get yerself into this mess, Connor? I always gave ye credit for more sense than this."

"Shut your mouth, brother, or you won't be able to breathe either."

Connor stretched his arms out to Egan, who grabbed both arms and pulled. "Lord, Con, ye weigh a ton."

"You're no lightweight yourself. Pull."

They reached the door and bust through it to the outside. Connor fell to the ground in a fit of coughing. The two men were covered in soot and ash.

Sinead stood, waiting for sight of them. As soon as she saw their shapes, she ran forward, grabbed Connor's wrist and yanked.

"Lass, you'll be pulling the arms from me sockets, if you're not careful," Connor grumbled.

"You're an ungrateful pig, Connor O'Malley. 'Twas a sad day when I agreed to marry you."

For some reason, Connor became angry. Here he was, sacrificing himself for the sake of youngsters he didn't know, and this woman was berating him. He expressed his thoughts aloud.

"Well, 'tis married we are. There's no help for it now. Maybe 'tis better I accept your carping and be done with it. You'd rather have me roasted than married, I suppose."

"Och, 'tis sorry I am to be chiding you. 'Tis just my nerves getting the better of me."

"Jaysus, will you look—at that—fire. 'Tis all-consuming, for sure," Connor coughed the words out.

Egan and Sinead turned to look. They stood with their mouths open as the building blazed behind them. Then, by pulling and yanking Connor, they were able to move him away from the building. They struggled to drag him farther from the heat, the smoke and flaming, falling debris.

Connor took deep breaths and cleared his lung with several chest-wracking coughs. He made them release him and sat up. "Just give me a minute to pull myself together."

"Don't take too much time," Egan counseled. "This building will be falling down on us far too soon."

"Help me to my feet and we'll get to the carriage."

Both Sinead and Egan tried to lift Connor, but his weight was too much for them. "You'll have to help us, husband," Sinead said, groaning with every pull of her muscles.

"Let me get on my knees. Then I'll be able to stand," Connor said, rolling over onto his stomach. He pushed himself to his knees, stretched each limb to loosen tense muscles then took more deep breaths of air and clambered to his feet. His body wavered to and fro. Sinead sidled up to him, put her shoulder under his arm and held him steady.

Connor started to laugh but coughed words out instead. "Are you — thinking — you can hold — me steady — by — yourself, lass?" His throat worked convulsively. He gulped in more air and said, "'Tis all right. I think I can stand by myself."

Feeling a warm flush rise to her face, Sinead withdrew her arms from around his chest and walked away from him.

"I didn't mean for you to be going away from me, lass."

She swung around to look at him. "You have a smart mouth on you, Connor O'Malley. I can't say as I like it. We haven't known each other long enough to be scrapping, so let's just forget it for now. My da is waiting for us, trying to hold the horses steady. He'll be anxious until we get away from this place."

"Aye. You're right. Just tell me this. Did the children get out all right? Are they safe?"

"Although terrified, many managed to escape out the back door. The older ones carried the younger ones on their backs. Most came out before the mob broke in and raced to the top," Egan offered.

"One little girl was killed by the falling furniture," Sinead said quietly, her eyes focused on the ground. "Come," she said, walking toward the alleyway and her father's carriage.

"I think Egan and I got some of the more frightened ones, from the upper floors, out before people ran up the stairs to steal or hack furniture and toys with their axes." Connor turned to Egan for confirmation.

"The mob set the building on fire. They forced the orphans to flee for their lives. I ran around the front to see if any children came out over there, but none did," Egan said, his voice displaying his utter disgust. "Firemen were attacked as they tried to put out the flames. 'Twas the most horrific scene I've ever watched."

"How could people be this way, especially Irishmen?" Connor asked of no one. "And they claim this is the wonderful country of America." He began to cough again."

"You wouldn't cough, Connor, if you didn't talk so much, "Sinead called back over her shoulder. "Oh. There was a young Irishman by the name of McCaffrey, I believe, who brought the last dozen children to safety. He took them to the Twentieth Precinct, I think."

Sinead reached the carriage. She nodded to her da and climbed into the back seats, noticing the remains of the fire on her clothing. With both hands, she brushed and scraped the cloth of her skirt.

Connor and Egan followed, staggering to the carriage, like drunks. "Connor, ye get in the back with yer wife. I'll help Bowes with the driving. We'll be at the Dewitts' house," Egan said, his gaze never leaving his brother's.

Connor nodded and stepped into the back of the carriage. He cast a surreptitious look at his wife, who smiled at him in a charming but decidedly smug fashion. He waited for her to make some sort of remark.

"You know," she said, sweetly, "Despite the mob pelting him with rocks and paving stones, the young fireman who brought the children to the police precinct took care of those children as if they were his own. He was as wonderful as he could be, and as Irish as yourself."

Connor laid his head back on the high part of the seat. "Your point is made, lass."

"And well, it should be," Sinead said. She smiled to herself.

* * *

On their safe getaway from the orphanage fire, Connor insisted they stop at the police precinct to inquire about the children from the Orphanage. When Bowes stopped the carriage, Connor rushed in alone.

The constable at the desk glanced up and seemed to recognize him. With a slight nod, he said, "All the youngsters were accounted for and are being brought to safety at a secret location." A deep scowl lined his face. "Except the young girl who died. You know the one," he added, "the one the big dresser fell on." His sigh filled the room. "I hate it when bad things happen to innocents…"

"As do I," Connor acknowledged. "Any other news?"

Another constable interrupted the conversation. "Let me warn ye. A mob attacked the Twenty-first Street Armory. Them bastards are tearing up this city," he said. "Irish gangsters they are!"

"Wait until ye hear this," added another, who rushed in from the outdoors. "They're no longer carrying just their brickbats and paving stones. They've got guns."

"Listen to me mister," the first one said. "You and yer folks need to be very careful. Get off the streets, if possible. Those folks are armed to their teeth and unthinkin' deadly when roused."

"We'll be careful, but we need to get through the city. A young son awaits us at home, and we need to make sure he's fine," a somewhat subdued Connor said with deference.

The constable added, "Then ye better see to yerself and the missus before ye see yer son. Ye're a bit of a mess, covered in soot as ye are. Were ye burned at that fire, boyo?"

"I don't believe so. Nothing hurts much, just my body aching with the need for resting itself."

"Well, then ye'd better do that soon 'cause I'm thinking there's more to come." He smiled at Connor. "I must admit, young fella', I've been hearing some splendid things about ye. Might ye be thinking of joining up with our forces in the most immediate future?"

"Thank you kindly, but I'm not a much of a man for power over people. I'm merely a horseman, raising nags for the sport of running," Connor replied. He smiled back at the man to soften the refusal.

"Och, if it's the horses ye're interested in, ye ought to be going to Saratoga. I've heard talk that some men are thinking of starting a racing course up there."

"I'll keep it in mind, for sure. I'm surely not liking the idea of staying in this city any longer than I can help it," Connor grumbled, turning toward the door.

"Well, if ye change yer mind, about joining the police, I'd be happy to talk with ye. Ye're a big man, and we could sure use more like yerself, right now, or even yer younger brother. We have no idea how much depth this disastrous day will have," the constable said, giving Connor a friendly pat on the back as he walked him to the door.

With a brief nod and smile of empathy, Connor left the building and joined the others at the carriage. He relayed the news to them then sat in the back with Sinead. His eyes closed of their own volition. He knew exhaustion marked his face and body, along with the remains of ashes and charcoal streaks.

Bowes drove on. The afternoon sun slipped behind gray clouds of smoke, its oppressive heat magnified by flames shooting up in distant areas and lighting the blinded sky. Shadows shifted on the streets even as the sun waned, above the flames. For the moment, the streets were hooded, barren.

* * *

The people in the carriage rolled toward their destination in utter silence. Each one was too sick inside to hazard any of their thoughts in inconsequential speech. Bowes turned the horses around a corner.

A gasp of relief passed Sinead's lips as the iron fences surrounding sections of Gramercy Park hove into view.

Connor's eyes opened. His gaze snapped to look directly into her face. He stared down into her eyes and noticed the gladness in them. She's lovely looking, he thought, even messy as she is right now.

Bowes broke the silence. "Listen. Here's me plan. I'll leave the three of ye in front while I take these fine horses to the back. They've served us well, they have. I'll secure them in a nearby stable. They can rest and have themselves a grand feed."

Egan nodded. "Aye, they've earned all that."

"That they have," Bowes said. "And with the way things are going, who knows when we'll be needing them again, fit and strong."

"Bowes, I'll go with ye and help with the horses. Two of us together are better than one of us alone," Egan said.

Connor sat straight in his seat and looked around. "The Dewitts live around here, in one of these fancy buildings? In the midst of all this wealth?" he asked, loudly, surprised at the sound of his own voice.

"That they do," Bowes piped, "and not a grateful bone in their bodies. Their daughter was nice enough, but neither one of the parents would give ye a thought or a drink if ye were parched."

"Da, stop that," Sinead said. A sharp edge rode her tone. "We don't want these lads to think ill of the Dewitts. I'll need to deal with the Dewitts for Robbie's sake. I don't want to incur their anger by putting bad thoughts into the heads of these lads. Such a circumstance will solve nothing."

Connor tilted his head to one side. "I'm wondering what they might have thought of our absence this entire day."

"They probably thought we were just getting reacquainted," she supplied.

"Reacquainted?" Connor arched a brow.

"Aye, my da told them we knew each other years ago in Ireland."

Connor stared at Sinead and then up at Bowes, who sat in the driver's seat with his shoulders hunched. "Well, did we?" Connor asked. When no answer came, he asked again. "Well, did we? Know each other in Ireland?"

Bowes swiveled around in his seat. "We'll talk about all this later, when things have settled down some. Let's just get through this day." His voice sounded choked. "Make sure Robbie is fine," he said in a very evasive fashion.

Dead silence greeted Bowes's response. Sinead must have picked up each nuance in her da's voice. Her hand tightened and tangled in the ripped cloth of her skirt. She closed her eyes for the moment.

Connor watched her reactions, trying to puzzle out what was happening. A strange, haunted look intensified in his wife's eyes when she opened them. He needed to get to the bottom of his wife's secret — or perhaps, her da's secret.

Even in Ireland, Connor suspected there was more to this hasty marriage and his da's relationship with Bowes Brennan than his da let on. He didn't mention his thoughts to anyone at the time, but, now that he was sure there was much more involved, he'd seek out answers.

Bowes turned a corner onto upper Fifth Avenue, west of Union Square. The avenue of commodious row houses and ornate mansions stood as silent sentinels of a lovely neighborhood, so far untouched by the hand of the gangs.

Many of the houses were made of sandstone, which turned them from pink to chocolate depending on their age. The houses were built by designers captivated by the Italian Renaissance, and the soft brown stone made for richly carved facades and lavish ornamentation.

The carriage horses stopped with a tiny tug on the reins and a gentle, "Whoa." Their heads drooped in their harnesses.

Connor heard Sinead's sigh of relief and glanced in the same direction she did. The five story Dewitt mansion, its chocolate color reflected in the waning light of the sun, was set back several feet from the roadway and stone sidewalk. A spiked iron fence with what looked like balls and arrows at different intervals separated the brownstone from other houses nearby.

The entire picture was serene. The property seemed untouched by the rioting in other parts of the city. Sinead drew in a deep, breath. She hesitated for only a second before she leaped from the carriage ahead of Connor. She nearly tripped over her full skirt and clutched the side of the vehicle.

Connor stepped out slowly, still looking up at the house. He held her elbow until she removed the skirt from beneath her shoe, then settled his hands on his hips and walked closer to the entrance gates.

Deadly silence permeated the building. It seemed deserted. No inner lights shone through the closed bottom-floor draperies. Connor took another step forward and tried to open the gate. It was locked.

"What's wrong?" Bowes asked.

"The gate is locked," Connor said, puzzled. "Do they always lock it?"

"Usually not until dark. I have a key somewhere," Sinead said, digging in her reticule for the object. "Ring the bell above the entrance."

Connor pulled the chain. The ring echoed over the quiet avenue. Drapes were pulled back from several of the surrounding houses. People peered from their windows. He looked up. Someone parted a curtain on the fourth floor. He rang the bell again, harder.

Sinead found her key, shoved it into the large lock and jiggled it around. Nothing happened. "How could they have done this? Locked the gate? They knew I was returning home today," she said in exasperation and turned her attention back to the job at hand.

Finally, the key turned in the lock. The gate creaked open. Sinead squeezed inside the narrow space, ran across the red bricks and under the small portico decorating the porch at the front of the house. She pounded on the door, bleating one name. "Robbie. Robbie..." She turned to Connor.

A strange, haunted look intensified in her eyes. No one answered her call.

CHAPTER THIRTEEN

No matter how hard Sinead slammed the heel of her closed fist on the door, no one hastened to answer it. Waves of terror rose. She sank to the porch floor, her long ash-splattered legs sticking straight out in front, and leaned back against a railing. Loose-limbed, she mouthed a frightened and exhausted groan.

Expressionless, Connor stepped over to lift her to her feet, effectively barring entrance to the door. Poised above her when she stood, he listened intently, ear against the wood. Uncertainties made him scowl, clench his jaw. He looked down at her, puzzled.

Looking up into the depth of his dark brown eyes, Sinead felt hot and cold at the same time. She took a step back, off the porch. The heat he generated was too much for her to bear. To avoid the shadows of exhaustion and puzzlement that darkened his eyes, she glanced up at the building's facade.

She noticed a quick movement, something she imagined she'd seen before. A curtain in the fourth floor window fluttered then hung limp. A small patch of white appeared near the sill and was gone in an instant.

"Someone's in the house," she whispered and craned her neck for a better view. "Why won't they answer the bell?"

A corner of Connor's mouth edged up with disgust apparent in every crease. One dark eyebrow arched. His expression remained reserved, even though he mustered a sardonic smile. "With all that's been going on in this city, whoever it may be is probably frightened beyond measure."

Leaving Egan to hold the horses, Bowes stomped up on the porch behind Connor and Sinead. "Here, let me try something." He gripped a long piece of wire and thrust it into the door lock with a quick, furtive motion. With deft fingers, he twisted it in several directions.

Connor stared at Bowes for a full minute without blinking. "And where did you learn this art?" he asked, unleashed anger in his voice.

His face serious, Bowes looked up and simply made use of the truth. "You'd be surprised how many men I've brought home when they were so far into their cups, they were lucky to know where the hell they lived," he said, with a grimace. "And, I can't be telling ye how many times their women locked them out of their own houses. Most often with damned good reason." He continued jiggling the wire and was able to push it in a bit further.

Connor stared and watched a slow grin roll onto Bowes's face, before he continued. "A nasty, mean man in his cups is not one to be fooled with. There's no talking to them. They have no amount of sense in their brains and far too little control over their actions," he grumbled.

Bowes gave the wire a final turn. Something inside the lock clicked. He gave a grunt of satisfaction. Sinead behaved as if what she witnessed was commonplace. Connor shook his head but couldn't stop himself from grinning along with Bowes.

He waved at Egan, who sat quietly in the carriage, waiting. Egan pointed to himself and Bowes nodded. Egan jumped out of the carriage, tied the horses to a post and trotted up onto the porch with the others. Bowes drew them together into a circle around him.

"I want the three of you to listen to me, and listen carefully, mind ye. Ye don't know who could be in that house," he said in a low, rough voice, emphasizing the undercurrents of the day. "The house seems deserted but we all sense someone's in there. For what purpose, we don't know at the moment, but I intend to find out. Here's what I want ye to do."

He lifted his hand and began to count off on his fingers. "Sinead, I want ye go to the back door. Leave it open for me to be getting in or for you to be gettin' out if ye need to do that in a hurry." He raised a second finger. "You lads stick together and go through this house floor by floor, room by room. Be alert. Examine everything and watch your backs."

When he raised his third finger, Connor interrupted. "Those were my plans exactly. Let's not take any chances. We'll not be able to help anyone if we're beaten down in a heap."

Bowes blinked once and nodded. "I'll be taking the horses round back now. I'll meet ye in the house as quickly as I can," he whispered over his shoulder while going down the short steps to the gate, which he closed behind him.

Without a good-bye to her da, Sinead turned the bronzed doorknob and pushed lightly. The door swung in.

Darkness blanketed the inside foyer. Silence greeted her. Desperate thoughts for Robbie filled her with dread. She opened her mouth to call out, but Connor put a hand over her mouth. He gently rubbed the bottom lip and put a finger to his own before removing his hand. Slowly, she looked up at him and felt dangerous emotions stirring. She nodded.

His hand fell to his side. "Let's do things as your father said. You go to open the back door. Egan, stay with her. I don't want her alone for a minute, until we know who's here. I'll look around this floor a bit until you come back. Go quickly!"

Connor saw Sinead grab Egan's hand and lead him to a small hallway that ended with a closed door. She undid the latch and angled her body through a narrow opening. Egan followed.

Left alone, Connor looked around in amazement at the display of useless wealth in a circular room twice the size of the manor's library in Ireland. Several mahogany tables on tall, thin legs stood to one side of the entranceway. Ornate silver trays were angled on top of them, one lying flat. A huge Oriental rug covered the floor at the bottom of what must have been the main staircase. It led to a landing that branched off with stairs going in two opposite directions to the next floor.

Three doors faced the room, the one Sinead and Egan had gone through and two double doors, facing each other across the room. Connor moved with stealth to the door on his left. He slid it open but moved back with a quick step. When nothing happened, he sidled slowly into the room, with his back to the wall. His eyes slowly adjusted to the lack of light.

A large fireplace in the room covered one wall. To one side of the grate, several fire utensils, including a long poker, hung neatly in a silver box. Cautiously looking over his shoulder with every footstep and his back to the wall, he navigated the room to the firebox. Heart pounding, he grabbed the poker from its hook and whirled around to face the room. The instrument was cool in his hand and gave him a false sense of confidence.

The sound of scurrying footsteps, someone running, along with the squeak of boots on a wooden floor, infiltrated the room from the large hall. Connor took a deep breath. He braced himself against the cool, dark brick of the fireplace and waited.

Egan and Sinead appeared in the doorway.

Egan whispered, "Connor, are ye there lad?"

"Aye. Straight ahead."

"Show yourself then. The room's dark with those draperies drawn."

Connor took a huge stride forward. "There's no one in this room," he said.

"There's no one in the servant's quarters either. The cook's gone and Hans isn't here either," Sinead commented, a puzzled expression on her face. She frowned and looked around her. "Nothing's been disturbed in here."

"That's good," Connor mumbled. "Well then, let's get on with our work. We'll check out the other room on this floor, but I sense no one's around on this bottom level. Perhaps, the help are hiding on the other floors."

"Let me call out," Sinead insisted. "There are only two staircases in the house. This one here," she said, pointing to the main staircase in the front room, "and the servant's stairway in the back. If anyone wants to leave in a hurry, those are the only two ways they can get down, short of jumping from a window."

"All right. But first, let me make some noise. I'm sure noise might scare up some birds out of their territory." Connor stamped across the foyer. He scuffed his boots on the bare wood floor and stamped loudly on the rug then stood and listened, his finger to his lips in a gesture of silence.

Nothing stirred upstairs. Sinead moved to the stairs, letting her heels click on the bare wood. At the bottom, she called up, "Robbie? Robbie, son, 'tis Mama."

"They must be gone," Egan said. "Afraid of the rioting, no doubt. And sensible they were to do so."

"No," Sinead said. "I'm sure I saw the curtains move on the fourth floor. Someone is up there. I just don't know who." She started up the steps.

Connor grabbed her arm and held her in place. "Lass, don't you listen to your own father? He said to stay together."

"Och, God, Connor. It might be a small boy up there all by himself. I think everyone else left. I can't stand it. Please, I beg of you. Hurry."

"Here's what we'll do. You stay close to me. Egan and I will go up the stairs with you in back of us. At the split in the landing, we'll each take a side. You stay behind me. We'll follow your da's directions to look in every room on every floor." Connor took a step up, turned and grasped her chin in his hand. "If the lad's up there, we'll find him."

He pointed in one direction to Egan and helped Sinead move onto the step with him. She quickly obeyed, putting her trust in this man, and watched Egan move to Connor's other side, giving his brother a single nod.

"It'll take hours to go through this whole house. And we might frighten my son more with the waiting." The color drained from her face and her eyes widened with fear.

"If that's what's you're thinking," Connor said, "then call the boy again, louder this time."

Sinead cupped her mouth and shouted, "Robbie, 'tis Mama Jane, darling. If you're upstairs, come down. I'll wait in the big hall. I have your da with me, so you don't have to be afraid, son."

"Mama?" The small, high-pitched voice echoed through the empty house.

"Jane, is that you?" Isabel, Robbie's governess, called from the head of the fourth floor stairs. "Jane?"

"Och, Isabel, 'tis you," Sinead gasped. Her knees seemed to slip from under her, and she sat on the stairs. "And Robbie. Alone here? Come to me. Hurry, please."

Suddenly, within seconds, no more, Robbie rushed to the main landing. The hollow sound of his small feet clicking down the stairway echoed in Sinead's ears. A lovely young blond girl, several years younger than Sinead, followed behind, her blue eyes glassy with tears. When Robbie saw his mother, he flew down the rest of the way and flung himself into her outstretched arms.

Sinead circled her arms around him, put her cheek on the top of his head and squeezed. He shrieked in her arms, part in youthful glee, part from the fear contained inside him for hours and part with love. He clung to her neck.

"Och, laddie, 'tis most glad I am to see you so very fit," Sinead said, rocking him back and forth in her arms.

The boy muttered against her neck, with a hint of tears in his voice. "You left me for a long time."

"I know we did and I'm sorry." She brushed his hair from his forehead and pressed her lips against his eyes. "Were you scared?"

"No." He turned to Isabel, who remained on the landing. "I wasn't scared, was I, Isabel?" Then, with all the single-mindedness exerted by a four-year-old with only one thing on his mind, Robbie continued, "You said you'd be back in the morning to get me, to take me riding."

He glared frowned at Connor. Connor smiled back at him, ruffled his hair and stepped onto the foyer level.

Happy to have the boy in her arms, Sinead grinned at him. "Aye, Rob. I did say that, didn't I? But sometimes, circumstances prevent folks from doing what they planned."

"What's a circumstances?" he asked, with a face screwed up with confusion.

Connor laughed aloud. He turned to the young woman on the landing. Egan was staring at her, his face appreciative of her loveliness. "Is there anyone else in the house, Isabel?"

With her gaze locked on Egan, she shook her head back and forth. Her hair fell loose from its knot in the back. She tucked it behind her ears. "They left us here. The Dewitts went to their summer home in Albany when they got word of the troubles. No sooner than they departed, the servants ran off and joined the people roaming the streets." Her voice trembled with fear and reaction to what happened.

"You were a strong, brave lass to stay here by yourself," Egan softly murmured, taking her hand and leading her down the stairs. "And it seems you took good care of the wee laddie, here."

Connor smiled and glanced at Sinead. "That you did, lass. Sinead and I are most grateful to you."

"What's grateful, Mama?" Robbie asked, clapping his hands in excitement at all the attention.

Connor laughed and swung the young boy up into his arms. "Now, here's a laddie I can take to…"

Isobel bobbed a small curtsy then, with a disapproving look, spoke directly to Connor. "You called Jane, Sinead. The Dewitts don't allow that in their presence."

"That's her name. We'll be calling her that from now on, I'm thinking." Connor smiled back at Isobel, whose face lit up with a big grin to match the one on Connor's face.

Robbie reached up to take Connor's chin in both hands. He edged it around to face him. "You're dirty, you know. Mama Jane will clean you up. She doesn't like dirt."

Sinead sighed and said, "Och, Robbie, you're the delight of my life."

Connor and Egan bellowed with a repressed gaiety. Everyone was safe, for the moment.

* * *

The excitement of their return to the mansion was over. Although exhausted, everyone had eaten his fill from the scraps left in the iceboxes. Once the food was consumed, Connor, Egan and Bowes were exiled to the upper regions of the house by Robbie to see his room and toys.

Sinead and Isabel stayed downstairs to clean the kitchen. "We'd better clean up just in case the mistress of the house returns." Isobel exclaimed, rushing to put things in their proper places.

"Well, I'm a bit miffed," Sinead countered, banging pots as she dried them. "Actually, I'm more than that. I'm downright angry." She slammed a metal dish on the counter. "To think they went off and left the lad, not caring what might happen to him."

Isobel nodded in agreement. "Why, no sooner than they got word about the rioting in the streets, they packed their belongings and half the household goods. At least, those with any value," Isobel snarled, scrubbing one of the already cleaned pots.

Sinead briefly stood stock still then leaned on the counter. She took a deep breath and let it out slowly.

Isobel's face reddened. She sneered then scowled at Sinead. "They were frantic to leave. They left some of the silver and all of the paintings behind. Took three carriages and four carts to get them on the road."

Sinead shook her head. Her Irish temper flew several notches higher, and she marched across the room, slapping a pan between her hands. "I just don't understand how they could leave Robbie behind. With such unrest in the city. Here. Alone. With just a young lass like yourself to watch over him."

"He wouldn't go with them. He stamped his feet and insisted they wait for his Mama Jane. Put on a real tantrum." A smile broke out on Isobel's face. "It was quite a sight to see." She briefly chuckled. "I have to tell you this, though. The Mister did try to catch the child, as he calls him. He was going to take him with them regardless of anyone's feelings in the matter, including the Missus. When the Mister reached out to grab him, Robbie slapped his hand away and ran out of the room. He flew up the stairs and hid in that upstairs closet off the linen room." Isobel straightened and puffed out her chest in a show of pride in Robbie. She smirked and waved her head back and forth in peacock fashion.

Sinead didn't know whether to laugh at Robbie's antics or cry. "Didn't anyone go after him?" Agitation made her stride to Isobel and glare with narrowed eyes. "Search for him?"

Isobel sniffed with disdain. "Oh, they pretended to search high and low. Sent that fool majordomo to seek the child out. Robbie stayed quiet as a mouse until I found him. I coaxed him out of the closet. By the time got him down the stairs, kicking and screaming, they'd already left the house. I couldn't find them anywhere."

Sinead gasped. She held her breath for a moment, distressed by the news, which she found incomprehensible. "They didn't try to find out if he was safe? They didn't wait?"

"No, they didn't." Isobel looked up at Sinead, her face filled with sympathy. "They took some of the servants with them, those that would go with them. The ones they left behind took off for the streets, either to protect what they thought was theirs or their relatives, I imagine."

A corner of Isobel's lip curled in a sneer. "Or to get into the rioting and looting. They'd already taken things from here." She turned away. "You know how they are sometimes…"

"But you stayed, Isobel—when you could have gone to your parents' home and possible safety." She touched the girl's arm and pulled her closer. "You stayed…"

"Of course, I did. I couldn't leave the little fellow alone with no one to look after him." Her eyes gleamed with determination, courage and pride. "If anything had happened to him, I'd never forgive myself."

"And I'll never be able to thank you enough," Sinead replied, taking hold of Isobel's hand and holding it to her cheek.

Squeezing Sinead's hand, with urgency, Isobel spoke softly. "Jane, now that you're here, I would like to go home to my parents. I'm sure they're probably worried sick by now."

"Of course. You go ahead. As long as my husband and I are here, we will see to Robbie's care. And he loves my father. We'll keep him amused." With sweetness and total sincerity, Sinead smiled down at the young girl. "You have always been kind and generous to Robbie, never more than now. I thank you so much more than you'll ever know."

Connor entered the kitchen. The room seemed to grow smaller with his presence. "Have you ladies done all you need do here? 'Tis time to rest and make plans for tomorrow."

The gaslights in the kitchen flickered, playing over his dark hair. Shades of brown with touches of red and yellow gave him a halo. He was handsome, almost to the point of taking Sinead's breath away. So very masculine were his looks. She could feel a blush rushing up the sides of her face, along with a fear of more attraction to this man.

"Aye, we're done here. Should we all gather together in one room?" Sinead asked.

"Nae. I think I need to talk to you first. Alone." He smiled at her, a look of wonder on his face, as if he were judging her by some secret standard.

"I'll go upstairs and get Robbie ready for bed," Isobel replied, a smile threatening to break out. She walked toward the door.

Connor put his hand out to stop her. "The lad is already asleep on a sofa in the library. I think we'll all sleep downstairs this night.

It's too dangerous for any of us to stay alone in the upper regions of the house."

Both women nodded.

Sinead mumbled, "Perhaps we'd better pack some of Robbie's clothes and bring them downstairs, just in case."

"'Tis a good idea, lass." Connor smiled at her with a tender expression on his face.

"I'll do it," Isobel said. "You do your talking..." She strode from the kitchen, trying to hide the smile on her face.

Sinead put a hand on her hip. All the resentment she'd built up over the past few months of fearful waiting, plus all the tumultuous activities of the past few days, culminated in the presence of the man facing her. She snapped, "Well, what is you'll be saying to me? I'm tired and in need of sleep."

Connor tilted his head in disbelief and stared down at her. "I've been talking to your da."

Frightened by the thoughts he conjured up in her mind, her need for sarcasm grew. She wouldn't allow herself to be beholden to this, or any, man. Not any more. "Och, that must have been an interesting conversation..."

Except for the narrowing of his eyes in response to her anger, the expression on Connor's face didn't change. He continued with what he intended to say. "Neither your da, nor I, believe this rioting will end with just one day of horror. We're sure there's more to come."

Sinead adopted even more of an ungrateful attitude. She was unable to stop herself. "And how would you be knowing that, after only being here for a few short days?"

"Short days? They've been the longest of my life." Connor's anger flared. "But enough of this carping with the long blade of your tongue. My instincts tell me people so aroused will not stop until forced to do so by a greater force than theirs."

"Och, must be your manly instincts at work. Well, 'tis those very manly instincts that got you into the trouble you've been having since your arrival."

"Lass, I'm not standing here to argue with you. You're my family now. I want to protect you and my new son." Frustration made his words harsh, as if he was forced to do his duty to his new family.

"The best way you can protect us is to go back where you came from — to Ireland. Once the Dewitts become aware of the fuss you and your brother created since you landed, they'll see to it Robbie no longer stays in my care, much less yours. Don't you understand? The child has no mother or father of his blood."

"Whatever the circumstances, I am the boy's father now. I will protect him, and you, with my life. I take my responsibilities to heart, whether you want me to or not." He crossed his arm over his chest, in a gesture of stubbornness. "Besides, going back to Ireland is impossible at this moment."

Connor snorted in disgust. "We're lucky if we can get out of this city before more tragedy strikes, as it did yesterday and today."

Sinead rested her palms on her hips, then squeezed them tight until her knuckles whitened. She bent her body toward him. Her eyes grew steamy and closed into narrow slits. She tilted her head in defiance. "We are not leaving this city, not now or ever. At least, not Robbie or me. You can go where you will."

A slow smile crept onto Connor's face, but his gaze mirrored the seriousness of his tone. "Your da and Egan told me of the devastation done by folks in the area of his boarding house. They saw it first thing in the morning and saw worse in the city when they were driving to reach us. It is their conviction more rioting will follow in the next few days."

Sinead's lips curled in a downward sneer. She lowered her eyes, tossing off a sharp grunt in his direction.

Connor leaned against a tall cupboard and crossed his arms chest-level. He appeared relaxed but something in his stance seemed tense and watchful. "Turning away from an argument doesn't accomplish anything. I'm willing to listen to your thoughts on the matter at hand."

"You don't understand." Her face flushed, Sinead spun to face him, her posture rigid. "I dare not leave or take my son away without permission. As it is, the Dewitts have plans to sue me before a magistrate for Robbie's sole custody."

"Sue you? The lad's mother?" Connor stared. "You're right, I don't understand or perhaps I understand more than you think I do." His stare intensified. "Why would they wish to do a thing so base?"

Sinead's pretended anger collapsed, along with her rigid posture. Tears slipped from her eyes and trickled down her cheeks. She wiped them away with the back of her hand. Almost in defeat, she said, "You don't understand. You just don't…"

"Try me…" He took a step toward her and held out a hand.

"The Dewitts' daughter and her husband were in a serious accident. Something frightened their carriage horses — you know the way horses are — and they ran away with the carriage. It overturned going around a corner. The driver couldn't control them."

"And?" Connor asked, waiting for her to continue.

"The Cavanaughs were tossed out of the vehicle onto the cobblestones. Mister Cavanaugh was rushed to the hospital, his neck broken." Sinead choked back a sob. "His wife went into labor, and Robbie was born before his time."

More tears of anguish slid from Sinead's eyes and over her cheekbones. She blinked several times in succession. Her breath caught in her throat.

Connor wanted to comfort her, to kiss the tears from her face. He almost laughed at himself, wondering why such a thought came to mind, unbidden. He managed to keep his demeanor stern. "Continue, please. I would know the entire story."

Her face bathed in agony, Sinead said, "Lucinda Cavanaugh died shortly after giving birth to Robbie. Her last words bade me to care for her son as if he were my own and to bring him up in a Catholic household, as she promised her husband."

Sinead took a deep breath before continuing. "When Lucinda, the sweetest, most gentle woman who ever lived, married Mister

Cavanaugh, she signed a paper agreeing to bring her children up in the Catholic faith. Even in her dying, she did not go back on that promise."

"And you've honored your pledge to her, haven't you?"

"Aye. At first, it seemed a burden, but then a pleasure. I did it with all my heart, for I love Robbie. He is the brightest light shining in the window of my mind."

Connor moved closer and resumed his probing. "I take it the care was in keeping with Mister Cavanaugh's wishes as well?"

"Aye. When he returned to Cavanaugh House he was so crippled and in pain, he cared not one whit about arrangements for his son. At first, he had no desire to even look at him, but within months, Robbie wormed his way into his father's affections and became his da's total reason for living." She looked up at Connor. "Robert senior doted on the lad."

Connor sighed. The story didn't please him. It sounded to him as if the Cavanaugh's made a young girl promise something far too difficult to comprehend. He wondered how he, himself, could make it right.

She went on with her story. "When Robert realized he was dying, he married me in order to leave Robbie in my care."

Connor frowned. "Then why are you living here with the boy and not in the house his da must have left you?"

Sinead looked up, surprised at Connor's questions. "Robert forgot to change the will he and Lucinda signed. The will stated that should he die before his wife, his house should be sold, his wife should return to her parents' home — unless she remarried."

She shrugged and, in a soft voice, pleaded with Connor for understanding. "They agreed the money from the sale of the house and whatever fortune Robert might leave be saved for the care of the wife and child." She hung her head in defeat.

Connor began to understand the problem. He wondered about the Dewitts. He tilted his head to one side and studied his new wife with wiser eyes. When he spoke to her, it was with gentleness in his tone. "The most important thing at the moment is seeing to the safety of us all. 'Tis with that end in mind we'll be leaving these premises in the morning, especially if there's danger afoot."

Like the good servant she had become over the years, Sinead shook her head and said, "I can't leave without permission."

"No magistrate living would be punishing you for seeing to the lad's safety, particularly since the Dewitts left him to his own devices at a dangerous time." Connor walked directly to her and lifted her chin in his hand. "Plus, lass, since you were Cavanaugh's wife when he passed and you have remarried, judges in courts might see your position in a new light."

Sinead's face brightened when the thought took hold of her. "Aye, 'tis true. I will think on this further."

"You may not have the time to worry about it if what your da thinks will happen does, in truth, happen." Connor placed an arm around her shoulder and drew her a bit closer. "It is only a matter of time before the gangs and crowds of riotous people turn on the wealthy inhabitants of the city. If they begin to invade this area, we leave."

"Where will we go?" Sinead held her ground, although very aware of Connor's arm. It felt very comforting.

"First, to the Dewitts' summer home in Albany, where we'll inform them we are going farther north to Saratoga." He stared up at the kitchen ceiling and sighed. "Although I'd rather just avoid them, manners dictate we stop to see them."

He lifted Sinead up onto the counter then smiled. "We will stay at your da's home there."

Sinead frowned and shimmied further back on the counter. "My da's home?" She chortled. "He has no home in…" Her voice faded with each word, and she stared at Connor with an inquiring squint.

He smiled down at her and raised one hand to rest on the cabinet behind her. "Aye, he does have a home there. He told me. And from the looks of you, you didn't know, did you?"

She groaned in disbelief. "Nae. Each summer since I've been

living here, the Dewitts go to their home in Albany. Robbie and I went with them last summer before Mister Cavanaugh's death."

She shook her head and smiled to herself. "My da never mentioned what he did during that time. I just assumed he continued with his carriage business, for I never saw him."

Connor reached out to put his other hand on her shoulder. Sinead stared at his hand for a second, and he removed it. "Obviously, your da kept watch over you and Robbie without telling you. We'll find out later, for sure."

"He has a house in Saratoga?" Sinead bowed her head in contemplation. "How very strange!"

"Aye, he does that. Strange indeed that he never told you." His mouth turned up in a crooked grin. "Well, there's no shame in it, and no matter how you fuss, that's where we'll be going until things are sorted out."

"And you expect trouble?"

"Trouble usually trips along in big doses." He put his hands at her waist, lifted her off the counter and set her on her feet. "We'll be leaving in the morning for the north. In any case, this city is not where I choose to live and work." He hesitated, watching her face for some reaction, but saw she merely seemed distracted and puzzled. "But we'll be discussing this at a later time. Agreed?"

Sinead smiled and bobbed her head. "Agreed."

"Then prepare yourself and Robbie for our early departure. I have no idea how much of a trip it might be. If possible, we'll retrieve my trunk from the hotel. I have most of my money with me." He moved toward the kitchen door. "If we can't get there because 'tis too dangerous, I'll cope with what I have with me."

Sinead smiled up at him. There was comfort in her eyes and the impression of trust in the lack of tension of her full lips.

Connor wanted to kiss that mouth but gave her a tiny shove toward the kitchen door instead. "Hurry to your chores, lass."

When she'd left the kitchen, Connor walked around the room, examining the layout. He opened several of the cabinet drawers. He looked at the huge table in the middle of the room. His gaze came to rest on a chunky wooden block with a set of sharp butcher knives protruding from it. Lifting several of the knives from the block, he hefted them in one hand, then put several back. Two, he wrapped in a cloth taken from a drawer.

"Are ye planning on hurting someone with one of those?"

Connor whirled around to face his brother. A corner of Connor's mouth lifted at the sight of Egan, his red hair standing on end and his head moving from side to side in teasing humor.

Egan laughed. "A bit jumpy, are ye?" A wide grin spread over Egan's face. "Well, well, getting armed I surmise."

Connor chuckled. "I didn't expect to see you in here. You took me by surprise." He continued wrapping the knives in cloth. "With all the activity today, I figured you'd be greeting the muse of sleep by this time."

"No more than you, brother. It seems this city has shocked the both of us into an unusual wakefulness, wouldn't you be saying?" Egan moved around the kitchen, taking in all pots and pan hanging from a wrought iron umbrella-shaped fixture secured to the ceiling. "The Dewitts must run a large household, judging from the amount of cooking utensils."

"From the little I've learned about them, they fancy themselves to be grand folks. But, the sight of that woman's reaction to Bowes at the docks on Saturday left me wondering where she came from."

Egan turned to look at Connor. "Ye've got your mind set on leaving this city, the grand folks like the Dewitts and those that are rioting? Ye're going to leave all this wealth around you?"

"Aye. You know me better," Connor said, stepping closer to his brother. "I won't live off the fruits of another man's labor." His voice deepened with concern. "Besides, I want to keep the lass and her son safe. This city is not the place to do that at the moment."

"I agree with all you're saying, Connor, but I have some plans of my own." Egan looked away, making Connor suspicious.

Then, remembering Egan's swift perusal of Isobel, a knowing

twinkle came to his eyes. "And what might they be, I would ask?"

"That maid, Isobel, wishes to return to her parent's home. She can't go across this city by herself, I'm thinking," he casually mentioned in a broad attempt to hide interest.

"So you intend to escort her there?" Connor smirked, "Ever the hero, eh, Egan?"

"Aye. That I am," he said, giving off one of his ready chuckles. "And once she's safe in the bosom of her family, I intend to join with the police department. Maybe I can't help bring some order to this place." Egan smiled in conjunction with Connor's ready laugh. "'Tis an exciting city, despite the troubles."

Suddenly Connor grew serious, anxious about letting his little brother go off somewhere without him. "And how am I to go on without you?"

"Like you always have, Connor." Egan put his hand out in a soft gesture. "You made most of the decisions on our journey here, just like you always did, even at home. You're the strength of the O'Malleys, laddie. Ye always have been."

He stepped closer to Connor. "You'll be doing what's right for your wife and the lad and for yourself. Of that I have little doubt."

In a voice filled with sadness, Connor murmured, "Da would not approve of our separating from each other."

"He thought it might happen, or so he said to me."

Suddenly, Connor thought of Egan as a man. The idea of his brother growing up hurt and he turned away.

"We like different things, you and me. Besides, it won't be for long, Con." Egan leaned his frame against a counter, stared at the floor then looked up. "Ye'll be coming back here to ship yer family over to Ireland."

"It seems there are a few legal impediments in the way — ones I didn't figure on. Da didn't tell me about them either. It might be a while before I can return, Egan." Connor put a hand on Egan's arm. "'Tis worried I'll be for you."

"Then I'll come to you whenever I can and as quickly as I can.

We'll not be separated for long." He stood straighter, more like a grown man. "I'll be as safe as I can be within the police organization."

Egan might act more grown-up, but the idea of leaving him behind still didn't sit well with Connor.

As if he understood his brother's worry, Egan's face grew sad. He softly murmured, "Beside Con, I have to take responsibility for my own life sooner or later."

"Aye, that you do, boyo." Connor ruffled Egan's hair then slapped his brother on the back. He brought his fist up in a playful gesture.

Egan swiveled away from the counter and took a fighter's stance, hunched over. The two began their usual playful tussles, before clasping each other tightly for a moment.

CHAPTER FOURTEEN

The day dawned hot and dry with an overlay of smoky residue from the day before. Moments after waking, Connor heard shrieks and screams rising in the distance. They penetrated his consciousness.

He leaped from the floor in the foyer where he had slept on a soft rug and untangled himself from the sheet he draped over his tired, bruised body. Darting to the front door of the mansion, he opened it cautiously and peered out, looking up and down the Avenue. Slowly, he eased himself out onto the porch, keeping his body pressed against the edge of the building.

The rumblings grew louder and more agonized. Connor realized crowds were crystallizing somewhere out of sight. The only indication of their whereabouts came from smoke rising into the sky near the piers, blocking off access to the water. Although Connor was not sure of the implications, it seemed to him the people's attacks were beginning to focus on areas of wealth. That meant they would come in this direction.

Not liking the outcries and clamor reaching his ear, he raced back into the house, slammed the door and shouted to Bowes and his brother on his way to the study. "Get up everyone. Hurry. 'Tis time to rise and leave here."

Bowes was the first to leap to his feet. Looking rumpled and disgruntled, he rushed to the back area of the house, calling out over a shoulder, "I'll have the horses ready in no time. The rest of you best be getting yourselves ready for a long, tedious journey."

Rubbing his eyes and stretching, Egan followed Bowes out of the room.

Connor knocked on the door of the study. "Sinead, Isobel, I believe crowds of people are coming this way. I can hear the voices, and I don't wish any of us to remain in the path of monsters."

Connor heard Sinead say to Isobel. "Please, could you get Robbie dressed and ready to leave here? I'll go pack some food." The knob on the door turned. Sinead appeared in the doorway.

Isobel called, "Jane, wait." She put her hand forward in a quiet gesture. "I'll help, then I'm going home to my folks." Tears streaked her face as she moved closer to the door. "I cannot travel upstate with you. I'm fearful for my family's safety."

Sinead turned and stared at Isobel. "I think you're foolish to try to cross the city in its present state, but I do understand. No doubt, I would be doing the same thing."

Sinead remained in the doorway and held her arms out to gather Isobel in them. The sobbing girl made Sinead fearful, but she hugged her and kissed both her cheeks. "Shush, lass. Don't worry. Ye do what you have to do."

Isobel went back into the study, calling, "Come, Robbie. It's time to get clothed. You're going on a fine journey."

"I'll see you as soon as Robbie and I return," Sinead said, crossing into the hall. "If everything is fine with your parents, find a way to come to me." She nodded to Connor, crossed the foyer and went through the recessed door to the kitchen hallway.

The kitchen looked drab and empty in the cool light of dawn. The Dewitts had taken most of the baskets from the hooks in the ceiling. Much of the food was gone as well. Perturbed, Sinead grabbed several tins, and bags, then reached to remove large pieces of ice from the icebox.

She shook her head. There were not enough. She grabbed a pick from the counter table and chipped away until she had enough to line the bottom of the tins. Opening the icebox further, she tossed slices of ham and beef on top of the ice. More ice tumbled in. Chunks of bread and cheese hung from ropes and wires strung up on iron bars. She tossed them into cloth bags she had grabbed upon entering the kitchen.

Her arms full, she staggered out into the hallway then stopped by the back door to lay the food down before continuing on into the big foyer. "I have some food ready to take with us," she told Connor.

"Good," he said, piling what little clothing he found into cases usually used for covering the pillows. "We'll look poorer carrying things like this."

"That's good Irish linen you're putting your things into."

"Don't worry. I'll replace everything we take with more."

Sinead was about to answer when Isobel appeared with Robbie, who was dressed and unusually quiet. "The boy's ready," she stated while staring at the linen sacks.

Connor nodded, moved to the front door and slid outside.

Egan ran in from the back of the house. "Bowes says to hurry." He reached down and grabbed some of the pillowcases from the floor. "Come this way. We'd better go out the back. Bowes has already put the food in the carriage." His arms full, Egan dashed to the kitchen hall, asking, "Where's Connor?"

"Stepped outside. I'll get him." Sinead hurried to the doorway.

Connor, who had run into the street to check on what was happening, came storming back into the house. "Folks are crowding the streets in front of the house. So hurry up."

Egan stopped in his tracks. "Then, it's true. Rioters are building barricades. One of the policemen patrolling outside told me the mob cordoned off the waterfront neighborhoods from the center-island districts." Egan paused, took a deep breath and furrowed his brow. "I guess they're not letting anyone through.

"How the devil are they doing that?" Connor questioned, anger in his voice.

"The policeman said they've cut down telegraph poles." Egan mimicked the action. "They're using those, along with carts, wagons, boxes, brick and any rubbish they can find to run lines along

First and Third Avenues."

"I'll be damned if this isn't the worst city in the world." Connor strode to his brother's side. He grasped him in strong arms. "If you're still intending to do what you said last evening, you'd best be setting out now. He glanced toward Isobel and tipped his head in her direction. "Avoid the crowds. Walk around them, no matter how far you have to travel. And for God's sake, be careful and look to your wits."

The two men hugged fiercely. Without another word, Egan transferred the sacks to Connor and took Isobel's hand. With gentle persuasion, he drew her to the front door, cautiously opening it. Within seconds, they had slipped around the house and away from Connor's view.

Connor's elongated sigh caught Sinead's attention. He stared through a slit in the door opening. His eyes were watery.

"Egan's not coming with us?" she asked, her voice hoarse.

"Nae. He must do what he thinks is right. Our da taught us that." Connor wiped his damp eyes with the sleeve of his shirt. "He's agreed to see Isobel to her parents' home. After she's safe with her family, he'll join up with the police forces until this rioting is done. When the time is right, he'll come to us."

"How will he find us?"

"He will. Somehow. Some way." He bent, picked Robbie up in his arms and settled him on a hip. Noticing the lad's quiet demeanor this morning, he said, "Do not fear, little one, your new da will take god care of you. Just hang on."

Robbie flung his arms around Connor's neck and laid his head against Connor's chin. He clung tightly.

Connor pulled Sinead's hand until it rested on his arm, hoisted the bundles higher in his other arm and started walking toward the back of the house. "Come lass."

She pulled her hand away. "Food. We have to take some more food. I was waiting until you could help me."

"We may not be able to. Come. We have to go through the back.

Your da will have the horses waiting."

Sinead looked around the area, perhaps, for the last time. "I can barely leave this place. It's been my home for what seems like forever."

"Don't worry, lass. We'll soon have another home for you and the lad."

Anger barreled through her. She swung around to face him, knowing that her life was being changed again without her consent. "I have been content here—with my lot in life. I don't want another home."

"We'll see what lies ahead—but after we take care of what's right in front of us." Connor paused, before asking "Has your time here been so happy?"

* * *

The horses were in their traces, ready for movement. They stood with the enduring patience an excessively hot day demanded, heads bowed and eyes half-closed. Bowes hated to work the horses in weather like this, when, most often, they would be grazing in a field near his Saratoga property during the summer heat. Keeping them in the city and working was a necessity this year.

Under great strain, Bowes's thoughts scattered in every direction. He paced beside the carriage, sweat moistening the skin beneath his eyes. With nervous energy, he wiped the sheen from his face with the sleeve of his flimsy undershirt. Sorrow engulfed him, nestled deep inside his guts and rubbed the ache in his stomach.

How have I gotten myself into such a sorry state? He no longer felt as cocky and sure of himself as he was before Annie's death. Her dying, without a single word of good-bye, at the feet of an animal he secretly coveted, had taken all fight and sureness out of him in a single blow. Then the death of his youngest daughter put a keener edge to his sense of loss.

The only thing left to him now was keeping this daughter safe. She had managed to live through disease and grief. Now, he must keep her safe from harm. His promissory marriage obligation to Annie, and now to Sinead, took precedence over everything. This daughter must be saved from all the disasters he believed his life had thrown her way.

While his thoughts scurried, he took a soft towel from the driver's seat and wiped the necks of the grays. He combed their manes again, impatient for those in the house to appear. Thoughts exploded in his brain.

Sinead's happiness, with Robbie, was of utmost importance. Its urgency made him contact Finn O'Malley to beg the man for one of his sons, never realizing he would put such a one in any jeopardy. He did it for his daughter in the hopes it might help keep Robbie at her side.

Bowes did what he always did when troubled over some aspect of his life. He talked it out with his two good friends, the grays. "Hell," he said to them, "if the marriage saves Sinead from a life of misery and regret, I'm glad." He ran the edge of the towel over the equine brow bands and continued his muttering. "The lad, Connor, seemed big enough and strong enough to battle for the lass and her son."

A modicum of fear raced its way through Bowes's body. He shivered in the heat. He thought back over the past week and stood polishing the side of the carriage with the now damp cloth. "You know," he murmured to the animals, "evening after evening, in many of the saloons in me Irish neighborhood, I heard the grumblings and worry of me friends — on a daily basis, too."

The grays turned their heads slightly and rolled their eyes to see their master. He watched the horses' ears perk up each time he spoke to them and smiled. "I have to admit, at times, I commiserated with those very same downtrodden men, particularly after a hideous day of catering to rich men who rode in me carriage, urging us forward."

He leaned forward to pat the neck of the slightly taller animal. "Hurry on. Hurry on, they'd screech at me and I sure didn't like it," he grumbled in a high-pitched tone.

He continued muttering to the animals in the way many horse-man do. "Obvious to any man who has some brains, those men so horribly discontent would attempt to clear the city of its wealthy individuals, of their homes and businesses." He hung the damp cloth on the side of the carriage. "I had no doubt, they would march on Wall Street. No matter 'tis the best-defended area of the entire city."

Bowes reached into the grooming box he kept under the driver's seat. The hard bristles of the brush he was looking for scratched his hand. He pulled his hand and the brush out together and blew on his hand. "I knew many innocents would die in these attempts to create justice for all. Let me tell you, death and dying are ugly things and poor alternatives to discontent."

Moving to the back of the horses, he brushed their tails with a practiced motion before tossing the brush back into the box. To keep busy, he straightened the horses' gear once more and moved around them, patting and murmuring soft words.

"Och, I saw the serious divisions occurring in the rioter's ranks. When I originally talked to me friends in the saloons about the draft, they mentioned a one-day anti-draft demonstration. Nothing more."

The results of yesterday's display had forced Bowes to abandon any thoughts of rebellion against the authorities. In fact, at this point, if he didn't need to get Sinead, the laddie and her new husband out of the city, he would have joined the authorities as young Egan prepared to do. He took the hoof pick from the tack box, bent to clean the horses' hooves.

Soon, he thought, volunteers would line up at the fire and police stations, wanting to defend their neighborhoods against the worst of the rioter and arsonists. In frustration, he grabbed the brush again and, with added vigor, assaulted a tail already hanging straight.

He sensed the diehard rebels would pursue black people. They would brandish poles and clubs to do far more damage than they already done.

The very idea upset Bowes so, he started brushing off the horses' legs with swift, sure strokes, talking to them again in a friendly way. "The bad ones, avengers, will hunt those poor people down where they work. Attack their homes and stores. Until some greater power comes and forces them to suffocate their rage."

As the dangerous times facing everyone worked to the forefront of his mind, Bowes thoughts drifted to his daughter and her dilemma. Her experience in both Dublin and New York had hardened her, but beneath the veneer was a fine young Irish lass. What she never realized, probably his fault, she was truly a country girl, with the gentle, proud ways of her mother. He was sure of it.

Those thoughts made him so uncomfortable his pacing began anew. It was with great relief that he saw his family exiting the Dewitt mansion, through the back door. He straightened to meet them.

Connor, with Robbie's legs wrapped around his waist, held the lad tight with one arm and juggled the cloth bundles in his other arm. He sped from the Dewitts' mansion and down the back garden path, leaving the wrought iron gate wide open.

Sinead followed, carrying bundles clutched to her chest. Barely able to see over what she carried, she darted across the alleyway on swift, silent feet.

No words were spoken as Sinead leaped into the back of the open carriage, dropping her baggage on the floor. Connor shoved Robbie into her arms then bound onto the driver's seat next to Bowes and sat back.

When Bowes saw everyone was safely secured, he climbed to the driver's seat, clucked to the horses, and flicked the reins to urge them to a brisk trot . Supreme anxiousness compelled him to move those he loved out of the city environs as quickly as he could. They headed north, to Saratoga and a different life.

Down the alley they went, far faster than they should have, until they came to the end, facing another alley between huge buildings bordering Fifth Avenue. A block away, loud screams and calls reverberated in the distance, and the occupants of the carriage could smell smoke hovering over the city.

The carriage scooted left onto the main part of the avenue. Fire bells rang and clanked behind them. Piercing blasts of whistles split the air, along with the rumbling shrieks of bedeviled people.

Connor stood, stepped into the carriage, and glanced over his shoulder. "Some sort of collision, between the rabble and the authorities, must be happening several blocks farther down the avenue."

Connor's thoughts and worries over Egan's welfare escalated. He knew his brother's thinking processes often moved quickly, sometimes with dire consequences. "Och, Jaysus, I pray Egan's bright nature and smart mouth help him make his way safely through the devastation prevailing in this place."

He sat back abruptly, his hands grasping his knees, his head bowed. Sinead touched his arm with a soft pat or two, her nose wrinkled from the smell of ash. Robbie scooted over in the seat to sit closer. Seemingly unaware of their attempts at comfort, Connor settled into bad memories.

It was shortly more than a month since Egan and he left their home in Ireland. On a balmy, serene Saturday morning in July, they had arrived in America at a New York City port. The wharves bustled with activity and noise, giving an indication of what life might offer here. That day, Connor had watched his wife faint at the sight of him, the very wife who had patted his knee only moments ago.

He shifted in his seat slightly to stare at her in an oblique manner. She sat as still as a statue, staring down at her hands folded and resting on her lap. Her hair, uncapped and clean now after her bath last night, rained delicate, soft copper curls around her face. Her light blue eyes, so unlike the sparkling sapphire jewels his mother sometimes wore, were huge with fright and roving over every inch of ground they passed. Yet, her back remained straight despite her fear, and she smiled at the lad who, thankfully, did not quite realize the seriousness of their situation.

Ashes descended over the carriage, and Connor batted them away. He lifted Robbie onto his lap, hoping to protect the lad from debris, but his thoughts were concentrated on his wife.

Och, she was brave, for sure, but cold-natured, he thought. Lovely to look at, but difficult to deal with if she didn't get her own way. Well, that would have to change. He shook his head and almost groaned aloud. How had his father talked him into such a baleful slice of life?

Bright streaks flamed across the sky to meet the sun, adding more heat to the day and further memories of the upsetting arrival in New York. Saturday evening, while waiting for Sinead's da, flashed before him. Egan and he had gotten into a brawl with Irishmen over something he didn't even understand. He did now.

The outcome of that battle was a jail cell, locked up by others formerly from Ireland. An embarrassment to him. He'd never been in such a place before.

The shouts of marauders on the street got louder. Bowes spurred the horses to a faster pace. Connor was unable to relieve the black memories, not even when Robbie climbed off his lap and crawled over to Sinead, who never once looked in Connor's direction but stared straight ahead as if navigating the way.

An especially loud shout from one perpetrator of misery brought the stinking, infested jail to mind. Sunday, when Egan and he were let out, they were put into the hands of those who controlled lives but who seemed to dislike the thought. Bruised and battered in body and spirit, he and his brother felt like refugees from a penal colony. Egan had gone in one direction, Connor in another. That evening, the only good thing in Connor's fleeting memory was the ability to bathe, to be clean.

The sound of racing feet and people tossing things into the streets assailed those in the carriage. The horses briefly shied but quickly righted themselves as they turned onto Fifth and tore up the avenue.

After hearing about the disturbances in the city on Monday, the family raced through several serious altercations, only to become completely involved in a flaming riot at an orphanage. They had gotten more bruised, burned and exhausted. Only the joy on the wee lad's face, when he saw them, made the day brighter for Connor, who was still concerned about what might come.

Police whistles sounded several block away. The whirr of sirens rent the air. Flames rose in the sky to streak the day with red tinges. Smoke and ash fell everywhere around them, carried softly on what little wind there was. Sparks hit the grays' rumps. The horses bolted forward.

Bowes clutched the rein with all the force he could muster. "Slow down, ye idjits." He touched their hind ends with a short whip. "Whoa. Pay attention, now. Whoa," he called in an elongated voice meant to reassure and soothe.

It was only Tuesday, the fourth day after Connor's arrival in America. He had lost sight of his favorite brother, each fleeing for his life in a different direction. Connor had an added group to tend. In this whole world, all he wanted was to return to Ireland, his family and his horses.

*　*　*

They had gone no more than ten miles when a vague indirect light spread from the far horizon they had recently vacated and blocked out the rays of the sun. Tongues of fire from downtown areas streaked through the sky. They lapped at the sun with claw-like fingers.

Gray smoke spread uptown, a surprise for such a cloudless, windless day. Soon the sky behind the carriage was dark with hot cinders and more ash, which floated over them from the south and east. The smell was cloying.

Connor spotted a mean-looking group of about seven unruly men gathering in the road up ahead of them. They carried large chunks of wooden cudgels and stood in a straggly line as if daring the carriage to pass.

A blood lust glittered in the eyes of several. A slight hint of madness contorted another's broad, sweat-greased face. They crouched, as if ready to charge the carriage like bulls in a blind rage.

Their crooked, deceptive grins and grimaces struck fear in Connor's heart. He looked around the area, hoping to find another possible avenue of escape but none appeared. They were blocked in.

A spray of blinding orange and blue sparks roared and shot into the sky, matched only by growls and snarls from the gang barring the roadway. Heat rose from the vanished sun, making fears magnified. The men screeched with gleeful fury, their eyes fixed on the flames, loving the sinuous undulations of it. One man with a dangerous sneer turned and refocused his gaze on those in the carriage.

Bowes stood, his hands clutching the reins, a whip in his free hand. "Hey there, Hogan, me friend," he shouted to one of the men. "Haven't seen ye in far too many days. Come on over. I would be having a word with ye."

The brute of a man called Hogan took a step forward. His crooked smile became a sneer then disappeared before he took another two steps toward the carriage. "Whatcha' doing here Brennan?" he asked. "Ye're not a fool. Ye must be knowing 'tis not a good time to be roaming the streets."

The shuffling crowd of men in back of Hogan bellowed with coarse laughter and spit bolts of coarse derisive remarks in the direction of the carriage. They quickly closed in behind the man who was obviously their leader.

Connor's hot blooded Irish temper rose in unreasoned anger at the folks who seemed to want to stop him from protecting his new family. These were the very same people who caused horrendous devastation around town on Monday. Although he understood he should not rile them further, he needed to get past them to some sort of safety.

Without turning around, he tipped his head to one side and slung words at Sinead, from the corner of his mouth. "Take the boy in your arms. Do not let him wriggle or speak. Make him pretend he's ill."

He leaped over the door of the carriage, knowing full well he was taking a terrible chance by approaching the group of ruffians on foot. They had heavy cudgels with which to fell him, but he barely stopped his forward movement, except to pat Bowes's knee and give orders. "If I can make my way through and move them from one side or the other, take the carriage by them with as much speed as you can."

Connor knew the danger, but rage churned relentlessly through him. The smile plastered on his face ached with animosity but he did not falter in his steady movements forward

Sinead called out, "Connor, come back here." When he ignored her, she poked her da on the arm. "Make him come back. They'll kill him if they've a mind to. We can't let that happen."

"Daughter, do what the man asked of ye. Take Robbie in yer arms and rock him back and forth as if he were sick or diseased somehow."

Sinead burst into ragged and uncontrollable sobbing. She swayed in her seat until she had control of herself and could reach out. With tears dripping down her face, she pleaded, "Robbie, lad, come to Mama, darlin'. Rest your wee head on my lap. Remember when you were sick with the terrible coughs. Your new da needs you to be acting like you're terribly sick. Can you do that for Mama, love? For your new da?"

With wide-open, terror-stricken eyes, Robbie flung himself down onto Sinead's lap and clutched at her skirt. He groaned and shrieked as if in pain, all the while never taking his eyes from her face. Tears trickled from his eyes in sympathy and fear. They rolled down his face to his chin, mixed with the ash floating in the air and mottled his face.

"Hogan, me daughter's having hysterics behind me here, wanting to get our laddie to a new doctor before it's too late. We need to be moving on. To save the wee youngster. With yer permission, for sure," Bowes shouted, using a smile and deferential movement of his head to indicate a way through the crowd.

Hogan strode forward belligerently. "Who in hell is this brute coming at me?" With a show of bravery, Hogan straightened, sneered then stepped to one side. He bent and clasped a large stump in his hands. He looked up at Connor with shifty eyes. "Well, who are ye?"

"I'm the wee lad's da. Me son is sick," Connor answered, not taking his eyes from Hogan's. "Ye need only to look at him, suffering in his mama's lap."

"If ye're the lad's da, how come I don't know ye?" one of the men in the crowd screamed out. He followed his question with a high pitched laugh, like a hyena's.

"I've just returned from the old sod. Me own da was sick and needed tending," Connor lied, without a blink. He was ready to fight if need be, hoping he needed no weapons other than his bare hands.

"What's wrong with the laddie?" Hogan asked.

"We're not sure, but we're thinking it might be the small pox or diphtheria. We're trying to get him out of the city before he infects more folks." Connor moved forward and put his hand out in supplication. "Now, I'm figuring Irishmen, like yerselves, will do for one another and a wee Irish laddie."

"Och, Jaysus. Stay away from me man," Hogan said, holding his arm straight out toward Connor. "You're likely carrying the disease yerself…" The man backed up until he stumbled into the men in back of him. "Move, ye stupid bastards The've got sickness there."

The others bumped and pushed each other back. Their fearsome animosity collapsed under the fright of possible illness. They stood silently in Hogan's shadow, grumbling amongst themselves, considering their options.

They were an incongruous blend of opposing forces, shaking their heads and waving their fists at each other now. Sides were chosen and alliances made there on the street.

Hogan made the final decision. "Man, get back up into yer carriage," Hogan instructed, his dark, destructive need for vengeance momentarily diffused. "We'll be making a wide path for ye."

He and his men moved to the sides of the roadway. He nodded to Bowes. "Go on through, man. And don't be coming back here until the lad and the rest of ye are free of disease."

"Aye, man. And I'm thanking ye, Hogan." Bowes moved the carriage forward at a slow pace. He stopped only long enough for Connor to mount the driver's bench. Then in the midst of a flurry of ash rising from the road, he pushed the horses into a fast canter. Dust and dirt climbed the air, going higher than before. It flew above the men on the road like cinders from the fires of the day before.

CHAPTER FIFTEEN

Traveling north through the upper reaches of New York City was a frightening experience for the members enclosed in Bowes's carriage. Minor battles with gangs of rowdy people, going in all directions, some fleeing the city, others seeking revenge on the blacks and rich, ensued every few blocks.

Shouts traveled through the air. Connor saw a gang running toward their roadway. He grabbed the reins from Bowes and made the horses gallop past. "Move on grays," he called. "Good boys..."

No sooner had they gotten passed one gang, another surfaced from a side street. They all brandished large stick which they waved in the air. They threw paving blocks at the carriage, several reaching their goal.

"On grays." Bowes clucked as loud as he could, hoping the animals could hear him. Again, the horses raced forward.

The carriage was assailed every few miles, until they were totally outside the city's environs. Fortunately, Bowes and Connor were able to jolly people out of doing damage to the carriage or those that rode in it.

Once totally clear of the city, relief overcame them. The horses, sweating profusely, slowed their pace to a walk. Bowes wheezed and coughed the effects of the ash into his hand. Connor groaned and leaned back in the seat. Robbie hiccupped and cried softly.

Sinead murmured soothing words to him. "'Tis all right, now, darlin'. Everything's fine. It will be just grand, our little vacation."

Robbie laid his head down in Sinead's lap. The people traveling together through the anguish of riots did little talking to each other.

During the first day on the route upstate, Robbie, deep in some secret child's place, refused to look at anything outside of the carriage.

No matter how Sinead cajoled him, "Robbie, look. 'Tis a blue bird," or tried to interest him in some unusual natural wonder, he merely clung to her skirts, fearful and weepy.

"Robbie. Look at the river flowing past."

No response came.

"The white sails on that cutter are blowing hard against the wind. See, Robbie."

Finally, at a loss as to how to console him and take away his fears, she let him keep his head in her lap or huddle in a corner of the carriage. She continued to murmur to him and tried to rid him of his angst with soft Irish lullabies.

Connor, sitting on the driver's seat with Bowes, was entranced by the sound of her songs. They made him nostalgic for home and seemed to heal a space left by the death of his beloved mother, a space he was not aware he had. He felt soothed and renewed by the singing.

The further they got from the city, the more the tension produced by the riots left them. Connor got out of the carriage and stretched his legs. In a bit of energy, Connor swung Robbie up onto broad shoulders and ran with him alongside the moving vehicle.

The boy gasped and hung on to Connor's forehead. Only then did childish fears leave the boy. With his short legs wrapped around Connor's shoulders, and his hands fully entrenched in Connor's hair, Robbie began laughing, grinning at Bowes and looking around at the scenery.

When Connor placed him on the ground, he continued to hold him close with a hand on the young boy's neck.

Thereafter, throughout what seemed like a long voyage, Robbie's little arms reached for Connor at every opportunity. Each time the lad returned to his place in the carriage, he would hug Sinead with gleeful, boyish intensity. "I love you Mama Jane. I mean, Mama Sinead. I like that better."

His outlandish giggles when Connor was around forced her to reevaluate the worth of this hurried trip out of the city and into the country. Perhaps, it wasn't such a poor idea, after all.

Again, Connor lifted Robbie from the ground, whirled him in a circle and deposited him in the carriage. Connor winked at Sinead, a broad smile on his face. Robbie hugged her then whispered, "Mama, I love my new da." His bright laughter soared in the air.

They made it to Albany in a matter of days, camping out or staying at inns along the route. Past Albany, the lower humidity and slight westerly breeze made the journey on the main road to Saratoga more comfortable. Sinead relaxed. She showed more patience with Robbie's boyish antics and total inability to remain quiet for more than ten minutes at a time. In fact, she was beginning to enjoy the journey.

She had a chance to think on the slow ride north, and on the subsequent nights huddled together sharing one big room at inns along the way. Many thoughts surfaced in her mind, most of which she pushed aside for a later time.

* * *

"Robbie seems terribly fond of Connor, already," she said to her da one evening while viewing the incredible sky, filled with stars of every magnitude. "Look at them cavorting down by the river."

"Aye," Bowes responded, "skipping stones. 'Tis almost hard to tell who the bigger laddie is."

Sinead laughed. "I think perhaps Connor fits that bill." One small ray of hope surfaced. "I'm just glad they get along." She put her arm on Bowes's and they strolled together down toward the two who were playing.

She shivered and pulled the shawl closer around her shoulder. Her mind taken up with the upcoming lawsuit over Robbie, she didn't give proper attention to the big step she had taken in getting married to a stranger, sight unseen.

Bowes poked her arm. "Look at them. Chasing each other, they are."

"Da, deny as I might like to deny, I saddled myself with the encumbrance of a husband. Being concerned about other things, I said little in how the marriage took place, or where, or even when. 'Tis my own fault, I guess."

"Nae, lass, I'm thinking I forced the decision on ye. But it was because of me own worry over the lad." He patted her arm. "'Tis glad I am to be having this talk with me favorite lass."

She chuckled then mumbled, "I'm determined to have a say in how and where this unwanted marriage is to continue. Perhaps the short sojourn in Saratoga will work just fine, but I have no intention of staying there beyond August." She added that fact to the list of demands written in her brain, a list her new husband would need to follow if he wanted her cooperation.

"Telling a man where and how he's going to live is not the way to get on his best side, daughter. Ease back a bit. Let yourself see his true value. Look closely..." Bowes watched his daughter out of the corner of his eye.

She saw the look her da flashed and smiled. "I'll try. My feelings about him changed since the day I met him at the dock, a week ago." What she didn't say to her father was that Connor provoked a strong and distracting presence, an attraction of sorts. With no intention of ever admitting her plans to him, she'd decided Connor was worth the bother and the risk of marriage.

Heat rushed up her body, her face growing hot with the strength of her thoughts. Confusion over revitalizing something never thought of — respect, admiration and possibly love — was a negative force. It stopped her thoughts in their track. How might she gain his true interest?

A swirling wind tossed a few fallen leaves up in the air. Robbie ran, trying to catch them in his hands. He laughed when they fell onto his bare knees and tickled him. Laughing, Connor picked him up, tossed him in the air once and slung the boy over his shoulder belly down.

Robbie pounded on Connor's back, screeching, "I'm gonna' get sick. I'm gonna' get sick."

"You better wait until I bounce you around a bit," Connor said as he heaved his shoulder upward.

"Ugh…"

Bowes and Sinead laughed and began running down the slight incline to the river. "Wait for us," Bowes cried. "We'll all play." He pulled on Sinead's arm until they fell and rolled down the hill to the others.

Connor put Robbie on the ground and went to help Sinead rise. Her face was flushed with excitement and lovely to look at. He took a deep breath.

Robbie ran to her and grabbed at her skirt. "Look Mama." He pretended to box the leaves away all the way back to the carriage.

Sinead's laughter shot out like a bolt of lightning. Connor turned around and smiled down at her. "I like the sound of your laughter. It pleases me."

"I'm thankful," she responded. "I think 'tis time we got on the road again, if we intend to make Saratoga before midnight."

"I still need to stretch my legs a bit. Would you be of a mind to walk a bit with me, lass?" he asked, raising his eyebrows in an effort at playfulness. His smile was easygoing, almost sheepish.

"Aye, I might like a walking spell myself," she replied with a quick, staccato beat. Her heart raced at the deep, masculine timbre of his voice. A prickling at the back of her neck worried her but she nodded.

A broad smile on his face, Connor turned, knelt and drew Robbie to him. The boy's small arms went around Connor's neck

"You have a choice here, laddie," Connor said in a stern voice, pretending grave seriousness. "You can either ride up here with your Grandda Bowes or you can walk with your mama and me."

"I don't want him sitting on the driver's bench," Sinead shouted, her attitude flinty, her breath blasting out in a rush. "He's too small." She wagged her finger at her father, giving off signs of her temper brewing. "What if he falls off, gets entangled in the horses' legs and crushed beneath their feet?"

"Och, daughter, stop yer fearful ways." Bowes met his daughter's furious stare. "I'll keep the laddie on me lap. Nothing will happen to him, for sure, no more than anything happened to you when you were young and I carried you on me lap."

"I don't remember our ever doing that," she retorted, her good mood spoiled.

Bowes ignored her and poked Robbie on the arm. "We'll drive this old carriage together," he said, looking at Robbie and shaking his head in the affirmative. "Come here on yer grandda's lap, me young boyo. Sit with this old codger, and we'll drive all the way to Saratoga together."

Robbie let Connor settle him on Bowes's lap then giggled. He reached his short arms and hands back around Bowes's neck and hugged him tightly. "I love you, Grandda. Even when I was very little I've wanted to drive the horses, but Mama never let me." He looked at his mama, put his hand up to cover his mouth and whispered into his grandfather's ear, "She's afraid of horses, you know."

Bowes nodded. "I know, laddie, I know."

"Why is she so afraid?" His childish words hung in the quiet.

Bowes weathered face crumpled. "It's a long story, lad, but I'll be telling ye someday."

Intrigued, Connor cocked his head to the side. "And a story I'd like to be hearing myself," Connor interjected, smiling and nodding to them both. He scooped Sinead up into his arms, swung her around and set her back on the ground with great gentleness. "There ye go, lass. I'll just hold your arm for a moment until you get your walking legs under you."

"Och, I'm fine already," she said, easing out of his grasp, a tingle racing up her arm to her shoulder. His eyes held hers in a strange way.

Robbie clasped the reins in his hands. His grandfather fixed them properly with the correct placement. Bowes turned in his seat and said, "We're going to take a bit of a run down the road here…"

"No!" Sinead turned to the carriage. "Da, you can't be taking Robbie if you're going to go fast."

Bowes scowled down at her. His lips twisted ruefully in a plea. "Ye've got to stop yer caterwauling, lass. The boyo has to grow to be a man. Take care of yer own problems for the moment."

Sinead inhaled sharply. "Problems?" Her voice throbbed low. "Da, I don't have problems."

"Aye, ye do, and he's walking right next to ye." He waved a hand, dismissively. "See to yer man, Sinead." With that, he snapped the reins and the horses moved forward at a quicker pace, leaving Sinead and Connor in a fine puff of road dust.

Sinead arched a brow, watched the carriage move away, then waved her hands around to dispel the dust settling over her. In doing so, she turned her face away from Connor and squared her shoulders.

"Come, walk on the grass. It'll be more comfortable for your feet and the dust won't be as bad."

Sinead hesitated, shuffling her feet on the grass behind him but not responding verbally. She merely did as she was instructed and looked up at Connor through narrowed eyes.

The two walked silently along the grass strip at the edge of the road. Connor reached and pulled a leaf from a low hanging branch. He held it between his thumbs and tried to make it whistle. Content with not speaking, Sinead studied his every movement.

Conner possessed powerful shoulders and arm muscles. The column of his neck was strong and sinewy, his mouth sensual, his nose long and aquiline. He was a handsome man, she thought, refusing to admit that to anyone, much less herself.

Everything about him was hard, though. He was a fit figure of a man but contained too much inner strength for her. She didn't want to be a lesser figure in this marriage. She sighed deeply, instinctively knowing that he kept Robbie and her safe. She coughed to get his attention.

Connor didn't notice. Other than a strong pang of homesickness for the lovely green fields of his Irish home, he strolled companionably along the road with his wife. *Wife*. The concept was difficult to fasten in his mind, other than his having a responsibility for her. He stared down at her, wondering what her thoughts might be but afraid to ask.

He enjoyed looking at her smooth body, the lovely flawless texture of her skin. He intended to be careful, to speak in guarded words about the issues they needed to discuss. He didn't want to rile the temper of which he'd seen flashes. Not now, at least.

"You know, lass, there are things we need to straighten out between us in order to make things right for the boy." Silence followed his opening gambit into serious talk. But her body betrayed her. It tightened with the expectation of a confrontation she was not ready for.

"I know you want to be kind…"

"Sinead, do not mistake kindness for weakness," he said, his tone harsh.

Her eyes flared with an unnamed emotion. Their color deepened. Her eyebrows rose. She leveled her gaze at him. "We don't know each well enough to converse about any subject, unless you wish to discuss the riots in New York."

Connor was taken aback. He sighted her like a hunter his prey and let his penetrating gaze bore into her, relentlessly. "Now why would I be wanting to discuss something I found a most horrendous, evil thing. I prefer not to recognize that in people, especially in those of Irish descent. It has spoiled all my illusions about my own people."

"But it happened, with most of our Irish folks doing great damage to a fine city, along with some of the Germans thrown in."

"I knew nothing of their discontent with the original populace who lived there. I only arrived a few days ago, and I've not experienced a pleasant day since. I neither condone nor sympathize with their actions."

"Then just be quiet about it," Sinead said.

There was an edge to her voice that surprised him. It was a quiet reminder that the peaceful conversation he envisioned had become just another battleground. He wondered why it bothered him so much but knew he needed to break the tension. He raised his head to sniff the air. A clean, fragrant scent of pine filled his nostrils and the sound of running water filled his ears.

"I hear a stream across the road. Perhaps, we should be stopping here for a bite of food." he suggested.

His hand dropped to her arm in order to stop her movement forward. She looked up at him with a puzzled expression and a halfhearted smile. The need to touch her rippled through him. The desire to posses her flashed within him. His hand tightened on her arm. He pulled her a bit closer but concentrated on what was missing from her smile.

She recoiled and rubbed her arm. He awakened something inside her, but what that might be was a mystery to him. There was a pull there, an attraction. At least on his part.

With no sign of her feelings, she scampered up onto the road, put her hands on each side of her mouth and shouted, "Da…"

Bowes had already turned the carriage around to wait for them. He shouted back, "Sinead, the laddie says he's hungry as a bear." Robbie tittered into his hand then waved to his mama.

Connor stood where he was and watched his wife run toward the carriage. He saw her take out a bundle tied with a dark brown cord and put it down on the road. Then she reached into the back seat again. A rug of sorts, one they used several times before for their lunches, flipped out into the dust.

Sinead walked away from the vehicle toward the stream, until she came to a small copse of trees. She shook the rug out then laid it on the ground in an area shaded from the sun by giant maple trees.

She waved to three standing by the carriage. "Come on, you

three. Da, bring the bundle of food over here. I'll lay it all out on the rug. Connor, would you be taking Robbie for a wash in the stream? Don't be letting him play in the water."

Connor nodded, came forward and took Robbie's hand in his own. Somewhat disconcerted at his wife's change of mood, he turned to Bowes. "When do you think we'll be arriving in that city of Saratoga?"

"Before dark. We'll settle into a boarding house there and, if we have time, we'll go look at the property I have and the small house I've put up on it."

Connor stared at the man who had become a significant part of his new family. He nodded an invitation for Bowes to walk with him. "Is it true what you told me about the racing track they're figuring on putting in on the way to your place?" Connor asked with great interest. "Whoever *they* are."

"Wealthy interests, laddie. Like I told ye, there's wealth in Saratoga Springs. Not quite the same as it was before the war started."

"What do you mean?" Connor asked.

"In the old days, people from the South came here to drink and play in the waters. Although, some of them still manage to sneak up here for a spell in the warm weather, 'tis harder for them now that they're in the midst of a damned war."

Robbie pulled on Connor's hand and was shushed momentarily. "In a minute, laddie."

Bowes continued as if he hadn't been interrupted. "An overgrown Irishman like yerself, by the name of Morrissey, seems to have taken over many of the gambling interests and sporting events, like the racing." Bowes winked and grinned slyly.

Connor grinned back at him, in agreement with the older man. "Now, Morrissey's a man I'd like to be meeting..."

"And I'll be seeing to that very thing, come morning." Bowes chuckled, picked up the bundle from the road and stomped off toward his daughter.

The carriage rolled on though the tidy, vibrant village of Saratoga Springs, stirring up a bit of dust under the wheels. Although anxious to get to the boarding house, the occupants of the back seat stared at everything with wide eyes, craning their neck to see and trying to seem inconspicuous at the same time.

Large trees and huge hotels lined the main thoroughfare like the walls of a canyon. Men in expensive black broadcloth and women in the latest fashions jammed the porches of hotels and brick paved walkways.

A parade of grander carriages than their own moved down the street, all with blankets of crimson velvet, lined with satin and edged in gold lace. They led a processional advance of even more elegant, well-dressed people, riding and strutting about, conversing, nodding to friends. The sound of music floated over the avenue.

Having made Connor sit in the back before coming into the grander parts of the village, Bowes sat alone, on the driver's seat, his body upright and his gaze straight ahead. He did manage to wave at several people who called out his name. Connor looked about with great interest, studying the magnificence of the surroundings and the people who seemed to parade and saunter to some unheard rhythm.

Sinead dusted off her garments and drew a long scarf around her shoulders. She looked to see if Robbie was presentable. He kept jumping up between Connor and Sinead, pointing his fingers at all sorts of new sights.

"Look, Mama. Look, Da." Everything in the town seemed to delight him. "Look here. Look over there." The barrage of excited words and pointed fingers, to which both Connor and Sinead answered, "I see. I see," was constant.

Without stopping, they traveled down the main street, took a right and turned into a quieter section of the village. Shortly, they reached the simple gray and white boarding house where Bowes had stayed while he worked on the house he was building. Even after his house was finished, he stayed on as a boarder, for he didn't like living alone away from all the action.

A woman with a round, pleasant Irish face and bright red hair, a bit younger than Bowes, greeted him as a long-lost hero. Her hug was grand, eloquent. "Och, Bowes, me friend, 'tis happy this Pegeen is to have ye back in the fold. I've missed ye, ye old buzzard."

Several well-dressed young ladies, who had been lounging in the sitting room off the main entrance when they arrived, rushed into the hallway to welcome him, obviously joyful at his return. They surrounded him.

"One yellow-haired girl cried out, "Bowes, you're here again. Will you stay a while this time?"

A dark-haired beauty screeched, "We didn't get to see enough of you last summer." She tittered into her hand when Pegeen glared at her.

Somewhat embarrassed, Bowes nodded and introduced his family amid much noise and exuberance. Several of the young women eyed Connor quite brazenly, and Sinead grew annoyed over his preening in front of them. His instant rapport with them was ridiculous, she thought to herself. He acted as if he had known them for years.

With almost no trouble, for they brought little luggage with them, the tired O'Malley family and Bowes settled into their upstairs rooms. While Sinead and Robbie ate a cold meal in their room, Connor and Bowes untacked the horses, brushed them down then fed and watered them.

The horses were ready for the short jaunt to Bowes's house, which was supposedly only a mile or so away, overlooking the shores of Saratoga Lake.

Although tired from their long journey, Connor, Sinead and Robbie climbed up into the carriage. Pegeen, whom Bowes had invited, sat next to him on the driver's seat. The horses grew a bit frisky for they sensed they were nearing a place they enjoyed. They entered the rutted road to the property with high-stepping energy, and the sound of Pegeen's laughter, almost a chortle, over something Bowes whispered to her.

The sun was almost down, but it was still light enough by the time they reached the part of Bowes's land where they could see the outline of the house from the road. A brooding straggle of stone, all gray and brown in the soft pink of fading light, clung to a grassy knoll overlooking a valley of green fields. The shape of the house seemed to move in many directions at once.

A bulky wedge of forest, with massive oaks, huge maples, several sturdy elms and hundreds of fir trees surrounded the back and sides of the house. Smaller trees grew at the front, just enough to shade the house yet grant a good view of the green fields below. A fast-moving, rocky stream ran through the largest and most level of the lower fields.

"My god, Bowes, what a wonderful place for the raising of horses," Connor excliaimed

"Aye, that's always been my dream. The winters are a bit rough on the beasts but they grow stronger, and most often, healthier," he said, glancing at his daughter under his lashes. "Just a dream o' mine, one I couldn't possibly do all by meself."

"If this is where you'd rather be, then why have you been wasting your time in the city for all these years?" Sinead asked, annoyed that he must have confided something of his dreams to Connor and left her out. It was not the first time he'd done that on their journey here, and she didn't like it.

"I would never be leaving Robbie or ye with those Dewitt vultures. Now, would I, darlin'? I had to get yer problem reconciled first." A foolish grin spread across his face, asking for forgiveness.

"Well, now that I have a husband in my pocket, so to speak, do you intend to be leaving me alone to the vultures, now?" In the space of a heartbeat, her anger surfaced. Her voice got more strident. "When I still don't know which end is up?"

"I think I'm leaving ye in competent hands. Don't you think so?"

His shoulders hunched forward as if protecting himself. He cast a glance at Connor, who, with Robbie on his lap, only shook his head and grinned. Bowes sputtered, "Those hands certainly look big enough to do a man's job from where I'm sittin'."

Sinead shrugged, disgusted with their bantering. "Och!" She stood up in the carriage, her hand blocking what was left of the glare of the dying sun from her eyes. "The house doesn't really look like it's been lived in, Da. It's got a sad, lonesome look to it."

"Sit down, child, and I'll drive straight up to it."

Sinead plopped back in place. She refused to look at Connor, wanting to wipe the silly grin from his face and from her da's. She sat on the edge of her seat and scrunched her face each time she was jostled by the action of the carriage on the rutted roadway. She clutched the door at the side of the carriage.

Connor said nothing but stared at everything. "Bowes, the place does have a deserted look to it. There must be some reason for that. Why haven't you lived here?"

"I couldn't just move up here by meself. I don't like living alone."

Pegeen chuckled. "You can say that again." She poked Bowes in the arm. "Do ye, man?"

Bowes smiled at her but turned his back. "I bought the place for Sinead and me grandson. For the time when they'd be free to live their own lives, away from the nastiness of the city. The Dewitts put a stopper on me dream, I can tell ye. I couldn't leave New York City without my daughter and grandson, now could I? What kind of man would ye think me to be?"

The truth burst on Connor with startling clarity. He saw the need in Bowes face, in his posture, in his voice.

Sinead did too. She snapped, "Then it's me you're blaming for not realizing your dreams?"

"Nae, lassie. 'Tis not yer fault that ye tried to be decent to the Cavanaughs and those others who have little to do with decency."

Connor interrupted. "Let's not argue amongst ourselves. There's much to be done to make this family a real and loving one. We'll all have to work at it and slinging vicious thoughts won't be helping."

The silence gave confirmation of their thoughts. The closer they got to the house, the more Sinead realized how big it was.

Suddenly, Connor saw the shape of it. A longing stabbed through his chest. He was shocked. "Bowes, it looks like O'Malley House at home. Different stone but so much like it. That's very strange," he murmured and stared at Bowes more closely. "Very strange, indeed…"

The carriage pulled up in front of the house. Bowes pulled back on the reins and murmured a soft, "Whoa."

Robbie, who was quiet for a change, asked in a soft voice. "Mama, can I go up to the house? It's like a castle. I like it, and Grandda Bowes said it was for me. And you, too," he added.

Connor leaped down from the carriage and lifted his hands. "Aye, son. Come down." He set Robbie on the ground, held his hand out and approached the porch at the main entrance. "This house is like my home in Ireland, only this porch goes all the way across the front. Mine in Ireland is smaller."

Bowes watched them circle the house. When they finally reappeared on the other side, he took mental note of Connor's expression.

"'Tis a lovely home, Bowes. You should be proud to live here, like a grand duke or something." Connor smiled up at him.

"Nae, 'tis not for me, laddie. 'Tis where Sinead and ye will raise young Robbie and the rest of yer family that's to come. 'Tis a house for a young person, a young family, a home to build on," Bowes said.

Connor's mouth hung open and, knowing his skepticism showed, he stared at Bowes in total disbelief. One didn't give away property and houses. They were the very things that sustained a man. "Why would you be giving a house to us?"

"Ye don't have one here, do ye?"

"Nae, but I have one in Ireland that belongs to my family. When Sinead, Robbie and I go there it'll…"

"What do you mean, when Sinead and Robbie go there?" Sinead stood in the carriage, her hands fisted and set on her hips. With teeth clenched and voice dropped low, she asked, "Whoever said I was going to Ireland, now or ever?"

Her nasty reaction drew Connor's complete attention and pushed him to the brink of anger. Why was she being so difficult? A horrible truth pierced deep into his soul. He tipped his head toward her, losing every bit of desire he felt for her, no matter how lush and vibrant she seemed. "You're a married woman now, lass. You'll go where your husband goes," he growled softly.

The message wasn't lost on her. "First of all, I'm not your lass. Second of all, going to Ireland was never part of this marriage scheme to my knowledge." A derisive smile crossed her face. "I married to save my son, who was given to me by his darling mother at his birth— then by his father who became my first husband. I will not leave Robbie somewhere nor shall I take him away from everything he knows."

"Be careful what you say, Sinead. You may regret it more than you expect," Connor whispered between tight lips, his anger at the forefront.

His whisper was a sinister reminder of all she stood to lose. Sinead pretended to ignore the jab. She climbed out of the carriage and strode directly at Connor, shaking her finger up into his face. "I'll not be staying here in this Saratoga, with you or anyone else. I'll fix up this house for you, and for my da. Then I will go somewhere and make a life for myself and my child."

Anger flooded her voice and lodged an ache in her heart. She looked at her father. "And I won't ever be living here in your house." She rounded on Connor. "You go back to Ireland by yourself if that's your desire. I'll not be going with you, for sure."

Bowes swung around in his seat. "Be quiet. The both of ye. Robbie is coming off the porch. I don't want him to hear yer tongues tripping over themselves. He's been through enough without the two of ye spitting in front of him like two fuming cats."

"Mama, come see," Robbie called out to Sinead. "You can look through the windows and see inside. I saw my room. It has a toy horse in it." Robbie ran to her and hugged her tight. "Is this going to be my house?"

Sinead and Connor stood toe to toe in a battle of wills done through their eyes. Connor's gaze bore more deeply into hers before flicking to Robbie. Sinead lowered her hand and kept it on Robbie's small form, holding him tighter than she might have wanted.

"Are you angry, Mama?" he asked, tipping his head up to see her.

"Oh, not at you darlin'," she answered, about to lash out at Connor again. She bent and put her arms around Robbie. "I'm just surprised. Grandda Bowes gave us his house. We'll have to do some fixing on it, but it will be yours, for sure, in the distant future," she said, glaring at Connor but surprised at herself, knowing she never planned on living in the country. "You don't want to make your other grandparents sad if you left them. You wouldn't want to do that, now would you?"

Bowes scowled but said nothing. He just stood back and watched the actions going on about him. Pegeen stared at the two combatants.

Connor tossed Sinead a baleful look that danced on the edge of a dangerous precipice. "I'll fix up this house until it's looking so fine you'll be wanting to live here forever. Then we'll talk — oh wife of mine." He stormed back to the carriage. "'Tis getting dark. We'd better be going back to the boarding house."

"I'll say it again. I will never live in that house."

Connor grabbed Sinead's elbow. She flinched then snatched it away from beneath his touch. He warred with the hard steel of reserve he'd just erected around himself.

"Aye, that's a good idea ye had, Connor. To go. Let's do it," Bowes said in a loud, hearty voice. "Come Sinead. Robbie. 'Tis time to go back to our rooms at the other place. Sleep has a power all its own. I think we'll be needing a bit o' that."

Sinead climbed into the carriage with reluctance. She was ready to see this battle to its end and send Connor back to his home in Ireland — without Robbie or her. This marriage was a farce. "I may sleep, but I shan't be changing my mind about staying here or going to Ireland."

Connor spun in his seat to face her. "We'll talk about this on the morrow…"

Pegeen spoke up from the driver's seat, next to Bowes. "I know it's none of my business but don't be talking in the presence of the laddie here." She pointed. "Look at the wee tyke. He's plenty upset already."

"Och, Robbie. 'Tis sorry I am, love. Your da and I were merely having a disagreement. You know, like the ones the Dewitts sometimes have, and the servants as well. It doesn't mean anything." She gathered him in her arms and rocked him back and forth.

Her eyes narrowed and her lips tightened as she glared at Connor. When she spoke, the words were for Robbie but the look was for Connor. "Don't you worry, my darlin'. Mama *Jane* will take care of you. Always and ever…"

CHAPTER SIXTEEN

Sunlight glittered through the trees and climbed the tall sash windows. A slight breeze ruffled sheer curtains, flicking them softly against the wood.

The sound penetrated Sinead's consciousness. She drifted drowsily from sleep to semi-wakefulness. She stretched her arms over her head like a lazy cat. Every muscle in her body ached from riding in the carriage for so many days and the tension she held within her since her husband arrived on the ship. Her groan shattered the peaceful silence of the room. She rolled to one side like a limp rag doll, opened one eye and noticed a delicate tracery of tree branches in shifting patterns on the curtains and shiny wood floor.

Where was she? Slightly puzzled, she looked around the room at the ornate furniture, the flowered wallpaper and remembered the trip to Saratoga. She sat up in bed and stretched again.

"Och, Robbie, love, 'tis a most beautiful morning. Perhaps your grandda was right. A good night's sleep solves many problems." Robbie fell asleep in the boarding house room as soon as they returned from her da's property and she not long after. Not wanting to move again, she waited for his answer, but none came.

She glanced at the small iron bed where she placed him last evening after he had fallen half asleep in her arms. Her body straightened and tightened up. He wasn't there. She rolled over and placed a foot on the floor. The child never went anywhere at the Dewitts' without Isobel or her by his side.

She sprang from the bed, panic rising to her throat, and pulled on the clothes she'd worn yesterday, clothes she barely was able to shake out before falling into the featherbed that beckoned to her. Half-buttoned, she sat on the bed and slipped her bare feet into her dusty shoes. She tried to fix the buttons of her shirt as she flew to the head of the stairs, calling, "Robbie? Robbie, darlin'?"

Frantic, not quite awake, she raced down the stairs then peeked into the sitting room. Seeing no one, she tore to the small dining room. "Robbie?" She halted just inside the dining room doorway. "Where is my son?" she asked of the three attractive ladies lounging around a dark, circular table in the center of the room. "Has anyone seen my wee son?"

"Wee?" cried one of the ladies, dressed in a feathery fuchsia nightgown with an untied silk robe drawn over it. She took a long, deep draft of a cigar and let it out in a stream of white smoke.

Sinead began to cough. The other women looked at her as if she were crazy. One shook her head in disbelief then stared.

Sinead looked down at her clothes. Half the buttons were undone and several were buttoned in the wrong place. The material gaped at inappropriate places, and it looked like she had slept in it.

"Och, my heavens," she cried. Tears burned her eyes. Self-consciously, she smoothed the crumbled material of the white cotton shirt.

Pegeen, the owner of the boarding house, who had greeted Bowes so profusely, entered through the swinging door from the kitchen. "Well, and 'tis a good morning to all you late risers." She nodded to the women at the table. Liquid from the cup she held in her hand sloshed to the floor. She put the cup down, grabbed a clean cloth from the sideboard and bent to wipe up the wet spots on the floor.

Sinead stood rooted to the spot and stared at the woman. Something in the voice and relaxed attitude tweaked a memory of the days before America. She tilted her head as if listening but continued to stare with wide eyes.

"And a right good morning to you, young lady. Did ye have a nice sleep?" she asked Sinead, while her light red curls bobbed with every motion. "Just sit right down at the table. I'll get ye some breakfast to fill those bones. Ye must be starved. Ye barely ate enough for a birdie last evening, you being so tired and all."

"Have you seen my son? He's gone from my room Do you know where he is?" Sinead asked, her voice accusatory and rising.

"Why, of course, I do, darlin'. He's gone off with the men folk, with yer husband and da. They went into the village to get new clothes and supplies, they said, but I'm thinking they went along to check things out and see what's going on." Pegeen smiled, a mischievous twinkle in her eyes. "This place is a hotbed of elegance during the summer. All sorts of activities go on for those who come to partake of the waters and those who come just to partake." Raised eyebrows punctuated the remark.

Coarse laughter erupted from the three women at the table.

The flush accompanying the embarrassment of being laughed at streaked its way up Sinead's body. "Why didn't they wake me?"

"Couldn't bear to wake you. They said you were sleeping soundly and far too exhausted. Two kindhearted gentlemen they are, for sure." The woman put her hands on her hips and sauntered toward the door to the kitchen. "And very handsome, too, I must admit. Made this old heart flutter with joy just for the looking at them."

The women huddled at the table laughed again, somewhat shyly this time, and murmured politely about Connor's and Bowes's handsome, masculine looks.

One woman from the night before said in a husky voice, "And your wee boy is delightful. He greeted us with such seriousness and a bit of a bow."

A younger, yellow-haired girl, with her mouth full of scone, added, "A boy that age is usually full of devilment. Your little fellow was so polite. By the way, I'm Esmeralda, better known as Essie. I have a room on the third floor, way in the back." Essie grinned shyly, her shiny, white teeth a brilliant flash of light.

Pointing at herself, the brunette stated, "And I'm known as little

Loralie or Lorie." She shot Sinead a big smile and fluttered her lashes. "And let me say that I think your hair is lovely, all soft and curling around your face." She glanced at the others. "What I wouldn't give for hair like that!"

Sinead ran a shaky hand through her tangled hair. "Thank you but yours is equally as lovely," Sinead replied, a blush stinging her face with heat, "all dark and shiny."

Lorie smiled at her. "Actually, men seem to prefer the red or yellow colors. You must be a star. Are you going to work here?" Not waiting for an answer, she shrugged, with a delicate movement barely lifting her thin shoulders.

Sinead replied quickly to the blunt question. "Oh, nae. I have a situation in New York City, taking care of several people in a grand house."

"Well, there must be money in that then," Essie responded, with a quick nod, looking at the others with secret understanding.

"Not really," Sinead quipped. "I'm afraid the money left to my son is managed by his grandparents." She laughed and shook her head. "I'm afraid they're not too generous, but I really don't mind. He'll have the money when he's grown."

"Hey there, I'm Helene," barked the oldest-looking woman, who had been quiet. She sat in an ungainly position, with her legs stretched out in front, her ankles crossed, her bright limed-colored robe dangling on the floor. "I live on the third floor, too," She added loudly, her mouth open in a wide yawn.

"Are you all related to Pegeen?" Sinead asked, turning her back for the moment in order to fix the buttons on her shirt. When she turned back, they were staring at her, their mouths agape.

Essie was the first to recover. Words spilled from her. "You might say we're related in — in — " She stopped, leaned back then seemed to study Sinead. "Your father didn't tell you — ?"

Pegeen breezed through the door, juggling a plate of food and an empty cup. A frown etched her face. Her eyes were as hard as gray chips of ice. "I'm sure her da never mentioned our living arrangements."

Puzzled, Sinead smiled and took the plate from Pegeen's hand. "My, that looks utterly delicious, but it's far too much for me to eat, especially this early in the morning."

"Well, eat as much as you can. Trust me, nothing goes to waste at this place."

"It's not early," Lorie said. "It's well past the noon hour."

"My word, I've never slept this late in my life." Sinead added, frowning.

Helene offered, "Well, ducks, there's a first time for everything."

The sound of the front door opening then footsteps approaching halted the conversation. Robbie rushed into the room, his arms filled with small bundles.

He ran to his mother. "Mama, look what I got. My da bought me everything," he babbled while hugging the packages, his eyes big and bright with joy.

"How nice…" Her breakfast left untouched, Sinead beckoned her son over to her and hugged him close. "Let Mama see. What did you get?"

Robbie sat on the floor beside her and began ruffling through his packages. He pulled a plain blue shirt out of one. "Look. And it fits me perfect." He held it up in the air.

The women exclaimed over it until he tossed it over his head and dug out another shirt, a fine white one. "This one, too."

He stood, held it against his chest, twirled it in the air and threw it to one side. He dug back into the packages and pulled out a gray sweater and a pair of long gray trousers. He clutched the trousers to him, his eyes all shiny. "See, Mama. My first man's clothes."

Bowes walked into the room. "Well, I can see 'tis the wee fella' who gets all the attention from you lovely ladies."

Pegeen stood. "Bowes, can I be getting ye something to nourish yer scrawny body?"

"Nae, don't bother. I'll just eat what's on this plate here," he said, indicating Sinead's plate.

"That's yer daughter's, but I'll make her another."

"Really, I thank you but I'm not hungry. I'll eat after I wake up a bit more." She turned to Robbie on the floor beside her. "And what else did you get? Tell me. Come. Show me everything."

"My da took lots of things back to grandda's house. He said I can play with them while he's working there. I'll have to go out and help him very soon." He spilled the remaining packages on the floor, pulled on her sleeve, hunched his shoulders gleefully and giggled. "My da got me a hammer. Just like his. And some nails and some boards and a pail and a shovel and a..."

"Whoa, Rob, don't be giving all yer secrets away to the ladies." Bowes gave all of them a genuine, radiant smile then sat and chewed on a slice of ham from Sinead's plate.

Sinead looked up in time to see his eyebrows rise in a flirtatious manner. "And for a bit of information, where might my husband be?"

"He's already out at the house, preparing to work on a barn first. He's got to build a barn quickly."

"A barn?" The word pounded a wooden stake through Sinead's heart. She knew he was a horseman in Ireland, but never thought he would continue the work in America. Well, she'd have something to say about that, she would.

"Aye. We met young John Morrissey on our travels this morning." He turned to the others. "You girls know John, the sportsman, don't ye now?" When they all nodded, he continued. "Believe it or not, the man and some friends are developing a race track off Union Avenue—just to handle something for the crowds during the summers. Anyway, the man has some fine racing horses that are needing care and training before the races he's scheduled for August."

"Horses?" Sinead stared at her da through hot and fevered eyes. She could barely contain herself. Hatred boiled within her and, with a rumble, roared through her body with enough force to almost knock her down, if she weren't already sitting on the floor.

"What horses? You know how I feel about those animals. I can barely ride in a carriage without a fear of the beasts charging through my body like a herd of wild elephants." She shivered.

Bowes's clean-shaven face flushed red. He couldn't meet his daughter's eyes, his muscles flexing in his shoulders and arms, his hands fisted. "Well, that's something ye'd best be discussing with yer man."

Sinead leaped to her feet. The certainty of it swept through her like a tidal wave. "I most definitely will." She stared at the floor in embarrassment.

The ladies, who had been watching the entire procedure with wide eyes, slowly began to push away from the table. They stood and seemed to huddle together. Stale perfume floated in their wake to mix with the sour acid taste rising in Sinead's throat.

Essie gave Robbie a wave. "I'll see you later, darling boy." In the way of an apology, she said. "I have a two o'clock appointment to get ready for."

Lorie stretched, her robe falling open. Totally unembarrassed, she walked by Bowes with the robe trailing after her. "Bowes, I hope we see you later this evening for the usual festivities. Bring your new son with you. It seems like he might be in need of some cheering up by then." Sneaking a scone from the table and popping it in her mouth, she smiled at Sinead and left the room. Gone less than a second, she darted back in, ran to Robbie and gave him a quick kiss on the forehead. One of her breasts fell out of her nightgown. She casually shoved it back in and said, "I need some rest before I greet my client. See you all later…"

Pegeen shouted, "Jaysus, you girls will be…" She glared after them then glanced at Sinead.

Bowes groaned in the back of his throat and swallowed the "Jaysus" on the tip of his tongue. He rubbed the scar on his throat, avoiding Sinead's gaze.

The last few interactions brought Sinead's head up. Her eyes widened as her mind hummed in an attempt to understand what her eyes had seen. She looked at the doorway where the women had gone, looked at Pegeen then at her da. A sore, bleeding ache spread to her chest. Sinead softly asked, in a mood clearly less than happy. "Da, what kind of boarding house is this anyway?"

Bowes started to walk away. He turned back, ruffling his hair then straightening it. He clench and unclenched his hands then examined his fingernails. "Well, now, Sinead let me tell you..."

She interrupted. "Aye. Please do." With a nod of her head in his direction, she moved slowly away from him and sat on one of recently vacated chairs. She folded her hands, her knuckles white, in the lap of her skirt. In a voice that seemed to demand obedience, she said, "I'm listening."

A fiery red blush invaded Bowes's face and circled to the tips of his ears. He plastered a potent Irish smile, deceptively harmless, on his mouth, yet with utter confusion he searched the pockets of his trousers, finally found a handkerchief and wiped his brow with the cloth. "Well, now daughter..."

This time, Pegeen interrupted. "Robbie, I wonder if you would be helping me in the kitchen. I could use a laddie's hand at me sink. It seems I have much to do and little help. Come, lad." She held her hand out and Robbie grasped it, his little face shining with importance.

His smile and the fire in his eyes lit up the room. "What about my bundles? I can't just leave them here."

"We'll come back in and get them after the kitchen is clean. How's that for a fine idea?" she asked, shaking her head, making her hair flow like a gaudy rose-colored banner.

"Okay..."

When Robbie nodded to her, she turned back to the dining room for a quick word. "You two can get on with yer conversation once we've left. I have a sad feeling this won't be the most pleasant of talks."

"I'm going, Mama." He gave Sinead a small wave and followed Pegeen into the kitchen.

Sinead said nothing, merely stared at her hands clasped tightly together, her lips curled in disgust.

Bowes shuffled from one foot to another and studied this daughter he loved to distraction. Full of rage and defiance, she is, he thought. Boiling with anger, a difficult woman to please.

He always tried to do his best for her, her sister and, now, the youngster. It was unfortunate her sister died, but it wasn't his fault. The disease took her away from them both. Sinead had no right to be angry with him, especially in this circumstance. He coughed into his hand to divert Sinead's attentive stare.

He found them a place to stay during the Saratoga Season, an almost impossible thing to do. He'd known only Pegeen would take all of them in, this late in the summer.

He was reluctant to speak to his own child. "Well, I suppose you want some sort of explanation…" His words trickled off. He shrugged his shoulders helplessly.

"Really, Da?" Sarcasm dripped from her mouth. "Only say as much as you feel is necessary…" Sinead didn't look at him, nor did she move a single inch.

His confidence in the face of her cold anger melted like ice in the noonday sun. "This town is filled to the brim during the Season. Places are taken well in advance of the summer. I knew we would be finding enough lodging for all of us, here. Pegeen doesn't use the boarding house as…"

"Then why didn't you have us stay in Albany?" Her words were level, her face calm.

"Several reasons. I have a home here."

Sinead snickered with scorn.

Instead of the embarrassed flush, Bowes's face grew mottled with anger. It felt overly warm. He stammered, "What if the Dewitts — found out ye were there — in Albany — and tried to take Robbie from ye then? What would ye have done? Run off foolishly is what ye'd do, for sure. Well, I saved ye the trouble. I did it for ye."

She laughed a small, tinkling, mirthless sound. "So your solution was to bring us to a house of ill-repute?" Her insulation from anger fled. Her heart froze, while tears stung her cheeks. A wet, choking sound erupted from between her lips. "Perhaps, Robbie should be taken away from the likes of you and me." Sinead brought her elbows up onto the table, and her head tilted to find sanctuary in her hands.

"Ye don't mean that for an Irish minute. Ye wouldn't be giving that sweet child up if yer very life depended on it. Would ye, now?" Bowes moved to her and put his hand on her shoulder in a profound, silent gesture. "Be getting hold of yerself, sweetheart. I'll think of something before long."

Sinead pushed his hand from her shoulder and wheeled around in the chair to face him. "You'll think of something. I'm through with you and your thinking for me. Look at the trouble I'm in already."

His temper boiled when she turned on him like that, plus, he harbored a wicked hatred for martyrdom. "Ye're in no trouble, lass."

"No? I still don't have control of Robbie. I'm married to a man I barely know. I'm sitting in a whorehouse with my child, and my father doesn't think of those things as trouble." Her voice was as icy and hollow as an empty grave in winter.

"Look at things positively for a change. Ye're married to a good man who will take care of ye and yer son. He'll fight for ye to gain Rob's custody. And, in turn, he's asked nothing from ye." He paced the room, his body straight and tense.

"Nothing from me, is it?" Sinead's voice reached higher notes than it had ever reached. She shouted at the top of her lungs. "He wants what every man wants, a woman in his house to cook and clean for him, a woman in his bed to gratify his baser needs and produce his children. And if I do all that, what happens to Robbie then?"

"Whoa there, lassie." Huffy at being attacked by his own daughter, without her having any true knowledge of their situations, Bowes whirled around to face her. "'Tis women like that, like yerself, with those thoughts, who force men to seek the very women ye're so against here. If there wasn't a need for such ladies, they wouldn't be here at all. And those here — ye've only to talk to them. They'd much rather be in yer shoes, missy."

Suddenly, Sinead met his angry gaze with a sad one of her own. She murmured, "You never mentioned to me that Connor was a horseman, a horseman with ambition. You seemed to have let the information slide somehow. I never heard a word about horses until I got that letter from him. Can't you just see me as mistress of a horse farm?" The laugh that tumbled from her body was anything but filled with humor. It reeked of the highest form of anguish.

"Don't ye think it's about time ye gave up this fear about the beasties? Like it or no, ye've been around them all yer life. Nothing's happened to ye." The memories Sinead faced almost brought Bowes to his knees. He sensed what she would say. His shoulders sagged.

"They killed my mother," she whispered.

"One did. It was an accident as I've told ye many times before. The poor stallion was only doing what comes naturally to them. Yer ma shouldn't have been sitting on that fence with a new horse in the paddock, one she didn't know anything about. She knew better than that."

"Well, she paid for her indiscretion with her life. And I had no ma growing up, no life that was ordinary, no friend until Lucinda Cavanaugh took me under her wing."

Bowes stopped and took a long look at his daughter. He studied her for a moment then spoke in a soft voice. "Sinead, I have to admit I don't like what I'm seeing in front of me, and I feel poorer for the picture. What has happened to ye, child? What have I done to ye so bad ye can't pull yerself together and get on with yer life?"

She gasped at what she considered harsh words, given the circumstances. She swallowed. Tears welled in her eyes.

He knew he should stop but couldn't. "I'm ashamed of yer whining about the things that have happened in yer young life, things that have passed ye by as ye claim. 'Tis yerself lettin' them pass ye by, stopping ye from doing the things normal to a woman yer age. Pull yerself together daughter. Get on with the life God gave ye—the business of living."

Sinead rose to confront him. "I think ye've said just about enough." She barely resisted blurting out more, allowing the hurt on her face to speak for her.

Bowes reached out to touch her, but she drew back.

A deep well of longing opened up inside her. She gave her father an unreadable look then stooped down and swooped all of Robbie's bundles into her arms. Her back straightened. She hurried through the dining room doorway, down the short hall and out the front door.

CHAPTER SEVENTEEN

What possessed her to attempt this foolish parade toward the possible destruction of her life as she knew it? To Sinead's everlasting misery, the tolerable kind of life had passed her by. She wondered if she was continuing to hide emotions from herself. No, she decided, firm in the convictions of what she didn't know for sure.

From the Circular Street boarding house — how could she call that place a boarding house? To the civilized end of Union Avenue was the longest walk she had ever taken alone. And she proceeded on this determined march, in the heat of red-hot, sorrowful regrets over her past simpering and sniveling temper, at what her da said to her, and apprehensive dissatisfaction with what she believed loomed ahead of her. Although disoriented, she fully intended to change her life, this very day, if she had a say in it.

When she strode past a particularly dusty section of the road, a sign informed everyone of the track being built for the racing of horses. She stood for a moment and watched, with a warped gaze. Men in the field, stirring up dirt. Drawing herself into a straight line and sticking her nose in the air, she spit on the ground.

Proud of herself for doing something she'd never done before, something disgusting and coarse, she turned and spit again, not caring if she were seen by anyone. The second bit of spit knocked the pride out of her. Her hand covered her mouth, and she staggered away in shame.

Her stocking-less thin boots were forming blisters on her feet and the sides of her smallest toes. The boots rubbed with every step.

Sinead felt her overheated feet slipping and sliding around, leather scraping at her heels. Unable to walk farther, she sat down by the side of the road beneath a tree offering shade. With a sigh, she leaned against the trunk.

Her reason for heading to her father's house was beyond her. Sinead wasn't the least bit sure what the skewed reasoning for going in that direction was. She couldn't understand her motivation. She needed to think. Her eyes involuntarily closed and didn't open until she heard the sound of carriage wheels on the road. Thinking it was probably her father, she stood and waved.

The large wagon, filled by five burly men in work clothes, went by at a fast clip then stopped, turned around and turned around again. It stopped again directly in front of her.

"Are ye lost little lady?" the driver, sitting on the high seat in the front, asked, his Irish brogue as thick as her da's. Sinead thought him older than her da so wrinkled and weathered was his face.

"Ah, er, no, I don't think I'm lost. I'm on my way to..."

The men sitting on the floor of the back of the crude wagon gave each other questioning looks. "Don't' think you're lost? Where might you be going, lass? The road up ahead is often deserted and not fit for a young lady to walk by herself," said a younger, yellow-haired man in the back. He smiled. His teeth were as yellow as his hair. Two were missing at the side of his mouth.

"Yeah," offered another, "tell us where you'd like to be going. We'll see that you get there safe and sound."

Sinead had never confronted so many men while unescorted. If this were the city, she would run away and find a large group. *Perhaps, I should run back to the track where those other men were working?* The very thought made her tremble.

"Cat got yer tongue, girlie?" a dark-haired man asked.

That angered her. "Nae. My tongue is in my mouth and ready to slice you for that sort of remark."

The men laughed and glanced at each other with knowing smirks. Sinead continued. "I'm heading to a certain property. Sitting somewhere above the lake, I'm told. I've only been there once, and it was dusk."

"Well, we're headed in that direction, miss," the older driver said, tipping his hat to her. "We'd be willing to give you a lift to where you're going if it's along our way."

"Harry, we have to get where we're going before half the workmen in the Springs do. I need that job," complained the dark-haired man to the driver. The man turned to Sinead. "Excuse me, ma'am, but my name is Jonah. I'm in desperate need of a job to feed my family. There's one opening up on a property by the lake, and we need to get there fast."

"Well, Jonah, you'd best be going along then. I don't want to be the cause of a man losing a good job." Sinead tipped her head to them and returned to the maple tree, relieved they weren't going to bother her further.

Harry turned and looked at the men in the back. "Ye can't be serious. Ye'd be leaving a young woman sitting by the side of the road? She is possible prey for any beast that might come along with bad intentions."

"You're right, Harry, as usual." Jonah scrunched around in his spot so he could face her. "Listen, missy, we're going to a place where they're raising a barn as quick as they can. Jack Morrissey told us about it."

Harry added, "'Tis Bowes Brennan's place. He always said he'd be having himself a horse farm when all is said and done. But you fellas know what a braggart he is, for sure."

As soon as she heard the name, a great smile spread over Sinead's face. "That's me da you're speaking poorly about." She laughed heartily. "And that's where I'm going, so I'd be happy to ride along with all of you. Harry, can I sit up top with you?"

"Oh my, lassie, ye sure can, after me speaking me mind so freshly. Let me give ye a hand to help ye on yer way to the seat here." Harry reached his hand down to her, but she could barely hobble over to the wagon, so badly did her feet pain her.

"Och, My feet are sore and swollen. Just give me a minute, please."

Jonah jumped off the back of the wagon and rushed to her side. "Let me help you up." He took her elbow and tried to assist her. When he saw she couldn't walk right, he swung her up into his arms and set her on the wagon seat next to Harry.

"Thank you," she said. "I truly appreciate the trouble you're all going to. I'll make sure you have jobs. 'Tis my husband who is giving them out."

"Oh, praise be." Jonah slapped his hands together before leaping back up onto the bed of the wagon. "Then maybe it's really going to be a barn for horses, horses that race."

Sinead turned and studied him. He was a small man and a bit darker than the rest of those in the back. He certainly seemed pleased about a job. She hoped he got one, although she had no idea what it might entail. She'd talk to Connor about it, for sure.

The wagon moved off. Sinead stretched her legs out on the bar rising in front of her, feeling her feet swelling inside the boots, she sighed with relief. "Harry, I truly am grateful for this ride."

He looked at her, his temple a strip of frowns. "I can't understand how come yer da let ye go off alone to the lake." He shook his head. "'Tis a bad thing to be traipsing on the roads like that, even during the daytime. Bad people do bad things at all hours of the day. I don't think yer husband would be pleased."

"Don't blame my da. It was my fault. We had a disagreement . I ran off, like the foolish lass I'm beginning to think I am."

"Well, don't worry any further. We'll get ye right to yer da's property and into yer husband's arms within an hour. You just enjoy the scenery."

Her husband's arms... She shivered with a sort of anticipation. Now why did that suddenly seem appealing?

* * *

Connor stood to the side of the rolling knoll below the house. His men had dug out half the hill for the barn's foundation. A portion of the barn would be below ground with just enough space at the top of the second floor for the horse's to see out the windowed bars he intended to install. He shaded his eyes with his hand while he watched the progress.

He was pleased. By putting part of the barn into the hill, it would preserve heat garnered from the horses. Someone told him the winter's here were dreadful, cold and snow-laden.

He planned to use the bottom floor for his tools, plows and maybe a few cows. He started toward the barn and the men working, continuing to plan for the winter. Sheaves of hay piled against the walls would insulate the barn a bit too, he thought.

Bored horses could cause much damage, as well he remembered, and he wondered what prompted the sad memory. He thought, perhaps, it was his wife's unreasoning fear of the animals. The fear was turning out to be a detriment to this marriage. It reinforced his decision to return to Ireland — without her.

Anxious to get the work done fast so he could leave, he continued planning for this horse farm. It was the least he could do before he left. Bowes, Sinead and little Robbie would be secure, with a place of their own. He tramped around the barn's foundation to make sure it was level and turned to look out at what would be the paddock.

He surveyed the land below with a knowledgeable eye. Men worked on fencing in a lower pasture, so the horses would have access to the stream. He moved toward it, looking for a place he could dam to bring the water in easier.

A hired man strolled to his side. "The men at the barn are ready to lay the heavy boards down on the ground for the floor."

"Aye, that's good," Connor replied, nodding to this bright-eyed young fellow.

"But more men are needed," the lad said with a tone of deference. "That is, if you want the floor leveled and all."

Connor didn't want to take the time to go into the village to hire more men. He hoped Morrissey would keep his word and send men out to the property. "I'll take care of it. I'm glad it's going so fast. The men are doing a grand job of it."

"I'll tell them. I know my father will be pleased to hear it."

"Ask him to keep the men working. I'm going up to the house to see what needs to be done there. I'd like to make it habitable for my family. Maybe I'll send one of you to town to get more men. The more we have working, the quicker the place will be ready." *And the quicker I can leave America.*

The youngster moved away at a run.

Connor started up the hill toward the building at the top of the property. Thoughts of repairs rushed through his mind. He'd need to put in stairs of some sort for going up and down the hill. After several steps, he turned to scan the land again.

The rolling hills reminded him of Ireland. Such hills were good for the horses. Bowes chose the site well. Connor laughed to himself. He intended to leave it all at the first opportunity. *Too bad...*

The men he hired worked diligently. Never in his life had he seen such a diversity of men, he mused, from all walks of life, of such different colors and different religious backgrounds, work together so cohesively. It made him proud they saw fit to work here for him, a foreigner to their land. He was nothing but a green Irishman from the old country, with little background in anything except how to handle horses.

When he reached the top of the knoll, he stood before the house, staring at it. He wondered what he could do to make it into a home fit for the lady and her son. He heard a wagon turn into the property and come up the long road toward the house.

The wheels pounding the ruts made him smile. If the wagon brought more men to work, he'd set some of them to working on the road, he thought. Connor waited outside for the wagon's arrival, watching the roadway. Waiting was not something he did well, so he paced the porch and studied the house from every angle. Its stone facade and its structure brought memories of Ireland to the forefront and filled him with a longing he couldn't control. While he walked, he wondered what he was going to do about Sinead's obvious animosity toward him? The marriage needed consummation, even if he went back to Ireland. He intended to go, with or without her, before the end of this summer.

He shrugged his shoulders and plopped down on the porch railing. Well, if she decided not to go with him, it would be her problem, not his. Lost in thought, he barely noticed the wagon had made it up the road and had pulled under the shade trees at the side of the house.

Someone called out to him. "Hey, mister! A group of us were sent here by Jack Morrissey, from down in the village. We came to work on the Brennan place. Do ye know where we can find the boss man?"

Connor moved off the porch then came around the corner of the house toward the wagon. Partially shaded by trees, the people in it had a better look at him than he did of them.

Sinead giggled and poked Harry. "That is the boss man. That's Connor O'Malley, my husband. Set me down and I'll be introducing you to him."

"Lordy, but he's a big one, now, isn't he, lass? Listen, missus, I can't set ye down with yer feet sore like they are. I'll bring yer to yer man," Harry said in a whisper.

Connor stumbled over an above ground root in the path. He jettisoned forward and looked back to see what tripped him. As he stepped forward again, someone stuck a bundle in his arms, a warm bundle.

Startled, he looked down. "Sinead. My God, what are you doing here? I never expected you to be coming by so soon. The house isn't ready for you. I haven't even been inside it yet."

Although something about this man often irritated her, causing slight chills to chase up her spine, she was determined to set things right between them. "Well then if I can take off these rotten boots, I can get started straightening things up. But first, I'd like to introduce you to my new friends." She smiled up at his startled face.

He couldn't stop his eyes from staring. "How did you get here, anyway?" Something about her made his blood boil like an iron pot over a campfire. It wasn't with anger.

"My friends." She pointed to the wagon. "They brought me." He turned away, not knowing where to put her down.

She assumed he was walking away. "Wait! You have to meet them."

"Lass, I have no time for socializing at the moment. There's too much to be done around here for any kind of polite interaction." He moved toward the house to put her on the porch.

She pinched his arm. "Connor, stop! Don't be getting up on your high horse. These are workmen. They need jobs. Come, they're waiting at the wagon."

"Workmen?" He snickered. "And where did you meet workmen?" He looked at her sideways, a twinkle in his eye and one eyebrow arched.

"By the side of the road, just beyond the new track that Morrissey man is building." She tried to smile.

Now, his temper began to tick. "By the side of the road? Are you crazy woman?" He peeled back his lips, showing his teeth.

His tone of voice and facial actions made her feel like punching him, so she did, on the shoulder, but she kept her face pleasant. "Nae. And you can put me down anytime you'd like. Just let me take off my boots first," she reminded him. She wriggled in his arms and bent to remove them.

"Take off your boots?" He realized he'd heard little of what she said when he held her. "What is going on here?"

Harry stepped forward. "Mister O'Malley, Jack Morrissey sent us here to work for you. That is, if you still have jobs open for the likes of us." He gestured to the men standing on the other side of the wagon.

At a loss how to answer, Connor looked down, into the sad, light eyes of an Irishman who reminded him of his father. "And who might you be, sir?"

"Harry Nolan, if the truth be known. From County Mayo I am." His chest expanded with the force of his pride. "And used to working with the huge beasties."

Connor fumbled Sinead around in his arms, hoisting her up and putting an arm under her bottom. He stuck out his hand to shake Harry's.

The men who waited behind the wagon moved closer, their hats in their hands. They stood in a group, looked at Connor and then at the ground, in deference.

Connor recognized the pleading eyes. He had seen enough of them during the famine years.

Harry backed toward his men. "This is Jonah. He has no last name. It seems his mama didn't know who his father was, so she just didn't give him a final name at all. And being so small, he sometimes rides for Mr. Morrissey. He's as strong as they come."

Connor studied him. In the racing business, being small was an asset. "Welcome Jonah." Again, Connor put his hand forward.

Still struggling to reach her boots, Sinead slipped to her waist in his arm. Her body pressed against him, one breast to the side of his chest.

He tightened his grip on her.

Harry continued with the introductions, as if he noticed nothing. "This young one here, and probably the strongest amongst us, is young Eddie Johnston." He pointed, to a blond youngster, with huge arms and muscled shoulders. The one in back of him is his older brother, Bobby, a fine hand with any kind of animal."

Harry pointed again. "And that's their cousin Fred, a bit long in the tooth, but spry. They're all good workers and will give you an honest job for an honest day's pay."

Their mute promise of support affected him but not as much as Sinead's position. He knew he would have to get away soon. "Fine. You're all hired. Harry, you seem like a good one to be assigning jobs. Go down to the barn or the paddock where the others are working away." Connor turned toward the porch, then turned back to add, "Oh, I'm also needing the ruts in the road leveled. That track'll be impossible to traverse if we get rain and it gets muddy."

Harry shouted after Connor's retreating figure, "Aye, sir. We'll be getting to the road promptly." The small group returned to the wagon.

With a nod, Harry assigned the three Johnston men to work on the ruts. They took some shovels from the back of the wagon and rested them on their shoulders.

Indicating some more loose tools in the back, Harry said, "Take those and leave the rest in the wagon. We'll take them onto the lower road below and unload the rest there."

Connor called back. "I'll be down as soon as I deposit my wife in the house."

Harry stopped him. "Sir, can I be letting me horse feed a bit on your grass before we head out tonight?"

"Aye, 'tis not a problem. The grass is rich and abundant. Just don't let him eat too much if he's not used to it."

With a wave, Connor carried Sinead to the front door but turned back once again. "And, please, call me Connor, or Con will do."

Sinead was hanging off his arm and calling out, "Good-bye gentlemen. I appreciate your fine gesture to me. Of the ride. I'll be seeing you all later." She swiveled back to Connor, her eyes glittering in the light. "I saw the lake. It's beautiful. I lived near a lake, once, a long time ago."

Connor's eyes widened at his wife's surprising gaiety. He gave her a quick squeeze. "My God, Sinead, what's come over you? I've never seen you like this."

She marveled at his strength. "Get me into the house and you'll see more." She pulled back to look at him, astonished by what she just said.

The frown and the puzzled look on his face made her laugh. His warm breath against her cheek gave her a quiver of expectations and a joy at being here on this property. She wasn't going near that boarding house. No matter what, she wasn't going back, nor was

Connor, if she had anything to say about it.

Connor replaced her in both arms and settled her close to his chest. He kicked open the front door and dropped her to her feet inside the door. Her screech of displeasure stopped him short. "What's the matter with you?"

"My feet," she cried as she crumpled to her knees and onto the floor. "You set me down so hard, they're stinging. You've hurt me."

Connor jumped and tried to pick her up again. "Och, Jaysus. Do I need this? Come. Let me see. Hurry, I have work to do." He beckoned her toward a horsehair sofa, placed against the wall.

Sinead fell onto her side, crawled into a ball and tried to rub her feet. "I can't move. I will not step on them again."

"All right," he said, picking her up from the floor. "I'll carry you to the chair over there. But I can't stay here. I need to get back where the men are working."

He had no intention of telling her that holding her in his arms like this was doing him a grave injustice, and serious harm to his mental and physical state. It made him think of their marriage with hope.

"Connor, are there beds in this house?" Sinead asked in a small voice.

He regarded her with something like shock. "What?"

"Are there any beds in this house?"

His knees turned to mush. "I'm pretty sure, but I doubt there are linens for them. What are you talking about, woman? What am I talking about?" he asked himself, turning around in a circle.

"Sit down in the chair, Connor." A mysterious, womanly half-smile crossed her face. "I'm wanting a wee talk with you before you set off again."

Slowly, she wound her arms around his neck. Being this close to him awakened new sensations in Sinead's body. Not knowing what to do next, she brushed at the hair near his collar with gentle fingertips.

He shoved a hand through his hair. He fidgeted, moving about in a rather aimless fashion, as if looking for some place to put his wife. Something was wrong, he decided, but there was little time to understand it all. His mind struggled with various foreboding thoughts.

He crossed the room with her still in his arms and tried to put her into an overlarge wing-chair near the windows, but she tightened her arms around his neck. Her heart thudded against his chest, a deep, heavy beat, matching his own.

Her lips curved into a cajoling smile. "I'll sit on your lap, if you don't mind?"

What was left of his mind was twirling in all directions, just from the feel of her fragrant body close to him. He took a deep breath and plunged down into the chair. He took her arms from around his neck and placed her hands in her lap. "What is the matter with you, Sinead?"

Not one to cower before a challenge, she pursed her lips, squeezed them into a round ball and turned them in his direction. "Nothing," she said lightly. "I want you to kiss me Connor."

He stared at her, at her mouth. The way she was posed assured him of her naivete. Her lips were drawn tightly together. He wanted to make them go soft and yielding.

"Sinead, have you ever been with a man?" he asked in a level voice.

Her eyes opened wide, and she glared at him. "Of course not! What do you think I am?"

"Have you ever been kissed by a man?"

She laughed, as if he just made the silliest joke. "Of course I have. Robbie kisses me all the time. My da always kissed me good night when I was small. Each night before I went to my room next to Robbie's, Robert Cavanaugh would kiss my forehead."

"Nae, I mean have you ever been kissed by a man who had more serious intentions regarding your person?"

"I don't know what you..." A dull red rose over her ears. "Och, you're talking about in a carnal way?"

"Aye, lass." His eyes flashed a warning. There was steel in his tone that insisted upon the truth.

Sinead bit back a gasp of outrage. "What do you think I am? One of those ladies from the boarding house?" The words flew out of her mouth before she considered the wisdom of saying them aloud.

She moved to stand, but as soon as her feet touched the floor, she winced and fell back onto his lap. "I have never allowed any one to take liberties with me. A few tried, but I smacked them down to their true size."

He stared at her, his face hot. "I thought as much."

"Well, you are so smart. Now, I have some other things to tell you." Her anger at full force now, she spit more words at him. "I am not going back to that boarding house. I want my son taken out of there as quickly as possible. My da can stay there all he likes."

"What is this all about?"

She jabbed a finger at him. "Don't pretend innocence with me, sir. You recognized immediately what kind of women they are."

His eyes narrowed. He arched an eyebrow. "And what kind of women do you think they are?" he asked softly.

"They're—ladies of the evening that sell their bodies for some man's pleasure." Her lips thinned with righteousness.

"Don't you think that's a bit harsh?" He stared at her. His voice was chilling. "Do you have any idea of why they might feel they have to sell their bodies?"

"They do it for their own pleasure, I'm sure," she countered, raising her chin a notch.

"If you believe that, then you have a lot to learn, lassie. I've seen women who have sold their bodies so their children will have food. Irish women. During the great famine. Learn this bit of philosophy before you learn about kissing. There are many reasons for doing all sorts of things. I think you'd better consider all the possibilities. Have such things happened to you? If not, you'd better make sure they don't."

"Are you threatening me, Connor O'Malley? If you are, I'm not afraid of you. And I don't want to talk right now, anyway. Kiss me," she ordered.

Again, she pursed her lips and kept them squeezed shut in a totally unappealing way. This time Connor decided he'd take the plunge into the icy waters indicated by her attitudes. He touched her mouth with his own. He did it softly with a feathery touch and could feel her heart pounding. He pulled away. "There. Are you satisfied?"

"You didn't kiss me hard enough. I hardly knew you were there." She frowned, confused.

He barely kept his mouth from curving into a smile. "All right, Sinead. We'll try again. I guess right now is as good a time for a lesson as any other." His lips curved with reluctant amusement.

He put his thumb on her mouth and rubbed her lower lip gently. Slowly, her mouth softened. He drew her to him within an arc of his arm and let her rest against his chest, her head beneath his chin. He kissed a side of her face and the bottom of her ear. She tried to turn toward him. Her eyes were closed. He reached for her cheekbone with his mouth and let his tongue touch the sharpest angle. His lips traveled up the side of her face, inching from one section to another.

Her gasp of surprise delighted him. He turned her face toward him with the gentle touch of one hand and laid his lips against hers, moving them ever so slightly over her mouth, taking small nips along the way. He continued pressing her to him, astonished to feel her back arch against his arm, to feel her strain against him.

He made every effort to control the hardening between his thighs. He crossed his legs, shrugged free of her mouth to break the kiss and sat still. He stared at her flushed face, her half opened eyes.

She looked relaxed, almost stupefied, like a sorceress who would fulfill his dreams. He needed to put some distance between them.

"I'm going to take you into the kitchen." He hazarded a glance at her face. "I want to take a look at your poor feet. Let's get your boots off."

"My feet?" Her mind couldn't follow his. She was confused, disoriented and numbed by the warm force of her feelings.

"Aye, your feet. You said they stung, didn't you?"

"I can barely feel them now."

"Well let's take a serious look at them, before you run around the house, cleaning, in your bare feet."

"Cleaning? Bare feet?"

Connor stopped himself from grinning. "Aye, won't you want to be doing some cleaning of this place. That is, if you remember what you said that you intend to stay here and not go back to the boarding house.

"Right," she mused. "I remember saying that."

"And lass, do you remember where you might have left the little laddie?" His solicitous questions startled her. "Won't you be wanting him here with you?"

"My da will bring him before long."

"Does your da know where you are? That you've gone away? I'm sure he's going to be worried."

She straightened. "Och, Jaysus. My da doesn't know! I didn't tell him when I ran off. Connor, I have to go back to get Robbie." She sat so still, in shock, twisting her fingers in her lap. "What have I done? This is the result of my own foolishness, not my da's. I've been such a fool." A glimmer of unshed tears flashed in her eyes.

"Don't worry, lass. I'll send someone to fetch them both."

"Och, that's so kind of you," she said, snuggling back into the comfort of his arms. You don't really have to do that for me."

He nodded. "I know, but I want to. I've been much taken with your father and the lad. They're fine folks, Sinead."

"Connor?"

"What is it now, lass?" He breathed in her sweet fragrance and tried to quell the desire rebuilding in his loins. "What?"

"Will you be kissing me again?" It was half a statement of her wanting, half a question for his.

"You can count on it, wife." His mind burned feverishly with images.

Sighing deeply, Connor stood abruptly and carried Sinead to the kitchen. He sat her in a high-backed wooden chair and removed her shoes. He examined her feet, massaging them a bit, despite her flinching at each touch. They were definitely blistered and raw.

Wishing he had the medicine he used on his horses, he filled a bucket with warm water and set it down in front of her. Slowly, he put her one foot in the bucket then the other. She let them sink to the bottom.

His heart nearly stopped at the dreamy expression on her face as she soaked her feet in the bucket He smiled down at her. The wondrous look she gave back to him threatened to make him cease taking the deep, regular breaths necessary to life. He grinned. Perhaps, his life was getting better.

CHAPTER EIGHTEEN

The day Sinead arrived on the property, Connor sent two workmen to find her father and son. It was an easy job. Believing his daughter to be having one of her infrequent temper tantrums, Bowes stayed at the boarding house with Robbie. They chatted and drank lemonade with the ladies when they weren't busy with customers.

The two moved into the stone farmhouse late that afternoon. Bowes was suspicious about his unusually quiet, his abnormally happy, his sweet-talking daughter. She showed little discontent with the home forced upon her, in a place she claimed to detest. He wondered if his words at the boarding house affected her so much she acted in a daze.

She kept Robbie close to the house, afraid he might be hurt by one of the three horses now occupying the paddock and barn areas. She dealt pleasantly with every worker who stopped at the house. However, she seemed nervous, as if constantly on the lookout for something, staring out the front windows for long stretches of time, doing little more than thinking.

Did his words made a cleft in the rock wall she placed in front of herself? Did it make her think of her present situation? Perhaps, he thought, when he noticed the difference in her demeanor. He noticed a change in Connor's as well. Bowes grinned.

* * *

Within two days after the family was established in the house, Sinead sent her father down to the new barn to get him out from

272

under her feet. He'd been gone less than an hour when Connor appeared on the porch.

He lifted Robbie into his arms, let him wrap his legs around his hips and marched the both of them indoors. He pretended to drop him. Robbie giggled and clung to the man's neck in pretended fear.

Connor said pointedly to Sinead. "The lad's grown in the last few weeks of traveling . He's gotten taller, lost some of his fat." Connor said, poking the boy in the ribs, "and gained muscle tone."

Robbie flexed his arm and felt a small bump of a muscle. Sinead wanted to laugh at the sight of his "John Morrissey" pose but didn't for fear of offending her son.

"Why he no longer looks like such a little round ball of a baby, nor does he act like one anymore. He's gotten quite manly," Connor said. "I'm going to start calling him Rob to fit his new size."

Connor put a hand under Sinead's elbow and snaked it around her back to untie her apron, which he let fall to the floor. He gave her a quick kiss on the neck, then, taking her hand in his, made her step over it. He led her onto the front porch. "Come lass. It's time to look over your new surroundings. You've spent far too much time in the house. It's time to show my new wife and son around the farm that is to be their new home."

When she gave him a surprised look, he added, "Although I've been busy, I've noticed what you've done to make the house look like a home. You've worked hard. You've turned this house into a lovely place, fit for a king."

"Don't be patronizing, Connor. Under our present circumstances, I only did what was best for Robbie."

"Rob, Mama, Rob. I want to be called Rob from now on. I'm gonna' tell my grandda, too."

"All right, darling." Sinead smiled at her son. "Rob needs a home is worthy of his new size."

The last thing Connor wanted to do was to start an argument with his bride, so he nodded in agreement. He understood she would need a bit of wooing but hoped it was not in vain. What he desired was to interest her enough to consummate the marriage and go back to Ireland with him.

Of late, the hours they spent in each others company passed far too quickly. It was difficult for him to look at her without feeling a stirring in his loins. He had to admit, he was getting quite fond of her, in a lustful way. Perhaps, the marriage could be a viable one if they just pulled together on some things. He shook his head to force himself out of this introspection. He was a man of action.

His thoughts strayed back again to the subject on his mind. Several things stood in their way. First, her overzealous concern, almost a stifling concern, was not good for the boy. Secondly, Connor couldn't envision a court, which would deny her claim of motherhood. But then, he knew nothing of the laws of this country.

He wondered how she'd fair in Ireland, at O'Malley House, where most of his brothers lived and all their horses were kept. He understood the need to interest her in the animals, somehow. Today would be the very first step.

"I'd like you to visit the barn and paddock the men and I constructed," he said, leading the way. "We've built everything so your da would have a permanent home to look forward to when we go back to Ireland."

As soon as he said the words, he knew he'd taken a wrong turn. In one instant she froze, became a stranger, making him aware how pleasant and open her expression was only moments ago.

"What makes you think for one moment we are going to Ireland?" she asked in a decidedly cool tone. "You must understand by now, the Dewitts will never give up custody and I..."

"Somewhere, somehow, a compromise will be reached. I promise you," he vowed. "There is something those Dewitts want, something other than this fine laddie, here." Connor squeezed his legs until Robbie laughed at the action.

"I need to discover what it is the Dewitts require. Egan and I discussed it." Connor looked into the sheer glory of her face but with a twist of lust in his belly. "Egan will learn their secrets. If anyone can do it, Egan can."

He shifted the boy onto his back and folded the skinny young legs over his arms. "Also, lass, I have no intention of living the rest of my life without those things, which keep me sane. I don't think I could."

"And what keeps you sane may I ask?" Sinead asked, beginning to draw back.

"My life with the horses. I have lived on a farm my entire life. The farm did nothing for generations on end but raise racing stock. It's a tradition in my family." A smile dotted his face. "I love the feel of a horse beneath my body, singing with speed, and me, with the wind whistling my ears…"

"There are horses in America as well," she snapped. "Och, this discussion is useless." Her face reflected her every passing emotion. "Let's see what you and my da rendered on this isolated piece of greenery and sand."

Connor led her to the steps he'd installed to reach the barn. He hitched Robbie up higher onto his back. "All right, laddie, are you ready to be seeing what wonderful sights await you?"

"Aye, Da. Take me. Mama won't let me go down to the horses by myself."

"Well, she'll need to be letting you go there with your grandda and me, now won't she?"

"I wouldn't bet any dinners on it," Sinead said, smiling to soften the harsh words and her tone of voice.

To Connor's disgust, the closer they got to the barn, the more nervous Sinead became. She trembled and shivered.

Standing on the level part of a knoll, the barn and the horses seemed gigantic, despite the difference in size. Going from the light, into the darkness of the barn, bothered her. The air was still and humid.

The smells of hay and horses were rank to her sensitive nostrils. Several horses were moving around in their stalls, chomping on hay and slopping water from their buckets. The noises seemed foreign. They frightened her. Sinead hadn't realized so many horses had arrived already.

A horse kicked out at the boards of its stall. It sounded like an explosion. Sinead shrieked, a female screech of terror. Her heart pounded within her chest as if it wanted to break out of her body. She leaped back and tilted drunkenly toward the ground, waving away Connor's hand when he held it out to catch her. She staggered up against a wall and refused to go any further.

Connor shrugged, let Robbie slide down his back and took his hand. He moved back to Sinead and put his arm around her shoulders. "Come, lass, the horses can't hurt you. They're in their stalls and eating. Sometime they get annoyed at each other and kick the sides of their stalls. 'Tis naught to be afraid of."

Although Robbie continued to hold Connor's hand, he jumped and pulled in his excitement. "Mama, look. See the horse. That's the one I like. The red one."

Connor smiled. "The red one is it? We call it a chestnut. Would you like to get closer and pet him?" Connor asked while drawing Sinead closer to the stall.

"Aye. Right up to him…" Robbie let go of Connor's hand and ran to the stall door.

"Don't be running at them, son. It frightens them."

As if Connor told him a foolish joke, Robbie giggled uproariously. "They're so big, nothing could frighten them."

"They're big all right, great big *babies*, especially the racing ones. If they get really frightened, their first instinct at the sign of trouble is to be running away from the fearsome object, as fast and as far as they have to. Wouldn't you do the same if you were scared?"

Robbie no longer paid any attention. He hung over the edge of the stall door and reached out to pet the horse. "Come here, laddie. I won't hurt you. I'm only a little boy," he bubbled. "You're much bigger than I am, so you don't need to be afraid. I want to be your friend."

"Robbie, come away," Sinead shouted, her voice breathy, her

eyes broad with terror. "He'll bite you if you get too close."

Connor whirled around and took hold of her arms to settle her. "Where did you get such foolish ideas, Sinead?"

He stood there, looking down at her and wanting to take her in his arms and kiss away all her fears. He knew his thoughts were written on his face.

Robbie stretched over the door from his waist on and grabbed for air with one hand. He scrunched up a bit closer on his perch, tipped over and nearly fell inside the stall, his feet kicking in the air and his hands pushing against the wooden half-door. At the same time, the horse moved closer as if to see what object was offering some amusement from the boredom of captivity.

Sinead screamed. Her hands flew to her mouth. She gasped in fear. "Oh my God, he is going to get eaten. If he falls, he'll get trampled."

She turned. "Connor, please, please, take him away from there." She was gagging. Sobs emanated from her mouth in great gusts. She wailed, "He's going to get killed. I know it."

Robbie froze on the top edge of the door. He turned around to look at her, his eyes blinking in the dim light. "Mama, don't cry. Don't be scared. This horse is my friend. He won't hurt me."

Connor shook her. "Sinead, stop it. The boy's not taken any harm. Even if he were to fall in, the horse would draw back from him." Connor glared at her, his annoyance growing into anger. "Good God, woman, you act as if ghosts sewed rocks into your dainty undergarments."

He dropped his hands from her arms, picked Robbie up from the door and held him in a tight grip. "It's really all right, son. It seems your mama is more afraid of horses than they are of her." He whispered in Robbie's ear. "Let's just give her a minute to compose herself."

"That's what Grandda Bowes says about her. He says she's got an af-fix-ition — or something like it. He told me she'll need to get over it if she's going to live here with all of us."

With her breath barely there and a slight hint of madness in her tone, she shouted at the two of them. "We're not going to stay here. Robbie, you and I—"

"Rob, Mama, Rob…"

"Are going back to New York City as soon as we can—as soon as I can drag your grandda away from here. Or we'll take a train," she said all in one breath. "That would be fun, wouldn't it, Rob?" Tears streamed down her face, pushing down bad memories.

She wheeled around, away from them. "My heart's been in my mouth most of the time I've been here. I'm leaving. I feel I can't breathe in this place. I can't keep track of my son, I'm afraid of the horses, and I want to go home." She clutched the wall in her distress.

Connor growled at the back of his throat. He fixed her with a cold eye. "This is your home, lass. It's what your da bought so you could be safe from those others you were so against."

She feverishly shook her head, back and forth. "Nae."

Her unbound locks could capture a man's desire, he noted with annoyance. This marriage was made for fools. She would never crave the simple life he did.

"I don't care about all that," she countered. "He never asked me what I wanted. I want to go back to the city."

"What are you going to do when you go back to Ireland with me?" Hope dawned in his expression.

She ignored his fleeting smile. "I'm not going to Ireland with you or anyone else," she mumbled quietly. A murmur of uneasiness slid throughout her body. A frown marred her brow. "How many times do I have to tell you?"

"Well, I guess you've made up your mind to it, but I can't stay here in this country forever. I have responsibilities over there that must be taken care of." He gave her another wry half-smile, one that failed to reach his eyes.

"You've got a father and brothers to do for you. This lad has only me."

"Because o' the way you've done it," he snapped, knowing there was no escape for their quandary, "you haven't allowed anyone to penetrate your tight little circle."

Her gasp filled the barn. "I'm not going to stand here and argue with you. The stench is making me ill. So are you."

"Then flee to the safety of the house. Live your bare existence if it suits you, but don't force the child." He resisted making a comparison between his own life, filled with family and friends, and this youngster's lonely life. "The lad and I are going to examine the rest of the property and greet some of these horses. Rob likes horses. He doesn't need to be kept away, just taught how to handle them as my da taught me."

"You're not taking him anywhere. He's going back to the house with me."

Robbie was watching the two of them argue. He grasped Connor's face in his hands and turned it as a mirror to his own. "Don't holler at my mama. Don't make her cry." He pointed a finger at Connor's nose. "That's not nice."

Heartbreak echoed in his words. Connor set him on the ground and hunkered down to his level. "Listen, laddie, I wasn't hollering at your mama because I don't like her. I do. She's a wonderful lady, but I don't have to agree with her all the time, do I now?"

"You're not going to spank her are you?"

"Nae, but it's a nice idea..." Connor straightened and looked at Sinead. Their battle was brief, brutal, but over. He preferred to bargain with her, plead, or perhaps, placate her but chose to tease instead. "Should I spank you for scaring this child far more than horses could ever do?"

Still fuming, Sinead refused to acknowledge her husband. She held out her hand to Robbie. "Come, son. We'll go up to the house and play in the sand."

"I want to see the other horses. Talk with them. I want to stay with my da and be teached about horses." Robbie put his hands on his hips, looked up at his mother and glared at her.

Sinead's shoulders sagged with disappointment. She wheeled around, her hands clenched into the folds of her skirt. "See what you've done. You've made him misbehave to his mama."

"Nae, 'tis his mama who has misbehaved. Now you can either continue on this little tour Rob and I are taking or go up to the house and sulk behind closed doors."

His curiosity of the word apparent, Robbie asked, "What's sulk mean?"

Sinead raised her finger and pointed it at Connor. "If anything happens to this child you'll be held responsible. It'll be on your head."

"I think I can handle it. Go sulk, lady. A good sulk might do you some good. Soften your belligerence," Connor groused.

Robbie yanked on Connor's pant leg. "Da, what's 'sulk'?"

The frown between Connor's brows disappeared. "Come laddie. I'll tell you all about it as we walk and talk. It's something ladies do quite well." He grinned at Sinead, a big, broad grin.

"So do men," she commented then fired a glance of loathing at both of them and stormed from the barn in a mood. Charging across the sandy entrance, the ground shifted beneath her feet but didn't slow her progress to the stairs. Halfway up the steps to the house, she turned and glared down at the barn.

She would like to put her hands around Connor's neck, she would. But in what fashion?

Chapter Nineteen

A week went by. By the thirtieth of July, two days short of three weeks since her husband's arrival in America, Sinead's life had changed, with incredible dramatic intensity. Each time she looked out the window, a myriad of tents, placed everywhere on the one hundred and six acre property, greeted her eyes. The city of tents obstructed her vision of the barns and paddocks.

Bowes and Connor allowed workmen, with or without families, to pitch tents on the grounds, until after the races in August. People were tucked into every available space on the farm, some living close to the woods but near the Kayaderossera Creek, others staying closer to the main house. The surrounding area, which could be seen easily from the house, resembled a carnival grounds or a gypsy encampment.

Two barns and two paddocks, built out of the very best lumber, stood like fortressed gates. Horses occupied the pastures but were put in the barns during the heat of the day and let out at night to enjoy time on grass.

Twice daily, morning and night, Bowes's two grays pulled a trailer over the lower road to cart valuable race horses from the farm to the training area. He drove with considerable care, forcing the grays to a walk when the horses in the trailer fidgeted. "Easy, lads. Let's not rile up the boyos in the back," he would call.

The former sulky track on Union Avenue was now Horse Haven, reconstructed by Jack Morrissey, the famed fighter and gambler. The track stood ready and waiting for the first legal four-day race program, starting August third. Morrissey considered it just another profitable way of amusing the free-spending summer guests.

* * *

"My God, 'tis getting crowded in here, what with all the workmen piling in to have their say," Bowes commented early one morning. Connor and he stayed in the largest tent, close to the barns and paddocks. The two men maintained a constant vigil that would continue until after the racing days.

"Everyone wants to talk about the horses scheduled to run on the new track," Connor supplied, "and to voice their opinions, I guess."

"And the care of those we have here. And the building or rebuilding of anything and everything," Bowes added with a snort of laughter.

Occasionally, one or the other would go up to the house for a spot of food, but they talked about little else but horses and racing stables while they were there. Their time at the house was further shortened by shouts from harried workers calling them away from meals.

Harry, growing increasingly fond of Sinead, stopped in for brief visits, as did young Jonah. Usually, each day, the local postman delivered what was turning out to be larger quantities of mail for everyone living on the premises. Nevertheless, most of Sinead's and Robbie's days were spent alone, something to which they were not accustomed.

This noontime, the postman came to the house. He knocked on the front door, instead of leaving the mail in the small, enclosed mail hut at the bottom of the road.

Pleased with the interruption of her otherwise boring day, Sinead greeted him kindly. "Och, Mister Sanders, have you come for a call?"

"No, missus," the thin, dour-looking man replied. "I've come to bring you a personal letter. Here," he said, shoving the letter at her, "it's addressed to you, under your father's name."

He frowned at her as if such a designation bothered him. "I figured it might be an important missive."

"Well, I thank you for bringing it to my door." She smiled at the discomfited man. "Would you be caring for a spot of cool lemonade on this hot day?"

"Why, I thank you, missus, but I think I'd better be bringing this package down to your husband. Is he in the fields?"

"Don't trouble yourself, Mr. Sanders. He'll be up for a spot of food shortly, and, if not, I'll take the package down to him. It's a small one and looks easy to carry."

Sinead took the package and other letters from him and placed them on top of a table by the door, except for the letter to her, which she put into her apron pocket. She watched the postman move off the front porch. She heard his "Hi there, young fella'" and saw him ruffle Robbie's hair.

She pulled her letter out of the apron pocket and glanced at the return address, one of the hotels in the village. The familiar handwriting, with its tight, precise letting, set her heart to pounding.

The post was from Adelaide Dewitt. Sinead knew it was bound to be bad news. Nothing pleasant ever came from Adelaide. A picture of Connor flashed into her mind. She couldn't bear to be alone while reading probable disastrous news.

She felt everything she gained in life was slipping through her fingers. No matter how fearful she was of the horses, she needed to go down to the barns, to Connor.

She yanked off her apron and flew out the front door, where Robbie was playing in the sand. Unable to leave him to his own devices, she grabbed his pail and a shovel and half dragged him with her down the steps Connor built to the first barn. At the bottom, she let go of Robbie's hand, admonishing him. "You play right here in the sand where Mama can watch you."

She stood on the bottom step, cupped her hands around her mouth and shouted like a fishwife hawking her wares. "Connor.

I'm needing to speak to you."

"He'll be with ye in a minute, lassie." Her da answered, unseen, from somewhere inside the barn. His position away from her, in a barn, and the sound of his voice calling out sunk deep within her memory. Although unable to focus on her own thoughts, the pulse in her neck beat rapidly.

Connor poked his head out of the barn and shouted, "I'm in the middle of something. What is it you're needing, Sinead?"

The deep timbre of his voice jogged her memory even further and caused her to shudder. She shook her head to dispel whatever it was crawling around inside her brain. She grunted, chiding herself for her foolishness, then laughed quickly. "And you might be in the middle of more, if you don't step lively. I need the two of you up at the house. For only a moment. Something's come up. I'm thinking I'll be needing advice."

She saw her da, who had come to the barn door, look at Connor and heard him bellow gleefully. "Did ye hear what the lass said, Connor? She might be needing our advice. Did ye ever think such a thing would occur in your lifetime, now, did ye laddie?" Bowes doubled over, laughing.

Annoyed at her father's bantering and using her as the butt of a joke, Sinead turned on her heels in a bit of anger. "Go to hell the both of you. Men!" she exclaimed. She grabbed Robbie's hand and marched him back up toward the house, grumbling the entire way.

"Mama, my pail," Robbie wailed.

"I'll get it later."

"But I was building a barn for the pony Da is going to get me," he whined.

"And what pony are you talking about? You'll not be getting a pony, for sure, young man."

Robbie sputtered, "But, he said…"

"Well, he's wrong. You'll not be getting any pony." Sinead looked down at him. His face was tracked with a fine line of tears, rolling from his eyes to his chin. Kneeling and gathering him in her arms, she whispered, "Och, my darling, I meant, you'll not be getting a pony until you're a bit bigger and older."

Belligerently, Robbie whispered back, "That's not what my da said."

"Well, he and I will discuss it, later on. Though probably not until the races are over, and he gets his mind onto other things than the horses he's caring for." The mere thought of those other things made her grin.

"You look silly, Mama," Robbie said in a loud, petulant voice.

She gasped. "Now, is that a nice thing to be saying to your mama?"

Connor, looking solemn, came up the stairs two at a time and stood two steps below them. Sinead barely needed to lift her eyes to stare directly into his face.

"Tell me, lassie, what could be so all-fired important for you to be calling me from the training of a young horse to the bit?"

When he took another step, he swung Robbie up on one hip and put his arm around her. Sinead felt a warm tremor start in her feet, and she moved up the steps at a quicker pace.

"Come into the house. I've something to show you."

Connor raised and lowered his eyebrows. "I hope it's something so interesting I won't mind leaving the horses for a spell."

Her gaze swept over him. A warm flush crept up her neck, her face and her ears. She was flustered, at a loss for a retort, so she mumbled, "Nae. This is serious. I have a letter from Adelaide Dewitt."

Robbie pulled Connor's face around to look at him. "That's my grandmother you know, but she doesn't want me to call her Grandmother. I have to call her Missus Adelaide, ma'am." Robbie giggled. "Isn't it funny?"

"Aye, laddie. Sure is funny." They reached the porch. Connor set Robbie down. "Why don't you play out here for a spell? I'll have Mama call you in when she's fixed us both some lunch."

"All right. I'm building a fort, under the steps, you know." Robbie pointed to a mass of sand sitting by the porch step.

"And, 'tis a fancy one, for sure," Connor said, examining the spot carefully.

Connor followed Sinead into the coolness of the house and closed the door. He halted directly behind her. Without letting her get far ahead of him, he swung her around, against his chest. "Where are you going, lass? 'Tis not often we have a moment to ourselves."

"Not with you staying down in a tent with my father, we don't," she grumbled.

Connor kissed her forehead and twirled a strand of her hair around his thumb. "And here, I thought you like it better with me away." Brushing her hair back from her temple, he kissed the bottom of her ear and brought her closer to him.

"Connor, please. Robbie may come into the house at any moment."

"And what would be wrong if he saw his da kissing his mama?" Connor grinned down at her. "I thought you might be wanting another lesson, maybe even needing one."

Sinead couldn't resist the lure of the bantering form of intimacy or the deep, soft tones near her ear. Affected against her will by his closeness, she raised one hand to his face. She allowed two of her fingers to trace the sharp ridges of his bones, wondering what submitting to his touch and possession might mean in her life. She stopped. It would make him far too important. Her other hand closed in a tight knot, along one side of her skirt. She'd touched hot coals before and wanted to draw away from the hot coal in front of her.

Connor stared down at her. A merry grin turned up one part of his lip. Unable to bear his searching gaze, her hand moved over his eyelids and closed them. Reaching up on the tips of her toes, she administered a quick, unsettling kiss to his mouth. He sucked in his breath. His eyes snapped open.

She skittered away toward the kitchen. One long arm reached out and caught her elbow, his body following like a snake. "Don't go, lass…"

Sinead battled with a depth of wanting. It spilled out of her and caused her to move back into his embrace. His breath was shorter now. She wanted to say something but her tongue felt thick.

An emotional attachment to this man, whose every intention of returning to Ireland as soon as possible, would be damaging and foolish. She was afraid to hope. Everything she'd ever cared about had, somehow, mysteriously been taken from her. Her mother, her sister, the Cavanaugh's — and now, the Dewitts were trying to take Robbie away.

Her light eyes darkened and shadowed with the torment of losing so much. The hurt was too much to bear.

"I can't stay here or be so close to you, Connor."

"Why not?" he asked, then skimmed his hand up the side of her neck.

Sinead tipped her head to touch his hand and arched her body closer. One minute he was a glacial-eyed hunter, the next he was a kind and loving friend. "You plan on leaving, going back to Ireland. Right?"

His big hand framed her face. He let his fingers dip into her hair. "Aye, but I'll take you with me."

Having heated her body against his warmth, those words froze her like a blast of ice. She hesitated, staring directly at his broad chest. "I won't go. I can't risk losing another thing in my life, like Robbie. That's what would happen, for sure, if I tried to take him out of the country."

"Sinead, please understand. I can't be losing everything I've ever loved, either. My country, my kin or my horses. I'm a stranger in a distant land," he said woefully, his hard-gained self-control slowly receding.

This was becoming a complicated web, with Robbie and her future like spiders at the very center. "I guess we both are. I know nothing about country-living. I fear and hate the very beasts you love to distraction."

"You'd get over it. They're nothing more than big, simple animals. They want to please. They look for your attention and affection, not unlike Robbie does. After the races, perhaps, you'd be willing to learn about them?" The question was a plea.

"I think it would be better for both of us if we didn't share intimacies. That way, when you return to Ireland, you can get an annulment in the church, all legal-like…"

Connor cut off her thought and dropped his hands from her waist. He spun around, away from her. "'Tis the damned letter you got today, isn't it?" He looked angry as if the change of subject hadn't suited him.

She snapped back. "You don't need to be swearing now, do you?"

"The only way you seem to understand or respond is through harsh treatment. Has no one ever treated you decently in your life?" Connor's brow knit together in a seamless frown. He shook his head in apparent disbelief.

Sinead shoved him with the force of her anguish. "My mam was killed when I was only four. I barely remember her other than the great love she bore everyone. Some memory of her accident lingers. It was something to do with a horse."

Sinead was so deep into relentless remembrances, she barely noticed Connor stepping back and looking at her peculiarly. "Only my da tries to do good for me."

She grunted scornfully then continued. "The worst part being, no matter what he tries to do, it seems to place me into more trouble than before. 'Tis how we came to America, wound up in New York City, and how I got mixed up with the Cavanaughs in the first place," she complained.

"Now, what exactly are you trying to tell me?" he asked in a caustic way.

Her cry of need, a cry for understanding, was swallowed by the sarcasm of his question and his insolent glare. She let a long moment pass. There was no more time for subtleties. Things were happening around her in a much too rapid fashion.

She moved to him and jabbed him in the chest with a pointed finger. "It means, when I was but fifteen my father saw fit to remove me from the Catholic School for Young Irish Ladies I attended, and press me into household service. He claimed he was lonely for his family — what there was left of it."

"Sinead, certainly it was not the end of it..."

Tightness welled up inside of her. "Nae, for sure. He drove for Robert Cavanaugh, for several years, and then Lucinda, when she married Robert. Shortly after the marriage, Lucinda felt the need of a personal maid. My da thought it was a perfect place for me." Sinead's voice softened, momentarily. "Fortunately, she was a gentle mistress, unlike her mother. When she died, Adelaide Dewitt took me into her home because she couldn't deal with her daughter's child."

Connor's eyes grew dark. "How come Robert Cavanaugh married you, his wife's maid?"

The suspicious tone of his voice was unpleasant. Connor was digging into her past with cold indifference. She didn't like it.

Her next words were spit at him with deliberate anger. "Again, my da dug into the scene. Robert was near to death from his crippling injuries by then. He didn't want his son to be brought up in a Protestant home by snobbish, anti-Catholic folks." A snort came from her mouth. "My father, who was helping around the house, convinced Robert if he married me, Robbie would always have a home with a Catholic family. And so, the marriage scheme came to fruition."

She stared at the floor. Connor was ferreting out her deepest secrets, exposing them to the light of day. He forced her to face an undeniable fact. She was a willing participant in her da's plans, all done to keep Robbie close to her since he knew no other mother.

She gasped and brought her hand to her mouth. Suddenly she saw her world through clearer eyes. What she saw in herself wasn't a pretty sight! She was doomed to be punished for her inadequacies.

"In my innocence, nae, stupidity, I went along with another of my father's scheme," she said in a somber voice. "Foolishly, I have done nothing more than exchange one man who didn't really want me for another who…"

Heavyhearted, she walked to the window of the front room and watched Robbie play in the sand pile by the porch. At the edge of everything in her mind, shame gnawed, for her own adult actions, piled on top of the misery she feared in losing Robbie to the Dewitts. Tears blurred her vision.

Connor came behind her and looked out the window over her shoulder. "Don't despair, lass. We are not finished yet. But let's take everything in order." He placed his hand on the back of her neck. "First, the letter. We need to take care of whatever ill-will it tosses at us. I'm still here and standing by your side."

Sinead turned to him. Facing her own truths cut her down until her anger dissipated into thin air. She risked losing all she'd worked so hard to gain if she didn't follow Connor's lead here. "Aye, let's look at the letter." She walked to where she's dropped it and picked it up. She held it out in her hand. "I just can't look at it."

Connor took it from her and slit the top part with his fingernail. He read it. "The damned thing is nothing more than an invitation." He turned the note over in his hand and chuckled. "Worded more like a summons, to be sure, but 'tis only an invitation." His own words awakened his wrath.

"An invitation? To what?" Sinead questioned.

Connor grabbed her and swung her in a circle until she was dizzy. "Dinner. The damned invitation is to a damned dinner with the damned Dewitts. Saturday, the night of the horse parade. 'Tis hard to believe. They're in Saratoga. At Union Hall."

"Well, I'm not going to dinner with them," Sinead said with vehemence.

"Aye, y'are. With me. It says right here," he said, tapping the paper, "you're to be bringing your new husband. For a look-over I would assume."

"I can't..." she tried to shove herself away from him.

"And why not, may I ask?" Connor smiled and set her on her feet but kept her close to him. He liked the feel of her against him, soft and warm. The smell of her was sweet, fragrant as the lilies in the fields.

"I'll not be going to the Dewitts like some subservient maid. I have nothing appropriate to wear to a place like the Union." She patted her skirt and tried to get the wrinkles out of it.

"Aye, you do. You're the same size as several of the girls from Pegeen's boarding house."

A burst of air came from her lungs. "Connor, I'll not..."

"Aye, you will. They have perfectly appropriate clothing to wear everywhere around this town, some of it quite elegant and proper," he said. The grin on his face almost convinced her.

"I couldn't wear..."

"You could. You have to. There's no time to have a new dress made for you." He paused. "Listen, some of their stuff hasn't even been unpacked, if what Pegeen says is true. Most of those ladies are decent. They've only come to their present profession due to unforeseen circumstance."

Sinead shook her head in bewilderment. "What circumstances could possibly drive a woman to sell her body?"

"Let me ask you a question. Wouldn't you do everything imaginable to care for Robbie if there was no other way to do so?"

A shiver tore through her body. Hadn't she ostensibly done the same thing in trying to protect Robbie and to honor a promise made to a dead man? She married a man sight unseen and pledged, before a priest, to honor him forever. "Oh, Connor, 'tis sorry I am for what I've done to you."

"You've done nothing to me lass." He pulled her back up into his arms and softly kissed her mouth. "At least, you've done nothing to me yet, lassie. But I do have hopes..."

Through tears of gratitude Sinead kissed him back, equally as softly. "You've been decent to me and to Robbie. I would like to..."

291

"I like the both of you." He put a finger to her lips. She wanted to kiss it. "And don't be making any promises, missus. We've a job to do, to convince the Dewitts I'm a proper da to the wee laddie." He cuddled her in his arms. "But first, we've got to get you dressed in the most elegant outfit there is. I'll send word to Pegeen, if you agree not to embarrass her over her profession."

"Och, I wouldn't hurt anyone deliberately." She bowed her head in chagrin. "You've pointed out on several occasions that such a profession is sometimes wrought from great sorrow."

"And 'tis the truth of it. Besides, Pegeen herself is much taken with your da. Like any man, he's not aware of it yet, but things are bound to change."

His last thought jolted her. "But, Connor..."

"Hush now, lass. It's time to take the offensive. I have a plan in mind to outwit the Dewitts and save Robbie from their clutches."

"The saints preserve us. Another Irishman's planning! I don't think my heart can stand it." She giggled, just like Robbie.

"Come here, me darlin' Irish beauty," Connor exclaimed, drawing her tight against his chest. "It's time for another lesson in kissing..."

Before his mouth came down on hers, he saw her eyes widen with expectation and interest. He moved his mouth with unerring skill, nipping the lower lip with delicate gentleness. The sweet caress of her breath mingled with his. He grew hard when her response indicated her willingness to participate in a game of love.

He ran his tongue over her lips and into the creases at the corners, and she opened them to him. The tip of his tongue played a peaceful game with the inside of her mouth, exploring, discovering. No other sensations interfered with the wholesome smell of her, the honeyed, hot taste of her.

Her shaking hands caressed the back of his head and neck. The tip of her tongue touched his in an agreement to their play. A bolt of lightning shot through him. The kiss grew deeper, more passionate. Their mouths molded together, breath static. Connor's knees were weak. He wanted to take her to the bedroom and ravish every inch of her body.

The front door slammed. "I'm hungry, Mama," Robbie said, in his little boy's voice. "Can I have something to eat? Please..."

They moved quickly apart as if caught in a conspiracy. Connor drew away from her with the upper part of his body. He didn't dare let go of her totally, at the moment, not in front of Robbie. "Aye, laddie. I'll just be giving your mama a lift to the kitchen."

"What's the matter with her? Can't she walk?"

Sinead coughed, trying to hide the laughter rumbling up out of her. Connor lost the fight with his. His laughter tumbled out and made Robbie laugh with him.

CHAPTER TWENTY

Preparations for the evening were in their most active state. Connor lounged in the front room, waiting for Sinead to appear. He heard her humming then chatting with Essie, amid giggles. Essie's voice topped Sinead's, with some foolish comment, for the two of them laughed gleefully over it, in some female notion of fancy. His worries over the upcoming evening festivities lightened with the sound.

During the past week, Sinead made peace with the women of the boarding house. While they might not travel in the same social circles, they would remain close friends. No longer would Sinead chafe at society's strictures nor cut the women down in public or private. Consequently, Essie was staying the night to care for Robbie.

Tiny spurts of Robbie's voice penetrated the house from the sand pit, now placed at the side. He played there often, with his pail and shovel, or with the children from the tent city, making a barn out of rocks, sand and water for the pony-to-come.

Connor promised the lad a pony. He only needed to be the voice of reason and persuade Sinead. He was firmly convinced, nae hoping, no one could be around the large animals for long without developing a relationship with them. Even someone as fearful as Sinead. No doubt, it would happen, but he would not mistake her concession for submission.

Shrieks and shouts from the children interrupted Connor's thoughts. The children's laughter made him chuckle. He drew a mental picture of their present condition. They should look a mess by now, covered in sand and dirt.

He stood and went to the door. "You lads, out there. Be careful. Don't get too dirty or your mamas will kill me." His words were greeted with hilarious, high-pitched screeching.

Satisfied he'd done his fatherly duty, he moved to the window and looked out on the wonderful spread of land that made up the farm. A smile creased his face. When he left, Bowes and is daughter would own a wonderful legacy.

Since Sinead and he last kissed, she underwent a startling change of personality. Her excitement and enthusiasm for everything, her patience with his long hours and the smell of horse he carried with him and her acceptance of the ladies of the boarding house served to enhance the change. Even her dealings with young Rob were easier, softer.

His heart swelled at what he envisioned might be the very next step. He called over his shoulder. "Ladies, hurry or we'll be later than we planned." Connor felt a sudden surge of confidence stamp the evening.

He whistled under his breath and idly perused one of the many agricultural books he'd bought in the village. He had hoped to read them all, during the time it would take him to prevail upon his wife to return with him to Ireland. Then all the ready agricultural knowledge could be applied to the O'Malley farm and its horses. Tired of the interminable waiting, he ran his hands through his hair.

A return to Ireland seemed likely at the moment. Sinead insisted at every opportunity she intended returning to the city of NY with their son. Now, she did so in a quieter, more deliberate tone. His thoughts flowed on like quicksilver. He needed to do some fast thinking and intense planning, if he were to gain her agreement to travel with him.

"Sinead, what in God's sweet earth is taking so long?" he called from the living room. He moved back to the chair and plopped down in the seat, his legs stretched in front of him.

When she didn't answer, he went back to his private musing. He leaned against the chair's plush back and closed his eyes. What kind of a marriage would it be with the ocean between them? Annulment was out of the question as far as he was concerned. Was it possible another woman might appeal to him, like the lass he left behind in the Irish village?

Sinead came rushing down the hall from her bedroom and burst into the living room, her face ablaze with excitement. "Och, Connor. Look."

Connor shot out of the chair at the sight of her. She whirled in front of him, her filmy dress floating in waves at the side. Her scent wafted on each turn and made him crazy. She was gorgeous, this woman of his.

"The dress fits like a dream," she whispered. "It was so kind of Pegeen to be spending so much time preparing it." Whipping her skirt around her like a Spanish dancer, she twirled again and cocked her head. "Well? Aren't you going to say anything?"

The first image of her entering the room had stolen Connor's breath away. He stood mute and still. His heart clutched and expanded at her very presence. All thought of other women left his heart the moment he looked into Sinead's flawless face. A solitary grunt, of a bull staking his territory, snaked within his mind. Shafts of desire spiked to lance through him.

The fitted gown showed every inch of her lush curves. Her face, beneath a slight tan, was pink with excitement, her coloring vibrant. Her eyebrows arched in a wicked, suggestive way. Her eyes promised with a coy look of sensual innuendo.

This was no pale and delicate woman, he thought. She looked wanton, in a purely innocent way. Very much the jade. About her lay all of the subtle ways of entrapment women fostered. He determined not to fall for such a snare, not now, hopefully not ever.

"Well?" she asked again, puzzlement dotting her face. She tilted her head. Suddenly, she seemed unsure of herself. "Don't you like the dress?" Her expression saddened into a bleak-looking frown.

Connor tried to hide the avaricious gleam he knew sparked his eyes. He felt like a rat seeking refuge from a prowling cat. His heart beat thickened with the fever within his chest. He felt the stirring of manhood in his trousers. If she accomplished this just by appearing in front of him, perhaps he was doomed.

"You absolutely take my breath away." He stared at her with the mind of a predator. His gaze drifted from her radiant face to the embroidery on the wide, square neckline of her dress and the tasseled trim below it. "You are beyond anything I could ever dream happening to me."

She drew back for a beat. His sincere words surprised her, but no more than they surprised him.

Essie came into the room, her bright yellow hair swinging freely. Her toothsome grin lit up the room. "Doesn't the missus look lovely? Dazzling?"

"She goes well past lovely and dazzling. Try heart-stopping," Connor said, not removing his gaze from Sinead. He let it wander and linger to its contentment.

"Well, I'm going outside to play in the sand with my small charge," Essie informed them. When no one responded to her or looked in her direction, she fled through the front door, chuckling loudly.

Connor heard her chiding Robbie for the amount of sand his body contained. His mind quickly blocked out her voice as he crossed the room to his wife. His arms slid around her waist. He drew her tightly against the full length of his arousal, delighted at the womanly feel of her. He teased her lips with his tongue and wondered how long he could keep his desire for this feisty woman in check.

A flare of heat grew in her eyes, but she touched his chest with the heel of her hand, pushing her upper body away slightly. "Connor?" She worried her lower lip with the edges of her white teeth.

The very gesture set Connor aflame. A line of fire shot across his back and down his legs. His arms folded around her tighter than before. Afraid he might overstep what she was ready for, he kissed her brow in a loving gesture. His hands gently rubbed her back and then smoothed the hair, hanging nearly to her waist.

The unexpected feel of its full length and its silky quality captivated him. She usually wore it tied in a bun wound around her head or at the nape of her neck. He crushed a wad of hair in his hand, kissed it then her mouth softly.

"We'd best be going, lass, or I'll not be able to keep myself from devouring you in some unseemly fashion." He turned to the door and took her hand.

Her smile gladdened him, made him feel lighthearted. She followed the smile with a rich, zesty laugh and moved in front of him to go out the door he was holding open. They walked across the porch in the direction of the carriage and Bowes's grays, which waited patiently in the long circular driveway.

On the porch, Sinead called, "Rob. Come say good night to Mama."

The lad ran from the side of the house and stopped before running into her. In a hushed voice, he whispered, "Mama, you look beautiful." He looked down at himself. "I'm all dirty."

"But the compliment you paid to your mama deserves something." She bent down, kissed the top of his head and patted his back. "You behave yourself, Rob, and take good care of Essie…" She smiled at them both, linked her arm with Connor's and gazed up at him with adoration in her eyes.

"You look pretty, Mama," Robbie called, in an admiring small, soft voice. "Like a flower in the garden."

Sinead chuckled, looked down at him, then said very seriously, "Thank you, darlin'. Mama feels very pretty tonight." She tossed her head and again looked at Connor.

He ruffled the top of Robbie's head. "Behave, son." He put his hand over the hand on his arm. They strode to the carriage, where Harry, dressed in his best livery clothes, looked very smug and proud. He sat perfectly upright in the driver's seat.

* * *

Bleakly, Adelaide Dewitt stared out the window of the far too expensive room Ludwig engaged for their short stay in Saratoga. Money was tight since their house in New York City had burned to the ground. It was just as well, she thought. The city was not the same since the Civil War had started, nor was Saratoga. When the elite from the South stopped coming, the ambiance of the village was ruined for Adelaide. She sighed and brought her hand up to pat her hair in place.

Fortunately for the Dewitts, they had fled their city home before it was destroyed. Most of their valuables, except for some paintings and furniture, were secure in their house in Albany. That house, close to Adelaide's family and used only in the heat of summer, was intact and, due to the extensive renovations they made on it every year, beautiful.

Deep in thought, she turned from the window. Perhaps, if they used more of the money Robert Cavanaugh had left to their grandson, another New York home would be rebuilt on the same piece of land as the old one. Besides, Adelaide wanted a newer house with more luxuries in it, but she didn't mind staying in the Albany one for now. She walked with aimless abandon to the unmade bed and fussed with the covers, placing them in a neater fashion.

Restless with energy, she moved about the expensive hotel room, worried about finances. Ludwig had decided they should treat themselves. The visit to Saratoga for the first running of a *legalized* Thoroughbred Racing Card was the perfect excuse.

Ludwig promised not to bet heavily on the races. Not for a minute did she believe he would keep the promise. He was addicted. Gambling on all sorts of sporting events, a habit taught to him by Robert Cavanaugh, was at the root of Luddie's present financial problems.

She clucked to herself, distressed. In a nervous gesture, she ran her hands over her hair, making sure her bun was in place. She picked up the remains of the newspaper, lying on the floor, straightened it out, refolded it and let it fall from her hand to the nearby table.

Sad but true, she thought, Luddie's problems became hers when they married thirty years ago. She was a mere sixteen at the time and often wondered if her life would be different if she hadn't conceived the first time the forbidden fruit of lust was tasted. Well, one never knew, did they?

She lost her appetite for Luddie when his affairs with gambling and the demon rum drowned his interest in other pleasures and diminished his performance ability. She shrugged.

If her fate had been different, their daughter Lucinda wouldn't have been born, a terrible thing for Adelaide to contemplate. She had loved her daughter dearly. If it hadn't been for the dynastic loins Robert Cavanaugh had forced upon Lucinda's delicate, suffering womb, the girl would be with her mother still.

Anger in her every footstep, Adelaide circled the room at a faster pace. She stamped the heels of her shoes on the floor, with little care about people in the rooms below. How she hated Cavanaugh! Secretly, she had enjoyed the effects of Robert's crippling accident, and she managed to ignore the son he'd fostered.

A lowering of her eyelids and a soft groan brought her back to her senses. Lonely tears skimmed her eyelashes. It did no good to relive the past.

"Luddie, hurry, dear," she called, just to hear the sound of her voice. "We don't want to be late, now, do we?"

She and Luddie arrived in the village two days ago. They spent the time greeting people they knew from previous seasons.

Old Mrs. Elizabeth Smythe, a white-haired lady from New York City, hurried to impart the first bit of gossip. "How grand to see you, dear. And you, Ludwig. I spied your Jane strolling about with your grandson just yesterday."

Adelaide managed to hide her surprise, keeping her face bland with a bright smile. "Jane?" She chuckled. "Are you sure? Or have your *old* eyes played a trick on you?"

"On the arm of a very handsome gentleman, I must add," Elizabeth said, smiling slyly.

Luddie pinched her elbow. They stared at each other, a bit aghast, to think Jane was here, in Saratoga Springs, with young Robert and her new husband.

"Er, that's Jane's new husband, as a matter of fact," Ludwig responded.

"Why yes," added Adelaide. "We're planning on meeting with them before the racing meet. Perhaps, we'll see you for a long chat before then as well." With a brusque nod, Adelaide marched down the stairs of the hotel to the street level.

After concerted inquiries and conversations with several other guests, they learned of the farm at the lake. Returning to the porch, they watched the parade of well-dressed women and men and remained quiet until Elizabeth approached them for a second time.

Elizabeth, who loved to spread stories, confided to Adelaide. "The place out by the lake belongs to Jane's father. Bowes Brennan, of all people." She wrinkled her nose.

"Is that the truth? I didn't know," Adelaide lied. She was having a hard time disguising her feeling of disgust.

"Of course, it is, my dear. Would I lie to you?" The smile she gave Adelaide was broad and deceitful.

With equal fierceness, Adelaide smiled grimly. "Tell me what else you've heard."

Mrs. Smythe rubbed her hands together. "It seems, one Connor O'Malley handles the operation of the farm. They board horses for some of the wealthier thoroughbred owners, I'm told." She tilted her chin in Adelaide's direction, obviously pleased to impart news she hoped would upset her friend.

Adelaide pulled on Luddie's sleeve. "What fascinating news." They glanced at one another, nodded to Mrs. Smythe and slowly walked across the porch to the main doors. "We'll see you later, my dear," Adelaide called over her shoulder.

With Adelaide's hand on her husband's arm, the two scooted

down the huge porch of the hotel and glanced back at their gossipy friend. She was conversing with another. They sheepishly sat in two empty rocking chairs, their heads close together. There they discussed several plans, each of which came to their minds with the ease of their long years together and several practiced deceptions.

Once a strategy was agreed upon, Adelaide remarked. "How might living on a horse farm appeal to our Jane who hates and fears the animals?" Adelaide was not particularly fond of them herself, but she clearly understood Jane's fear and knew whence it came. "I doubt the marriage to her Mister O'Malley will go all that well."

* * *

A day later, Adelaide waited for Luddie to come out of the bathroom, She realized she was glad Robert was alive and well. Several times, other friends mentioned they saw him in the village with Bowes and the man Robert now called his da. No matter what the child called anyone, he would come back to New York with Luddie and her, she determined. They couldn't afford to lose the child's inheritance to some lowly Irish washerwoman. Not at this late stage in their lives.

"Luddie, hurry," Adelaide called to her husband. He was dallying with his evening shave, no doubt rereading the racing card for the tenth time. "They'll be here any minute."

"I'll be right along, dear. We need to consider, and think about what's going on in this town, in order to converse with those people with any sense of propriety," he shouted through the closed door. "Tonight, the game must be played for our success."

"Well, hurry."

"I'll be right there, my love. If you like, start down without me. If you should encounter them in the lobby, do not discuss anything important with them until I arrive."

"I'll wait," she answered begrudgingly. She slid onto the window seat, her knees crossed in displeasure, her foot tapping air.

Her nerves were frayed. She couldn't even bear to look out the window again, so she watched the bathroom door, waiting for her husband to appear.

Ludwig waddled out of the small room, his waistcoat stretched tight across a belly that led the way. His full mustache and long sideburns were still damp but freshly combed and waxed.

He tweaked the mustache with a certain male satisfaction. "Well, my dear, I must say you look very relaxed. And quite lovely I might add."

"Thank you, Luddie. Every compliment is pleasant, indeed. But I'm really quite anxious about this evening. We know nothing about this man our Jane married other than he stands to inherit property in Ireland. Fat lot it will do us over here in America."

"Addie darling, please, have some faith in this husband of yours" He flicked his wrist over the sleeve of his jacket to chase off a piece of suspected lint. "I've checked out this young fellow. He's a horseman of some note in Ireland, plus the eldest son of a titled father. With the gossip in this town, I'm sure he'll be equally famous here."

"But will he stay here? In America? If the rumors are true, after what happened to his brother and him in the city, I doubt he'll return to live there."

"I'm sure our little Jane will be able to persuade him to stay. She's quite a tasty piece of goods or haven't you noticed, Adelaide?" Ludwig leered.

"Don't be disgusting, Ludwig. This teasing will lead me to fancy something went on between the two of you." A rush of heat rose to her face.

Her husband bellowed with good humor. "I would be most flattered if you thought so, my dear. But you do understand it takes someone like you, with your beauty, your intelligence, to make a mockery of this man and turn him into a pile of quivering jelly."

It was Adelaide's turn to laugh, although her lips turned downward as the sound burst from her body. "Come," she said, keeping a smile plastered on her face. "Let give those two devils their due…"

With her hand linked to his forearm, the two left the room and strolled toward the stairs, prepared to make a grand entrance into the gigantic center lobby of the hotel. As they promenaded, they continually nodded, in a condescending manner, to people they passed, as if the DeWitts were far grander personages than those they greeted.

Faced with the final wide staircase, Adelaide drew her petite frame up to appear more imposing. "Luddie, walk me to the banister. I'll hold on with one hand and keep the other on your arm. I think we'll make such a refined picture, don't you?" She smiled up at him.

Ludwig tipped his head to his wife of many years and took her elbow. He brought her to the handrail with a sliding motion, offered her his arm and gently, with much deference, led her down the stairs.

From the steps, Adelaide saw Connor and Jane, waiting in the lobby. They were speaking to several men she knew on sight, many of them important financiers. She wondered how they became connected with such illustrious people.

Suddenly, she squeezed Luddie's arm and let air hiss between her teeth. A most unimaginable sight greeted her eyes. Bowes Brennan stood with them. A very attractive woman, even more petite than Adelaide, clung to his arm. He was talking and making grand gestures to the gambling house owner, John Morrissey. The shock over Brennan's even being allowed in the grand hall of the hotel brought Adelaide up short.

Her voice, pitched high, carried clearly across the wide expanse of the lobby area. "There they are." She rushed gracefully down the remaining steps, sweeping her gown in back of her, as if anxious to see the young couple. "My darling Jane," she gushed as she hastened to enclose Jane in an embrace.

Connor turned, nodded and reminded politely, "Sinead is her name."

"Ah yes, Sinead. Dearest girl, I am so happy to see you." With a great show of affection, Adelaide kissed both her cheeks. Sinead drew back, her eyes narrowed. Adelaide took the opportunity to toss a barb at her. "And you look so well. The outdoor climate seems to have put some color into your pale cheeks."

While his wife greeted Jane, Ludwig extended his hand to Connor. "My boy, how grand it is to finally meet you face to face." He nodded to Bowes. "And Mister Brennan. How nice to see you again."

Ludwig turned back to the woman he considered young Robert's governess. "And Ja—Sinead, you're looking quite fit."

Sinead looked at Connor and her da. She shrugged and gestured. "Have you all met Mister Morrissey? He's been so kind to us since our arrival."

Irish Jack Morrissey tipped his tall hat to them. "'Tis nice to be meeting ye. The O'Malley told me ye own a grand house in the City."

"We did," Adelaide said sharply, glaring up at a man she deemed most common. "Irish rioters burned it to the ground. We've nothing left but the land it stood on."

Morrissey smiled down at the woman who challenged him. "Och, 'tis a sad thing then. But to me countrymen, the land is everything good and glorious. Ye were lucky to have it. I'm sure 'tis waiting for ye still."

He looked around to include everyone. "Well, I'll be bidding ye good day. Have a pleasant dinner. Connor, lad, I'll be speaking with ye during the parade of the fancy horses. Should be an interesting event."

Adelaide, her eyes narrowed with dislike, her lips turned up in a sneer, watched the man tip his hat to her again and leave. Her eyes followed his bulky figure, greeting people on all sides, until he went out the large doors onto the porch.

She turned to Connor and Jane. "Let's repair to the dining room. My husband and I reserved a special table at the front." She quickly preceded them then whirled around, her gown twisting around her

leg. "I am sorry to be so rude, Mister Brennan. You haven't introduced us to your lady friend."

"Aye, Missus Dewitt. That be the case, but I'll do so this moment.
Pegeen lass, come forward here, for a minute of yer time. I'd like ye
to be giving the Missus here a big smiling nod, being as how she's
Robbie's grandmother."

Pegeen moved to his side with great caution. She popped a quick
curtsey to the Dewitts. "Sir. Ma'am."

"Will you be joining us at dinner?" Adelaide inquired, impo-
litely.

"Och, nae, Missus Dewitt. Bowes and me, we've already supped.
We'll be on the street, waiting for the show of horses."

Adelaide turned slightly. "Well then Ja—Sinead, Connor. Come.
We've ordered a delightful dinner. I certainly hope you're both hungry." As she moved off, she turned back to Bowes and Pegeen. "Perhaps we'll meet again somewhere."

Pegeen bobbed again and said sweetly, arching a single eyebrow. "Och, I'm hoping we will." She watched them troop single-
file into the huge room off to one side of the lobby hallway. "Like
hell I do. Perhaps when the place down there freezes."

Pegeen felt the heat of her face. "Bowes, me love, that rotten woman
chilled me to the bone. I couldn't have eaten in her presence for all
the tea in—och, you know the place."

Laughter blasted from Bowes small frame. He embraced Pegeen
and swung her around.

"Och, ye're making this old woman dizzy," she whispered in
his ear.

"Aye, and ye've been making me dizzy since the first I ever laid
me eyes on ye, years ago." Bowes set her on her feet. "I think I'm half
in love with ye."

"Half would never do me, Bowes. I'm an all or nothin' kind of
woman."

Bowes put his arm around her waist and pulled her close. "Well,
then lassie, would ye be wantin' to marry with an old man like

me?"

Pegeen frowned. "Bowes, I don't take kindly to that kind of teasing."

"Well, now. I don't think I'm doing such a fierce thing." His expression became serious. "I've been missing the warming nature of a woman."

He took her arm and walked slowly with her onto the porch. He situated her under one of the large lanterns hung for the festivities. "When me Annie died, I had me girls to take care of. I had me a livin' to make. Having been in love with a warmhearted woman in my youth, others didn't appeal to me for the longest time."

Pegeen's gaze shifted to the wooden slats of the flooring. "Ye don't have to tell me these things, Bowes."

"Aye, I do. I'm not saying I didn't have me a lass or two..."

"Or more..." Pegeen smiled at the man she'd loved for a number of years. "Perhaps, I'd better be listening to yer story."

"Pegeen, I wish ta hell I met ye years earlier." He drew in an elongated breath. "Me Sinead was brought up with coldness by them nuns in the school I sent her to. The cold streak followed her into her adulthood. 'Tis making her life a misery. And mine along with it."

Pegeen patted his arm. "Don't be too worried. I think she's found an extremely warmhearted and lusty man. She already loves him." Pegeen laughed. "She just doesn't know it yet."

"But she needs a woman's guidance. Someone she can talk to with confidence." Bowes pleaded. "Ye wouldn't want her to be telling her troubles to the woman ye just met, now, would you?"

"Bowes, I'll do the best I can for the girl. I like her. I truly do. But I'll not be having some man marry me for his child. I did it once and ...Well, ye see how I ended up."

"Nae. 'Tis not what I meant at all," Bowes added quickly. "Don't be misunderstanding me on purpose, Peg girl. I, too, want a warmhearted and lusty person in my life. I merely meant... well, with the both of us as one, we'll be able to cherish and guide those young ones."

"I don't know…" Pegeen shook her head.

Bowes swung Pegeen around and grasped her as close to him as he could. The kiss he placed on her mouth made her knees weaken with desire. She kissed him back with all the fire in her.

Everyone on the porch began to clap their hands in glee over the wonderful spectacle they watched with growing interest.

"Marry him," shouted one woman.

A man exclaimed, "Ah, just another show added to the Saratoga list of events. How absolutely fitting!"

Shouts rang out from all ends of the huge porch. All were positive with excitement.

Pegeen broke the kiss and flung her arms around Bowes's neck. "Och, ye kissed me into it."

"Then ye'll marry with me?" he asked, incredulous and thrilled.

Everyone surrounding shouted in unison. "She will. She will."

Then realizing the fuss they'd created, Bowes and Pegeen scrambled down the porch steps and disappeared into the welcoming dusk of the lamp-lit street. The people on the porch screamed and hooted with laughter.

One man cried out. "Let's make this a tradition…" He got on one knee and proposed to the woman at his side.

She, in turn, laughed louder than the other guests. She bent and kissed his mouth. "Fool, we're already married…"

CHAPTER TWENTY-ONE

The grand dining room at Union Hall seated about a thousand. Tonight, due to the upcoming parade of horses, tables were packed into every corner of the room, leaving little room for maneuvering. Dazzled, both Sinead and Connor took a step back. The excitement emanating from the room was very different than their simple life on the farm.

The décor was extraordinary. Hanging crystal-globed chandeliers lit the room with soft, sparkling perfection. White tablecloths shone with snow-white purity. The colorful dresses, worn by the ladies, enhanced the room with bright, brilliant colors. Sinead wanted to point.

Male waiters, holding trays of spicy, fragrant dishes high above their heads, rushed between and around the long tables. Everyone was served with fawning efficiency, great respect and a modicum of charm. Supreme gaiety filled the room. Sinead didn't know where to look first. She stared at the trays the waiters carried and watched as they danced, bowed, and removed the silver covers from over the food-laden plates, with a flourish.

The Saturday evening's fare was the kitchen's crowning glory for the entire week. The meals themselves were sumptuous.

"Look. The meals. They're as good as meals served by finest restaurants of New York City. Or any large city throughout the world, I'm wagering," Sinead whispered to Connor, holding her hand up to cover her mouth.

"I can barely hear you, but I do know what you mean," he added, giving her waist a tiny squeeze of agreement.

Guest vocalized their content with the meal, giving forth loud sighs of delight and excessive patting of stomachs. Their murmurs changed to a buzz and got louder minute by minute.

Seated at a table, which gave her a view of the porch, Sinead examined the people wandering about outside and in the dining room. The hotel was crammed with folks from all walks of life.

She tried to start a conversation, so the meal would not be so solemn. "I assume many of the folks here arrived in Saratoga to watch the horses perform."

"Along with the rich," Ludwig contributed with a smirking snort.

"Some come praying to be noticed mingling with their betters," Adelaide said, lifting her nose higher in the air. "Some of the young women you see, not unlike those from the boarding houses, appear on the scene with the hopes of attracting wealthy husbands or benefactors."

Ludwig added, "Some come for the social activities or what they can find in the way of goods to be bought, bartered or stolen."

Adelaide's tinkling laugh rose high above the table. People sitting at nearby tables glanced over. Adelaide politely nodded to them. Connor stared for a moment then peered at Sinead and raised an eyebrow.

Ludwig leaned over and said to Connor. "The new and legalized racing card brings a new and totally different element to the Springs this year. The turf crowd! They've come from sections of the North and the West. A few from the South, too, despite the devastation wrought by the War."

Connor replied with a bit of rancor. "I imagine horsemen convene on the village in great mass. I've spoken to several from Canada who arrived to contend for the racing purses. I'm caring for some of their horses."

Ludwig's eyes narrowed. He pointed to a group on the porch. "See those people?"

Both Connor and Sinead looked out onto the huge veranda but

saw nothing unusual.

Ludwig tapped Connor's arm and pointed again. "No, there. Those men in a huddle, fingering the racing card. Gamblers and bookies clustered together. Placing their bets, I would wager."

"Aye. I believe you have the right slant on the matter. I've spoken to many of them during the past week." Connor sat up straight in his chair and looked at Ludwig from a great height.

"Any good tips?" Ludwig asked. A crooked grin accompanied the strange light of eagerness in his eyes.

Excitement prevailed at the tables around them, making it difficult for Connor to answer quietly, so he shook his head, "Nae. I do not," he mumbled.

Throughout the rest of their meal, the conversation at the Dewitts' table was desultory at best. The older couple never mentioned their grandson's name, not even to inquire about his health. Other than a decided lack of appetite, the biggest problem for Sinead was the noise. Hundreds of people conversed in ardent tones one on top of another. They made her ears ache. She longed for the solitude and peace of the farm.

While waiting for dessert, Connor began the discussion to follow. "I'm wanting to thank you both for this kind invitation to dinner. The meal was delicious, but all through it I've been thinking of the purpose behind it. I presumed the dinner was for discussing something you felt was important."

Ludwig laughed then smiled at his wife. "I told you, my dear, this young gentleman was bright."

"I take it your answer is in the affirmative?" Connor softly inquired.

"Yes." Ludwig pushed his chair away from the table a bit. In a clumsy movement, he placed an elbow on the table. Adelaide touched his arm. He withdrew the elbow and sat up straighter. "I did wish to speak with you both, regarding our grandson."

"He has a name. 'Tis Robbie," Connor mentioned.

"Robert," Adelaide snapped.

Connor turned to her. His smile was cold. "We feel Robert too grown-up for a wee laddie. As a matter of fact, he now prefers to be called Rob. He feels Robbie is too babyish."

Sinead lowered her eyes so she didn't have to look at the Dewitts. "Och, Connor. I don't care what they call him. Let's just discuss what we have to discuss and be done with it all."

In a fit of temper, Adelaide slapped her napkin down on the table. "Let's go onto the porch. Ludwig wants to have a good vantage point when the horses are paraded in front of the Hall." She turned to her husband, her face a mass of wrinkles. "I told you talking to them would do no good."

"Adelaide, calm yourself, my dear. Our talk is not finished, just delayed. Isn't that right, Connor?" He turned to him to garner some manly support.

"Aye," Connor answered, "Besides, I'll not be wanting to miss all the excitement either or to see the horses react to the crowds."

"Whatever for?" Adelaide asked. She smiled at her husband, but there was an edgy sound to her words. "My husband thinks by looking at the animals today, he'll know how to choose them on race day, two days from now." She shook her head, her mouth turned down in scorn.

Sinead ignored the play between the Dewitts. She pinched Connor's thigh. The rock-hard muscles jumped at her touch. His huge hand settled over hers.

His face showed no expression whatsoever as he stood and helped her to stand. "One of the race horses boarded at the farm the past week. He was a bit spirited."

"Heaven knows how the beast will act on the day of the races. Crowds will cover the race track — with shouts and constant movement. A distracting lot they'll be, I'm sure," Sinead mused, standing close to the husband, whose strong physique enveloped and protected. Connor glanced down at her.

Her face grew warm, yet she shivered, flustered by the turbulent desire she saw flashing from his eyes. "I've heard such thoughts elsewhere." She gave him an embarrassed but wan smile.

Connor leaned in toward her. "But, so true…"

Ludwig stood and patted his rounded paunch. "Come ladies. To the porch…" He helped Adelaide to rise and kissed her cheek. She moved in front of him and circled the entire dining room before going into the long central lobby and onto the porch.

Connor and Sinead followed, slowly. Connor put his arm about her waist and drew her closer to him.

"Connor, careful. What will folks think?"

"They'll realize this man cares for this woman. Cares a bit too much, perhaps." Thoughts brought a red flush to his face and he laughed. "He's letting his emotions run away with him, I'm fearing."

"Those very same emotions will slip away as soon as you're back on board a ship to Ireland."

"I have no desire to argue with you tonight, lass. I'm wanting to hold you close to me. There's no crime in that, now, is there?"

Sinead sighed, stared up at him. She let her eyes fill with the essence of him, his scent, his even disposition and his sturdiness. She found she trusted him, his judgment on all sorts of things. Nothing would stop him if he wanted to go so badly. *What am I going to do?* Letting Connor leave would not be an easy task, but she knew she could never leave Robbie behind.

Outside, Sinead studied the sights on Broadway, the main street in the village. Flanked by the huge elms bearing lanterns of every description, the street glowed and shimmered with life. The center of the roadway was clear of all carriages. They now lined both sides of the thoroughfare for as far as she could see.

Sinead searched for their rig and, recognizing it parked nearby, waved. Harry sat on the driver's seat of the carriage, and vigorously waved back. Bowes and Pegeen sat in the 'box' like royalty. A farm hand stood at the horses' heads, although Harry, his hands relaxed on the reins, easily controlled the grays. Just below the carriage, the farm's wagon, containing many of the workers, snuggled against a particularly thick elm.

Sinead started in their direction. With a squeeze and a nod, Connor drew her attention to the Dewitts, who had established themselves directly beneath a soft pink porch light. He guided her through the crowd, eager to seek a good vantage point for the show to come.

John Morrissey stood on the steps talking to several Kentuckians, including John Clay, son of the famous Henry Clay. He looked up just in time to see Sinead and Connor crossing the porch to join the Dewitts.

He shouted up to them. "Connor, me lad, I just got word from some of me friends. You'll be having a surprise. Some good news tomorrow. One you'll be enjoying to the fullest."

"That would be nice for a change," Connor fired back. "Do you mind the telling me the importance of this great surprise?"

Morrissey let loose a booming laugh, bent down and whispered something to John Clay. Lifting his head, he grinned and shouted to the porch again. "If I told you then it wouldn't be a surprise, now, would it, laddie?" With a chuckle and a wave, Morrissey moved off the porch and down toward the roadway.

Connor shrugged and walked over to where the Dewitts had planted themselves. He placed himself directly behind Sinead and touched her elbow. She leaned against him, her soft bottom brushing his thigh. His arms went around her. With gentleness, he kissed the top of her head.

Adelaide had managed somehow to get a chair for herself. She sat, fanning her herself with what looked like a newspaper. Her eyes seemed focused on the roadway.

Ludwig stood by her side. "I don't suppose there's any reason for delaying our conversation. You two are fully aware of what needs discussion, so I'll make this short. We want our grandson. He belongs with his blood family."

"How come you left him in the city, with only a young girl to care for him?" Connor countered. "You left him and the girl to fend for themselves during an uprising. What if we had not been able to reach them? They would have burned along with your house."

Connor's words brought an angry reaction. Ludwig's face grew red. "The boy refused to come with us. We chased him around the house for hours. He insisted on waiting for his Mama Jane."

"And you left him." Connor refused to skirt the seriousness of the situation. His tone was terse. "He's content where he is, and he'll be staying there."

Ludwig drew himself up with an arrogance born of privilege. "Well then, let me make this plain. Adelaide and I will take this to a higher authority. Right into a court in Albany."

Although slow to anger, because of his size and the possible damage he could do to those smaller, Connor grew quiet. "You've intimidated my wife with those threats long enough. I'm thinking 'tis time you blew the sleeping volcano to the winds."

"You'll lose the boy then. He's our blood, not yours." Ludwig stamped across the porch.

Sinead leaped to the attack. "Blood? You two left the child while the city erupted around him. Gangs ran through the streets. Looting and burning everything in sight. The poor wee tyke. How could you be so uncaring and callous?"

"Hush, lass." Connor pulled her closer. She burrowed into his body, her face streaked with tears of outrage. With one arm around her, he faced the Dewitts. "Do your worst, old man. The lad and I developed feelings for each other in a very short time—feelings stronger than the relationship you've been building with him over years."

"You know nothing about it. You're just listening to the mad ravings of an unsatisfied woman." Ludwig stood with his hands clenched on his hips, like an old bawd. He nodded at Sinead. "The boy belongs with his rightful family."

She spat, "You don't want him. We do."

Connor continued, "I can only assume you have other reasons for keeping him in your custody."

315

The look passing between the Dewitts was all the confirmation Connor needed to be sure of his instincts. He hugged Sinead to him. "Come, lass. Let's go down to the carriage to watch the parade."

Sinead nodded. "Thank you, Connor."

He wiped the streaks of dampness from her face. "No thanks needed. I love the wee rascal." Connor guided her to the step. He turned and shouted back to the Dewitts. "Any time you'd be thinking of visiting with the laddie, come out to the farm. You'll be welcomed like visiting royalty."

* * *

Just as the horses came down Broadway from their starting point, Sinead and Connor settled into the carriage with Bowes and Pegeen. In order to see every step of the horses' progress over the roadway, the older couple climbed onto the rear seats. They pushed their knees into the soft backing and hung on to the low railing at the end of the carriage. They laughed and hugged each other with excitement.

Connor stood in the middle section and helped Sinead struggle to her knees on the cushioned seat in back of him. Trying not to slip off, she leaned against him. Her arms wound loosely around his neck, his shoulders holding her steady. His head nestled between her breasts. Every movement he made, in any direction, created a vibration in her belly, one she hoped he wouldn't notice.

She drew in a deep breath. The masculine scent of him, the residue of leather, of the outdoors and the spicy smell of the cream he had put in his hair to control its habit of spilling onto his face, conspired to heat her blood. Something within her sprung to life. Without thinking, she placed her lips on his hair for the briefest of moments.

He turned, an innocent grin of pleasure crossing his face. Sinead flushed and felt heat travel through her entire frame to the very tips of her fingers. The feel of his sturdy back against her body made her want more from him, a closer connection. Knowing she contained

316

little knowledge of lust, she used a great deal of imagination and felt exceedingly warm.

The internal thoughts cut off abruptly. The crowd's cheers swelled to a roar of loud approval. The pageantry before them began. The silky sleek running horses approached. Twenty-seven of them, from fourteen different stables, paraded down Broadway, past the piazzas and porches of the crowded hotels. Everyone shrieked with delight. The noise hurt Sinead's ears but she watched closely.

Each horse was ridden by a male, dressed in a bright racing costume. Black and white jockeys struggled to keep their mounts in control. Many of the horses and jockeys had been in the national spotlight throughout the country. The crowd hooted and hollered as the horses passed by them.

Dressed in a bright shirt, Jonah, Connor's recently appointed exercise lad, sat atop one of the lesser mounts. Although he would not be racing on Monday, his excited grin flashed with the pride he felt at riding one of the horses in the parade.

The loudest yells of encouragement from the crowd were for the favorites, the most well-known horses of the lot. Captain Moore, a reddish bay colt from New Jersey, considered by many to be the best colt of the year, skittered over the roadway. He set most of the other horses to dancing and bucking.

Lizzie W, a dark bay mare, caused the crowd to swell forward, trying to touch her, for luck. Men swarmed toward her, calling her name over and over. Men stationed on the road itself vigorously shoved them back to the tree line.

Momona, a bay mare of five, from Kentucky, and a record holder at an American mile, seemed to have her own section of fans. She drew gleeful shouts from knowledgeable race devotees. She twirled in place as if she understood the crowd was jubilant about her. Thunder, a four year old gray from Canada, who received his share of greetings, looked around as if bewildered by all the activity.

Morrissey's horse in the parade was a four year old bay. Having recently bought the animal from John Clay, the Irish fighter renamed the thoroughbred John B. Davidson, either to honor a benefactor or to disguise the horse's true identity. Only the wisest horsemen, like Connor, Bowes and Harry, knew the difference.

The spectacle was as the crowd expected. They hooted and screamed out the names of their beloved horses or cherished jockeys. They turned and talked to anyone who would listen. The entire concept was an extravaganza of great magnitude to those fortunate enough to witness it, a ribald event to add to Saratoga's already glorious history.

The closer the horses came to the carriage, the tighter Sinead clung to Connor. When the last horse went by, she sighed with relief, hoping her fears were not obvious to everyone. Glad the excitement was over, she was happy to get away. She wanted to be with Connor. *Home… Alone… With Connor.*

Slowly, he turned toward her as if drawn by an inexplicable pull. His hands moved to her waist. He threw two quick kisses, one at the inside of each breast, before she could move away. She was stunned at the fluttering sensation. Her nipples instantaneously hardened and rubbed against her dress. Her breath stuck in her throat.

With a look of longing on his face, Connor drew her head closer and placed a long, lingering kiss on her mouth. Sinead sucked in a breath and his lower lip with it. She was shocked at his behavior in front of such crowds and even more shocked at her own reaction, her sudden disregard for others. It was as if the people around them vanished, and Connor and she were alone.

Bowes interrupted the moment. Trying desperately not to chortle at their dilemma or his daughter's flushed face, he coughed loudly several times. He cleared his throat. "Er…"

In an attempt to get their attention, Pegeen stood beside Bowes, pretending to cough as well. "We have something we'd like to tell you…"

"Aye," murmured Sinead, finally catching her breath enough to make a sound.

Bowes poked Pegeen in the side. He nodded to the young couple who could barely look at anything but each other. "I see," she said. "Trust me. 'Tis for the good."

Bowes leaped off the seat, helped Pegeen down and moved to the carriage steps, nearly knocking Connor aside. "'Tis not of any importance at the moment. We'll stop out tomorrow to visit."

"Aye," Sinead answered, barely hearing a word anyone said.

"Pegeen and I are going out on the town. Ye're welcome to join us." While he spoke, Bowes helped Pegeen down the steps to the road. The two stood by the side of the carriage, waiting for an answer.

Connor stared at Sinead, letting her make the decision but fearful of the answer. Held spellbound by her gaze, he was unable to remove his hands from her waist. In turn, she fell into the liquid pool his eyes created and answered with a force of sheer energy.

"I think we'll be going home. There are still some horses on the property, and probably some of the others will be coming back in tonight. It would be better if I were there." Connor seemed to ramble on. "And I'm sure Sinead will want to check on young Rob." Some heavy-lidded, sensual expression made his words sound contrary.

Alarmed by the strength of her feelings, Sinead's tense muscles suddenly unknotted. Tears made her eyes shiny. Expectant, she willed anxiety away.

Connor barely raised his voice as he stared at Sinead. "Harry, do you mind taking us back to the farm so early? You can come back into town after, if you like."

"No, Con, I'm not minding, for sure. In fact, with all the noise here, 'tis about ready I am to be turning in meself." He turned slightly in his seat. "We'll just be takin' a leisurely drive past the lake on our way. Give us a fair chance to rest the grays from the excitement of the evening."

"Thanks, Harry..." Connor settled Sinead in the back seat and sat next to her, his arm draped over her shoulder. "Are you comfortable, lass?"

"Aye..."

Harry clucked to the horses and moved them from the lineup of other carriages. At the corner, he crossed Broadway and headed toward the lake road.

Sinead shivered, thinking, hoping, rethinking what might happen tonight. Was it worth it, she wondered. He'd be going back to Ireland and going without her. If he stayed, it would be torture for him. She wanted him so badly now, she'd risk most anything—anything, but Robbie. Just thinking of letting the child go sent a wave of nausea coursing through her. The whole arrangement of circumstances was a sin against hope.

"Are you cold?"

"Not really."

Nevertheless, Connor removed his broadcloth jacket. "Here. Put this over your shoulders. It'll give a wee bit of warmth once we get lakeside," he said in a hushed voice.

"Thank you, Con."

He chuckled, squeezed her shoulder then lightly rubbed it. "I believe, madam, 'tis the first time you called me Con."

"I hear the men say it all the time." Sinead couldn't think of another thing to say. She leaned back and tried to make her breathing sound even. She quickly realized it wouldn't work.

The carriage barely made the turn onto Union Avenue when Connor's lips met hers. Her heart rate increased. It pounded in her chest, in the groove of her neckline. A roar started in her head. It grew louder with each clop of the horses' hooves on the road. The excitement she felt knew few bounds. This was so unlike her.

"Hey Harry," young Jonah called from the side of the road.

Connor and Sinead pulled away from each other like two children caught in a foolish battle. Neither had heard a horse approaching. "Jonah...," they mumbled together

"Hello ma'am. Con. The owner of this horse wants to put the beastie in our stable until the race on Monday."

"What did you tell him?" Con asked.

"I didn't think you'd mind, since we have open stalls in the second barn. We can keep him separated from the other horses."

"Good enough. We've got the room," Connor said in a business-like tone. "We'll be leaving the gate to the lower road open. We'll set out lanterns. Be careful, going into a strange area. You have a young horse under you."

Harry spoke up. "Con, I'll do the gate and all. I'll be waiting for the laddie down by the gate, in case the horse acts up. And I'll be checking the other horses as well. If anything's wrong, I'll be calling ye quick as a hare."

"Aye, Harry. 'Tis good of you, for sure. About time I was trusting me own men to do their jobs. Just be careful with the colt there, Jonah. Don't let his playful tricks get the best of you."

"I'll be careful. I promise. He's a nice mount. Kinda' quiet."

"Be careful he doesn't surprise ye."

Harry picked up the reins and sent the grays forward.

No sooner than the horses moved, Connor curled Sinead in waiting arms and bent to her mouth again. This time he delved deeper, tickling her tongue with the tip of his own. The response thrilled him. If he continued this on the way home, taking whatever liberties he could, he wondered if she be ready and willing for the final act?

Chapter Twenty-two

Parts of Saratoga Lake, the shoreline thick with trees, lay covered by a soft mist. It crept over the rippling water, creating gentle pictures weaving in and out of the shore like threads of gossamer. Velvet blackness, lit only by a hovering full moon sliding behind an occasional thin cloud, drew a deep breath from Connor. He was further soothed by the steady hoof beats of the two carriage horses.

Moonlight reflected off Sinead's lips after his mouth left hers. The romantic scene suited and filled his mind with images of what might come next. The suspense of the conquest of this woman was to be savored and enjoyed. Sinead's graceful neck, stretched and open to his lips, was tempting. He was about to kiss its creamy expanse but stopped when Harry swung the carriage off the lake road onto the main road to the property.

The road looped and curved like a silvery skeleton in the dim light. The broken rhythm of the grays jarred. They pranced a bit, sensing the closeness to home, where food, shelter and rest were in the offing. Harry controlled them, brought them back to a slow trot and drove on with an expertise surpassing Bowes's.

"Harry," Connor mumbled, his voice hoarse and gravelly with lingering passion, "take the horses down onto the lower road. Leave the gate open for Jonah. Bed these two down well. They've worked hard since they've been here and, from what Bowes told me, this was to be their holiday for the year."

"I'll be doing it, Connor lad, but don't..."

Connor cleared his throat. His voice dropped to a conspiratorial level. "Sinead and I will walk up to the house. A bit of fresh air will do us both good," Connor said softly, wondering if he could stand upright with the tight erection pushing away at his trousers.

He winced with pain, struggling to control urges. In the well-enlightened landscape of his mind, everything centered on his groin and its gratifying fullness. Never had a woman excited him more.

Sinead was warm, loving and strong of spirit. Her interest in culmination of this night was immense, yet innocently adventurous. She tantalized and maddened him until he felt quivery with the force of lust. Not wanting to ruin the eagerness she displayed, Connor determined not to hurry her. A walk by the creek might give him time to cool.

Harry stopped the carriage at the darkened lower barn. He leaped from the driver's bench to loosen some of the attached harnesses from the vehicle. Connor stood, adjusted himself the best he could and stepped from the carriage in a bound.

He turned in time to help Sinead, who tripped on her skirt and fell into his arms. "Well, Missus O'Malley, don't you think you're being a bit forward here? For sure, you're trying to entice me from my innocence."

Harry chortled but kept about his business.

Embarrassed, Sinead pushed away from Connor and tried to be humorous. "Get on with ye, O'Malley. Leave me be."

The tone was far more serious than he expected. "Well now, missus, will you be walking with me, down to the creek? There's a fine rock just waiting for us to sit on it for a spell."

Connor reached over, took her hand and gave it a slight tug. "Come, lass. 'Tis but a short step from here. The breeze will cool our tempers some."

"Tempers?" Harry muttered to himself before snickering.

"What, Harry?" Connor asked, knowing full well the man made a mocking comment. He shook his head, figuring it was a remark meant for the male of the species. Such remarks were expected from friends.

"Nothing, boss. Just a whisper to one of the animals here…"

"Aye, 'tis sure I am, friend."

Connor laughed and pulled Sinead along a walkway the workers fashioned out of flat stones. The path wound around a copse of birch trees, hiding the creek from view. They could hear the creek bubble and dance with abandon on its voyage toward the lake.

Coming out from behind the shadow of the trees, the rock, partially covered by ferns and moss, loomed into view. Its large, flat surface hung over the cool, sparkling liquid of the creek, that laughed aloud as it tumbled over the boulders in its path.

Sinead moved straight to the rock, which clutched the ground with an arm flung above the water. This time, she pulled Connor after her. "Och, Connor, the moon is so bright. Each time it passes a cloud in its way, it acts like some sassy wench winking at her fellow."

He breathed in sharply, took the remark as a boon and turned her toward him. "Are you intending to be my sassy wench?"

A blush moved from bare throat to face. She laughed and gave him a big wink, her mouth wide in a grin. "Was it sassy enough, husband?" she asked, winking again and again, first with one eye then the other.

She stopped in mid-wink. "Or is this better?" Her arms slid around his neck. She stepped into his embrace. Standing on tiptoes, she initiated a kiss, lips open a smidgen, inviting.

Desire coursed through Connor, sharp as the cutting edge of a scythe. He lifted her to press hard against his body. Within seconds, the kiss deepened. They couldn't get enough. Mouth groped with mouth, angling for position. Tongue fought with tongue, tasting, dueling for supremacy, neither or both being the winner.

Connor's initial erection magnified to a throbbing degree. His breathing grew erratic. Sinead gasped for air. A moan escaped her warm and open lips.

Connor went to his knees on hard stone and drew her with him, closer to where the rock protruded over the water. He lowered her gently onto a patch of moss. Still kneeling on the rough surface, his lips traveled all over her face up to her ears.

Heat rippled through him. "You are the most beautiful woman I know…" His arm cradled her shoulders.

A childish pout curled a corner of her lip. She muttered, "Have you known that many, Connor?" The question came from some deep-seated worry, although she lay back on the carpet of moss and his arm. She stared at the stars blinking from their lofty perch.

Connor settled himself on one hip and an elbow. He stared down at the beautiful face beneath him. "How many women I might or might not have known matters not. You are lovely, a true beauty, inside and out." He lightly kissed her mouth.

"Sinead, I want you to know I understand your devoted protection of young Rob. I've come to love his sweetness, his innocence. I also see what the Dewitts are about, their veiled threats. I want to protect you and the lad." He paused for a moment, considering. "I sense there's something the Dewitts desire even more than their grandson at their side."

"Connor, I'm frightened." She looked small and sad. "I've come to rely on you so much of late. My heart will break if you return to Ireland or seek some other woman. I know I haven't pleased you the way a man likes to be pleased, but I'm afraid…"

His naked gaze afforded ample fire with which to destroy or claim her. "What are you afraid of? The act of mating?"

Sinead sat straight up, nearly knocking him over. "Nae, I truly believe the *act* is a simple thing. Or so I've been told. 'Tis the other possibilities in life."

"What? I don't understand you." Connor sat up and examined her dour expression in the dim light.

"Connor, what if we mated and I carried your child? It would leave two children without a father." A shuddering breath made her lower lip tremble. "Have you given any thought to that possible occurrence?"

The anger beginning to rise in Sinead's voice took him aback. Nothing was on his mind this night but the planned seduction. He tried to ignore what her words and tone of voice did to him. He concentrated on his lusty intentions but felt them slipping out of his grasp. *A child of his without a father?*

Sinead stood up. "I've loved kissing you, loving you, however little was accomplished to your satisfaction."

She brushed the skirt of her dress, surprised to find clingy moss refusing to let go. "I think I'll retire for the night. I'm so sorry to disappoint you yet again, Connor. I can not take the chance of you leaving me with another child to care for and no man." She stepped off the rock and walked through the copse of birches, holding on to each tree as she passed it.

Forlornly, Connor followed behind her. "Let me see you to the house. I'll stay in the tents. I have some serious thinking to do."

"Aye, Connor, I believe ye do have serious thinking to do."

Out in the open field, Sinead spun around to face him. "I cannot go to Ireland. I cannot take Robbie away from his *natural* grandparents, however bad they seem to you or me. They sustained the two of us since Robert Cavanaugh's death, and they deserve some remembrance of the daughter they loved so dearly."

With dogged persistence, Connor grasped her arms and drew her closer to him, wondering how he possibly could explain his feelings without hurting. "But they don't want you, Sinead." Her eyes closed with uncertainty, her expressive face distraught.

She stared at him for a long moment, shook herself loose from his grasp but stood directly in front of him. The silence between them lengthened. In that silence, worlds of communication sped through them, touching each with dramatic fingers.

"Neither do you, Connor O'Malley. Neither do you…" Her eyes filled with tears. "You don't want me either…"

She ran past him, across the first field, then across the second, past the barn. At the base of the stairs to the house, she wanted to turn to look, to study the man with a dispassionate eye, but thought it would shatter her heart into pieces.

Sinead sensed he was standing where she left him, not moving an inch to come after her. She trudged up the steps, head hanging low, mind a fury of conflicting thoughts and desires.

My God, I'm in love with the man. She loved him with a fury and a passion she'd never felt before. Through the terrible riots, excessive traveling and watching his easy way with Robbie, she had learned to love. Her heart danced at the very sight of Connor O'Malley.

The realization chilled and heated at the same time. What she wanted was Connor's arms around her, to become the wife she felt he deserved. Was she going to be alone forever in this world? Never to have anything she wanted? What was to become of her?

Wavering, she turned around to look then chastised herself. Something snapped. She forced herself to stand stiff, spin on her heels. She marched up the steps with more purpose, running to hide the burning in her body.

Besides, she loved the child with an intense fervor. Robbie would be cared for as she promised his father. No one could break the deathbed promise. Connor and she needed to arrange an annulment through the church, either in Ireland or here. The place where the marriage would be dissolved no longer mattered.

Sinead stood in the doorway of the house, knowing they had nothing more to say to each other, then went inside. Closing the door behind her, she leaned against it for a moment, hoping for strength in the decision. With a new resolve, not to be broken, she held onto the wall for balance in the darkness and tiptoed down the shadow-draped hallway to her nun-like room at the far end of the house.

The way her body shook, she seemed like a devout old Irish woman staring into the eyes of a banshee. Without bothering to undress, she flopped on the bed. Huge gasping sobs racked her body, the strangling sobs ripping across her nerves.

* * *

Running his hands through his hair, Connor watched Sinead charge away. Chilled beyond belief, he felt like he was standing naked in a vast field of ice.

Sinead's gentle, quiet demeanor, overburdened with a sadness she couldn't hide, filled his mind. Love warred and wept in his stone cold heart. He wished to melt into the earth, wondering if he would again feel the beloved familiar warmth following a thaw.

Sinead had awakened an unexpected, reluctant admiration in him. It made the taste of the defeat in their relationship most sour. She admitted freely and openly that she cared for him. He hadn't been as honest. Those facts, along with the grandest and slowest-fading erection he'd ever experienced, did nothing to improve the moody temper beginning to build despite his admiration for his wife.

As he walked toward the tent, where Bowes and he stayed when first on the property, his thoughts wandered. He searched his heart. He could run after Sinead, groveling like a pup awaiting scraps from the table, grateful for whatever small favors she promised this night, or…

"Didn't I dance enough, beg enough and sweat enough in my pursuit of her?" he grumbled. "Running after her, begging for more, will only strain my pride and prove the increasing weakness I get at the mere sight of her." He knew those emotions were something he needed to negate if a return to Ireland was planned.

Ireland… it was too strong a pull to turn down. How he longed for the peace and security he found in his father's presence, in his father's home, he thought, as he tramped through the damp grass.

He stopped mid-stride. His da…wasn't it his da who got him into this mess in the first place? The damned lottery! Bowes Brennan! The name was familiar somehow, lurking in the back of old memory somewhere. There was some connection he hadn't seen before.

Connor picked up his speed. He ran toward the tent, hoping

Bowes had returned to the property. The tent was empty. His damp shoes made tracks on the wooden floor. He flung them off and rolled onto one of the cots, still dressed.

His thoughts would keep him company tonight. The need to come to America and give up all he held so dear bore heavily on that lottery in Ireland. He determined to figure out the connection between his da and Bowes and the lottery, a connection which had sealed his fate.

Connor needed to think things through tonight. There were decisions to be made, decisions that affected every one of them.

Nervously, he pushed hair from his temples. He began to feel the magnitude of what he stood to lose: the home in Ireland, the close family ties, the beloved horses. Or a new home in America, American horses and a new wife and son. Everything needed sorting. He had to find some kind of logical order, see reality without his usual inclinations toward daydreaming and grandiose visions.

First, the horses. What did they mean to him? What of the breeding program he had started at O'Malley House? Could Bartley and the twins handle the tasks needed to make it a successful venture? Pain came with the admission that they could do it, and easily. Didn't their own da train them all the same?

Besides, there were fine horses in America. Even he admitted some were equally as good as his Irish horses. Would he be able to establish an O'Malley Stud farm here in Saratoga? He didn't know the answer. Only time would tell.

He already knew going back to New York City was not an option for him. He hated everything involved with the place. But could he convince Sinead to stay with him here? He doubted it.

And what of Sinead? Of Robbie? His wife was right. Why bear more children without a da to love them? It didn't make any sense to him either. Perhaps, he wasn't worthy of being any child's sire — that is, if he didn't already consider Robbie his.

For the entire night, Connor floundered with the fragments of dreams. When he woke the next morning, he was positive he would help Sinead get total custody of the wee laddie who counted so heavily on her love. He would uncover the secret the Dewitts harbored and save the two people who meant so much to him.

CHAPTER TWENTY-THREE

Yawning and stretching, Connor nearly fell from the narrow, hard and far-too-short bed. Slightly disoriented, not being where he expected to find himself — in the marriage bed — he rolled onto one side. Muscles aching from a restless sleep made him uncomfortable. Mindless annoyance rose with each movement.

He raised one eyebrow then opened both eyes to a gray dawn. His eyes itched and burned. He sat up and rubbed the sleep particles from them, barely keeping his lips from curling into a snarl. With supreme effort, he pulled on boots and stood, groaning like a wounded animal.

The bowl of clear water he'd set there the night before while he dressed still graced the table to the left of the cot. He sloshed his hands in the cold water, dashed some on his face without bothering to dry it, and glanced around at the depressing and restrictive environment of the tent. What a lousy way to live, he thought, and made a mental note to put up houses for the permanent help.

He stopped short. Thoughts of the evening before came racing into his mind. Had he make some kind of decision? He wasn't aware if he had come to any conclusions regarding the problems existing between Sinead and himself.

Suddenly, the picture of a chestnut horse jumping over a high, restrictive fence and knocking a woman to the ground popped into his memory. Trying to catch the scene and make it firm, he squinted, fumbling with mental fingers at images flashing by and escaping his grasp.

"The horses on the property?"

The sound of his own voice startled him. With pounding heart, he flew out of the tent onto the damp grass. Taking one deep breath, he scanned the area. Some horses were turned out in the large field and serenely grazing on lush grasses. Harry stood in the middle of the smaller paddock, with a longe line, exercising a mammoth bay gelding in a circle.

He turned and sent a salute to Connor. "Con, here's a horse for you. Big and powerful."

After nodding, Connor shrugged his shoulders, heaved a sigh of relief, pleased to see the horses being taken care of without his express orders. He turned away and stared up at the house, sitting peacefully on the crown of a grassy knoll.

The first flush of sunlight appeared over the horizon. It was time to go and face Sinead. He swallowed the lump in his throat and tried to absorb the shock the mere thought of her brought him. Perhaps, they could work out some compromise, something that might not jeopardize either of their futures.

Raising an arm in a salute to Harry, to indicate where he was going, he started off across the fields at a jog. He slowed as he neared the stairs. A grand-looking, one-horse carriage Connor didn't recognize had wheeled up the drive and stopped in front of the house. Connor increased his pace and flew up the steps three at a time.

John Morrissey sat calmly in the driver's seat, studying the house. His gaze swept up as Connor came up the last step onto the landing. "Laddie, thought ye might stop at me establishment last evening," John shouted.

Connor crossed the roadway. Morrissey stepped down from his perch at the front of the vehicle and stuck a hand out in greeting. "I told ye I'd have a surprise for you today."

The men shook hands and cuffed each other on the back.

Puzzled, Connor tilted his head to one side. "Och, aye. You did mention a surprise last night. I forgot. Other things took up space in my mind," Connor said.

Someone sat in the shadows at the back of Morrissey's canopied carriage, just beyond where the sunlight swept in, and chuckled.

"Too much into yer cups, were ye, laddie?" Morrissey asked, a sly grin dotting the broad, handsome face.

"'Tis not much of a drinker I am," Connor offered in response, wanting to discover who was in the back. The laugh sounded familiar.

"Well, 'tis of no importance whether ye remember or not. I've brought the surprise with me this morning and intend to be leaving it on yer doorstep. Come, laddie. Climb out of me carriage so I can be on me way."

A young man, red hair shining even in the soft light, leaped from the carriage and ran in a straight line at Connor. "Con. My God, 'tis good to lay me eyes on yer ugly body."

Connor gasped, stunned. Tears clouded his eyes. He fought back an overflow of strong emotion. One shriek, "Egan," and Connor's brother was clasped in huge, strong arms.

Exploding with laughter, Connor grasped Egan around the back, lifted him with a mighty groan and swung around several times before allowing Egan's feet to touch the ground again. "You've gained some weight there, brother." They slapped each other's back in their delight to be reunited.

"Aye. And ye're still as big as a horse. As strong as ever..."

Without letting go, Connor held Egan away from him in order to take a better look. Egan's freckles stood out against the light-skinned face. He had filled out, grown into the man he promised to be.

A hug was in order, but how did you continue to hug a grown man? Connor stared at his youngest brother. Something inside him cried out, nearly vocalized, to the young lad Egan used to be.

"And where's yer beautiful wife?" Morrissey asked.

"Aye. Where's Sinead?" questioned Egan. "What with all yer hollering, I thought she'd come running to the door to see what ailed ye."

The door squeaked open. The three men turned as one. Sinead peeked out, her face wistful, pale and distraught. Robbie was directly behind her, unsure, grabbing at her skirt. Still dressed in clothes from the evening before, her hair was messed. The dress looked like she slept in it. She looked disheveled, ill at ease.

The men stared, first at her, then at each other, speechless.

"I'm here. Rob and I watched and listened to your male moans and groans. We didn't want to disturb a meeting of the clans," she murmured.

She sent a brief smile to Morrissey. "Mister Morrissey." She nodded to him then turned her attention to Egan. Her face was wreathed in a lingering grin. "Och, Egan, 'tis glad I am to see you. So fit and healthy besides."

Morrissey took notice of the dress Sinead wore. He turned to Connor and gave him a peculiar, inquiring look. But the Irish in him forced him to be charming. "Och, missus, ye're just as lovely to look at in the morning as ye are at night. Dressed in yer fanciest garments to greet the day, are ye?"

Her eyes downcast, Sinead's face flushed and turned a bright pink. The color traveled slowly up to her ears. The supreme discomfort under which she labored was apparent.

Morrissey kept the conversation going. "Well, lads, 'tis off to church with me wife, I am. When the two of ye are more settled, join us on Sundays. I'll introduce ye to the most devout Father Michael. A grand young man he is, too."

Morrissey climbed back up onto the driver's bench. He tipped his derby to Sinead. "Missus. Gentlemen. I'll leave ye to yer reunion." With a mighty cluck to the horse, he maneuvered the carriage around on the circular roadway and waved at them. With another resounding cluck and slap of the reins, he was off down the road at a rapid trot.

A strange expression of bewilderment froze on Egan's face. He stared at Connor then at Sinead. As if he quickly summed up the situation, he queried, "Aren't I to get an embrace from me favorite sister and me new nephew?"

"I'm your only sister, if what my da tells me is true. A while back, Da mentioned there were just the five O'Malley brothers and no lasses. Of course, I only know of you two."

"Do ye mean to tell me, Connor has not spoken of his family to ye?" Egan turned and glared at his brother. "What's the matter with ye, Con? Are ye ashamed of the boyos?"

"Whoa, there, brother. First there were the riots to speak of, then the long travel time to this place and the setting up of it. Sinead and I had little time for genteel conversation. Besides, I'm missing them all with such a fierce ache I can't set it aside."

As he made the statement, Connor realized how true it was. He and Sinead never really talked about things of importance. They threatened each other with what was most prevalent on their minds, her custody of Robbie and his desire to go back to Ireland at the earliest opportunity. With a sad, searching gaze, he stared at her.

Unable to withstand the penetrating stare, Sinead leaned down and whispered something in Robbie's ear. The boy giggled, sped out the door and threw himself at Egan. "Mama said you're my uncle."

Egan scooped the lad up and bear-hugged him until Robbie cried for mercy, giggling all the while. "That I am, young fellow, that I am. 'Tis Uncle Egan I am, for sure," he said, tickling Robbie for emphasis.

About to place Robbie on the ground, Egan turned. Another carriage pulled by a large chestnut gelding entered the drive at a leisurely canter. Bowes and Pegeen sat in the driver's seat together. "That's my grandda Bowes."

"Just saw Morrissey on the road," Bowes shouted. "He told us Egan was here. I'm wanting to speak to the lad." He stopped the carriage in the circular roadway. "I want Pegeen to meet him." He swiveled in the seat and put an arm around Pegeen. "This redheaded wonder is me son-in-law's brother, Egan. Laddie, meet Pegeen Riley."

With Robbie still in his arms, Egan moved to the side of the carriage and extended his hand. Sinead came out of the doorway like a shot, ran across the porch and tried to grab Robbie from Egan's hold.

He wheeled around to face her. "What's the matter with ye, lass?"

"Don't take him near the horse, please…. She stepped back, wringing her hands. "He'll get hurt."

"From this old nag," her da teased. "'Tis all right, Sinead, child."

Connor leaped into the fray, taking the boy from Egan. Robbie's little arms went around Connor's neck. He put his face so close they touched at the brow.

Robbie's face scrunched into a pout, his lips turned downward. "I don't like my mama, right now. She's being naughty."

Sinead gasped. Tears filled her eyes. She turned away and moved to the porch.

"'Tis all right, son. She's just having a bit of fear for you," Connor said walking to the horse's head with deliberate steps.

"I'm not afraid, Da," Robbie said, shaking his head.

"I know, son. 'Tis something we'll take care of right now. We are going to prove to your mama horses won't hurt you." Connor lifted Robbie up and put him on the chestnut's back. "Hold tight to the horse's mane. Good boy." He patted him and called out, "Sinead, I want you to look here."

Stealing a glance at her, Connor saw she was frozen in the spot. He took a short step toward her. "No matter what the cost to me in forcing you to do this — do this you must, for the lad's sake," he said softly.

Sinead's body trembled as if diseased. She gasped audibly then moved like a snail, her eyes so large everything was reflected in them. She sobbed in a breath before stumbling into Connor. She felt the pressure of his arm holding her steady.

Robbie held on to the mane with one hand and waved to her. "Look, Mama. I can sit here and I'm not even hurt. Please, Mama…"

The sight of him atop the huge horse sent a renew stab of fear to her heart. She clutched Connor's hand tightly, though it meant humiliating herself, and struggled to adjust her expression to one of pleasure.

"Sinead, look at your son." Connor urged. "He's delighted to be where he is. Look, lass. Give him the pride in himself only a mother can give."

Knowing the others were watching her, her face ignited into flames of rushing heat. Her body shook, closing off breath until it ran short. She looked up at Connor. Unable to bear his searching gaze, she pleaded, "Help me…"

A strained pause held them all enthralled. Her glance over the roadway barely connected with Robbie's before shifting back to Connor's. Her body was depleted of all its strength. "Help me…"

Sinead plunged into frigid, stultifying fear of horses. She needed to clear her mind of her mother's accident or lose some tenuous grasp of her son. "Con, help me walk over there — to Robbie — to the horse. Please, Connor." She looked up at him, begging for a boon. "Do this for me and I'll not be asking another thing of you."

"Sinead, darlin', ye can do it. For yerself," Bowes said softly, his voice barely touching her. "When ye were a wee lass, ye loved the big beasties, as ye used to call them. I couldn't keep ye away from them, nor yer mama neither. I know it was her undoing, but it doesn't have to be yers. Take some of yer mama's spirit back for the laddie."

Connor turned a bit and gave her da a strange look. Sinead straightened, lifted her chin. Although she didn't let go of Connor's hand, she walked gingerly to the horse and her son. She came close enough to feel heat emanating from the animal's sturdy body and halted. Connor stood in back of her, his legs braced. She leaned against him, briefly closed her eyes and stretched out a trembling hand to touch Robbie and the horse.

Robbie grinned. "See, Mama. It doesn't hurt."

Now wide-eyed, she touched the horse. His hide rippled under her fingers as if she tickled him. "Why, he's soft—he's…" She looked up at Connor. Tear flowed down her face, unheeded. "Connor, he's soft, so soft."

She turned and rested her head against his big frame. Connor folded her into an embrace. He rained kisses on her temple and both cheeks. "Och, lass, 'tis proud of you I am. You're a brave, generous girl and deserve to have a laddie like Rob."

He cradled her in a one arm and took Robbie off the horse with the other. "Good, boyo. That's what you are, Rob. My very good boyo."

Sinead stared up at the two of them. "Why, Connor, you've tears in your eyes."

"They're tears of pride in my whole family."

Pegeen, who had been silent until then, spoke up. "What ye did, Sinead, was most glorious thing I ever did see." Tears rolled out of her eyes. "And now if you gentlemen wouldn't mind, I'd like to be speaking with the lass by meself. 'Tis time I told her a bit about me own plans."

"Good thing," Egan said, laughing to break the tension. "I'd like to be speaking to the men folk. I have some news of interest to all of us."

Sinead took Robbie from Connor. His little legs encircled her waist. "Pegeen, come with me. Essie's still here and we'll have a cup of tea between us."

"Me, too, Mama."

"Milk, for you, laddie. With some grand, sweet raisin cookies. Go ahead with Pegeen, love. I'll be right with you." She set him on the ground, where he placed a hand in Pegeen's.

Bowes and Egan removed the horse from its traces and started down the hill with it. "We'll be taking him to the barn, Con," Bowes shouted, making the horse jog for a bit. "Meet ye there to talk."

"Connor," Sinead shouted to stop him. "Don't go yet. I need to thank you…"

"For what?"

"For your patience, perhaps. For your kindnesses, your consideration." She looked at the ground. "For everything, since we…."

"You've no need to be thanking me, lass. I'm your husband."

"And I'm thinking I'd wish you'd stay that way..." Unable to meet his gaze, she turned and ran into the house without glancing back at him.

Chapter Twenty-four

In the afternoon, they celebrated Sinead's brave contact with a horse, her first in twenty years. Robbie kept running over and hugging her skirt then running back to Bowes, Connor and Egan as if he were one of the men.

"I'm proud of my mama," he cried out at one point and looked at Connor. "Aren't you, Da?" When Connor agreed, he also got hugged.

By evening, they moved onto a celebratory dinner for the upcoming marriage of Bowes and Pegeen. Discussion of everyone's plans for the wedding remained at the forefront.

Not to be undone by her new life, Pegeen told them of some necessary steps she'd already taken. "The arrangements are made for the ceremony to take place on Saturday evening, following the racing program. Of the damsels at the boarding house, only one elected to stay in her present business," she said quietly, her gaze avoiding everyone. "The others, Essie included, are taking different options open to them in less dangerous life styles."

Bowes patted her hand. "All of them, but Essie here, intend to leave Saratoga for bigger cities where there are more opportunities for employment. I know Peg will miss them. They've been good boarders and never practiced their trade at her doorstep, regardless of what some people might think."

"Da, you know I'm sorry about the mistake I made," Sinead said. A flush crept up her face. Her ears burned. "I didn't really know —

or understand…"

Bowes continued. His words filled the void. "I intend to set up a small livery stable and blacksmith shop on a piece of village property I own, behind one of the big hotels. The land is in the village itself and near to Pegeen's house. I'm willing to do your shoeing for a paltry sum, Con," he added with a smile.

"I'm not sure how long we're going to stay here," Connor said. His gaze rested on Sinead. "When we leave, you'll be taking the place over."

Egan assured Connor. "I'll go back to Ireland whenever ye want to return. In the meantime, I'm planning to go back to the City of New York. There are untold opportunities there for a fast-minded lad."

"Not a job I'd be imagining for you, but I suppose it works all right for the time being. How's life in the police department?" Connor asked in an extremely serious tone.

"Based on my short friendship with Morrissey, I've made a speedy rise within the department in barely two weeks. New York City and its police department have become my home away from home, but there are other things in the offing."

"Would you not trade it all for the green hills of O'Malley Stud?" Connor asked in a surprised manner, his longing for home obvious.

Egan grinned at his older brother. "Ye know, I think this Irishman has a taste for the political life, believing he can do good things for our fellow countrymen." His face grew serious, mouth turning down. "Con, ye have no idea the squalor the Irish live in. By the force of those who think them scum. Bad circumstances debilitate the men. The women and children cry out in anguish, daily."

Egan shook his head and took a deep breath. "Well, enough of depressing facts." He turned to Essie. "And what are you intending, lass?"

Essie beamed her answer. "Since you asked, I'll tell you. I'm going to stay with Pegeen and Bowes, and help out with the new boarding house. I can read and do numbers."

"And where did ye get all the learning?" Egan asked, giving her the full benefit of one of his glorious smiles and dancing eyes.

Her rather obvious attraction to Egan, and her subsequent shyness because of it, touched them all in different ways. "In the very city you were talking about. Before she died, my most dear mam taught me those things."

Pegeen interrupted. "'Tis a fine hand she has, too. We'll need her in the spring and summers. Bowes and I decided we'd only open for some of the race crowd, those with horses of their own. We plan on putting notices in local papers — and in the city — wherever."

Bowes added, "It'll bring me more smithy duties, too. That's when Peg will need Essie the most."

"And I'm going to help Sinead as well." Essie leaned over and ruffled Robbie's hair. "Take care of this favorite tyke of mine. And in the winters, maybe I'll get me a job in a dress shop — if one will take me."

Egan grinned. "They'll be lucky to have ye, too, lass. I'm betting on it."

"Has everyone had enough?" Sinead asked. She pushed away from the table. "There's still some cake left on the counter."

"I'll have it, Mama," Robbie shrieked. When everyone laughed, he asked, "What's so funny?"

Connor stood up and lifted Robbie from his chair. He rested him on one hip. "There's nothing funny, son. 'Tis just big people. Once their stomachs are full, they like to laugh."

Robbie giggled and hugged Connor, as if his da said the most astounding thing.

Everyone came away from the table, carried dishes into the kitchen and said their good-byes. The celebration was over. Bowes and Pegeen went back to the village. Connor and Egan went down to the barns, and Robbie settled in bed.

After telling Robbie a long story and kissing his forehead in a good night gesture, Sinead went into the kitchen to help Essie clean up. The job completed, Essie took off for her bed. Probably to dream of Egan, Sinead thought, strolling into the main room.

For the longest time, Sinead stood by the window and looked down at the land below the house. A light glowed in the tent and created shadowy, ghostly etchings of figures moving around. Somehow, knowing the brothers were there comforted her.

She sat down on the long sofa, trying to search her heart for a solution to the problems besetting her. It made her morose, so she grabbed an agricultural magazine from the side table. With a sigh of discomfort, she flipped the pages, noticing little but pictures, as the details of her life came into clearer focus.

Her eyes grew heavy. She leaned against the hard back of the sofa. Exhausted by all the emotional upheavals, the highs and lows, since first meeting Connor, today's bout with the horse sapped her last reserve of energy. She fell into a deep sleep and awoke in the middle of the night, darkness momentarily shading her vision.

She bolted upright on the sofa and swung her feet to the floor. Someone had tossed a coverlet over her, loosened the buttons of her dress and placed a feather pillow beneath her head. Alert to the absence of any noise, her heart slammed against her ribs. One ragged breath followed another. She dragged air into her lungs in great gulps. A cold sweat trickled down her neck.

The light of the moon lit the room with eerie silken shapes. They flickered, shimmered and wavered before her eyes. Sinead leaped to her feet, her heart still racing for some unknown reason. She staggered to the window. Other than the moon's reflection, there was no light anywhere else on the property.

With no regard for her state of dress, she rushed to Robbie's room. He slept peacefully, little warm breaths issuing from his mouth. She tiptoed out of the room and listened at the door of Essie's bedroom. Soft exhalations in spurting sounds greeted her ears.

The uneasy feeling refused to leave. *Connor!*

Her every instinct told her to get him, bring him to the house. The place was as much his as hers. She moved slowly toward the front door, unsure of what action to take. Even if he were not going to stay here long, she should make him her husband in fact, express the love she knew she had for him. Her deepest respect and love for him grew with every day she spent in his company.

She chastised herself mentally for her past behavior toward him. When did she fall so deeply in love with Connor? Was it the moment she saw him? When he greeted Adelaide, thinking her to be his bride? And she chortled over Essie's adoration of Egan, she thought with a snicker at herself.

Every handsome feature of Conner's face came to mind. Those features plagued her then faded into picturing the power of his bright blue eyes, the size and strength of him, his kind nature. How might he have looked as a lad? As a lad? Sinead grasped the wall of the hallway she traveled. What made her think of him as a youngster? As a lad of ten or eleven?

The vivid, sharp image of Connor O'Malley at eleven, when last she'd seen him, flooded her mind. She closed her eyes to draw the image closer and clamped her teeth over her lower lip, in concentration.

"Och, God, help me!" To her own inner anguish, she remembered. Remembered the large, brawling family of O'Malleys, mother, father and sons, her own mama, her da and her wee sister! Remembered it all! It was far clearer in the darkness of night, her most ancient of enemies, than her mind ever allowed her to envision before. She slid to her knees

No wonder Connor always seemed so familiar to her. His occupancy of her heart was uncontested. She loved him long ago, much as she did now, followed him, day after day, like a dogged spaniel worrying a bone. How many times did he trip over her, not knowing she was standing there at his side? How many times did he reach down and pat her head? How many times had he saved her from a high-stepping, playful animal's buck, fraught with danger?

Sinead came to a dead stop in the long hall. Her body folded upon itself. She rocked back and forth, as memories assailed her.

And the accident? In her vision, her mama sat on the fence, laughing, her tangled hair whipping around her features. She turned to Sinead. The chestnut horse leaped to meet her and toss her to the ground. Her mama was carried into the house, and a door closed, ending the horrific moment.

Sinead gasped at the force of the memory and what came next. She remembered. "Aye, I remember so much more." Sobs wracked her. She couldn't stop her swaying nor could she rise to her feet. "Dear God, I remember…"

Sinead had broken away from her da's embrace. Her small legs darted like quicksilver toward Connor, only to see him standing with a gun in his hand. She stopped running, held her breath and watched him shoot the chestnut. The horse crumpled to the ground in a heap and cast a last trumpetlike breath. Connor tossed the gun away and plunged headlong onto the still warm carcass. He cried his heart out in fear and terror as only a young boy could when faced with the fierceness of a man's job.

Sinead floundered in the fragments of her images and bent over her knees. Her hands came over her mouth to smother a fit of sobbing, so heartbreaking that little breath remained for breathing. The very person by whom she judged all other men was Connor. Sweet, strong Connor. He was hers for now, but she would lose him again.

Her eyes screwed tightly shut, she mumbled incoherent sounds of distress. "Too soon… Much too soon!"

The sound of her own voice crept through her mental cobwebs. She needed to tell Connor what she remembered, throw herself at his feet. Go back to Ireland with him, if necessary. Even if he didn't remember her, Connor felt something for her. She sensed his concern.

But Robbie, what of wee Robbie? A sweet, innocent child. He knew nothing about any of this. He didn't even understand about his real mother dying to bring him into this world, or how his da died in a last attempt to preserve Robbie's heritage from the Dewitts.

Lasting sobs wracked her body, in part for the wee lad, and part for herself. She slumped to the floor and let the coolness of the bare wood help shoulder her burden. She'd go to the Dewitts, beg them for a release. She'd promise them anything to balance the scales, visits every year, money. Anything…

Tears hovered. She sucked back a sob and wiped her face. Another thought intruded. Last night, Connor offered her a part of himself. Her worries about being left with two children and no father to raise them had set her off. She had run. She had refused his attention in fear of a totally unknown future.

She rolled over on the floor. She slapped her head with the heel of her palm, once, in misery. How foolish to give up such an exquisite part of her life! If she took a chance, perhaps, she would bear a child by the very person she'd loved since she was four. She'd survived so far without things. She'd survive even if he left…

Sinead pushed herself up to a sitting position. She cocked her head as if she were listening to something. She vowed to pit herself against everything or anything that frightened her. Ideas churned through her.

Slowly, she wiped her face with her sleeve, rose to her feet and looked around her. She could stay here, in this house, on this farm. She'd learn to love horses again. Her da would help her. He'd never turn her away.

With lighthearted steps, she tore through the living room to the front door and flung it open. She gulped the air. It felt cool, its smooth velvet darkness soothing, opening her up. Her breathing became less erratic.

She marched toward the stairs with sure steps. At the top, she halted long enough to gather her nerves together a bit more closely. With great purpose, she descended the steps lit by a deceptive glow of the moon.

She went directly to the barn and called softly, "Connor, Connor? Are you there, Con?" All she heard was the sounds of the horses, munching on hay or stirring in their stalls.

Her brows knitted. She shook her head to reaffirm her decision.

Connor and Egan went to sleep in the large tent, she remembered. She tramped through the damp, spongy grass of the field. At the tent, she called softly, "Connor? Egan?"

Slightly annoyed that neither answered her, but glowing with the joy of life rushing through her, she lifted the flap. "Can't either of you answer me?" Her voice echoed in her ear like a song, faltering in her throat.

She stepped over the threshold with plans to roust them both and froze in mid-step. The tent was empty of humans. In fact, it was empty of everything, all Connor's personal goods, except the two cots. Sinead sank to her knees and pounded on the raised wooden floor, a heart-wrenching wail echoing in her mind.

He was gone!

* * *

Despite the moonlight shining brightly, the road to Albany was rutted and treacherous, the distances melting into one another. Both Connor and Egan kept their horses going forward, taking turns at the lead. Connor was determined to reach Albany before dawn. If he was to keep to his intended schedule, he needed to get before a circuit court judge no later than ten, and he set a killing pace.

"Connor, ease up a bit. Ye're pushing too hard. The horses are plain winded."

Forced to swallow his temper, Connor thought to spur his brother on. "Understand, please. You've brought the ammunition I need to get the deed done. 'Tis important for everything to go forward as quickly as possible." He grumbled, "The lass has served penance long enough. Why let her suffer one second more at the hands of the Dewitts?"

Connor worked hard for all he'd gained in life. Even living through the famine was small compared to what Sinead endured with Cavanaugh and the Dewitts. At the same time he wished he could quench this constant need to please her.

"Connor, I don't want to be telling ye again. The horses need a

347

bite of rest and a swallow of some cool water. That's what we have to be doing. Right this minute, or ye'll not be having these horses on the road home."

Reluctantly, Connor willed himself not to crush his horse's spirit and slowed the big bay Harry was training, to a walk. "We'll let them cool down a bit. Let's see if we can find a stream of sorts."

"Aye." Egan rode up alongside Connor and slowed his horse to a walk. "I've never known ye to be so all-fired anxious to do a good deed. Or to work a horse beyond its capacity. What's really wrong, Con?"

Connor growled in frustration. "I've finally put much of it together. Bowes's description of the accident, the loss of his wife and their family's troubles thereafter, set me to remembering and worrying about things. Dreams of the accident long ago, and my part in it, have haunted me for years. Still does to some degree, I guess."

"I can remember yer nightmares, and Ma running to yer room to calm ye down, while ye fought with yer inner demons." Egan leaned over and patted his horse on the neck. "Och, laddie you've been such a good mount."

Connor sighed deeply. "I remember it, too, all too well. But I blocked the most of it out of my mind the day Bowes took off in the wagon with those wee lasses sitting atop all their worldly goods. Their sad faces haunted me for years."

Egan shook his head. "Funny, little as I was, I remember that day meself. I remember ye holding on to me while I cried."

Anger surfaced in Connor's voice. "Our da's complicity in the lottery scheme perturbs me. What if you or one of our brothers won the damned thing and were forced to go to America for a deed I did?"

"You did nothing." Egan suddenly howled with laughter and turned in his saddle to face Connor. "And all the time...I thought you thought...it was a punishment. This coming to America, to marry a lady sight unseen."

Connor smiled. Egan's ability to make him laugh at himself was good medicine. "No more…"

Still chortling to himself, Egan moved ahead of Connor and cocked his head to one side. "Con, listen. Over there." He waved his hand. "On the other side of the road. Hear it? 'Tis a stream bubbling away." Egan pointed to a splash of silver they could see from where they were.

Connor brought his horse to a stop and got off. "'Tis better we walk our horses over. In case something jumps out of those trees," he said, pointing to a small path across the field. He started moving in the direction of the stream, cutting through a broad field, his gaze focused on the ground. "Thanks be to God in all His glory for that moon."

Egan followed. The two tramped swiftly to the water, keeping their horses close. Connor slid the bit out of the bay's mouth and controlled him with the reins around his neck. Egan did the same. The animals were eager to reach the stream and drank their fill of the cool water.

Connor put the bit back in the bay's mouth and handed him to Egan. "Here, hold him for a minute."

He moved to the creek, cupped his hands to reach down into the cool water and drank. He lifted more liquid into his hands and tossed it over his head and neck. He rubbed more on his face then held Egan's horse. When finished, the brothers walked back to the road with the two animals.

Connor put his foot in the stirrup and eased himself above the horse's saddle. He slid into it softly. "We'll walk the horses a bit more."

Watching Egan swing up and on with ease caused Connor to smile broadly at his youngest brother. "'Tis glad to see you I am. I hadn't realized how much I'd missed your fiery temper, your constant joking and teasing."

"'Tis glad I am to be with ye, too. I've missed ye, big brother. Had to take a leave from me duties on the force, ye know. I didn't plan to leave the City for Saratoga, not so soon, Not even for the racing.

Although I admit, I'll be glad to be watching some of them."

Egan sighed with no posturing or pretense in his demeanor. "Wish we had one of our horses in the field of those races. It would almost make staying in America worth it." Egan chuckled to himself. "Who'd ever think I'd say I miss the grand beasts?"

"Me." Connor supplied. "Now, tell me something. I know you didn't want to say too much in front of Bowes. How did you find out about the stolen money?"

"Morrissey," was Egan's swift response. "He's had dealing with Ludwig Dewitt for years. The man owes him a great deal of money. Ludwig gambles in big chunks, if what I heard from Morrissey and the banker is true. Neither one would have cause to lie to me."

"And that's what the Dewitts have been using young Rob's money for? Gambling debts? I know our too-trusting Sinead never considered the idea there was wealth involved in transferring the lad to her custody."

"The Dewitts must have kept the terms of Cavanaugh's will from her." Egan looked sideways at Connor. "Do ye intend to tell her?"

Connor nodded. "Aye. 'Tis the lad's money and hers to use as they need. The decision, of where they might want to live and how, belongs to them, regardless of how it might affect me." He cast an anxious glance at the sky, the diminishing stars and descending moon. His desire to set things right for Sinead, down to the smallest detail of her life, urged him on. Perhaps, then she could love him freely. He legged his horse and shouted to Egan in almost a challenge. "Let's pick up the pace…"

Egan shouted back over the sound of fierce hoof beats on the hard packed road. "Have ye made up yer own mind, Con? About Sinead, I mean."

"Aye. But first things first," Connor shrieked into the wind made by the fast pace. "Let's see the judge, hand Sinead the papers, rightfully hers, and see what she has in mind for the rest of her life."

"Do ye love her?" Egan screamed to his brother.

Connor let loose with a laugh that traveled backwards to Egan and his horse. It bounced off the misty woods near the road. It sent both horses to skittering and picking up their pace another notch.

"I think the question is, how much?" he answered.

Chapter Twenty-Five

Monday, August 3, 1863

Sinead passed the remainder of the night going from the house to the tent and back again. Every muscle ached from all the excess walking, climbing the stairs and struggling through the spongy grass of the field, not to mention the lack of sleep. Memories warred with her misery and impotent fury with herself. It was difficult to keep her slowly sagging spirit up.

Dawn came and left the makings of a glorious day for the race program. Shortly, it, too, was gone in a blaze of hot, bright sunlight. Still no sign of Connor.

With a measure of mercy, Robbie was quiet, not questioning everything, as if he sensed the unease. In a state of mindlessness and, while blinking back tears, Sinead went through the motions of motherhood and fed both Robbie and Essie breakfast. She ate nothing herself but sipped several cups of tea. Between each cup, she stood, stared out the living room window and watched the activities below. No Connor in sight.

She took a bath and changed her outfit several times, in an attempt to look like nothing was wrong in her life. Now, it was time to pull herself up by the laces on her short boots. She'd played with fire by getting herself entangled in a poor scheme. Well, she'd got burned, but life went on and on and on…

By nine in the morning, Bowes and Pegeen returned to the house. Pegeen made Sinead change to yet another dress, one more appropriate for a race day. Pegeen picked out hats for the both of them, telling the girl, "Shade will be a necessity, child."

When Sinead continued to move through the room, a broken puppet on a string, Pegeen asked, "What's wrong, child?"

"Nothing...Nothing is wrong," Sinead responded.

Pegeen stared at her strangely. "Well, I can understand you might not want to confide in me. Perhaps, it would be better to wait for your da and the men. Let's retire to the main room to wait for them."

"There won't be any *men*, other than my da," Sinead said quietly as she left the bedroom and hurried to the front of the house.

No sooner than she settled in a hard-backed chair, when her da flew through the door Robbie, no doubt, had left open. "Where are the boyos? I searched the barns for them. Looked everywhere, called out..."

"They're gone," Sinead replied.

"Gone? What in hell's name do ye mean, gone?"

Pegeen came into the room. "Bowes, hush, man."

"What do ye mean 'hush'? The lads are gone, she's saying," he said pointing to Sinead. "I sure as hell am wanting to know what she did to the glorious gentleman I picked out for her."

"Bowes, please. The lass is hurt. Can't ye see for yerself, man?"

Sinead decided to end the conversation, the discussion going on about her. "'Tis not what I did, more like what I didn't do..."

Her father glared at her. Then his expression changed. She knew her eyes were red-rimmed, her face haggard, but she didn't care. Nothing meant anything at the moment. She just wanted to get through this day to the next.

"Well, let's us go ahead to the races. I'm sure the lads will show up before the end of the first day," Pegeen said. She took Bowes arm and practically dragged him out of the house.

Sinead called, "Robbie. Essie. I'll see you after the races..."

Robbie ran into the room for a hug. Sinead kissed the top of his head. "My darling boy. At least, I have you."

"Where's my da? He usually comes to tell me good-bye."

"Well, he's gone missing today," Sinead responded, hearing the tears in her voice. "Go out and kiss your grandda Bowes instead."

"I want my da. He's going to get me a dog. A red and white one. He told me so."

"Later, darling. I'll get you one. Go play."

It was ten before they left. Essie in charge of Robbie, and Harry in charge of the barns. Pegeen, Bowes and Sinead squeezed into the single-horse shay and were on the road to Horse Haven, Morrissey's new rendition of the former Saratoga Trotting Course.

By the time they neared the track, their progress stopped as carriages flowed up Union Avenue, one after the other in a parade. Large signs nailed to trees proclaimed the opening of Saratoga's first thoroughbred race meeting.

The occupants of carriages, dressed in the most splendid finery, vied for position to get through the gate. Those on foot managed get through with considerably more ease.

At the sight of some of the wealthiest people in America, riding to the track with them, Pegeen squealed, "Och, Sweet Jaysus, this is the most exciting thing I've ever seen. I don't believe I've gazed on this many of the rich, all in one place." She giggled once, brought her hand to her mouth but couldn't stop the lilting laughter.

Sinead said nothing. She remained motionless, fading away from all activity. She didn't want to be here, perhaps needing to fend off the questions about Connor's absence from the sport everyone knew he loved. If she could carry off this day with dignity and skill, she'd survive the experience as she did so many others in her life. Each time her composure left her, she struggled to regain it, yet tears of despair threatened to spill from her eyes at any moment.

Bowes stopped the carriage at the opening gate and paid the three dollars for race cards, handing one to Pegeen. He gave one to Sinead, who let it fall to her lap. She put folded hands over it.

The carriage moved ahead and slowly caught up with several others. Dust flew into the air, tossed by carriage wheels. The excitement generated by the noisy racing crowd was a palpable force, moving in undulating waves like the tides of the sea.

Pegeen laughed and clapped her hands together. She pointed to several of the woman who had arrived earlier and placidly sat in carriages along the route. "Look at their outfits. Seems like each one is trying to outdo the other and start a new elegance in fashion. Who would be wanting to wear a ball gown to a dirty, dusty place like the races?"

Sinead looked around, without responding to Pegeen's enthusiasm. There was no place to sit, no grandstand. The three of them would need to stay in the carriage, which Bowes settled as close to the track area as he could.

Most of the wealthy, or famous, received the best places to park. Many men deserted their women and strolled about the grounds, exclaiming about each new feature they found.

"The views are terrible," one husky man, wearing a large, bright diamond pin on his checkered vest said.

Another, whose hair was slicked back with grease, shrieked. "Look there."

A third companion, as tall and thin as the other was hefty, wore an almost identical outfit. "Those buildings are in the way. We'll not be able to see the whole race."

Another group of well-dressed men, clustered by the rail and discussed the track's inadequacies quietly.

A gray-haired man spoke first. "Those recently-planted pine trees are in the way as well as those barns over there. They'll need to be taken down if we're to continue using this track." He turned to a young man who wrote in a notebook. "Are you taking all this down?"

"Yes, sir, Mister Wheatley. Yes, sir," said the man taking notes.

"The stables will need to go somewhere else, too," Wheatly said. "They block the view."

Another in the same group added, "The track is not laid out too well either."

"Hell, Anderson," Wheatley retorted, "what do you expect when the track was built by a gambler, not a horseman?"

Anderson laughed. "At least the opening race will be historic, a winner-take-all sweepstakes for three-year-olds."

The young note taker added, "Two major races today, starting with the best-of-three one-mile heats and followed by a two-mile dash." Anderson and Wheatly glared at him and he grew silent.

Wheatly leaned over to speak in Anderson's ear. "Eight of the owners contributed two-hundred dollars to enter. Morrissey himself put in an additional three-hundred. Six of those entered already cancelled and will pay a forfeit fee." He shook his head and chuckled.

Someone in the crowd jostled him and he, too, grew silent. Nothing deterred the waiting, watching crowds, who moved in great clumps along the rail and the infield, elbowing and shoving others out of the way in their anxiety to see the races started.

Finally, at 11:30, the horses went off at the word, "Go."

Sinead heaved a sigh, glad the action started, and people stopped analyzing each other. Everyone would watch the race, their eyes focused on the track itself. Hopefully, no one would glance in her direction.

The screaming and shouting all around her, throughout each race, was deafening. She shrunk from the noise. Its cacophony reminded her of the shrieking gangs in New York City during the riots.

Fortunately, after each race, the horses were walked and cooled down before the crowd for about twenty minutes before they were tested again by running in the second heat. The noise abated some while folks chattered together in more normal tones.

Sinead knew she, too, would be caught up in the excitement of the crowd if she wasn't looking for Connor. Every tall, well-built man she saw gave her heart a solid kick. Connor was no where to be seen on the grounds. The races were nearly over. He had missed most of them.

That fact alone impressed upon her the awareness that he was truly and finally gone from her life. The thought carved at her innards with a vengeance born of lost hope.

Suddenly, a glimpse of bright red hair caught her eye. Her heart skipped several beats. Egan? She wanted to wave to him, to call out but was mummified with fear. Perhaps, the O'Malleys, came to enjoy the races with no intentions of coming to her. If it weren't for Egan's red hair and superior height, she might have missed seeing him.

* * *

Connor turned away from the track and leaned against a railing, put there to contain the crowd and give horses enough running room. Taller than most, he scanned the crowd.

Sinead stood, put her hand up a little way to wave but pulled it down before Connor saw her. She sank back down onto the seat. It hurt her to look at him.

Pegeen leaped to her feet. "Connor. Egan. Here we are," she shouted, and waved with vigor.

Sinead watched Pegeen step out of the carriage with a light step and search for Bowes. "Bowes, wait for me. I need to speak with you," she called, her voice trailing off the farther into the crowd she went.

Connor materialized, at the carriage, his jaw clenched. "Sinead, love…?" His voice sounded breathless, shaky and ground her soul to nothingness.

Her heart flew out to him. Without thinking further, all thoughts of dignity gone to dust, Sinead leaped from her seat and launched herself into his arms to still her trembling. Her lips closed in on his neck, and she mumbled into it. "Och, Connor. I've been so worried. Where have you been? I thought you had left—left me, to go back to Ireland."

She tried to catch her breath but couldn't stop talking. "I have so much to tell you. I can't bear it all." Standing on the tips of her little boots, she pulled his face toward her and rained kisses on it, afraid if she stopped he would disappear from sight again.

"Easy, love, 'tis only a moment until the races are over and we can have a private chat. I've much to tell you as well."

Never was she so eager to give herself wholly to anyone. "Connor, there must be hacks for hire outside the track. Let's take one home. Let Egan stay here to wait for Pegeen and my da. I need to get away from this crowd. I need to be with you. I'm suffocating with the worry inside me." She kept kissing his face.

"All right, lass. You stay here. I'll make the arrangement and come back for you." The kiss he gave her promised more to come — before he was finished with her.

* * *

Connor paid the hack driver and said, "Wait here. I want you to take my son and his nanny to the Bide-with-Us in the village. 'Tis on Circular Street."

He lifted Sinead down and said, "Wait on the porch. Let me handle Rob and Essie." He disappeared inside the house. Within minutes, he reappeared with Robbie and Essie, both carrying small sacks of clothing with them.

"Mama," Robbie screamed, dashing to her. He clutched her skirt in a hug. "Da says he's going to take you to a big party tonight, so Essie and I are going to Grandda Bowes."

"That's lovely, darling. You'll be having a grand old time yourself, with Pegeen, too. Be sure to be a good laddie…"

"I will. And he's going to get my dog after the races are over," he said in his squeaky little boy's voice. Connor went to lift him in and Robbie swiveled around. He stared up at Connor. "I can do it. I'm a big boyo now."

He turned back, clutched the sides of the carriage and drew himself up onto the step. There he turned and waved at them before jumping up into a seat. Essie followed him up and waved to Sinead. "Have a lovely time."

"Och, she will. I promise you."

The hack rolled down the drive. Connor looked at Sinead. There was a gleam in his eye. "I need to see Harry and make sure the horses are taken care of properly. Why don't you go inside and fix us something to eat? Essie said you didn't eat this morning. I've been too busy as well. But we'll talk and talk."

"Connor, I don't want you to be leaving me again."

"I won't, lass. This time I promise. It was necessary last night. I couldn't tell you I was going. You slept so peacefully, I didn't wish to be waking you out of a sound rest."

"Was it you who covered me and slipped the pillow under my head?"

"Aye."

"I would much prefer if it was your arm beneath my head," she said, giving him a shy look. She turned, went into the house and disappeared from view.

Connor wanted to follow her in. Every bone and muscle of his body concentrated on Sinead. His heart pounded against his ribs until he needed to move or fall down in a heap. What an extraordinary woman his wife was!

CHAPTER TWENTY-SIX

Sinead puttered around the house, trying to distract herself from plaguing thoughts. How could she resolve the dilemma facing her and the Dewitts? She readied a cold platter for dinner, placed it atop the block of ice in the kitchen and covered it with a cloth. She moved to the big parlor room and sat wrapped in considerations.

The sun left the sky and sunk into the horizon before she was aware of it. Finally, as the room darkened, she grew cognizant of the day's demise. Surprised to see the day gone, leaving only wonder is its wake, she stood and went to the front door.

Connor was nowhere to be seen, but this time she was not fearful of his going off. She concluded he must be in one of the barns.

Stepping onto the porch, an immense panorama of sky opened before her. The stars twinkled in a message of majesty and love. The moon shone with a fierce brightness and lit the land around the property. Distant mountains glistened like polished stones.

Feeling an affinity for the outdoors she hadn't felt in years, Sinead dragged in huge breaths of air, saturated with the honeyed scents of life, of grass, flowers and new-mown hay. Seemingly motionless, the air only stirred slightly, mostly in vibrating drifts of sound from activities in the village. Music and laughter rose over the lake.

Filled with a sense of well-being, she decided to surprise Connor by daring to go down to the barn and paddock areas while there was still activity. With no escort, she took a tenuous step from the porch and approached the stairs above the rolling mounds below.

Her heart fluttered at her bravery as she took the first step down.

There was a light in the first barn and she headed for it. Each step closer caused her breathing to labor a bit. At the last step, she put her foot forward onto the spongy turf. The tiny heels of her boots sunk into its softness. She plopped down on the step and undid her boots. They came off with surprising quickness. She flung them to one side and curled her toes into soft blades of new mown grass.

The sensuous feel of her bare feet against the bit of life, that sprang back to meet her, caused her to shiver with delight. Memories of her first home in Ireland, of the safety and security she felt there, raced through her. A warm sensation flooded her body. She rose and moved toward the barn with a purpose she never felt before in her entire life.

"Connor?" she called at the entrance. "Connor, are you there?"

No answer came from within. Sinead turned to stare out into a darkness lit only by the moon's brightness. She could vaguely discern some figures in the pasture. One was obviously a horse, but the tall shape of a man next to it drew her attention.

She ran, her feet dancing on the grassy and sandy patches of the earth. She ran toward the one thing she wanted above all other things. Connor!

* * *

His back to the house where his thoughts were, Connor concentrated on brushing the huge bay in front of him. "Stand still, you damned fool. Chester, quit your dancing…"

Slowly he worked himself from the side of the gelding's body to his neck. He pushed the mane to one side and stroked knotted clumps, one by one, with the stiff brush, until they settled smooth and silky against the animal's neck.

The horse stretched his neck forward, giving Connor ample room to do the job. Suddenly, the horse jogged a bit. "Whoa, boy. In a minute, you're going to be standing on my feet, big lump that you are."

"Connor…"

His wife's voice rang out in the stillness. He was surprised, proud, that she had come down there by herself. His attention to the horse in front of him wandered.

"Connor…? Answer me."

Ears straight up and attentive, the horse snorted and leaped to one side. He tossed his head in fear of the strange noise he couldn't see, clipping his master smack on one side of the temple. The hit stunned Connor momentarily. He sank to his knees before sitting in the grass. Chester stood quietly, looking at the man on the ground.

"Och, my God…" Sinead shrieked from the fence line.

Connor looked up in time to see his wife tuck her skirt between her legs and climb over the fence, struggling with each rung. He wondered if he were awake or dreaming, but the figure sprinted toward him, waving its arms.

"Go way, ye beastie," Sinead cried. "You robbed me once. You'll not be robbing me again."

He saw her. Sinead, little Sinead who had chased horses away from crowding him when only a tiny girl, unafraid of the animals.

Connor didn't know whether to laugh or cry. His head was sore but not for the first time in his life. Laughing won out. His body shook with muffled joy.

"Go, go beastie…" she waved the horse away, as if there was no fear of them left. She fell to her knees. "Och, Connor, love, are you all right?" Her hands traveled over his face, until she touched the round, stone-like bruise growing on his brow.

He winced. "Easy, love. You'll be making a dent in my brain if you're not careful," he crowed, the laughter bubbling out of him.

Sinead leaped to her feet. "You think it's funny, do you now? You frightened the heart right out of me." She turned on her heels and marched back across the field.

Connor jumped up. "Wait, Sinead, wait."

He could tell by the set of her shoulders she had no intention of turning back to him or waiting for a single minute. He leaped the fence, charged after her and swung her off her feet into his arms. "Did you think to get away from me? Och, there's no chance of it, lass. You're mine and we'll work things out together."

Her arms went around his neck. Her mouth nestled at his throat where she placed several warm kisses. Chills ran down his spine. Connor knew if he didn't get to the house soon, he'd lose everything and take her in the grass.

"I'm going to set you on the top rail of the fence, Sinead. I don't want you to move an inch."

"It's the way my mam died, you know."

"Aye, I know. I finally remembered," he said, placing her on the top railing. "But it's not going to happen to you."

"You killed the horse, didn't you?" Her voice was soft.

"Aye. That I did. It broke my heart, lass, but your mama's death broke it more."

Connor heaved himself over the fence. The desperate look on Sinead's face made him step in front of her and take her hands in his. He placed a soft kiss in her palm.

"Connor, I've only just realized some things in the last few days."

Connor climbed back onto the top rail next to his wife and straddled it. He took her in his arms, her body between his legs. "Perhaps, you should be telling me about it now, for I may not listen well later."

He pulled her in close to him and let her lean back on his chest. Perhaps the things she had to say could best be said with her face looking away into the distance.

"I closed off all my life from the day my mama died. I punished my own da for her death. Year after year, I tortured him."

"And how did you do that? You were but a wee lass at the time."

Sinead kept talking as if she couldn't stop. Connor let her finish without interruption. "The fact he still loved horses. A horse killed my mother. The very thought made me go after my da, and the animals, in a perverse, opposite way. I truly talked myself into being afraid of them, to punish him. I missed out on so much."

"Aye, you did. You missed the pleasure of sitting on them and loving them, as they, most often, love folks who are kind to them. Like your da."

She turned in his arms and looked up into his face. "Connor, I know I did wrong to my da. I'll make it up to him somehow."

"I think being happy might make all the difference in the world to your da. And to Robbie. So much of your troubles were not of your own doing, Sinead. You punished yourself, even more than you punished others. But I'm here now. We'll muddle through this business of life, together."

She leaned forward. Her mouth settled on his. The simple movement took his breath away. He inhaled strongly, enjoying the scent of her. "Wife, there's more to settle between us. I still need to tell you certain things, important things…"

Her mouth met his again. The tip of her tongue tickled the sides of his lips. His arms went around her. The kiss deepened. She melted into him.

Connor slid off the fence with her in his arms. He couldn't put her down. He couldn't stop kissing her. Her breath came faster. It blew across his face. Her arms tightened around his neck. He could feel her heart pounding against his own. The steady drumming was about to drive him crazy. He was ready to take her where they stood but moved toward the stairs to the house instead.

She gasped to catch her breath. She took his face in her hands and kissed every place she could find. Suddenly she stopped. "Connor, your bruise. 'Tis all swollen. It needs doctoring."

"Aye, lass, to be sure, but a different kind of doctoring is on my mind."

He raced for the stairs and went up them two at a time, charging across the porch when he got to it. One hand reached for the knob. He turned it and kicked the door open with his foot.

"Set me down, Connor. I can walk."

Connor never uttered a word. He pressed his lips against hers and fell onto the sofa in the living room, her on top of him. He couldn't let her go, not now, never. If ever he was in doubt before, he wasn't now.

Her response to his kisses thrilled him. He savaged her mouth and wanted to cry when she returned the favor.

Her breasts were warm against him. His need to touch them overcame him. The softness of them fired his desire for this woman. Their size filled his hand. Her sigh of pleasure, along with a moan, nearly undid him. He stood, never letting her mouth go, and carried her to the bedroom, which would be theirs forever more.

Throughout the night, she matched his every movement, gave back every kiss with a deeper one of her own. Their tongues dueled in a constant battle as they raced across each other's body, discovering and exploring. Sinead stretched and arched, sighed and gasped, struggling for a fulfillment never before realized. When it came with swift and deadly force, her world opened up as never before.

* * *

The morning dawned light and dewy. So did Sinead. At a late breakfast, neither Connor nor Sinead could manage more than a few nibbles. Slowly they gravitated to the big double swing on the front porch, their eyes were locked together. Their hands were clasped in an effort to keep touching each other.

Connor, eager to impart the news he'd held within him for far too long, ran his fingers reverently up and down his wife's arm. When Sinead shivered with delight, he smiled down at her.

"First, let me tell you, no one will come to the house here, until after we put in an appearance at the races, later today. I'm sure Egan told your da and Pegeen. I told Essie myself. Harry will care for the horses until further notice. I wanted a chance to explain fully where I was yesterday."

"I would appreciate it. I'll not be telling you again of my devastation when I discovered you and Egan gone from the farm. All your belongings as well…"

"We didn't want to wake you. While we stripped the tent, there was no need to tell you anything. I hoped to surprise you."

"Aye, you did that …" She nestled against him.

He squeezed her shoulder and placed a kiss behind her ear, garnering another shiver. "You never stirred when Egan and I roamed the house, bringing up all my things from below. You slept too deeply for me to disturb you."

Pulling away from him to look him in the face, Sinead said, "You could have awakened me as you did last night."

"In front of my brother? I think not…" Connor's laugh sailed across the porch to the trees of the forest. He pulled her back to his chest and hugged her tightly. "Och, Sinead, you've become my world." He trailed soft kisses up the side of her neck then leaned back with a sigh. "My things are stacked, rather messily, in one of the extra bedrooms, just waiting to be straightened out, after we are."

"My God, your things were here in the house the whole night?"

Connor nodded and brought her palm to his lips for a kiss. Her trembling, instant response thrilled him. She curled her fingers around his lips. The fire that flashed in her eyes matched the one he felt inside.

"Con, I never knew. I didn't understood anything about you. I never truly blamed you. Just myself. When you left, I truly thought you'd decided to see the last of me."

"Never…"

"But how could you run off without telling me you were going somewhere?" Her body tensed beneath his hand and arm.

"I was doing something for us, for you and Robbie. It was all I could think about." Connor swung around to face her. "And I didn't want to get your hopes up."

He leaned forward and placed a hand on her knee. She didn't draw away from his touch as she had so many times before. It was all the encouragement he needed. His mouth met hers and, with their lips sealed, their kiss contained even more meaning, more promise, than it had last night.

"Connor, stop. You constantly distract me. Tell me your news."

Connor rose from the swing. He saw the surprise on her face. Her arms stretched out to draw him back. He held up a hand. "Wait. I need to get a piece of paper to show you. Sit still. I'll be right back." He raced into the house.

Sinead settled back on the swing and gave it a bit of a push with her foot, closed her eyes and hummed.

Connor came out seconds later, waving a document in his hand. "This is it. The solution to all your fears and desires for Robbie."

"Nothing could be so easy…"

"Well, it was." He stood in front of her, attempting to hand her the document, then taking it back, smiling with a foolish grin. "Here's what I've learned. Robert Cavanaugh, Senior, was born and brought up in the City of Albany. He grew to manhood there before going to New York." He looked at Sinead whose face was serene. "Did you know he was quite a bit older than Lucinda Dewitt?"

Shaking her head, Sinead responded with a clipped, "Aye. Older than me, too."

Connor couldn't stop himself. His eagerness to tell the story overwhelmed him, as if saying it out loud would put it in better perspective. "Well, in his youth, he knew Adelaide, who came from Albany as well. He sought her out when he went to the city. It's how he met Lucinda in the first place. Ludwig sought placements for him until Robert became well-established in the financial community. When Robert secured more monetary success than Ludwig, he married Lucinda, much to her parents' despair."

Sinead frowned. "I always knew Adelaide didn't like Robert, especially after Lucinda's death, but… I appreciate your telling me all this, Connor, but I already know most of the story, first from Lucinda's mouth, then Adelaide's. The stories are different, I admit…"

He shook his head. "Nae, you don't know the most and the best of it. Egan brought me the news when he arrived. We owe many thanks to Morrissey, who got the information through his sources in the city."

Sinead patted the seat next to her and Connor sat. He took her hand in his. "Please listen. When Robert Cavanaugh married you to secure a proper Catholic upbringing for his son, he made sure the papers were recorded in both cities, New York and Albany. He stated in those papers how much hated New York City. He hoped you'd move away from there with Robbie."

Sinead groaned, "And how was I supposed to do such a thing, with no money or the prospects of getting any?"

"He left you a fortune."

"What?" Sinead leaped to her feet and paced the porch, talking, almost to herself. "He left just enough money to take care of Robbie until the laddie could be established on his own. As long as I provided care for the child, as if I could ever do differently, I would be provided for."

Connor stood up and walked beside her. "And who told you that story? The Dewitts?"

Sinead stopped in mid-step. She swerved, cocked her head and looked at Connor from the corner of her eye. "Aye." He lifted her up and swung her around.

"Put me down, ye ape of a man. You'll be making me dizzy."

He turned her to face him but refused to take his arms from around her. "Sinead, do you ever remember signing a paper for Robert?"

Her eyes grew wide. "Aye, I signed several when Robert's hands were crippled."

"Those were adoption papers. You are legally Robbie's mother."

Sinead's mouth opened. She gasped. "You mean I've been his legal mother all along?"

Tears gathered in her eyes. Holding her hand to her mouth, she pushed Connor away and went to stand at the porch railing, shaking. He followed right behind her.

"What a fool I've been, listening to those folks all these years!" She swung around to face Connor. "What should I do different? What do I do now?"

Connor lifted her and placed her on the sturdy railing, holding tightly so she wouldn't fall. "Listen to me Sinead. I've more to tell you, but first I want to tell you this. I love you. With all of my Irish heart and soul!"

"As I love you. So dearly." Tears filled her eyes again and threatened to flow down her cheeks. "But, please, understand, Connor, I cannot take the boy away from his blood grandparents." She took his face between her hands. "A journey to Ireland, often, would be right and proper, but, for them to never see Robbie again would be pure malice."

"I'll tell you the rest. Egan and I went before a magistrate in Albany, with all the information Egan brought with him, the adoption papers, the will and the proof the Dewitts swindled you and Robbie of money rightfully yours, and his."

Sinead shook her head. "Nae, they would never do such a…"

"They did. 'Tis not the money, Sinead. I'm wealthy in my own right. I can easily care for you and Rob. But listen and listen carefully. The Dewitts did cheat the laddie and are still doing it. Ludwig is in terrible debt, due to his gambling."

Sinead pushed herself from the railing and stood as tall as she could. She faced Connor, her bearing proud and resolute. "All I want is Robbie to be cared for. I don't want their damned money."

Connor cupped her face in his hands again. "The money is yours. Robert left it all to his wife, which is what you were when he died."

Sinead snaked her arms around Connor's chest and laid her head against it. "What would make my life complete is to be with you and Robbie, together, forever. It's all I want. I don't want to lose you to Ireland or any other place in this world. I'm in love with you, Connor O'Malley. The idea of living without you is more than I can bear…"

Sobs wrenched her body. This time she trembled in fear and privation rather than in passion. "What am I to do?"

Connor picked her up in his arms and cradled her. "This is what *we* will do. We'll pay off all of Ludwig's debts and…"

Sinead looked up at him and snaked her arms around his neck. "You'd do that?"

Connor kissed her lips in a pledge. "Aye, and more." He turned to toward the fields. "Look out there, lass. See the land spread out in front of you?"

Tears glistened on her face. She scanned the rolling hills, the forest areas, the barn and the paddocks. "Connor, 'tis lovely here. You've made a home here, a home to be cherished."

"And 'tis ours. We'll live here, bring up Rob and perhaps others, and raise horses. How's that for a life plan?"

Sinead squealed, "Then you'll stay? Here? With us? In America?"

"Aye, lassie. We'll work things out together. 'Tis my home now. Here in Saratoga."

With her arms around his neck, Sinead kissed his face all over, making sure not to miss his ears. Her mobile lips went from his ear, to the tip of his nose, and landed on full lips. Their kiss grew deeper. Their dueling tongues met. Connor groaned. He slid her down the length of his body. Sinead gasped. She strained against him.

They took a breath. Connor murmured in her ear, "I think we'll be a bit late for the races today." He swung her up into his arms and rushed into the house.

The End.

ABOUT
DORICE NELSON

When I took an early retirement from teaching, my husband and I moved to the Adirondack Mountains of upstate New York. I knew I needed a new "life" goal. Having done a bit of writing in my other careers, I selected fiction writing as my new challenge, never realizing the effort involved. I charged into the world of writing with both feet and freely admit it's the most difficult but satisfying career of my life.

Now my husband and I have moved again, to a small Hudson Valley village, not far from my beloved Saratoga and horses. We now have a new house, some acreage and two rescued English Setters.

More information at http:www.DoriceNelson.com.

Editor's Note: Readers may contact the author at: DoriceNelson@aol.com.

GREAT HISTORICAL ROMANC

FROM

www.cambridgebooks.us

Clan Gunn: Gerek
by Dorice Nelson

To become chief of his clan, Scotland's "Beast Battle" must marry before the end of his thirtieth ye It was how things were done, or so Gerek Gu thought...until he met his betrothed. "Action-pack Historical Romance filled with excellent writing, cre ible characters and a good story line." — Molly Mart Scribes World, Five Stars, Reviewer's Choice Award

Mystick Moon: A Novel of Old New England
by Terry L. White

A sweeping historical novel set in colonial Mystick where they hanged more witches then ever they trie in Salem. Travel with Rebecca as she starts her new lif in Puritanical New England.... How will having the gif of "second sight" affect her in the New Land?

Killraven
by Arline Chase

Two people reluctantly fall in love while an isolated island community on Chesapeake Bay is outraged by murder and violence. Hope Voeschell, a young woman brought up to believe in nonviolence, and DeCoursey Rogers, a man who has known violence firsthand.